Deep in the Palo Duro . . .

"Hello, the camp!" Cass called out.

"We're friends!" Riley hollered.

In seconds they were surrounded by a score of rough-looking men. A man in high boots stepped out on the porch. Cass tried to keep from looking around too much; he had to make himself appear hard. Riley was doing the same.

An outlaw raised the head of one of the dead men slung over the horse. "It's Virgil," he announced. "Shot dead. They got Skiff, too."

"This is a terrible cargo you've brought in here," said the man on the porch, his eyes flint-hard. "I believe I shall hang both of you."

"These men are dead through their own doing," Cass said. "They didn't challenge us or announce themselves. They just cut loose on us."

"They had orders to."

"Then they should have shot straighter," Riley said. "It appears you were poorly guarded—"

DI

Acclaim for
Bruce H. Thorstad's First Novel

THE GENTS

"Riley Stokes and Cass McCasland, ex-Union and
Confederate soldier knockabouts, gamblers and
dreamers, really *are* gents of the Old West . . . likeable
and memorable. . . . This is the first book of the
'Gents' trilogy and I'm thinking of calling Thorstad
up to tell him to hurry up with the other two."
—Dale L. Walker, *Rocky Mountain News*

"A great read . . . breathtaking authenticity . . . *The
Gents* has a delightful comic quality and two unforget-
table heroes. . . . This is a grand book by an author
who is destined for the top."
—Richard S. Wheeler

"Thorstad has woven a complicated plot through
which a whole mess of characters, good, bad and ugly,
ride. Read *The Gents*. You won't forget any of them."
—Robert J. Conley

Books by Bruce H. Thorstad

Palo Duro
The Gents
The Times of Wichita
Deadwood Dick and the Code of the West

Published by POCKET BOOKS

PALO DURO

BRUCE H. THORSTAD

POCKET BOOKS
New York   London   Toronto   Sydney   Tokyo   Singapore

This book is a work of fiction. Names, characters, places, and
incidents are either products of the author's imagination or are used
fictitiously. Any resemblance to actual events or locales or persons,
living or dead, is entirely coincidental.

An *Original* Publication of POCKET BOOKS

POCKET BOOKS, a division of Simon & Schuster Inc.
1230 Avenue of the Americas, New York, NY 10020

Copyright © 1993 by Bruce Thorstad

ISBN: 0-671-75905-1

First Pocket Books printing July 1993

10 9 8 7 6 5 4 3 2 1

POCKET and colophon are registered trademarks of
Simon & Schuster Inc.

Cover art by Tim Tanner

Printed in the U.S.A.

For Holly and Eric,
a couple of pretty good kids.

And a big Texas "much obliged" to Harper
Creigh, the Honorable Judge Roy Bean, for the use
of his surname.

PALO
DURO

1 · RILEY STOKES

THREE DAYS BEFORE RILEY HAD HEARD OF THE CREIGHS, OR HAD heard much about the Barlows, he swayed in some farmer's hay field, wielding a pitchfork. The afternoon was humid as a dog's breath, a kind of weather that Riley found irksome, especially since Texas came advertised, at least by Cass McCasland, as being so naturally dry a person could not work up a sweat if he tried. The region's supposed dryness had something complicated to do with being crossed by the 90th meridian—or was it the 98th?—which had to do with latitude and longitude and things best left in books.

Riley wasn't trying, but he was surely sweating now, even with his shirt hanging outside his britches in the hope of catching a breeze. The shirt, sweat-plastered to his back, tugged at him as he worked, while chaff from the hay he was ricking found its itchy way between the fabric and his skin. And as he pitchforked, and as he sweated, Riley called himself fool again, for the true facts according to Cass McCasland had a way of turning out as insubstantial as smoke.

Riley looked up when the hayrick creaked. The farmer had grasped the near mule's bridle and was leading his team perhaps a rod ahead, the man galumphing in big boots and encouraging his mules in Danish. Coming late in a long day, when a worker grasped at any distraction offered, Riley found the farmer directing Texas mules in a foreign tongue an interesting sight—at least twice as interesting as looking at the next scruff of hay Riley was about to fork up. Maybe that was the secret to handling mules, Riley reflected; here all along they savvied only Danish.

His momentum lost, he straightened his spine, then leaned on the pitchfork and set his hat back, causing sweat to settle in his eyebrows. He sighed from heat. He grabbed his shirttail and mopped his brow. The shirttail came away grimed and soggy.

Searching for respite, Riley's eyes found at the plains' rim a vague demarcation of horizon, where dark clouds—root cause of the day's mugginess—were shouldered up, apparently conspiring. If Riley were truly lucky, wild rain would stop the work before suppertime. Were he luckier still, which would require luck practically of a magnitude of Cass McCasland's, the rain would give them tomorrow off, till the hay lying cut on the prairie had dried enough to be fit again for the rick.

As his eyes located the girl, Riley acknowledged that keeping track of her had become his pleasant habit. She came toward him with a water bucket, moving down the line of pitchforkers, stepping blithely barefoot through the hay stubble. Her hair, except where it hung damp against her brow, was as gold as morning.

Riley glanced at the farmer, who was forking with vigor as an example to his workers. Then Riley looked again at the girl, seeing that if the workers between him and her did not dawdle too long over their drinks of water, he could stand blameless and resting till it was his turn with the dipper.

As though feeling Riley's eyes, she looked up. She started a smile, then obscured it as she blotted her forehead with a sleeve. When her arm lowered, the smile was generous, and served up all for him. It's hot, the smile said.

To prolong the girl's eyes on him, Riley pantomimed his sweltered condition as broadly as a minstrel player: shrugging, dropping his jaw in pretended exhaustion, rolling his eyes heavenward in supplication for a cool breeze. He made himself Riley the Amuser. Her smile on him held.

"Inga!" The farmer barked the name, so that it sounded so different from the way she herself said it. She had told Riley her name a day earlier, pointing to herself and pronouncing singsong syllables, ending in a girlish upturn— to Riley an intriguing music. But coming from the father, the name was a command.

The farmer-father looked from his daughter to the inter-loper Riley Stokes, whereupon his eyebrows lowered as powerfully as carpenter's clamps. The eyebrows spoke of the coming rain clouds, of the work that would be delayed; the eyebrows damned Riley for standing idle, propped on his pitchfork; they glowered at the notion that he, a hired hand and stranger, a smooth English talker and shiftless town man, was communicating through private looks with the farmer's golden daughter.

Riley's response was an innocent half-shrug, apparently causing the farmer's scowl to lift like bad weather, and his gaze, now showing surprise, to resettle far beyond Riley. So much happened on the face that Riley swiveled to look behind him, finding the novelty of a one-horse buggy skirling along the double track of road. The rig was towed by a little roan, proud-stepping despite the heat, coming merri-ly toward them and raising listless, muggy dust that settled quickly.

The buggy driver was some town fellow with tabby hair, Riley saw, some lucky bastard riding coolly hatless under a shading roof, a long-limbed and trim-bodied gent in striped pants and shined boots, white shirtsleeves poking from his vest as fresh-looking as if straight from a Chinese laundry.

Were the man a lightning-rod salesman, arriving to cash in on the coming storm, Riley had to own it was an admirable piece of timing. In fact, Riley was about to say as much to the worker laboring next to him, but then remem-bered the man was another thick-talking Dane. Heck, they all were. Riley turned to look again at the town gent in the covered buggy. Abruptly, familiarity jelled around him. For cripes' sakes, it was Cass McCasland!

Cass turned the roan mare—Cass doted on mares—into the hay field, letting it pick its way over the stubble a ways before reining up, naturally, in front of the Dane girl. The roan eyed the girl's water bucket and then shook itself, rattling its harness. Cass, ever the gentleman, got out of the buggy with an unfolding of long legs. He offered her a

"Good afternoon" as elaborately as if he'd come courting. Then he came up with "It's right hot," as if maybe she hadn't noticed.

The girl said something, although she spoke only Danish so far as Riley knew, and then Cass said something Riley didn't catch, although he nearly threw an ear out of joint trying. And then Riley was damned if Cass didn't get offered a dipperful of water as though he'd been working in the sun all day right along with the rest of them! Worse, he took his drink with her holding the dipper and him bending down from his height of six foot whatever and the girl giggling at what spilled over his chin. It was like maybe they were lovebirds, getting mirth out of any silly thing they did together.

"Inga!" the farmer said sharply, with alarm in his voice, and for once Riley agreed with him. Cass looked up startled and wiped his chin. Suddenly wary of her father, Inga backed from Cass, the bucket held girlishly in both hands and its weight pressing her dress against her.

Then Cass found Riley among the line of hayers, and his face went straight to amusement. His eyes ticked from one to the other: father, daughter, Riley. In some wrath, Riley planted his pitchfork tines eight inches into the sod, figuring he might as well go see what fool scheme Cass had for him this time.

The farmer barked in Danish to his Danish sons and neighbors, using the same tone that sergeants used. Instantly, the line of hay pitchers unposed from their surprise at Cass's appearance and bent to work, flinging hay into the rick. Riley, figuring he couldn't be held responsible for understanding foreign tongues, kept walking, although he took the precaution of keeping his eyes off the farmer.

"If you don't look like some damn granger," Cass said in pretended disgust. Which smart comment, Riley considered, did not deserve an answer. "I figured you for having more pride," Cass said. "Look at your hat, sweated plumb through."

Cass, who was South Texas born, used cowhand expressions like "plumb through" when demonstrating his superiority over anyone who stooped to ground work. Riley knew that, and knew he was being baited, but the hat was a new one; so before Riley could think of an answer having the proper starch to it, he took the hat off and examined it. Cass was right: a dark, jagged stain like the outline of distant mountains had spread from the hat's brim toward the crown. When it dried, its former frontier would be demarcated by a line of Riley's salt. *Damn.*

"A horsehair band would cover it," Riley decided.

"No better than a sodbuster," Cass said, pretending disgust again. "For pete's sakes, go get your horse."

"Can't."

"Why ever not?" Cass looked around for it.

"I lost it," Riley said. He was beginning to feel sheepish, standing in his sweated clothes, with Cass in white shirt and vest. The girl smiled at both of them. Her father, though, was wielding his pitchfork in a fury, as if demonstrating how well it would serve as a weapon.

"You lost a whole horse?"

"It's a long story," Riley said, but then decided he should not have to explain at all. By rights, it was Cass who should do the explaining.

"You," Riley said, pegging a finger. "Four whole days! After you promised to be gone only *two.*"

"What promise? That was more in the nature of a prediction," Cass said. "It happened I had to go all around Robin Hood's barn. You know how those things go."

"So did you get buffalo wagons or didn't you?"

"Not exactly, no."

"We're not going hunting at all, are we?" Riley said. "Last week all you could talk about was how the future lay in buffalo hides. But now plans have changed—I can tell by your face."

"I've got a line on something better," Cass admitted. "Just get in the danged buggy. I didn't come halfway to nowhere to leave without you."

"No sir," Riley said. The farmer was glaring at him again,

then looking off to the ugly clouds massing in the northwest, then back to Riley, making a connection clear enough for an ox to understand: Get to work before the rain comes.

"You go through the same song and dance every time," Cass said. "In the end, you'll give in anyhow."

"Is that so?" Riley decided he'd put his foot down. Stubbornness was one of his weaknesses. "In that case, I'm staying."

"In this heat?"

"Farming's honest work—not that you'd understand the satisfaction of that."

Cass, whose own weaknesses ran quicker toward impatience, said, "Oh, get in." To demonstrate, he got back into the buggy.

"I danged well mean it," Riley said. "Here you take our money and go looking for a buffalo rig. Naturally when you're gone that long, I'm going to get in a game. What else can a person do in a two-bit place like Jacksboro?"

"You could've had a little faith I was looking out for our interests," Cass said. He looked up at the buggy roof like he'd got out of the sun in the nick of time.

"I don't cheat at cards like some I know," Riley said. "There's times luck runs against me."

"It does every time, on account of you lack the knack," Cass said. He sighed. "So you got in a game and went broke, and then hired on to a farmer."

"The hotel kicked me out. I got hungry. I took my best offer."

"All right, you did your best. Now just get in."

"No sir, and that's my last word." Riley backtracked and yanked up his pitchfork for emphasis. Sometimes he wished he weren't the kind to go in for big stubborn acts. But then he wished Cass were a lot of other things too. As his hands reacquainted themselves with the pitchfork's weathered handle, he recognized his blisters would burst by suppertime. By tomorrow they'd be sore as blazes.

The farmer called out something in Danish, a harangue.

known the man spoke English at all, "he who partakes of liquor, he shall not sup at my table."

"Beer's not liquor," Cass noted, then swigged again.

"Also, I pay only for da whole day of vork," the Dane said. "Stop vorking now, you get notting."

"There's two bottles here for each of us," Cass said. "Once you're refreshed, I'll tell you all the particulars. You're going to agree this idea's a lulu."

Riley looked at the girl, the other pitchforkers, the glaring farmer, the beer.

"Better make up your mind," Cass said. "I only hired this rig till nine o'clock tonight."

2 · HECTOR GARZA

UNDER A GREASED-PAPER SKY, NO SHADOW COULD LIVE. SOMEwhere, rain would visit this night—somewhere, Hector thought sourly, but perhaps not here. When it came to rain, he was a pessimist.

He drew up his horse, then tugged his hat lower to rest his eyes against the glare of a bright and hazy day. Rolling a cigarette took a minute's concentration. He lit it, then squinted through smoke at his afternoon's work, his face bearing the critical look of one who is sleepy.

The cattle were scattered in loose bunches, with here and there a broad-hatted rider showing above the animals' backs. They were doing simple ear marking, culling out Halfmoon newborns from the newborns of their neighbors, the BR's in particular. It was lazy work, a patch-up business till the fall roundup and branding, and it caused the day to clock slowly, all the more so without the markers of sun and shadow.

These were spring calves, next season's yearlings, and soon after, the producers of what Hollis Creigh—and

Hector, too, for that matter—hoped would be the biggest crop of Halfmoon animals yet. The eventual goal was enough four-year-old steers to warrant the first trail drive gotten up on their own hook and using their own vaqueros. What the Halfmoon had done in years past, raising steers to be drovered north on a shares basis by other ranchers, was the way to build a herd, but only by driving its own animals did an outfit take in top dollar.

Hector sighed when he thought of trail driving. On the one side, he was edging fifty, and he did not relish sleeping short nights on hard ground for two months at a stretch. Yet on the other side, Hollis Creigh, Hector's brother-in-law and the Halfmoon's owner, had lost a leg in the crazy fighting of northern Americans against southern. This meant that whether Hollis chose to go or not, Hector, as Halfmoon foreman, would be the true boss of the journey. And on that same side also, the picture Hector made—of himself and his vaqueros driving steers past startled Kansas town dwellers—was a picture to savor.

But again on that first side, what would he be boss of? Perhaps no more than a *ponedero,* a nest of troubles, and himself the mother hen. Trouble was all too likely between Halfmoon men and any gringo drovers they met along the way, for English-speaking cowboys and Mexican vaqueros approached one another with rivalries well established. And then was the matter of *Indios,* wild rulers of the Territory, and also of black-coated Kansas marshals, who held white Texans to be vermin, and vaqueros lower still. Pah, Hector thought, and spat.

And also, among this same nestful of Hector's troubles, was this *gallo,* the rooster Roberto, Hector's nephew, son of Hollis Creigh and Dominga, Hector's sister. In age, seventeen years, and still mad over missing the chance to prove himself in the big *yanqui* war, and so all the more eager to prove himself against those gringo drovers, those *Indios,* those marshals, or anyone else he came across.

Hector said pah! aloud this time, and called himself a woman for fretting over that which had not yet happened.

He tossed the remaining fraction of cigarette and ran his gelding indifferently over it, figuring there was not enough grass in August to sustain a cow, much less a prairie fire. Then his eyes settled on a low spot, low enough to be greener than elsewhere, testimony that it did rain in Texas, despite much evidence to the contrary.

In that pocket four riders had collected, a waste of manpower considering the light duty of ear marking. Hector made out his nephew Roberto by the boy's quick movements. Miguel was another, distinguishable by his peaked sombrero. Who the other two were, Hector could not guess, but their identities did not matter so much as that they were there at all. No task Hector could think of required four men in that hollow.

Hector gave his horse a touch of his big-roweled spurs, setting it to a trot. Most likely the congregation had good reason; Halfmoon vaqueros were rarely slackers, a testament to Hector's careful hiring. He only hoped he wouldn't find a cow down. Accidents were accidents, and happened no matter how closely cattle were nursemaided. Disease, though, had a way of spreading.

Hector was nearly into the low spot, seeing it for an old buffalo wallow, when he made out Nash Wheeler, foreman of the BR, a sprawling neighbor to the Creighs' southwest. The remaining rider coalesced into young Cole, son of Libba Barlow, the BR's owner.

Hector's back straightened; he pursed his lips so that his mustache bristled. The ugly business this young one, this Cole, had caused at a dance that summer was with Hector *estar sangrando*—a festering wound. As why would it not be, for everyone had talked of it? The target of the ugliness had been Angelina, Roberto's sister, niece to Hector himself and in all the world his favorite.

To Hector's mind, it had been a Spanish affair—the house was Spanish-speaking, the music was their music. That Cole had been there at all was a thing to be noted. But to come in thus, among people not his own, and then to show disrespect for a landowner's daughter. . . . *Ay!* Men died for less.

In Hector's wild days, he would have cut Cole Barlow with the blade he used for castrating young bulls. But years had seasoned him, and English-speaking Texas law had become more watchful. For both these reasons, Hector had learned to postpone his vengeances, taking them in appropriate times and places.

Still unseasoned, however, was young Roberto. Only Hector's quick anticipation had prevented Roberto from shooting Cole Barlow on the spot. The incident sharpened old contentions between the Creighs' Halfmoon Ranch and the Barlow family's BR over range and water rights. And contention, Hector considered from the ripeness of his decades, was something both young Roberto and this *mocoso,* this Cole, had too great a taste for.

Feeling urgency, Hector loped the last twenty rods, collecting the men's attention as he reined in. Whatever trouble had come up, it was Hector's place as Halfmoon foreman to look into it.

"Mr. Wheeler," Hector said in the reserved way in which he spoke his English.

Wheeler acknowledged. "Hector."

Hector let his eyes touch on Miguel, as steady a vaquero as Hector had ever hired, then he shifted to his nephew Roberto and to Cole Barlow, seeing hard faces.

The men were looking at a black bull that circulated with stiff-legged intent among the cattle. The steers paid him no mind, but the cows were wary, breaking from his approach into short, rocking-chair jogs and then standing moon-eyed and fearful, switching their tails.

"What thing is this?" Hector said. He'd begun in English with Nash Wheeler, so he stayed with it to address his nephew.

"It's all with him," Roberto said. He executed a nod of his hat brim, pointing out Cole Barlow.

"The hell it is!" Cole said. "It's that randy devil bull of yours. Me and Nash caught it mounting a BR cow. Damned sure my ma don't want our calves tainted with wild Mex blood."

Hector felt his face go baffled. A bull did what a bull did: it mounted. This was a bull's whole usefulness.

"You see? You hear that?" Roberto said. He shook his head in private disgust, then muttered in Spanish that Cole Barlow had a picket pin up his backside. Miguel sniggered in appreciation.

"*¡Silencio!*" Hector said. He turned to study the bull, which was outsized, as black as gunpowder, and all horns, hooves, sinew, and bones, even more so than other longhorns. Yet, it was no devil—only a bull. "*Merde,*" Hector said. "These young roosters."

Nash Wheeler laughed. "I guess Hector hoped you two was scratching over something more interesting than true love amongst cattle." Wheeler meant it for humor but none of the faces altered.

"I am frigging well serious," Cole said, his features fisted in annoyance. "You work up a herd with some quality, then let an animal like that in with them? It don't make sense. It's like to taint the whole bunch."

Hector scowled at this talk of tainting. He supposed he knew little about breeding, a subject all the bigger ranchers were talking about these days. But himself, he liked the looks of a bull like that. The animal was a reminder that cattle could have their own fire and spirit—that they were something more than walking meat.

The bull's flank carried a smudged brand that stood out poorly against the blackness of its hide. Hector asked Wheeler, "It is certain this one is ours?"

"What are you, blind?" Cole said. "The BR wouldn't never let an animal that ugly keep its oysters."

"Pardon, señor—the boy speaks much crazy," Miguel said. He too addressed Wheeler, as though reasoning with Cole were not worth the effort.

Cole said, "Boy, hell."

"The animals have run together free always," Hector pointed out, "no matter what brand is on them. I think each one is another's brother or sister."

Wheeler took off his hat to wipe his forehead. "Cole, to

my mind, what Hector's saying is about the size of it." He shrugged. "I figure a longhorn's daddy is nobody's business. If any's pedigreed, it's the first I heard of it."

"It has always been thus," Hector said.

A lot of mad was bunched in Cole's face. "Damn it, Nash, they're a *Mex* outfit!"

"What's that got to do with it?" Wheeler said, which sounded to Hector like an honest question.

"How do we know the Creighs ain't using for seed bulls a bunch of bull-ring killers?" Cole said owlishly.

Young Roberto laughed, mustering up elaborate scorn. Hector was tempted to laugh too, but since he had ridden in to play peacemaker, and since Cole's temper was the first thing anyone mentioned when his name came up, it seemed a bad idea. Instead, he looked away, seeing a couple of riders watching from a distant rise. He couldn't tell if they were BR men or somebody else's.

Of course Cole was manufacturing trouble; range bulls mounted any cow they fancied. But Cole Barlow, being himself, was bound he'd be a trial on everybody. He sat now giving his big gray a feel of his spurs, and at the same time reining back, making the horse dance against the bit. It was a useless action that Hector found irritating.

"Much work waits before suppertime," Hector said. He was tiring of so much talk of bulls.

"I expect you could rope the damn animal and haul it back toward your place," Nash Wheeler suggested.

"I am not the one doing this," Miguel said, as if the job would fall automatically to him. He shook his head, making the sombrero rock. "The bull is not broke his eggs yet. Mr. Barlow stop him and he is all mad about it."

Wheeler tried out a laugh about the bull's eggs, but it didn't come to much. Hector looked again at the bull, taking in the wicked horns, the hulking shoulders. The day was too humid for fighting, whether it was men or bulls or anything.

He thought of suggesting that if all five riders put their reatas on the animal, they could do anything they wanted with it. But before he could speak, the rangy bull bellowed and rose up on hind legs to mount another cow. The cow went wide-eyed and tried to plunge away, but the bull, bellowing again and its nostrils flaring, pinned it with urgent forelegs against its pumping belly.

Cole shouted, *"Well, damn it to hell!"* and wheeled his horse. Seeing bulls mount cows was never pretty, but this one, Hector had to admit, had the look of the kind that mounted and killed in the same act. He'd seen it before; any cattleman had.

Cole Barlow spurred. His startled horse shot straight at the rangy bull, now coupling savagely. Two jumps and horse and rider were beside it, the horse going to side-stepping, unhappy to be so close.

Before Hector could think to yell or to do anything, Cole swept out his revolver and fired, the muzzle four feet from the rutting bull's shoulder. The report nerve-pulsed through Hector's mount and through his own body.

Cole fired again. He yelled, "Son of a bitch!" as his horse reared at the shots. Bawling cows scattered, their eyes peeled wide. The men's faces were blank with the suddenness of it.

As his gray's hooves touched back to ground, Cole fired three times more, his arm locked out straight and the long barrel close to the bull's ear. At each report, the gun kicked back and spurted flame against the bull's hide. A stink of powder and scorched hair rose up sharp and hellish.

The bull snorted, its eye rolling white. Its forelegs lost their grip; the cow got away from underneath it and cantered off.

"Frigging killer bastard!" Cole shouted as his horse reeled. He pulled his mount a few yards off and jerked it to a standstill.

The bull stood on splayed legs, its head swaying, all its dim processes focused behind the eyes somewhere, as though assessing inner damage. It hooked a horn at some imaginary enemy. Then a foreleg buckled, and the bull's great head and forequarters thumped heavily to the ground. Miquel said, "¡Dios!" in a hushed voice.

The bull wheezed bloody foam from its muzzle. It struggled against the earth to regain its feet. In the bull's last movement, the hindquarters collapsed and the carcass rolled to one side. Cloven hooves swung up briefly in momentum, then subsided.

"Bloody Jesus!" Nash Wheeler said.

Cole looked at them wildly. A muscle twitched alongside his mouth. Then, what had been awe in his eyes evolved to triumph. "Damned devil killer," Cole said, his voice lifting in elation. His revolver still trailed smoke.

Nash Wheeler was shaking his head. Miguel was caught in horror. Roberto was behind Hector, but Hector did not have to turn to read his nephew's intentions; he read them in Cole Barlow's eyes.

Hector jabbed spurs and wheeled, shouldering his horse into Roberto's. The boy's gun was drawn and cocked. Hector grabbed for it, got a poor grasp around the cylinder, and pushed the muzzle skyward. For seconds they wrestled in earnest, their booted legs touching. When the gun blasted, the fire spurting between the cylinder and barrel singed Hector's hand, and the noise set his ears ringing. Angered, he jerked the gun away, nearly unseating his nephew with the force of it.

"Damn you!" Roberto said, annoying Hector all the more because the words came in English.

A space opened. Hector tried to pop one ear to get hearing back into it. He came aware of Cole, sitting his horse and aiming his pistol at Roberto.

Cole said, "Lookit there, Nash—I would've had Roberto before he even got off a shot." Then he eased down the hammer, and, showing satisfaction, shoved the gun into its holster.

Hector puffed for breath. With his hand afire and one ear still ringing, he decided he would shoot the next man to draw a pistol, just to save himself aggravation. While he puffed, he examined the blackened welt across his palm where the powder had burned him. It amounted to little; branding irons often scorched him worse.

"Is your boy cooled a mite?" Nash Wheeler asked him.

Hector turned to see Roberto still angry enough to trail smoke. For his answer, Hector stuck Roberto's pistol into his own belt.

"All right," Wheeler said. He steered his mount toward the dead bull, not giving the horse slack to fight him. Then he swung off, moving as gravely as a man who is drunk and is taking pains to hide it.

"Nash, I would've had him clean," Cole said again.

"Hell you would," Wheeler said. "Your gun's empty." Miquel managed a laugh. Wheeler tossed dirt at the bull's staring eye, testing for life. The eye, however, was already dull, its moisture dried. Hector saw it would not blink again.

"I guess that showed old toro what cow to hump," Cole said. He rammed empty cartridges from his revolver and began putting in fresh ones.

"You're twice the fool," Roberto said. "That cow the bull had was one of our Halfmoons, not a BR."

Cole said, "Like hell," but the fact that he jerked around to look showed he was in doubt. Hector looked too. The gun noise had scattered the nearest cattle to a distance of thirty paces. One cow, already grazing, wore a clear-burnt BR brand; another standing placidly beside it had the Creighs' Halfmoon and single ear notch.

"It's done now anyway," Nash Wheeler said. Standing afoot among mounted men made him look small. He seemed to feel it, for he swung back into his saddle and immediately looked relieved.

"Someone shall pay for this animal," Hector told him. "Mr. Creigh, he will require payment."

"Creigh can keep his frigging seed bulls off Barlow range," Cole put in. "His half-breed whelps, too."

The term rang like a slap. All the men looked at Roberto, who sat disarmed and seething. "Tio Hector," Roberto said, "you give me my pistol."

"No pistol," Hector said.

Cole started to speak, but Wheeler said, "You done enough with your six-shooter. You'd best keep your mouth out of it."

Hector turned to Cole for the first time. He was more man than boy, despite his actions, bigger than Roberto and probably more than a match for him. "You fixing to say something?" Cole demanded.

"I will say that besides paying for this animal," Hector told him, "you also can skin it. One may see you have a knife."

Cole snorted. "Anybody who thinks I'm skinning their stinking bull is loco."

"Such a hide brings two dollars," Hector said. "Mr. Wheeler, you are the foreman. You must tell him."

They looked at Wheeler, Hector with them. His claim, Hector knew, was just. Cole skinning the animal would be one step toward smoothing the matter. What Hector wanted was Wheeler's ruling on the incident as the BR's foreman.

"Hell," Wheeler said, "I give up trying to boss him a year or two back. All I do is work for his ma."

Hector, disgusted, shook his head. "So then I must talk to Hollis Creigh, who must talk to the mother, who then must talk to this one like the *niño* he is."

Cole shifted a hand to his revolver butt. "Cole!" Wheeler said.

There was a space in which no one moved; then Cole Barlow wheeled his cow pony, coming out of the turn with the animal facing uphill. He jabbed spurs to its flanks and pounded to a gallop, riding up out of the hollow with his back rigid.

"Yes, you run," Hector said. "He runs from being a man, this one."

Cole could not have heard it, but he turned and called back, "This ain't over by a long shot."

"Once more, we will ask Mr. Wheeler for *justicia* in this," Hector said.

Wheeler shrugged. "You fellers do what you think best. I've wasted enough time on this." Hector saw another thought cross Wheeler's eyes. "Hell, Cole being just another BR cowhand is let's-pretend and everybody knows it,"

Wheeler said. "You do like you said and have Hollis take it up with Cole's mama. I expect Libba will pay the bill."

Roberto said, "By God, somebody's still going to skin this animal."

Wheeler's face took on amusement. "The young bucks are all het up today, Hector."

Hector saw it was an invitation for him to ally with Wheeler against the younger men—Cole, Roberto, even Miguel. "Roberto speaks correctly in this," Hector said seriously. He shrugged to show that facts were facts.

"Well, me, I've cleaned up enough of Cole's messes," Wheeler said. "It's time somebody else took their turn at it." He turned his horse and loped away.

While Hector watched Wheeler's diminishing back, Roberto came up at Hector's elbow. "Uncle, I request now the return of my pistol." Roberto spoke formal Spanish, suggesting sarcasm.

"Yes," Hector said, "perhaps tomorrow you may have it."

Roberto's face knuckled. He kicked up his horse and rode out of the wallow, taking the opposite direction from Cole and Nash Wheeler.

Hector was left with Miguel. He tried to roll a cigarette but was annoyed to find his fingers trembling. There was no fear in it; it was anger, unvented. He put the tobacco away while Miguel regarded the bull mournfully. Hector's ear still buzzed like locusts.

"Miguel, I am sorry it is you who shall skin this animal," Hector said in Spanish, "but thus are the circumstances."

"I also am very sorry," Miguel said, and swung a leg off his horse and got down.

3 · CASS McCASLAND

THE ROAN MARE HAD SETTLED TO A WALK, AND THE DOUBLE TRACK had fed into a wider track and then into the rutted road to Jacksboro before either of them said anything. The landscape was the stretched-out kind Texas was famous for, allowing him a sweep of country for miles in every direction except northwest, where brooding clouds were bunched up, obscuring the sun.

The muggy air kept the clopping of the mare's hooves bottled up against the buggy. After a stretch of listening to it, not speaking became a strain. At one point Cass formed up in his mind a humorous comment on how sweated Riley was. But then he thought better of it, remembering Riley was in a mood, and anyway, Cass had smelled sweat plenty of times. Besides which, if they'd wanted a life featuring regular baths, they wouldn't be spending time in a place like Jacksboro.

"Those little old clouds won't amount to a thing," Cass said. "All they're doing is making it muggy." Cass knew that long years on a Kentucky farm had bred into Riley an enduring interest in weather. Whenever Riley got sulky, weather was usually a safe bet for coaxing him out.

"Um," Riley said, which Cass considered better than nothing.

"Look at that—heat lightning. Still and all, I bet it doesn't come to anything."

Riley looked to where Cass pointed and sipped glumly on his beer. Cass thought the edges on his friend's expression maybe appeared rounded off a little, which was progress. Glum was better than mad, Cass thought. Glum he could handle.

"Ever heard of Coronado?" Cass said. "One of those Spaniard explorers who traipsed around this country?"

"I don't care if I have or haven't," Riley said. "I only came along on account of the beer."

"It was in the real olden days, even before the Mexicans came in. Texas must have been something back then."

"It's mostly empty now," Riley pointed out.

"Anyhow, that's what some of the *hombres* in town tell me. The old legends, dating way back to—"

"You speak Mexican?"

"I speak Spanish, sure. I grew up with Mexican families. They lived all around our place."

"I never knew it," Riley said.

"Well, these old fellows were explaining about Francisco Coronado, how he'd found so much gold he couldn't carry half of it. And then his men started dying off from fever. So what's old Coronado to do but bury it?"

Riley could sometimes be a trial to read. Right now he wasn't giving away anything.

"So, being cautious," Cass said, "he makes himself a map that he carries next to his heart. Only by the time he gets back to Spain, somehow the map doesn't."

Riley turned; on his face was the stamp of conviction. "Don't tell me you bought a treasure map." Cass blinked. "Gol dang it, Cass, that is the oldest trick in the book. The first time some feller offered me a Spanish treasure map, I got mad and kicked the slats out of my cradle."

"What do you mean, slats in your cradle? I'm talking the genuine article. Wait'll you see it, all old-time parchment and—"

"Excepting part of it is smudged," Riley said, "or maybe burnt. And the man selling it has been hunting that gold for years, only he can't quite find it on account of the burnt part. And all that's needed is somebody new to look at the clues from a fresh angle."

"How'd you know about the burnt part?" Cass said. His collar button was beginning to feel tight.

"I swan," Riley said, disgusted. "The same feller come up to me about it."

"Naw. This was kind of a short Mexican."

"That sure narrows it down."

"Could be any age," Cass said. "Looks like he spent thirty years prospecting."

"Or ten years drinking," Riley said. "One I saw had two gold front teeth you could hardly take your eyes off of."

Cass said, "Damn."

"It's what puts the shine on his pitch—you standing there listening and eyeballing those gold teeth. Puts you in mind of golden treasure. Only I wasn't having any. I told him to go jump."

Cass said, "It doesn't necessarily mean—"

"The whole thing sounds like something you yourself would've cooked up," Riley said. "Only now you're the swindled one. Or rather, you and me both. If you didn't believe in pie in the sky in the first place, you wouldn't be so gullible."

Cass sat in silence. The map was still fact; he had it tucked away in a hotel safe. "It's still worth following up," he said. "Just think of that much gold."

"Believe me, the gold in the teeth is all you'll ever see," Riley said. "You never used to be this dumb up in Kansas. Texas being your home country, you must've let your guard down. Anyhow, better gee up that mare, or we're going to get soaked."

Thinking back on it later, Cass realized that sometime during their conversation the clouds must have changed from the kind that mass up with no notion of doing anything, to the kind that mass up and roll at you with the bloody intent of a buffalo stampede. At the time, though, the first change he noticed was the wind picking up.

"We turn around now, we'd be back at that granger's in thirty minutes," Riley said, raising his voice on account of the wind. "I'll bet for ten cents he'd let us sleep in the barn."

"This will blow right on by," Cass said, but to humor Riley, he chucked the mare to a trot. "Besides which, I don't relish sleeping in any Swede farmer's barn."

"Danish," Riley said, at which point a swirl of dust came down the road, followed by a whole fuss and ruckus of it, making them grab their hats. In a minute, Cass could hardly hold the mare into the wind; she wanted to shy off onto the prairie.

"Better find a hole to hide in!" Riley shouted. He anchored his hat with one hand and gripped the seat rail with the other. It was suddenly dark as dusk, though only five o'clock. *"There's a low spot by those trees!"* Riley pointed toward a pair of cottonwoods, both whipping like clothes on a line.

Cass started to yell he surely wasn't lying down in any dry wash in his vest and suit pants, when, through the murk, he made out the writhing, hell-bound snake of a Texas twister, fat and black and coming straight at them. It came on like a locomotive, sucking everything in its path, about ninety percent of which at that moment was the rig and the roan and Riley and him.

"Cyclone!" Riley shouted, and bolted off the buggy, his hat shooting away like a passing bird. Cass jumped out to follow, whacking the mare a good one as he went by to get her out of the twister's path. As he bounded for the wash he saw the mare turn from the storm's fury, leap straight to a gallop, and run off, dragging the rig. Spears of grass were whistling past like bullets when he dove into the wash.

They lay on their bellies, trying to burrow into gravel. The noise was total—a howling within a roar, five trains colliding, steamboats exploding, hell's furnace erupting. Then there was a tremendous *whoosh!* that nearly sucked Cass's brains out. And then the twister was past, bringing on its heels great cracks of thunder that shook the earth and then lightning that stabbed around them—twice, three times. The fourth crackling arrow of lightning exploded one of the cottonwoods into a shower of sparks and shivered kindling not forty feet from where they lay.

"Cripes!" Riley said, for torrents followed. By the time

the worst had spent itself and eased down into no more than wild rain, they were as soaked as bathers. As if the rain had not been enough, the dry wash filled up quickly; then a little wall of water rolled down on them, turning the wash to a creek, turning Cass and Riley to drowned fish. They stood up in the last of the swirling rain, amid smells of brimstone and split cottonwood. Despite the rain, the shattered tree still smoked.

The horse had run east, going with the storm, but though the plains were as featureless as a spread blanket, Cass could see neither horse nor high-topped buggy. It was as if the twister had wanted them.

Cass resisted tallying up the cost of a roan mare and a high-topped rig. More than a hundred dollars, for damned sure. He said, "I doubt we'd have made the granger's place anyhow."

"Just don't say a word," Riley said. His face was all ridges, like chipped rock. He slogged through the wash, now a creek, and when his boots struck the road he turned west and started walking. Cass heard anger in every boot squish. He called to Riley gently, "Would you rather be by yourself, or can I walk with you?"

Riley had to huff air out of himself before he could say, "McCasland, I don't care what you do," putting way too much enunciation into it. Then he walked straight on, managing considerable dignity in spite of the squishing.

Cass hurried to catch up. The western horizon looked as clean as fresh-washed windows, so that Cass could make out the roofs of Jacksboro a good six miles off.

Without turning, Riley added, "Just don't say one single, blessed word."

4 · NASH WHEELER

NASH FOLLOWED THE YOUNGER MEN ON THE PUDDLED DOUBLE track out of Jacksboro. He rode with the sun in his face, his back slumped and his mind banked to mere embers. He was disgusted with himself. From then on, he'd let his horse do his thinking.

His own thinking, right up till late afternoon the previous day when young Cole had announced his ma, Libba Barlow, was letting the hands off early, had run along the lines of saving up his pay. Saving for what, Nash wasn't sure, but it was high time he set something aside against the ticking years, for years had been on his mind lately. The fact was, though he'd given no hint of the occasion to anybody, this morning marked his forty-fifth birthday.

Not that forty-five was some alarming height, particularly, from which he could see approaching infirmity, then death and a lonely grave. Yet it was a point affording a certain perspective—of how, if a man weren't careful, real age could one day creep up on him.

Nash had lately caught himself using the younger hands as a yardstick, and had frowned to notice it, figuring a need to make comparisons was in itself a sign of age. He didn't see why he should concern himself; he worked, after all, the same long day the hands did, sunup to dusk, often later. If he'd begun practicing economy in his movements, if he'd given up breaking devil-eyed horses, a man with salt in his hair could concede that much to maturity and still keep his self-respect. As BR foreman, Nash spent more time herding men than cattle and horses anyway.

What the years cost him most painfully was a kind of mental ledger work. In one column stood the forty-five years, foursquare and unalterable, balanced against which he could set little more than his situation at the BR.

Certainly Nash's portion of what a man could put a price to tallied a bare notch above nothing. Between sawbuck boots and a three-dollar hat, he wore fifty cents' worth of shirt and britches. He owned a gunbelt, a Colt's revolver, and a tailor-made Hope Tree saddle. In respect of his foreman's job, he had private use of a lean-to room off the harness shed, with a hayburning stove, a buffalo robe on his bunk, and a patent liniment calendar on the wall, none of which belonged to him. He didn't even own a horse.

Where had he spent so many years? Mostly in siding Coleman Barlow, before the war in the days of open range, and again after it in great drives to the Kansas railheads. Nash had had the sand for all of it, and for the war besides.

But besides sand, Coleman himself had had the grand notions, and also the knack of studying a thing out beyond its apparent horizons. Then, once he'd married Elizabeth, called Libba, Coleman Barlow had had capital as well, and soon after, the sprawling BR, two-story ranch house and all, carved out of supposedly free land with the help of expensive lawyers.

With Coleman Barlow in his grave, Nash rode for Libba, a situation about which he was of two minds at least. Cowhand wisdom said a man who worked for a woman might as well marry her, thus becoming entitled to certain compensations. What Nash ought do was court Coleman's widow, with an eye to becoming heir to what, if sweat were coin, should have been part his by now anyway.

But he thought then of Libba Barlow, Libba and her steel-edged laugh, and knew he couldn't suggest so much as a buggy ride without her seeing through him. Which was another way of saying he'd be damned if he'd do it.

No sir, the thing was to pile up a nest egg, either for assembling a few cows of his own some day, his late start notwithstanding, or to ease his way to greener pastures—to a town like Fort Worth, maybe, or even St. Louis, where he could take his one big swing at faro or poker, and maybe cash in big.

But then, on that previous afternoon Nash was still

thinking of, young Cole had ridden up, pleased with himself as a coyote pup, saying he'd got them off early. The hands had whooped and raced for the bunkhouse to put on clean shirts, and Nash had felt the town's old tug. Soon a night in Jacksboro beckoned so strongly that saving his pay seemed a caution for old men. Nash was damned if he didn't have some howl left in him.

Now they were six BR riders—young Cole Barlow leading, then Quirt Hanson and Lew Christmas, then Nash, then Corny Powell and his brother Tom, not one except for Nash out of his twenties—heading back to the outfit after a long Saturday night in town. Tom Powell, a kid of seventeen, was the worst off, having upchucked his liquor in a whorehouse parlor, and now half blind and half dead with headache.

Nash himself, still having some drunk in him, was feeling better than he knew he was going to in a couple of hours. Of course he was broke again, and sore at himself for so quickly losing his resolve. He felt horse-dragged from whiskey, and his eyes hurt like wounds. But the secret of having attained forty-five years cheered him in a grim way, like when a man has predicted the worst and the worst goes ahead and happens. He faced into a dawning, fast-stoking sun, feeling ancient and dangerous. He sang disconnected bits of "The Old Chisholm Trail" and was damned glad it was Sunday.

Cole was still drinking. "I bet you boys didn't get off early on Saturday when my pa was running things." He said it twisting in the saddle and looking back at them. Nash figured it would have been easier on the boy's neck if a couple hands would ride abreast of him.

At the comment the men looked at Nash, understandable because he went back on the Barlow place decades further than any of them. Hell, Nash had trailed cattle with Coleman Barlow before there'd been a Barlow place.

"Wouldn't have for a fact," Nash said. "We had to show that man calendars just to prove it was Sunday." It raised a general laugh, though not from Tom Powell, who rode with his eyes closed and his chin bumping his chest.

"Let's remember it was me putting in a word with my ma

that got us off at four o'clock," Cole said. "You don't get off till late and it's hardly worth going to town." He tipped up the bottle and drank. Though what Cole said was true enough, Nash figured the BR hands hardly needed reminding. For someone who hankered to fit in as one of them, Cole mentioned his ma too often.

"I'm sure we're all eternal grateful," Nash said. "Especially young Tom there."

It drew Cole around again, eyes dull brass from drink. "You don't like it, Nash, you can by gol set fence posts of a Saturday night." It was the kind of remark, Nash recognized, that only Cole got away with. Regular BR hands did not rebuke Nash Wheeler.

"Oh, I am tickled all over about it," Nash said mildly. There was an empty stretch in which six horses clopped tiredly and Nash felt eyes on him. He shrugged them off, not feeling like playing foreman this morning. Like he'd told Hector Garza, Cole being one of the hands was a let's-pretend business. Cole had no formal rank over anybody, but Coleman Barlow the father had been in his grave four years now, and Cole junior—though you did not call him junior—was Libba Barlow's remaining son, the older one, Hamp, having been killed at Shiloh. The plain fact was, Cole would eventually be the BR's owner, thus boss over them all.

Nash considered he was handling it the way Coleman the father would have wanted, bringing Cole up on the hard end of the cattle business, not cutting him slack. But since he'd gotten his growth, Cole was prodding here and tugging there, beginning to stake out the authority that would inevitably be his due. Hell, Nash reflected, that was probably to Cole's credit.

One thing Nash was sure of: when the time came that Libba ordered him to call Cole boss, that was the time, by gol, he would quit the BR. Whether he'd saved five hundred dollars or five dollars or no dollars at all.

The road angled, climbing a rise. When the sun hit their

faces, Tom Powell fisted his eyes and groaned. "Some sure can't hold their liquor," Cole said, and took a slug from his whiskey bottle, making sure they all knew who could.

"At least he made it upstairs first," Corny said, referring to his brother's upchucking in the whorehouse parlor.

"If he even did anything," Cole said, and sniggered. "Just talked, probably."

"Tom did fine," Corny said.

Cole rode another minute, then swiveled in his saddle. "Speaking of Rosie's, one thing I want clear as branch water. I'm staking claim on that little Mex—that Veronica." He stayed twisted around, looking for a challenge.

"I'm setting it out plain," Cole said. "I ever hear somebody in this spread's been fooling with her, they've got trouble with me." He pointed to himself with the hand that held the bottle.

Lew Christmas said, "Nobody's saying different, Cole," with his voice coming through a yawn.

"Why, Cole, I ain't noticed your brand on that greaser filly, particularly," Nash said, which brought Cole's face back around in an instant. "And I expect I've seen about all of her."

Lew's and Quirt's laughter was tired but genuine, a contrast to when Cole tried to joke them. Nash figured he shouldn't provoke Cole like he did, but the boy bridled up so quickly that riding him was a satisfaction.

Cole observed, "You're kind of a son of a bitch this morning, Nash."

This time Nash laughed, clear to his belly. "I'm a son of a bitch *all* the time," Nash said. "Fact is, I'm the original."

"You'd like to think so," Cole said, so as to have the last word, but he'd let a kiddish petulance into his voice. To cover it, he looked off, pretending some interest in the northern horizon.

Nash laughed again, enjoying himself. Cole Barlow passed for wild, but folks nowadays were forgetting what wild was. Coleman Barlow the father, or Nash himself in his day—there was wild for you. That country in those days had had space for all kinds of oats sowing.

As Nash saw it, young Cole, rather than being truly careless about how he had his fun, was antsy to prove himself, and that got him into corners. He had a way of sticking to fool positions, stubborn as an oak stump—like that business of killing the Halfmoon bull, where Cole had worked his mouth to a place he couldn't ease down from. Nash could admire backbone, but it helped when backbone had some judgment behind it.

Nash supposed Cole's pa having been one of the first Texicans and later the biggest rancher along the North Trinity was cause for that streak in him. Nash's own pa had owned nothing and had left it all to Nash. And worse, damn him, had taken off one moonless night—going out as ordinary as if to the privy, only he kept right on going— leaving Nash's ma and a brood of kids to shift for themselves. The man was no account to begin with, Nash supposed, and a drunkard to boot. Now he was little more than a bitter memory, but certainly nobody Nash had to live up to.

"Anyhow, that Veronica is one hot pepper," Cole said, making Nash shake his head that Cole was still harping on it. "I figure she belongs to whoever can make her swoon the loudest. Which is me. Any crib girl in Jacksboro can tell you I got the knack for pleasuring women."

"You pay her double, she'll yowl like a cat," Nash said, at which Lew Christmas whooped and slapped his thigh and got scowled at by Cole, whose face had blooded up dark. Corny Powell and Quirt traded looks in merriment.

Then Tom Powell stopped his horse. Moving as enfeebled as an old man, he slipped a leg over his saddle cantle and more fell than dismounted. He fetched up on the short grass beside the road, his face pale as catfish belly and one boot in a puddle, left over from the storm. Nash reined in, then they all did.

"Geez, Tom." Corny Powell said it disappointed, as though his brother were letting down the family standard.

He swung down and collected the reins to Tom's horse, and then stood uncertainly.

"You fixing to die on us, Tom?" Nash said.

Cole, now a rod ahead of them, drew up and glared around to see who was or was not following. Tom Powell groaned again, and draped a lifeless forearm over his eyes. Corny Powell said hopefully, "You can ride, can't you, Tom?"

Cole took another swig from his bottle, gaining time, Nash figured, to think of another jab for one of them. They were on the lip of the rise. Beyond and below it were the crossroads and the Coover Stage Station. Cole looked like he might say something, but then Corny Powell said, "You all go on ahead," sounding resigned about it.

"I'm all right," Tom managed.

"We'll just stay here a spell," Corny said.

"You ain't my mother," Tom said, in about one-tenth his regular voice.

"Another drink's the best thing for him," Nash said. "Clear his head enough to get him home, anyway."

"I expect that's right on the money," Corny said. He looked at Cole Barlow, and then they all did.

Cole bristled. "Damned if he's getting my liquor." He examined his bottle, which held two fingers of whiskey. "Sending good whiskey after bad," Cole said. "He wasted enough already."

With an air of demonstration, Cole raised the bottle and drank, glugging twice. Then, with all eyes still on him, he pulled his revolver with his right hand, and with his left tossed up the bottle by its neck.

Corny Powell said, "Son of a bee, Cole—"

The bottle looped lazily into the sunlight. Cole yelled, "Nash!" as though performing only for him, and raised his gun and fired. The bottle passed undamaged through the top of its arc. Nash dropped a hand to his gun butt, then resisted the urge to show off.

"Damn," Cole said, and recocked. Halfway down, the bottle flashed as it caught the sun. Cole's second shot sounded of hopelessness, triggered when the bottle had plummeted to within a yard of the ground. The glass smashed when it hit the prairie.

"That second slug hit!" Cole said. "You all seen that much!"

Nash, embarrassed to have once been Cole's age, and at that time probably just about like him, looked off to the northwest to hide whatever expression his face might have carried. Cotton-boll clouds, signaling an end to restless weather, had puffed up beyond the North Trinity.

Cole said, "Quirt—dang it. You saw it!"

"I ain't sure. I guess it could've touched it."

"Could've? What are you, *blind?* Tell Nash I frigging well hit it!"

Lew and Quirt looked at Nash—helplessly, Nash thought. He was suddenly weary of them. In the war, he'd ridden with Quantrill, Jesse James, and the Youngers. It occurred to him that in the compadre department, it'd been a long slide downhill.

Cole said, "Well?"

"I expect both shots hit plumb center," Nash told them. He kept poker-faced and looked at Cole, but it cost him an effort. He felt suddenly older and tireder, as though the year had just then turned for him.

Cole's expression smoked. "By God, every time we take him with us, he sets us one against the other!" Cole danced his horse like he liked to do—giving it some rowel and holding it back at the same time. He glared at Nash, then he jerked the animal around and jumped it to a lope, going over the little rise.

"What did that have to do with anything?" Quirt said in amazement. Nash wondered too. Maybe there'd been some part of the conversation he'd missed. Or more likely, Cole had been having a conversation the livelong morning all by himself.

Nash looked at the Powell brothers. Tom was sitting upright, alarmed by the shots. Corny stood with reins in his hands, letting their horses graze. In some disgust over the wasted liquor, Corny said, "We're all right. You go on without us."

Without answering, Nash kneed his horse and went at a walk between Lew Christmas and Quirt Hanson. He started over the rise, taking the lead. Within ten lengths they saw the snake track of creek with its wooden bridge, then the Coover Stage Station, a collection of tumble-down buildings huddled into the crossroads. Cole was still loping, going downhill, his horse's hooves throwing mud. Beyond him, a rancher's two-horse surrey was making steady progress in his direction.

The rig, Nash knew, would belong to his old saddlemate —one-legged Hollis Creigh, owner of, or at least chief claimant to, the Halfmoon Ranch, a modest spread neighboring the Barlows' BR. Nash canted his hat for a better look. The passenger would be one of the Creigh hands, or maybe Hector Garza, Creigh's foreman and brother-in-law. The driver most likely would be Hollis himself, since going to town was a chore a one-legged rancher could handle.

Nash thought of Creigh and let himself be needled. Creigh was the one man Nash had heard of, not counting Yankee carpetbaggers, who'd made the war pay off. Though you had to give him credit too, on account of Creigh cared so little what people thought of him, hooking up with Mexican town and refusing to be apologetic about it. A lot of men went and had their fun there, but Hollis Creigh had married in.

Cole was already reining up in front of the Creighs' rig, blocking its progress, when Nash remembered the day was a Sunday—meaning the Jacksboro mercantiles would be closed, giving Hollis Creigh and his foreman no reason to go to town. Therefore, the rig would be carrying somebody else. Hollis Creigh and Hector Garza could take care of themselves, against Cole Barlow or anybody. But the figures in the buggy were likely not Hollis and Hector.

"Expect we better keep Cole out of trouble," Nash told Quirt Hanson glumly, and set his horse to a trot. By the time he was halfway down the rise, he could see it was indeed not Hollis Creigh at the reins but a younger man—in fact,

Hollis's son, Roberto. And the front-seat passenger was not a man at all, but a dark-haired girl in a Sunday dress, peach in color. She was the boy's older sister, Angelina, aptly called Angel. In the surrey's rear seat sat a black-clad figure, probably Dominga, Hollis's Mexican wife. The Creigh boy, Nash figured, was taking the women to church.

Nash stepped his horse up to a lope. Young Roberto Creigh and Cole Barlow were a bad combination; they were natural rivals anyway because of the disputed range between the two families. Nash also remembered some bad business between Cole and Angelina at a dance that summer. Then, three days ago, the Halfmoon bull that Cole had killed.

Nash resisted showing too much hurry. He held the horse to a lope, like he was just enjoying a little run, but he reined up alongside Cole Barlow feeling late, feeling words had already been said. One look at the faces told him that much.

"Christ Almighty," Cole was saying, and then turned to Nash with that sneer of his, the anger over the missed bottle or whatever it had been evidently all forgotten. "Guess how much he wants for that damned bull I plugged?" Triumph was in Cole's face and voice, as though he'd argued Roberto Creigh were crazy, and new evidence confirmed it.

Nash noted Roberto's and Angelina's tight faces. From the surrey's backseat, Dominga Creigh jabbered something in rapid Spanish.

"Thirty dollars!" Cole crowed. "Purely loco. Hell, they already got the frigging hide!"

"You mind your mouth," Roberto said. "Somebody ought to teach you your manners."

Cole said scornfully, "Who, *you?*" and at that point drew his gun—not fast, like he did when practicing it, but deliberately, like he was giving them a look at it. He said, "I expect anybody who wants to try can damned well get down." In the buggy, the three Creighs went stony, all watching Cole's gun.

Nash blinked, trying to take it in. He figured get down meant they'd settle it rough and tumble. Nash approved of that much; rough and tumble never killed anybody. Besides which, entertainments came seldom to cattle country, and he was in no hurry to get back to his bunk anyhow. But if it were to be fists and feet, then why had Cole pulled his revolver?

From the rear seat, Dominga Creigh wailed something high-pitched and alarmed. Angelina said, "Robbie, don't let him bait you." Nash threw a look over his shoulder, taking in Lew Christmas and Quirt Hanson trotting up, still five or six rods out and unaware of the confrontation. The fact was, they were grinning like apes on account of pretty Angelina.

When Nash looked back, Cole still sat his horse, his gun angled negligently toward the Creighs. On his face was the same thin smile you saw on him a lot. Then Cole cocked the gun, costing Nash a surge of alarm. At that point, Roberto bent forward, which looked harmless enough; Nash figured it was to drape the reins over the splashboard, the natural first movement in getting out of a buggy.

But from the surrey floor Roberto came up with a nickeled revolver. Nash's mind, whiskey-slowed from his long night, was caught mulling what Cole meant with his damned gun cocked—whether he was going to shoot to scare the Creighs' horses into running, or shoot to bluff somebody, or what.

Before Nash could blink, the opposing revolvers detonated together, the concussion hitting like a slap and the billows of smoke merging. Angelina's cry was lost in the roar. Mrs. Creigh clapped her palms to her ears and screamed.

Cole's horse reared up because of the gun noise, and to Nash's amazement, Cole slipped from the saddle, his left hand clawing for the horn and missing and the rein running through his fingers. He landed heavily in the double track, causing his horse to shy away, wanting him out from under its hooves.

Roberto grabbed up the surrey reins and demanded speed from his horses. Cole's spooked mount shouldered into Nash's, giving Nash a handful for a moment. Roberto Creigh, working his buggy whip, fixed Nash with a stricken look when he went by, but what stayed in Nash's mind was Angelina, a slender hand gripping the seat rail and her face dismayed—and looking at him, Nash Wheeler, as though he were a mortal enemy.

Roberto sped his rig in a wide arc, its wheels spoking bumpily on the prairie, aiming to intercept the north road to one side of the crossroads. Nash had his hand on his pistol butt, but he didn't see what good more shooting would do. He controlled his horse, then swung down and jogged to Cole, who lay on his back with a look of consternation, like a person grappling with oversized problems. His chest was heaving, and a splotch already the size of a dinner plate was growing on his shirt.

Behind Nash, Quirt and Lew drew up in a scuffle of hooves. "What in hell happened?" Quirt's voice said in wonder.

Nash Wheeler, in the war a rider for Quantrill and then Bloody Ben Poole, had seen a thousand wounds. Now his mind worked. He stepped over Cole to pick up the boy's gun. He stuck it in his own belt and kept his back turned.

"Help me pick him up," Nash ordered. He squatted and got Cole's head up and slid a hand under his back, feeling warm blood where the bullet had exited. He threw a look behind him; the BR hands were on the ground, Lew holding all the horses and Quirt coming up, hotfooting.

"Is he bad?"

"He's bad."

"Did Cole pull on him or what?" Quirt's voice sounded young and strained.

Nash bent again to Cole. The bullet hole was placed where it would have done a lot of damage. While Cole ebbed, it seemed to Nash that he himself had two minds—one there witnessing, a second one racing ahead.

"Cole drew," Nash said, "but slow, like he wasn't fixing to start anything."

"Well, bloody hell—that don't figure."

"Damn it, Quirt, help me get him to Coover's Station. We'd best carry him afoot."

"Did Cole shoot or not?" Quirt said. "I thought I only heard the one."

"He never shot," Nash said, grunting. "The Creigh boy must've been hair triggered."

5 · HOLLIS CREIGH

AT NINE O'CLOCK ON SUNDAY MORNING HOLLIS LOWERED HIMself to a chair on his front porch and tried to get comfortable. It was a struggle, but then so were a lot of things. He set his one foot up on the porch railing to take weight off the stump and leaned the crutches against the corner post.

The air was still fresh two days after the storm; even so, it did not take much crutch work to break him into a sweat. He sighed and with a shirtsleeve blotted perspiration that had collected in one eyebrow. He adjusted his spectacles, then opened the Bible.

His wife had raised their son and daughter in the Roman Catholic religion. The three of them were off to town that morning for Mass, held humbly enough in his wife's cousin's parlor, for there was no proper church in Jacksboro. Hollis himself had never cared for that brand of faith, seeing it as a lot of foreign mumbo jumbo that got in the way of sacred instruction. He'd been raised up Baptist, but he didn't care much for the shouting Baptists either.

What Hollis liked better was reading the book for himself, drawing lessons where he could and applying them in his own thinking. Hollis figured he could read the Bible as well as any pope or preacher—or any Yankee president, for that matter, remembering Grant was supposed to have a fondness for the Good Book right along with his famous cigars and whiskey.

He read a passage in Judges about Samson's vengeance and was reminded inevitably of the war. Soon the Bible lay in his lap while he followed memories, chasing down his old exploits till they turned bitter, cider to vinegar. God, what a business war was.

Some vaquero in the bunkhouse was strumming a guitar and trying to sing a *corrido* in a wrenching voice, wringing all possible emotion from it. It was that new man, Miguel something or other. The strumming was all right, but the singing wasn't. The singer kept hemming over the words, which ruined the song's intent, which was to be bold and impassioned. Hollis's Spanish wasn't strong enough to follow a *corrido* in any case. They were long and frequently doubled back on themselves in refrains, and usually dwelled on tragic subjects. The last time he'd asked what the words meant to a particular *corrido* had been at his wife's people's place, and he'd asked it of his wife's mother. Old Señora Garza told him apologetically that it was a true and sad story about the Tejanos taking over the country from the people, meaning the Mexican people. Hollis had gotten embarrassed and had never asked about another one.

He listened awhile longer despite himself, not much caring for the *corrido*. He liked a guitar because it made strong, rhythmic music, but even so, it was not his music. Given his druthers, he'd take popular songs on a piano.

Hollis must have achieved at least some degree of comfort, because when the rider galloped into view down the long track leading up to his buildings, he groaned at the thought of having to get up again. The rider pounded, maintaining all speed, coming on like wild Comanches.

To confirm what he was seeing, Hollis took off the reading glasses, then called, "Hector!" toward the tiny log house skirting the yard. But of course it was Sunday, and Hector was off who knew where, tomcatting in town most likely. Hollis could have yelled down to the bunkhouse for a hand or two, but what with the guitar and *corrido* music, his voice would not have been heard. Then, just as he realized he would have to do the welcoming himself, he was struck by the utter wrongness and strangeness of the horseman galloping toward him.

Hollis got a grip on the porch railing and hoisted himself, spilling forgotten dregs of coffee. He swore, then stood upright, supporting himself against a post, to study the black horse and black rider coming on like the devil were chasing them. He hopped two porch posts to his left, two posts closer to fetching a rifle from the house. The rider streaked past the corrals and bunkhouse. Within eighty yards of the porch, his features resolved.

It was Hollis Creigh's own boy, Roberto, hatless and riding bareback in his Sunday clothes, his heels thumping one of the matched blacks they reserved for the surrey. Alarming Hollis all the more, the boy gripped the revolver Hector had given him for his birthday.

When the hoofbeats went by the bunkhouse, Miguel, the *corrido* singer, erupted from the doorway, the guitar in his hand and his stance a question. Roberto aimed straight for the porch, looking like he would ride up the steps and into the parlor. At the last instant he wheeled the black, the animal's legs bracing against its momentum and churning dirt. The dogs rushed up, ecstatic. Roberto slid off onto the lowest porch step and waved away the horse, which was wild-eyed and badly foamed.

"What?" Hollis demanded. *"What?"*

Roberto gulped for breath. His eyes were dazed. He managed to say, "Cole Barlow."

"What on earth? Cole's on his way here?"

"He's shot. He stopped us on the road—"

"Shot? *Dead?*"

"Hit square. Fell flat off his horse."

"And you did it," Hollis said, and before the boy could answer, the world changed.

"Pa, the bastard taunted me. He pulled his gun. He'd been drinking. Then he cocked it. I thought he might do anything."

"Your mother and Angelina—they're safe?"

"At the Martinez place. I drove them in the buggy, then I cut loose one of the blacks and hightailed it."

Hollis looked out beyond the porch. Miguel still stood in the yard. The ranch road was deserted—but it wouldn't stay deserted. "Fetch me a rifle while I study this," Hollis said.

"Pa, I couldn't help it. I really thought—"

"Fetch it!"

The boy bounded past him into the house. Hollis, sagging a shoulder against the wall, heard him rustling at the gun rack. In a moment his son was back, filling the doorway.

"Robbie, I've got to know. Was it a fair fight?"

"He was fixing to shoot, Pa, I swear. I pulled mine and we fired right together."

"Ah. Robbie, Robbie."

"First it was killing our bull. Then this. The bastard was foul-mouthed and playing his eyes over Angel. I'd had enough of him. But I was defending all of us. You can ask Mother. Ask Angelina."

"It was Cole alone?"

"At first. Then some BR hands came up behind him— Nash and Quirt Hanson and somebody else. They saw it, or at least Nash did."

"Nash?" Hollis said. A hand strayed to his brow. "Robbie —*damn* it."

"What?"

"Nash Wheeler. You don't know. You—"

"I know he holds some grudge against you."

"He'll twist it," Hollis said. "This plays into his hand. He'll make it worse to get at me."

"But Ma and Angelina saw it."

"On a witness stand, family doesn't much count," Hollis said. "You run in and find some trail grub. Take some clothes. I'll have Miguel catch you a fresh horse."

"You mean I should run?" Roberto said, and what tore at Hollis's insides later was that the boy had never thought of it.

"They'll be coming for you," Hollis said. "My God, you killed Libba Barlow's son!"

"But I never meant—"

"Git!" Hollis said. "Food and clothes! Cartridges!" The boy's face changed, then he vanished into the house.

Hollis wheeled, nearly falling. He shouted for Miguel. The new hand tucked the guitar under one arm and jogged a few steps closer. Hollis told him in a mix of two languages to catch and saddle the best horse he could find, and catch another for a pack horse. And tie a rifle scabbard on the faster of them.

"Sí, Señor Creigh."

Hollis looked out the ranch road, still seeing no one. In a moment, Roberto was back beside him. "Where will I go?" he asked, and at the same time broke open the revolver. He plucked out one fired casing; Hollis heard it ring on the porch floor.

"I reckon in the Nations somewhere," Hollis said.

"Way up in the Nations?"

"No, by God—*Palo Duro.*" The idea hit him full-blown, carrying its own conviction. With Roberto following, Hollis negotiated himself down the steps with clever hopping, the rifle held out as ballast.

"What's that mean? Palo . . ."

It seemed to Hollis there was a succession of sons in the yard in front of him—Roberto as infant, boy, youth, and now. "Palo Duro Canyon, on the lower Panhandle. It's a deep cut made by a fork of the Red. I saw it before the war, a green place with grass and water. Good game. It's vast, but you'd practically have to stumble over the rim to find it."

"You're saying go there?"

"It used to be a Comanche stronghold. An old pal of mine is supposed to be back in there, someone I rode with in the war. Someone who'll hide you."

"An old guerilla fighter," Roberto said, seizing on it.

"He is that. Last I heard he called himself Jackson. You run into anybody in Palo Duro, you ask for him. Tell him you're Hollis Creigh's son. He'll hide you."

"You're that sure?"

"He owes me ten times that," Hollis said. "Just call him

Jackson. His real name leaks out and his safety's threatened, therefore yours. He's on the run, too."

"You mean he's still evading Federals? An unreconstructed Rebel?"

Hollis scowled. "You let him hide you, Robbie, and that's all. Don't go making him some dashing gray rider. The war's been over ten years."

"But it sounds like you're saying he's a—"

"He's a criminal. I'm warning you now. I'll be working to clear you of a murder charge. Don't you get in deeper."

"All right."

"Once you strike the Red and the country starts climbing, stick with the lower fork till you hit the big canyon. It's a place a man could hide for years." Hollis scowled again, hearing his own words. "As long as it takes, anyway."

"It sounds perfect," Roberto said. "Just so it's somewhere the law can't—"

"Robbie—" Hollis caught his boy's shoulder and looked into dark eyes, seeing Dominga. "For God's sake, understand this much. It's not the law I'm worried about." The eyes questioned. "If Libba Barlow wants you bad enough—and she will—she'll post up some big reward."

"Bounty hunters?" Roberto said.

Hollis nodded. "They'll be expecting the Nations. You'll fool them."

"All right. I'd better help Miguel."

Hollis let go reluctantly. The boy dashed for the corral, as though, in his mind, it was all some adventure. "Son of a wolf bitch," Hollis said, and stood alone in the ranch yard amid pocked hoofprints. A minute later, he watched his son kneeing a tall horse out of the corral, leading a second.

"Ride at night when you can. Watch for quicksand in the bottoms."

"I sure will."

Hollis stood braced against the grounded rifle, then

elevated his face, not caring if tears showed. He had something more to say.

"I'd better git."

"I wish to hell I could go with you," Hollis said. He did not look at the truncated leg, but instead glanced away, seeing Miguel standing amazed by the corral gate.

"I know, Pa. Anyhow, you've helped."

"We'll get you word when something changes." He still clung to some hope, he supposed, that Cole Barlow had survived. He gripped the boy's knee for a last touch of him. He said, "Go with God."

Roberto, looking scared and game at the same time, encouraged the horse and went out alongside the house, past the lilacs and then the woodpile and the privy. Behind him, the pack horse trotted awkwardly with its head extended. Hollis watched his son angle for a low, oak-bristled ridge that would take him off Creigh land. Despite the recent storm, the tracks Roberto would leave in the chalky hills would be blunt and anonymous and, with luck, would be washed out by another rain.

Hollis watched his son a long time, till Roberto topped a rise, waved, and then was gone. He stood a moment longer, feeling ancient, the rifle barrel an irritation in his armpit. Then he turned and motioned for Miguel to approach him. "Miguel, you savvy me? I never learned too much Spanish."

"Much English, señor."

"All right. Give me a hand up the porch steps, then go in and fetch a rifle for yourself and ammunition for both of us. You know where the gun rack is."

"A rifle, señor?"

"That's what I said. I expect we'll see trespassers before this day's over."

6 · RILEY

"HERE. THERE'S SHOD HOOVES COMING OUT OF THE CREEK RIGHT here." Cass coaxed his horse up the bank and slid off to look closer. Riley got down and massaged his knees. "Take a look," Cass said. Riley supposed he might as well. He walked over to see that many of the hoofprints had smeared in the soft mud. Others were superimposed, blurring the impressions.

"What makes you think they're his prints?"

"Range horses wouldn't likely be shod like these are. And a man doing cowboy work would have no reason for keeping to the creek."

"Might be he's a normal human being who prefers shade to sun," Riley said. He fanned himself with his hat. "Might be he's from someplace where they have other kinds of weather than just hot and hotter."

"I still say it's him," Cass said, nodding, "on account of he's riding one horse and leading another. A cowhand working this close to his outfit's headquarters wouldn't need two horses."

"Depends how far he's headed." Riley stayed unconvinced. He tied his horse to a cottonwood trunk, keeping the halter rope short so the animal couldn't tangle itself; horses tied to trees got into the damnedest fixes. "Just as likely, it's some feller who's hunting the killer same as us."

"I could track better without your discouragements," Cass said.

"You could track better with an Indian," Riley said. "I don't know what you drug me along for." Cass didn't answer, which Riley soon found an irritation. "And if these tracks aren't the killer's, we've made no progress all day." Riley sat down on a tree root that the creek was undermining and looked at the water. There was just about enough of it for cooling his feet.

"For the sake of argument, we'll say it's him," Cass said cheerfully. "I figure you've got to follow what leads you're given." He poked a finger into the tracks like he knew what he was doing. "The rider came out of the creek here and went up that dry wash. And lookit here—the horse he's leading has got this little chip out of one shoe, the off rear." Cass interrupted his new streak of enthusiasm to look up. "What's ailing you today anyhow?"

Riley thought about it, deciding he felt whirly-headed. "I feel whirly-headed," he said.

"Probably sun-tetched. You spent too long in that hay field."

"No sir. It's from you changing your mind so much. Last week the only thing worth doing, according to you, was hunting buffalo. Then it was looking for Spanish gold."

In response to Riley's accusation, Cass tipped his hat over his eyes and hid, all sheepish. "You showed me the light on that one," Cass said. "I'll admit I was lucky just to sell off the map."

"Now it's man hunting. I swear, Cass, in the time it takes to fry eggs, you come up with another scheme for making easy money."

"It sounded like a tall story to me too," Cass admitted. "I mean, such a big reward. But this Barlow woman had sent a man to town to spread word about it. Five thousand cash reward for her boy's killer. The offer's bona fide."

"How do you know she's even got five thousand?"

"They're big cattle people, the Barlows, with holdings just below here on the North Trinity. Don't tell me you haven't heard of them."

"I heard of the one that got killed. Liked to shoot at whorehouses from the inside."

"She'll stand good for it," Cass said. "Five thousand dollars."

Riley had nothing against five thousand dollars, but he didn't care for the reverent way Cass pronounced it. It

meant Cass was counting his chickens. "But doggone it—
bounty hunting!" Riley said. "I never thought we'd sink that
low. Besides which, every shiftless buffalo man and cowpoke will be after that reward." He puffed out a breath
afterwards.

"I already told you our advantages," Cass said. "Buffalo
runners and cowpokes have a regular line of work. Which is
why in a few days they'll give up the chase and go back to
doing what they do otherwise. Us, we're not nailed down.
We can stay on the trail as long as it takes."

"Then we'll get beat out by professional bounty men,"
Riley said. "A big money pot like that's going to draw them
like blowflies."

"That's where we're sitting pretty. We'll outlast the ama-
teurs, but before the big boys can even show up, we'll have
the man collared."

"Anything figured that fine is going to go wrong someplace," Riley predicted.

Cass said, "Says you."

Riley looked owlishly at the creek water. Tugging his
boots off just to cool his feet would be an awful lot of work.

Cass tied his horse near Riley's and followed the dry wash
away from the creek. "Come on, why don't you? Help me
find a couple more prints."

Riley groaned as he stood up. "Once he veers off into the
short grass you can't follow him anyhow. What you need is
an Indian."

Cass didn't answer. Soon both men were in the sun, Cass
searching along the wash bottom, which held little except
gravel and sun-crisped cow pies, and Riley trailing listlessly
behind him.

"Hello now," Cass said. "Here's a clear print right here."

"Signifying what?" Riley said. He looked down, but what
he saw was a teeming river of ants, some streaming one
direction and some the opposite. His boot had dammed the
flow, so that ants were milling on both sides of it, trying to
get around him.

Being focused on something as fine as ants made the shot

all the more surprising. Dirt jumped on the wash bank and a report sounded, then they both dove for the shelter of the wash's low banks. Riley yelled, *"Holy Hades!"* as another bullet zipped and spouted dirt. They heard it whine off beyond them.

"Half a day into this and we're getting shot at already," Riley said miserably. Cass lizarded forward on his stomach. He stuck his revolver over the embankment and triggered off two shots. It wasn't much of an embankment—barely knee-high. Riley said, "Killed them all, I imagine."

"Letting them know we're armed," Cass said. A return shot spurted on the bank, showering dirt. "Where're those shots coming from?"

"I'd say the trees. You could stick your head up if you're that curious."

"Whoever's shooting could work their way closer to our horses and have a straight shot up this wash," Cass said grimly, which Riley did not like to hear. Riley figured since bounty hunting had been Cass's idea, it was his place to point out where things could be worse. With Cass pointing out bad things, the situation was downright alarming.

Riley changed positions, grunting. He kept his revolver pointed toward the creek and its line of trees.

"We wouldn't have any cover at all," Cass said.

Riley saw he was the only one trying to look on the good side. He said, "Every one of those bullets is hitting the same place. I think they're only shooting to scare us."

Instead of answering, Cass yelled, "What do you want?" The response was another searing bullet.

"Dang!" Riley said.

"Let's talk this over!" Cass hollered. He was elbowing around again. Once he got settled, he said, "Riley—cut my sleeve off."

"What?"

"For a white flag. Cut it off, damn it." So Riley oofed around on his stomach like a sleeper in a busted bed and got out his clasp knife.

"Ow—cripes!" Cass said. "The sleeve, not the arm!"

"Well, dang it—hold still. We ought to have a stick to tie it to."

Cass said, "Stick, hell!" and stuck his arm up and waved the sleeve. A bullet zipped in, but it kept a certain distance. "I think you're right," Cass said. "They're only shooting to scare us."

"They're making a good job of it," Riley said, and was thankful Cass had switched to the optimistic side again. He breathed a moment. He was thinking a person doesn't notice how hot the sun is till he lies in it. Right then, it was like having his shirt ironed while he was wearing it.

Cass yelled, "We give up!" and waved the sleeve again. "We're throwing out our guns!"

"Now just a danged minute," Riley said.

"You got a better idea? They got us cold. *We're throwing them out!*" Cass hollered. He tossed his revolver up on the bank. "Yours too."

Riley puffed from aggravation. He weighed the gun in his hand. A new Colt's six-shooter was a fifteen-dollar item in any St. Louis hardware; in a frontier place like Jacksboro, it would go for twenty-five. But Cass gave him a hard look, so he tossed the gun up on the bank. Another rifle shot spewed dirt, and they pulled their heads in turtlewise. "Lot of good that did," Riley said.

"Damn it, you've got us!" Cass yelled. "Quit your shooting!" Then, all too recklessly, Riley thought, Cass stood up. His knees were bent like he was ready to drop down quick, but he was standing nevertheless, and waving his silly shirtsleeve.

Riley said, "Idiot."

No shot came. "Get up," Cass urged. "Show that you're disarmed."

Riley said something that would have set fire to a Methodist. He got up gingerly in the new quiet and raised his hands over his head. Down in the creek bottom, a haze of gunsmoke drifted across the cottonwoods.

A voice called, "Step away from those guns!" Riley looked

at Cass. It was not the kind of voice he'd expected from a drygulcher. He didn't have long to think about it because a bullet zipped three feet in front of Cass's boots, making him high step like a cancan dancer.

"Walk forward!" the voice ordered. They stepped to it. Movement showed alongside one tree trunk. A figure ventured into the open, peering at them down a carbine barrel.

Riley said, "By gosh, it's . . . Wal, she's a—"

"She is," Cass said, "but was I you, I wouldn't mention it." He raised his voice to call to her. "It appears we're good and corralled. What's your idea next?"

The woman was slim and young and dark-haired. She wore a broad hat, men's canvas britches, and the kind of ordinary blue shirt any cowhand would wear. To keep her rifle mounted at the shoulder, she had to advance in small steps, but she came on with purpose.

"I ought to shoot you like coyotes," the woman said, showing dark, snapping eyes. She began reciting what she had against them: they were trespassing on her family's land; they were out for blood money on the trail of her brother, who was innocent of crimes and had only fired his pistol in self-defense; she despised bounty hunters in general and them in particular. The fact was, she had a whole lot to say about it.

Cass said, "Can we put our arms down?"

"No." Cataloging what evil men they were got her worked up all the worse. She appeared more tempted to shoot than ever. "Hold still!" she ordered Riley.

"Can't," Riley said, and it was true. "Ants," he said, hopping. *"Dang it."* The ants had got inside his pants legs and were running in both directions again, only this time on him.

"You'll never get your blood money!" she told them, and then cheeked into the rifle and looked down the sights. The alarming part was when she closed one eye.

"Gol dang!" Cass said, and shielded his face with his forearms, as though that would stop a rifle bullet.

They heard thudding hooves and looked up to see a pair of riders, Mexicans by their hats, galloping over the hill toward them. The lead one, a man about fifty with a mustache that shamed a paintbrush, reined up, looked from Riley and Cass to the girl, and then back to Riley and Cass. He declared, *"Sangre de Cristos,"* with much breath in it, sounding practically religious. Then he spurred again, and rode down on them, drawing a big Colt's pistol as he reined up.

"Angelina," this man said. He tipped up his hat brim using his pistol barrel, and puffed his cheeks while he looked at them. Then he said, "Angelina," twice more, becoming more sorrowful each time, as though she were often the ruin of his peace of mind.

The young woman said, "Bounty hunters," and gestured needlessly with the rifle. While dismounting, the Mexican spoke to himself under his breath. Then he set about scolding her in Spanish, at Gatling-gun rate.

Cass caught Riley's eye. "'Disobeys her father and ages her poor mother prematurely,'" Cass translated. "'Even he himself, when he hears so much shooting, is made sick with worry.'"

"You shut your mouth," Angelina told Cass. The Mexican still ranted, gesturing back over the hill many times. The second Mexican, a man much younger than the other, sat his horse behind a saddle horn as big as a tree stump and smirked at everybody.

"'And she herself would feel very bad in the confessional to admit of killing unarmed men,'" Cass said, again translating the older man's flow of Spanish. "'But he himself, he has many times admitted such things to the padre. Thus, he knows how.'"

"Oh, wonderful," Riley said.

The man subsided like a locomotive steaming down. At the conclusion of it, Angelina shrugged. She said in English, "I caught them, didn't I?"

Then the man looked Cass and Riley over, and the longer

he looked, the less he seemed to like them. Finally he said, *"Mercenarios,"* with great distaste, and then sighed to show what a trial it all was. "I could shoot you for trespassing or hang you for rustling. Which do you choose?"

"We're no rustlers," Riley said.

"¡Gatos furtivos!"

" 'Sneaking cats,' " Cass translated.

"You've got your gall," the young woman said, "hunting an innocent man on his own property."

Cass said, "I wasn't quite sure where we were."

The Mexican laughed, but it was not comforting. He ordered the younger man, called Miguel, to pick up their revolvers, then brusquely told the woman to fetch her horse. Then he marched Cass and Riley at gunpoint toward the creek and their own horses. While they were walking, Miguel was directed to lope down ahead of them and remove the rifles from their saddle scabbards.

The Mexican told them in English to get on their horses. Shooting them if they tried to run, he said, would bring him great amounts of joy. For good measure, he made them swivel around backward on their saddles. Then Miguel had to take up their stirrups and hook them on their saddle horns so they couldn't get their feet into them.

"Now, why don't you try to get away from us?" the older Mexican suggested. He told Miguel, "This is the way for handling rustlers," as though it were all a part of his vaquero training.

7 · NASH WHEELER

A COUPLE OF BR COWBOYS PLAYED CATCH WITH A BASEBALL. THE
regular slap of horsehide against bare hands was a rhythm
Nash absorbed without hearing.

He sat by the window in his room off the shed, with the
door open and after-rain air as green as new hay wafting in
to cut the leather smells of harness and saddles, smells that
were sweet and oily and underlaid with a fishy taint. The
light of dusk was not much to work by. When one of the
hands whooped, causing Nash to look out, the sky's afterglow dazzled his eyes, so that he turned back to his task
momentarily blinded.

Nash, of course, could have cleaned a rifle with his eyes
shut; the patterns his hands followed were that familiar to
him. He tore patches from what had once been underwear
and moistened them with hot water from the kettle. Setting
a fresh patch on his cleaning rod, he pushed it through from
muzzle to breech, feeling the spiral-cut rifling bite into the
cotton. When lighter resistance told him the rod had
emerged at the breech, he angled the rifle so the dirtied
patch dropped out. After running four water-dampened
patches, he switched to oiled ones.

The wolf scalps, little fur caps with the ears sticking up,
lay on his table, giving him a shored-up feeling like money in
the bank would. The Stockmen's Association paid two
dollars a scalp without argument, for which Nash's only
expenses were a single cartridge per wolf and just enough
strychnine to salt down the beef carcass.

Poison meat too much, and a smart wolf would only circle
it, while the foolish younger ones ate and sickened. Then
they'd crawl up to die in a *maleza* of thorns somewhere and
cost a man his bounty money.

But Nash knew to apportion the right amount, so that the

animals would fight among themselves for a turn at the flesh, then sicken gradually and be driven to water, giving Nash an easy chore of riding out to a creek bottom and taking his shots. So as not to waste ammunition, he gave each poisoned wolf a single .44 bullet, fired from fifty paces. If the slug did not do its job immediately, Nash was content to wait. Strychnine cost enough by itself; he didn't care to whittle down his profit with any needless expenditure of cartridges.

After wiping with a last patch, he took the rifle by the barrel and raised it toward the window, intending to look down the bore to ensure that it was clean. But then he noticed the cowhands, how they'd stopped throwing their baseball and were looking off toward the big house, their interest captured.

Nash repositioned himself. Libba Barlow, tall and erect and wearing a black dress uncomplicated by a woman's usual crinolines, threaded her way among silvered puddles, her skirts hiked, her direction averaging toward Nash's lean-to room. He recognized for the hundredth time the strength in her face, edging out beauty. She was coming to see him.

Nash had only time to lean the rifle against the table and wipe his powder-stained hands on what was left of the rag, then straighten the blankets on his bunk. His first thought was that, by her standards, his room must seem a lair. His second was, to hell with it; Libba knew how he lived.

She slowed for her last few steps, then stopped in the doorway, her silhouette eclipsing much of the remaining light. They regarded each other in this new element, Nash's territory. Finally, he said, "Libba," in a way that acknowledged the novelty of her coming to him.

"I watched for you to come back," she said.

"You could've sent a man out." He'd skinned his wolf pelts beside a waterhole no more than four miles from the house.

"I've got plenty of time for waiting."

"Want to sit down?" Nash said. He gestured toward his lone chair. For a response, she turned and must have regarded the ball players. Nash looked out the window to see them beginning to trail away, looking back at his lean-to room and her figure framed in the doorway.

"I've been widowed long enough to have gotten good at it," Libba said. "People talked enough about you and me in the old days."

"They maybe still do."

"Then we hardly need circle each other like dogs meeting, do we? We've known each other long enough."

"I reckon we have." He repositioned the chair and sat down, then looked up at her, her face too silhouetted to give away anything. "Libba, I'd like to say again how, how bad we all feel for you," Nash said. "Anyhow, how bad I feel."

"Thank you. I will note your sympathy's only for me. I was aware your opinion of my son was never exactly the highest."

Nash shrugged. "He had a streak in him. You see it a lot at that age. Given time, it would have worked itself out."

"Cole was not given time, though, was he?" Her tone was sharp. He looked up as though rope-jerked and saw she had closed her eyes and was absorbing pain. She stood cleanly in profile, her chin defined, her hair pinned up and head erect. He was reminded Libba was the kind called handsome. A lot of them started out pretty, but Nash figured it was how a woman held up to the years that determined handsomeness.

Then she swallowed, and Nash figured if she were going to cry, she would have done it then. True to Libba, she did not.

"I'm sorry," she said finally. "I wasn't really asking you that question." Nash, baffled as to what he might say, made some useless gesture. She said, "It's possible a mother doesn't know a son the way other people know him."

"Could be," Nash conceded. He thought of young Cole and his Mexican whore, of Cole wasting his whiskey when Tom Powell needed a shot. "Pretty much any youngster's in a big rush to grow up," Nash offered. "Cole might some-times have got ahead of himself."

"Yes—as if growing up is such an achievement. A mother would prefer a boy awhile longer. But everybody told Cole his pa was such a giant. His memory of the man was getting blotted out by people's stories. It was brag talk, mostly. Have you ever wondered how Coleman might have wound up had he and I not married? You knew my money built the BR."

"I expect about same as me. A saddle bum."

"You're hardly that. Think he'd have been better off?"

"No, you steadied him."

"We knew him as the same man, you and I."

"Coleman was pretty well the same man around every-body," Nash said.

"Yes. And you doubt my Cole could have measured up, but he could have. The side of Cole I knew could have."

"I never claimed different."

"It hardly matters now, though. Either way." She exhaled, with catches in it. "Well. I've thought about this, and what I don't want is a trial. Because it'd be as much a trial of Cole as of his killer. We'd get sidetracked hearing about how wild he was. That business with the Creigh girl at the dance this summer, and so on."

"I expect that's about the size of it," Nash said.

"And damn it," Libba said, "Cole can't be here to defend himself. My son deserves better."

Nash heard they'd struck the real subject. He extended a hand, meaning to light the candle, but then changed his mind. He redirected the motion to heft the rifle, laying its weight across his knees. "I can see how a trial'd be awful for you."

She nodded. "So, the summer drive's long over, and ear marking is nothing. With the number of steers we sent to Kansas this year, even fall roundup won't amount to much. As for more rain, we'll either get it or not. Nothing you can do about it."

"You're telling me I should go after Roberto Creigh."

Her voice became husky. "Nash, I'm asking."

It was what he'd expected, so his answer was rehearsed. "Everybody from here to Austin's heard of the reward you posted. I work for you, but you want him that bad, I figure you can offer me more than my wages." The dark had made it easier to speak his mind than he'd imagined. He looked up, expectant.

"Posting that reward was ill-advised," Libba said. "Even as we're talking, some cowhand might haul him in for the reward money. Bring him in alive, I mean."

"It's possible."

"Or the Creigh boy might hear of bounty men after him and turn himself in. Either way, there'd be a trial. And for what reason? Roberto fired the only shot, didn't he?"

"The sheriff must've told you that."

"He did better—he showed me your statement. You said the empties in Cole's gun had been fired at a whiskey bottle."

Nash's hand strayed to the wolf scalps; the fur cozied his fingers, making a comfortable feeling. "I didn't just say it, I swore it," Nash said. "I'm just glad the sheriff got it straight."

She said crisply, "In that case, Cole deserves justice, and by God, so do I."

"If you don't want a trial, suppose we start with exactly what you *do* want," Nash said. "It'll make it easier to settle on a price."

Libba said, "What I want must be plain by this point. To get it, I'm prepared to be very generous."

8 · ANGELINA CREIGH GARZA

THE BOUNTY MEN MADE A COMICAL SIGHT RIDING THEIR HORSES
backward. It was like a stunt someone would do in a fiesta
parade—riding backward to be funny and throwing favors
to the children. The bounty men, though, did not look
amused about it; they wore grim faces and gripped their
saddle cantles as though riding backward upset everything
they knew about horsemanship. When one tried to talk with
the other, Angelina's uncle Hector told him to shut his filthy
mouth.

The tall one was fair, with a rusty mustache and oak-
colored hair—tawny marbled with brown. He had pulled
his shirtsleeve back onto his arm, but of course it was still
detached at the shoulder. It gave him the look, she couldn't
help thinking, of a man wounded in war.

The shorter one had dark hair and no mustache; she
thought of him as shorter, although he was taller than
Hector or Miguel. They were town men, she decided,
judging by their smooth hands and the somber clothes they
wore for walking on boardwalks, except that for comfort in
riding, both had wide-brimmed drover's hats and tall,
stovepipe boots.

On the whole, they looked rather prosperous, although
with their expressions guilty and miserable, as was only
fitting, having been caught at their cowardly pursuits. Had
she seen them in Jacksboro, perhaps noticed them crossing
the street while she sat in the Peña family's restaurant
having coffee and a sweet with her mother, she might have
followed them with her eyes. She might have wondered, too,
what they did for their living, to be dressed up so when most
others went about with the dirt of the land on them.

Which only showed how easily looks could deceive, Angelina decided, for these men were refuse, they were manure. What they did for their money was hunt men like animals, and turn them in, draped dead over horses, to evil sheriffs that they knew.

At that point, Angelina's eyes troubled up; the picture of a dead man thrown over a saddle was hard for her, and she was sad for her brother, now running like a deer. To keep the bounty men from seeing sadness on her face, she nudged her mount ahead and rode abreast of Miguel, despite the hungry way he often looked at her.

9 · RILEY

THE DAY WAS COOLING, AND THEIR SHADOWS WERE STRETCHED and black as India rubber as they rode in among the corrals and buildings. A pair of dogs raced out to announce them; the dogs, in turn, brought out Mexican cowhands, who jeered at the strangers riding at gunpoint and sitting their horses backward.

Once they'd stopped, a woman burst from a low ranch house. She called out to the girl Angelina in an anguished voice, then dashed into the yard with her shawl floating behind her. The woman was surely Angelina's mother, Riley thought, for despite wounded eyes she was a shorter, darker version of the girl. She ran straight to her daughter, who swung off her horse and let herself be embraced and scolded and her hair stroked like a lover.

A grim-faced man on crutches had appeared on the porch. "I caught them, myself alone," Angelina called to him in English. "They're killers after Roberto."

"It's true?" the man asked, his voice carrying. His eyes ignored everyone except the Mexican, Hector, as though Angelina's word on the matter counted for little.

"Mercenarios," Hector said, seeming to get the same bad taste from the word that he'd gotten earlier.

Riley had found riding backward enough of an indignity without having grinning vaqueros making comments about him. He told himself he no longer cared if he got shot or not. Without looking at Hector, Riley swung a leg over his horse's rump and slid down. He was immediately swarmed over by the dogs until Miguel ordered them off. Once the dogs were restrained, Cass must have figured it was safe to slide off too. They stood stiffly, Riley resisting a need to massage his tenderer parts. A saddle sat backward had been far worse than none.

Angelina's mother, still scolding, towed her daughter to the porch. "You and I will talk later," the one-legged man said as Angelina approached him. "I've had enough of you riding around the country with rifles."

"What will you do with them?" she demanded.

"You brought them. What'd you expect I'd do?"

"They were hunting Roberto."

"Yes, and there'll be others. You can hardly stop all of them."

"You should hang them as rustlers," Angelina said.

"As simple as that."

"Yes." She stepped up on the porch and for a moment faced him. They were of equal height, the man on crutches and the girl who resembled him except for darker hair and complexion—although if the man could have stood unsupported, he might have been inches taller. The girl's mother tried to draw Angelina into the house, but she protested in Spanish, and then lingered in the doorway to watch what would happen.

The vaquero Hector had the knack of herding men with small movements of his pistol barrel. Cass and Riley advanced almost to the porch steps before Hector stopped them.

"Mr. Hollis Creigh, whose son you hunt like the wolf," Hector said, introducing. "You do this man a great measure of wrong. He perhaps shall shoot you himself." Hector went up the steps and extended to Creigh his revolver, rolling it in his hand so that it came up smartly, butt first.

To Riley's great relief, Creigh looked at the pistol with his mind clearly elsewhere, then waved it away, showing irritation. Like Hector, Creigh was about fifty, a lean man despite thickening in the body. His right leg ended abruptly above the knee, and his pant leg had been cut off and neatly sewn to shroud it. Ox-yoke shoulders testified to much use of the crutches. His face was two-colored—sun-browned from the eyes down, the brow white where a hat usually shielded it—looking in that regard like any other rancher.

Creigh's eyes settled on Riley, making judgments, then rotated to Cass. "Hector and my daughter have a good argument," Creigh said. "I could hang you or shoot you either one and get away with it—even under the circumstances." He meant, Riley supposed, of his son being sought for murder. "We've dealt with rustlers before," Creigh added.

Riley had chafed enough at being thought a bounty hunter; being branded rustler was too much. "By gol, we never rustled an animal in our lives!" He said hotly. "Just because you caught us traveling on your—"

"Silence!" Hector thrust his revolver muzzle in Riley's face. Riley tried to look scornfully at it, but the dark hole of the bore was daunting.

"Hector." Creigh raised a hand. *"Hermano."*

"It doesn't make us rustlers," Riley said.

Creigh was unmoved. "I expect we all know what you came for. I didn't figure cattle. Tell me one thing—how much blood money is Libba Barlow offering?"

Riley looked at Cass, who appeared apologetic. "We heard the reward was five thousand," Cass said.

"My God," Creigh said, barely audible. "So much as that." From the doorway, the mother began wailing something, her words distorted by grief.

Creigh lowered himself to a porch chair as though his strength had left him. One crutch tipped away from him; he grabbed out, but it clattered to the porch floor. He said, "Damned things." Angelina came forward to retrieve it, then stayed to put a hand on her father's shoulder. "Go comfort your mother," Creigh said.

When Creigh looked up again, the blue eyes had taken a set. "You've got brass, hunting my boy on my land. Either brass or no sense at all."

Cass said, "I'd like to say something."

"I'd not care to hear it," Creigh said. "Hector, get these trash out of here. Their kind makes me sick."

"And do what with them?"

"Short of killing them, whatever you like."

"Just a danged minute here," Cass said. "We were between situations, there's no crime in that."

"That's right," Riley threw in.

"We don't know your son from Adam," Cass said. "Your daughter seems to believe he's innocent of this—"

"Of course he's innocent!" Angelina said. "To men like you, what difference does that make?"

Creigh's voice was weary. "Angel, don't bother with them."

"By gol, it'd make a whole slough of difference," Riley said. "If we thought he hadn't done it, there's no way in hell we would've—" They were all looking at him, making Riley feel he'd done something terrible and uncaring. That he'd trampled people. The mother's eyes bothered him most.

"Look, I'm Riley Stokes, from Kentucky. I'm right sorry to meet you under strained circumstances. We both are."

"Sorry!" Angelina said.

"I'm Prosper McCasland," Cass put in. "Called Cass. My people ranch down around Uvalde, just north of the *brasada* country—"

"What do we care about your people?" Creigh said. He looked at Hector and angled his head. Hector cocked his revolver and began making herding motions.

"Just hold your horses," Cass said. "If we're in the wrong, it doesn't make us killers. All right, we were looking to trail your boy—five thousand is a lot of money. But I give my word we figured to bring him in for trial. We're no judge and jury."

Creigh's face twisted. "Your word."

"My word," Cass said, "as a Confederate cavalryman."

A space opened. One of the vaqueros behind them said something—probably translating Cass's words, Riley thought. Another said, *"Ay—caballero."*

"Second Texas," Cass said stoutly. "Sixty-one to sixty-five. The duration."

"Anyone may lie," Hector pointed out. Creigh was studying Cass. Hector, disappointed to be ignored, eased down his pistol's hammer with a sound of steel parts meshing.

Creigh said, "I'd say you're looking at a one-legged man and making tall assumptions."

"Am I?" Cass said. "You're the Hollis Creigh, I would wager, who rode with Quantrill. Your name was familiar—I just now realized why."

Creigh considered the statement. "Quantrill and others," he said. "Getting to be a long time ago. You are young to have been in it."

"Some were younger."

"Some were," Creigh acknowledged. His eyes went to Riley. "Him too?"

Riley looked warily at Cass, who must have figured it a good time, for once, to stick with the truth. "On the other side," Cass said. "That's nothing against him."

"No," Creigh said, "I don't reckon it is." He let out a long breath. "Do I also have your word you'll leave off trailing my son?"

Angelina said, "Papa, if you love Roberto, don't take their *word!"*

"You have it," Cass said. Riley let out a breath as profoundly as Creigh had. He was glad to think they were no longer bounty hunters. The five thousand had been pie in the sky anyway.

"Then *adiós,"* Creigh said. "I'd suggest you find a line of work that's worthy of a Confederate cavalryman."

"This is . . . *crazy!*" Angelina protested. "So you were in the same war. What does that make you—lodge brothers?"

Cass and Creigh looked at one another, assessing. Riley, feeling little kinship with Confederates, kept out of it, instead giving the mother and Angelina what he hoped was a look of sympathy.

"In a way it does," Creigh said. "Hector, return their rifles."

"*¡Ay!*—always this war," Hector said. He gave his revolver another twirl and flourish. Riley found the scuffing sound comforting when the gun slid into its holster. Then Hector spoke in Spanish to the vaqueros, causing Miguel to return Winchesters to their saddle scabbards, his forceful movements suggesting great unhappiness about it. Meanwhile, Hector sat down on a porch step and rolled a cigarette, taking care with it to show his disappointment.

"We are right sorry to have added to your family's worry," Cass said. Creigh accepted the apology with a perceptible nod. "So what is it you are saying here?" Cass asked. "That your boy never killed the Barlow youngster? Or did it in self-defense, or what?"

"There's no argument Robbie shot him," Creigh said. "But Cole had pulled a gun and threatened him. They fired together. My wife and daughter were right there."

"Shows you there's two sides to everything," Riley said. He wanted to ask for his pistol back besides his rifle but was wary of pushing his luck.

"Yes," Angelina said bitterly, "there's right and there's wrong."

What Cass said next nearly popped Riley's eyeballs out. "What you ought do in that case," Cass said smoothly, "is tell us where your son's hiding out." Cass slid Riley a cautioning look. "I mean before some real bounty wolves catch up with him."

Creigh snorted. Angelina said, "Of all the sneaking—"

"I mean it," Cass said. "Let us bring him in safe for trial. We'll collect Mrs. Barlow's five thousand and turn over half to you." Riley's head reeled; a minute ago, he and Cass had been on their way safely out of there.

"That much money would buy good lawyers," Cass said.

"You two ride out," Creigh said. "I could change my mind about that hanging."

Riley said, "Cass . . ."

"What I'm offering would be the best thing for him," Cass said. "If it was really self-defense." He looked from Creigh to Angelina. When he saw he'd made no progress, he shrugged and turned.

Riley, trying to hold himself calm, did not look at anybody. He went to his horse, moving like wood, and took the stirrups off the saddle horn. Cass swung up on his mount and gave Riley a look brimful of meaning. Riley didn't even want to interpret it. Instead, he swung up too.

"Son of a bitch," Riley said under his breath. *"Don't you say one other word."* He turned his mount and inwardly rejoiced when Creigh's vaqueros opened an aisle for him. He figured a man had only one neck; he could always buy another Colt's pistol.

From the porch came a scrape of chair legs. Cass swiveled in his saddle, so then Riley had to. Hollis Creigh had pulled himself erect along the porch railing.

"What I'll do is pay you six hundred now and another six when Roberto is safe with the county sheriff," Creigh said. "Libba Barlow's five thousand you'll turn over to me."

"Papa—no! Think what you're saying!"

"I am thinking," Creigh said. "Clearing Robbie with Libba's blood money kind of appeals to me."

"Is he hiding close in or somewheres far off?" Cass asked him.

"I'm not saying either way."

"If it's far, we'd have expenses," Cass said easily, for there was nothing he liked better than negotiations. "We'd need eight hundred now and the same when he's brought in."

Riley heard doom bells. Here they'd nearly been shot, or hung, or both, and now Cass was dickering with the fugitive boy's father like they were trading in horses.

Hector blew out cigarette smoke in an exasperated way and shook his head. The mother looked as frightened as Riley felt. Angelina erupted. "You can't trust men like these!"

But Creigh told them, "We'll talk it over. You swing off your horses and come on in the house."

Cass looked at Riley, flickers of satisfaction in his eye corners. Riley thought, *Horseshit*—hooked again! And when Angelina stormed into the house and slammed the door behind her, the sound echoed in Riley's mind like a hanging judge's gavel.

10 · ANGELINA

ANGELINA CARRIED DISHES AND SILVERWARE INTO THE PARLOR. Angelina's mother, though, did not look up from her place at the cookstove. She stood silent, her back made small and ashamed by what her husband was doing.

The bounty men sat with Angelina's father and talked stupidly of their bloody war, as though matters concerning it still needed settling. Angelina supposed it made a safe enough subject while the women were around. Certainly she herself did not care to hear war talk.

She carried the food—pan-fried beefsteak, rice with peppers, and Indian corn *posole*—into the parlor and set it on a window table. As she left them, her father looked at her with stern implication, but she would not dish out her mother's cooking to men who tracked her brother.

She closed the parlor door behind her to shut out their words, then immediately regretted it. With abrupt movements she made tea for her mother and moved the lamp from the cookstove to the table, in her anger agitating the coal oil so that its light wavered and then slowly settled on the tabletop. The closed door shouted with importance, but Angelina would not open it, would not admit she burned to listen. Her father was letting himself be hoodwinked by evil men.

Instead, she prayed over the food with her mother; then she ate without tasting, hearing the men's voices alternating, occasionally rising. At one point, one of the bounty men laughed.

Her mother sat distanced by tragedy and ate slowly, accompanied by noises of the cooling stove ticking and the firewood chunks subsiding. Angelina commented in Spanish that the table required a new oilcloth, and to demonstrate tapped a fingernail where the fabric showed through. Her mother's hand, on a frail-looking wrist emerging from a black sleeve, slid out and captured Angelina's own.

"What does he do with them?" her mother asked, damaged eyes beseeching. Angelina shook her head; she wished she could tell her.

Her father's voice called. "Angelina!"

"He wants now the whiskey," her mother said in English. "It is how he does his business."

Angelina knew well enough. She got the bottle from the sideboard. She balanced three tumblers on a serving board, took the bottle by its neck, and went in to them, using her hip to nudge the door open.

The taller, lighter-haired one said, "It's all mighty good, ma'am," but Angelina did not acknowledge him.

Her father said, "Angelina, if you'd sit with your mother in the bedroom . . ." leaving his reason unstated. She understood he did not want to be overheard.

"I shall if she wishes it," Angelina said, speaking Spanish, she supposed, to punish him. She took as many of the dirtied dishes as she could manage and left the others, deciding she would not go back in for any reason.

Angelina closed the door behind her, but the door would not stop her. Hearing her husband's request for privacy, Dominga Creigh had obediently removed herself to the back bedroom. Angelina stood falsely in the bedroom doorway and told her mother she had to see about her horse, that she'd run him hard that day and had to know he'd been rubbed down properly. Of course, the vaqueros knew how to rub down horses. But whether her mother accepted it as truth or not, Angelina did not care; it was enough that she did not argue.

Angelina slipped out the backdoor into thin moonlight, still wearing her boots and men's canvas breeches. The dogs came up and happily nosed her. She stilled them, then went around the house and along the wall toward the front, where the men's voices rumbled from the parlor window.

She slipped into the corner by the stone chimney and put her head against the logs' roughness. At first the voices were undifferentiated—merely low murmuring. Then she distinguished her father's voice, and the tall bounty man's voice from the shorter one's. Making out the words, however, was more difficult. She heard the shorter one say, "He isn't?" in evident surprise, and then the voices went back to murmurs. To understand what her father was telling them, she would have to put her ear against the glass.

She changed position, crossing a rhombus of light cast by the parlor window. When a work-roughened hand slid over her mouth to prevent her from crying out, the surprise of it stopped her heart.

"¡Dios! ¡Tio Hector!" Even then she had the presence of mind to whisper.

"What foolishness now, *pollita?*" Tio Hector spoke in Spanish because he could do it softer and with greater agility. Though his face stayed in the shadows, she knew he was angry; he'd called her *pollita*—little chick—as though she were twelve instead of twenty-one. "Have you not found trouble enough for one day?"

"It is that Papa . . . it is that he's telling them where he sent Roberto!"

"He has changed his mind, your father. He does that rarely, so his reason must be worthy."

"Telling *them!*" she insisted. "When he won't even tell *me!*"

"Because you would ride straight to him, in this way leading others behind you. Men who would kill our Roberto."

"I'd be careful."

"You would be careful, but you would be followed," Hector said. Their faces were a foot apart. Angelina felt great urgency, but her uncle, she saw, was no longer angry. He was playing with her.

"For once, listen," Hector said. "Your father has sent Roberto to a place of great safety. But now he wishes him returned. I do not know why he wishes this, but he thinks it best."

"He's letting those damned bounty men talk him into—"

"Hush, *niña*—such words! He does not let them do anything. He does it himself. Come away from spying at windows. Go in and sleep."

"I'm too worked up to sleep."

"Then we will walk down the road together in the moonlight, uncle and niece, while I smoke my cigarette. Come, your shoulders are shaking. We'll get you a jacket."

"Because I'm angry. What he's doing is terrible!"

"We will get you a jacket, and you will not be so angry," Tio Hector said.

With her legs at first stiff and resisting, she was drawn away from the house. A horse neighed from the corral. Lower down in the yard someone bumped the bunkhouse door shut. From the parlor window, the men's voices went on murmuring, like a low wind heard from inside a house.

11 · CASS

"YOU CAN BUILD A FIRE IF YOU FIND IT CHILLY," CREIGH TOLD them. "The evening cooled right down."

"Not for me," Cass said. He was warmed by the room's confinement and the hot smells of tallow candles, for one wall of the Creighs' parlor was a shrine to the fugitive boy. Somebody—Cass figured Creigh's Mexican wife—was keeping alive a rank of stubby votives under a painting of the Virgin. Other religious trappings decorated the walls: palm fronds, a picture of a baleful saint looking heavenward, his body bristling with arrows. On a wall by themselves hung daguerreotypes of the family, each image framed in dark wood.

"That picture is some years out of date," Creigh said, following Cass's eyes. The boy in the photograph could have been a freshly minted version of Creigh himself, though darker. "Roberto's soon eighteen, quite the young man." Creigh's eyes drifted, then returned, and he remembered to sip his whiskey.

Riley had selected a straight-backed, black leather settee that had a lot of Spanish in it. Cass inhabited a rocking chair, which had made cutting his beefsteak a tippy business.

From a vest pocket Creigh produced a pipe, then took his time filling it. "A man's going to make his mistakes," Creigh said. He paused to puff his breath into the rising smoke, diffusing it. "My Roberto might've made one in shooting Cole Barlow. Then again, he might've ended up the victim and Cole the killer. He may have made a mistake by running, but I doubt it, on account of after Roberto took out of here a bunch of bloody-minded BR riders showed up. It would have been bad if they'd found him. The sheriff didn't get here till evening."

"Running's understandable," Riley said.

"The mistake I made," Creigh said, addressing the pipe, "was in the place I sent him. Oh, it's safe enough—nobody's going to stumble over him. But for a moment, after Roberto rode in here and in the excitement and whatnot, I underestimated my worst enemy." He looked up. "Nash Wheeler."

Cass said, "Seems like I've heard the name."

"Foreman of the BR—in other words, Libba Barlow's man. But he wasn't always that. In the war, we were bordermen together."

"Bordermen," Riley said. "Which was . . . ?"

"Confederate guerillas," Cass said.

"Confederate *irregulars,*" Creigh corrected. "Bushwhackers, the Federals mostly called us. Hell, we used that term ourselves."

Creigh turned to Cass, the pipe now a pistol. "You were right that I rode with Quantrill. But after he fell out with George Todd, and the two of them took shots at each other, Quantrill's leadership . . . I don't know, I guess we just quit taking the man's orders."

Cass said, "I'd heard he lost his command."

"Some of us drifted to the regular Confederate forces. Nash Wheeler and I—we were saddle partners in those days—we rode off to Arkansas intending to join Sterling Price's outfit, only we wound up with Colonel Ben Poole. Bordermen was Poole's term for us. He never liked saying bushwhackers."

Riley was startled. "Bloody Ben Poole?"

"Bloody Ben indeed—only at first we didn't know just how bloody. Quantrill you'd call a bold leader, but he kept his hands clean personally. Bloody Ben, he had a grudge. His sister had died in Federal custody. Some say an accident —others, that it was deliberate. What we knew was Ben Poole carried a silk cord and tied a knot in it for every Union man killed by his own hand. And that cord was a mass of knots."

"Jesus," Riley breathed. Cass knew Riley had been volunteer infantry, and probably found it hard to imagine war on such terms.

"Now I remember," Cass said. "You and Nash Wheeler were Poole's captains."

"True enough. In time he called us majors—old Ben was a great one for handing out rank. The fact was, no one ever made him colonel excepting Ben himself.

"But by God, the men we had," Creigh said. "The Younger brothers, little Arch Clement, Frank and Jesse James—hellhounds, all of them. And the outrages done on both sides." Creigh's eyes ascended the wall, maybe seeing some of it. "I reckon war is war, but things were done that should never happen even then.

"The fact was," Creigh continued, "after the stories got around, the regular Confederate forces disowned Ben Poole, which gave the bluecoats excuse to hang our bunch as spies and criminals anytime they caught one of us. That was all fine with Bloody Ben. He never fought anything but his own private war anyhow."

"From what I've heard of the fighting along the Missouri and Kansas border," Riley said, "a lot of it was that way."

"For a fact." Creigh shifted in his chair, seeking comfort. "It got to where it wasn't war at all—just looting and killing, and us no better than renegade Comanches. Nash and I fell out about it, him being more keen on prosecuting the fighting. For a while, he even collected dead men's watches."

"I heard of worse on our own side," Riley admitted. "Ears."

Creigh nodded tiredly. "Anyhow, a few months before the end, a blind man could see where it was headed. Men started drifting away, particularly since we were hanged if we surrendered. I've not told this to a soul, but on the day this happened"—Creigh touched the stump of leg almost fondly—"I had it set in my mind to ride away from it. You could call it desertion, though I didn't. We weren't doing anybody any good anymore. I'd had enough."

"Good for you," Riley said.

"But I lingered too long. A Springfield ball went square through the bone. I lost the leg the day before Bloody Ben got killed. Then, with him gone, the whole outfit broke up. Nash went back to Texas while I was laid up in Missouri. He hasn't said two words to me since."

Riley asked why.

"I'll get there directly. But first, about the mistake I made. After Robbie killed Cole Barlow, I sent him to a pal of ours, Nash's and mine, a rider from our old outfit. This man owes me a debt, and I don't mean money. He'll shelter Robbie, and Libba Barlow's bounty hunters won't find him, I'm sure of that much."

"Then what's the mistake?" Cass asked.

"Nash Wheeler." The pipe had gone out, and Creigh set it on a table. "Nash is going to consider what he'd do if he was me, and he'll remember hearing about the same place I did, where old Rebels are still hiding out. I don't know why I didn't realize it before sending Robbie off. In a stew about BR riders coming, I guess."

Riley said, "This Nash Wheeler hates you enough to go after your son?"

"He'd do it for Libba's reward. Understand this—it's not hate he's got against me. More like suspicion and envy. And the whole reason is Greenville."

"Greenville, Missouri?" Cass figured Riley said it for both of them.

"I wasn't in on it, thank God. I was off scouting out hideouts, what we called friendly houses. But Bloody Ben and maybe two hundred riders hit Greenville the way Quantrill had hit Lawrence. Yelling 'Osceola,' which was our war cry, shooting up the town, looting, basically doing whatever they felt like. According to Poole, Greenville was a nest of abolitionists.

"So the boys found a warehouse of whiskey, and just when a lot of them were good and liquored, in pulls a Federal troop train, except mostly empty."

"That was the one with twenty-four unarmed troopers on it," Riley said, "all heading home on furlough."

"He remembers the numbers," Creigh told Cass, and shook his head. "I won't deny it. Arch Clement took it on himself to make those soldiers strip naked. Then he shot every one, borrowing pistols to do it. I wasn't there, but I must have featured it up in my mind a hundred times since. It was a black day for the Confederacy.

"Anyhow, eighty thousand in Federal army pay was on that train—I know on account of later I saw it. And after Bloody Ben was killed, the money never turned up."

"Never?" Cass said. "You mean in all that time . . . ?"

"Nash Wheeler believes I got it," Creigh said. "He's convinced himself. I ask you, does it look like I'm sitting on thousands of gold dollars?" He indicated the low-ceilinged room, the smoke-darkened wallpaper. He allowed a grim smile, then reached for the whiskey bottle.

"Hell, I can see where he'd suspicion it," Creigh said. "Nash and I were hardly speaking by that time. Bloody Ben always had a friendly farmhouse somewhere nearby, and he had one near Greenville. Me being a major, Ben put me in command of the place. A day later, my leg got blasted. A day after that, Ben was killed. I guess Nash convinced himself Ben had entrusted me with the money.

"Anyhow," Creigh said, "the few times I've seen Nash in ten years since the war, I can tell the thought of that money just eats at him. He came back to a foreman's job at two dollars a day. But he saw old Coleman Barlow—that'd be young Cole's father, who died a few years back—he saw Coleman set up comfortable, getting to be a big rancher. And me, I'm setting on this place with a family and no complaints. Meanwhile, Nash is going noplace working for wages. Like I said, it's envy and suspicion."

"Eighty thousand," Cass said. "What do you suppose happened to it?"

"Either Bloody Ben buried it, and it's still there, or somebody else got it. In any case, Nash is going to see Libba Barlow's five thousand in reward money as his big chance. And he's damned well going to take it. Protecting my boy from Nash is ninety percent of what you'll have to worry about."

"So just where do we find your son?" Riley asked.

"My question first. When do you propose to leave?"

"Right now—tonight," Cass said firmly. "In daylight we'd be too easy to follow. Chances are, your place is being watched."

Creigh showed approval. "I'll get Hector's men to rope a couple spare horses. With spares, you can travel all the faster."

"Good," Cass said.

Creigh struggled to stand. Riley gave him a hand up and he settled into his crutches. "Nash is an old borderman,"

Creigh said. "But only old enough to be at his most dangerous. He'll shoot on sight. Worse, he's the best white tracker I know of. He's got all the tricks."

"We know a few ourselves," Cass said, then feared it sounded like tall talk from men who'd let a girl capture them.

"You'll need them," Creigh said. "Nash might already be ahead of you, guessing where I sent Robbie. More likely, he'll come up on your back trail. But it's dead certain he'll be there somewhere. You count on it."

12 · ROBERTO CREIGH

THE COUNTRY WAS CLIMBING, INCLINING AWAY FROM THE RIVER bottoms into gravelly arroyos, which led to mesas, their tops sparsely grassed and pocked with prairie dog holes. Odd rock formations tombstoned the horizon. And while rising, while turning increasingly rocky, the land was drying, evolving toward New Mexico territory along the Panhandle's western border.

Roberto hugged the rivers, thankful for their occasional screens of plums and elms and cottonwoods, once risking a rifle bullet at a roosting turkey, which dutifully plummeted out of low branches to feed him for a day and half. His father had advised him to ride at night, but since Roberto had seen no one in two days, at least no one within hailing distance, he told himself he was safe enough in the light of day. Daytime travel was faster, for one thing, and also made it easier to cover his backtrail, which he attempted by riding on rocky ground wherever possible, and keeping to streambeds for miles at a time.

One day he sighted far-off wagons clustered on a rise, their canvas covers dimpling like sailcloth. Soon he heard booming rifles, the shots regularly paced, attesting to the grim monotony of buffalo hunting.

The next day it was Indians, young Paneteka Comanches almost surely, ranging out from their reservation at Fort Sill in the Territory. Spying them, a dozen riders, strung out in a creek bottom more than half a mile off, Roberto quickly pulled his animals into an arroyo and sat with his heart thumping loudly enough, it seemed, to draw enemies to himself by the pounding alone.

He was grateful the country was sparsely populated, for people were a reminder that he was on the dodge, fair game to anyone with enough sand to hoist a gun at him. He slept, when he slept at all, in the anxious, outer rooms of sleep, dreaming about his family. As he rode, he imagined himself being trailed by posses, which kept his head and eyes sharp and his stomach tight. And he imagined, too, the great canyon his father had described for him, picturing it as a deep cut, with walls so towering that as he rode between them, only a distant slash of daylight would show above his head.

But most of all, he imagined the mysterious gray rider, Jackson, or whatever his name would turn out to be, and the outlaws surrounding Jackson that would provide Roberto shelter. Criminals, his father had called them, but it was important to Roberto's thinking that the men not be criminals at all—rather zealots, partisans in the noble cause of an independent South.

It seemed to Roberto, who'd been seven when the war ended, that he'd missed out on the adventure of a century. In his arrogance, he imagined the Confederacy's effort had been all the poorer because he, Roberto Creigh, had not been a part of it. A rising new rebellion, a resurgence of that great spirit of the eleven embattled states—it was something he'd nearly die to help foster. No, not nearly, he told himself; he *would* die, and gladly.

Six days out of his family's ranch, Roberto followed a creek he hoped was the Prairie Dog Town Fork of the upper reaches of the Red, watching for rising walls that announced the canyon. Where the creek kinked, Roberto kinked with it, finding that a rising embankment on his side would force him to cross the current. Hoping it was the beginning of Palo Duro Canyon, he backtracked a few rods, seeing no other way in. Then he motivated his mount into the churning water. As he looked behind him, concerned that his pack horse follow willingly, a gunshot sounded. A bullet skipped off the water so near his mount's legs that the animal reared up and dumped him.

Water washed over him, seeming to rinse the sky. In a terror of Comanches, he got his feet under him, was up and drawing his revolver. Then, in waist-deep water, he charged as best he could toward the bank he'd just left, with the current resisting, holding him to the slowness of a nightmare.

Thrashing in desperation, Roberto reached the stream's edge, which rose abruptly and was undercut by current. He gripped a handful of weeds to help haul himself onto dry ground. But when he got one knee on the embankment, he heard the authoritative click of a man-made mechanism. He looked up into the muzzle of a repeating rifle held by a broad-hatted man, who, whatever else he may have been, was certainly no Comanche.

"Drop that pistol in the water," the man said. *"Drop it, damn your hide!"*

Roberto's mind clawed till the words registered. Then he let the nickeled Smith & Wesson revolver Tio Hector had given him pivot on his forefinger and drop into the creek. His horses had continued on across without him. They clambered up the far bank with a lot of thrashing, then stood dutifully, the gunshot scare forgotten.

"I expect you got a hideout gun on you," the man said. He was ragged and dirty and stood crouched over his rifle as though ready to spring. Despite his wariness, his expression suggested he was pleased with his own cunning.

"Just my rifle in the saddle boot," Roberto told him.

"I'll bet a toad sticker then."

"Only a pocketknife. It's not much of a knife."

"You're thinking to best me," the man said. "Get the drop. Only I'm too smart for you." Then he sucked in a breath and yelled so abruptly that Roberto jumped. "Virgil!" he yelled. "Virgil—where you at?" The hollering did not echo and the gurgling water soon covered it.

"Say, where's the rest of your party?" the rifleman demanded.

"There's just me," Roberto said, then wondered if admitting it was a good idea.

The man's eyes bugged. "You're traveling in Comanche country by your *lonesome?*"

"I'm looking for Palo Duro. The canyon."

"I ain't seen it," the man said, so quickly that Roberto got the notion he was lying. The man inclined his head and yelled again. "Virgil!"

It crossed Roberto's mind that the man in front of him might be part of Jackson's command, although he certainly wore nothing to suggest a military unit. It was true he carried guns, but so did almost everybody. The important thing was that the man was there at all, guarding the stream that was supposed to lead to Palo Duro.

"I'm to ask for somebody named Jackson," Roberto said. *"Jackson?"*

"—and to say my father sent me. Hollis Creigh?" Roberto pronounced the name with care, then stood expectant.

"Don't think I keep track of everybody's old man. What you wanting this Jackson for? Hunting him, I expect."

"I'm afraid I'm on the run," Roberto said. It was the first time he'd admitted it aloud, and saying the phrase made him feel older and more serious than he'd ever felt before, despite facing a gun barrel. "This Mr. Jackson and my father are old friends. They fought in the war together. For the South," Roberto added, making that part of it clear.

"You look kind of tender to be running from the law," the man said. "What'd you do, steal candy?"

Roberto considered. That he'd killed a man seemed something he should admit only to Jackson. He was saved from having to answer by the appearance of a rider coming down the creek, a larger man than the other, carrying a Spencer carbine and wearing a ragged black Hardee hat with the brim tacked up on one side, which, to Roberto's eyes, looked more like Union cavalry than Confederate. The rider came straight down the creek but was still on the opposite side of the main current. When he crossed over, his horse floundered a few steps. Roberto could see the point where the horse went to swimming, its head jutting forward, committed, and the eye flaring with fright.

"Took you long enough," Roberto's captor said. "I like to yelled my head off." He let his rifle barrel pivot and settle anew on Roberto. "I caught me some kind of Mexican. Speaks American, though."

The new man, Virgil, dismounted and stood looking doubtful. "Never heard no yelling. Alls I heard was a shot."

"Well it was me," the smaller one said with satisfaction. "I spooked his mount, and it dropped him in the crick." He nodded toward Roberto's horses, which were chuffing grass on the opposite bank. "See for yourself how wet he is."

"You mean you missed."

"The hell. I missed deliberate."

"I expect the question is where's the rest of his party?"

"He says he's by his lonesome."

"Alone?" Virgil said, acting just as astounded as the other one had.

"I am," Roberto told them. He felt that the fact that he was asking for Jackson was being forgotten. "I was told to ask for a man named Jackson," he said for Virgil's benefit.

The new man, Virgil, seemed rocked by the name. He pursed his lips in thought. "I believe you ought to've just kilt him, Skiff. I do believe it."

"Well, I doubt it's too late," the shorter one, whose name seemed to be Skiff, said. They both mulled it awhile, grimed fingers consulting their beards. "So let's say I kill him," Skiff said. "Then what?"

"I reckon you bury him."

"Says you. Burying's work, and us without no shovel. You got a shovel?" Skiff asked Roberto, who quickly shook his head. Then he looked at Roberto's horses. "I expect we'll just drop him in quicksand," Skiff said.

"Any fool knows quicksand won't hold a murdered man," Virgil scoffed. "He'll pop out again in a week or two. Then old Shad or somebody finds him and learns all about it."

"I guess I didn't think," Skiff said.

"Mr. Jackson and my father are old friends," Roberto offered. He felt this, too, was information worth repeating. Again, the name Jackson seemed to stun them. "From the war," Roberto said. "They were bordermen together."

The men looked at each other. "Beats all," Skiff said.

"My father is Hollis Creigh," Roberto said stoutly. "He lost a leg in Missouri while riding with Quantrill and later with some others."

"Whoa up," Virgil said. "Hollis how much?"

"Creigh."

"You heard of him?" Virgil asked.

"Not me," Skiff said. "This feller does seem to have a certain portion of information, though. He sure got it from someplace."

"We bring in a new man and you know who answers for it," Virgil said. "I expect burying's best. Then it's like we never saw him."

"It's a lot of work, though," Skiff said. "In particular without a shovel."

Roberto did not like more talk of burying. "You'd be making a big mistake. What you don't know is, I was sent for."

The two men swiveled to read each other like handbills. "Can't say I know what to think," Virgil said. He took his hat off and ran a hand through greasy hair.

Skiff said, "He's plain lying, I expect."

"But what if he ain't? Cripes, I wisht you'd a shot better. Now we're saddled with all this decisioning." Virgil put his hat back on and stood looking sad-eyed. "You're sure old Shad never mentioned nothing?"

"Not to me," Skiff said.

Virgil sighed. "He's apt to be mad if we do and mad if we don't," he said miserably. "Either way, he's apt to be mad."

Skiff lowered his rifle's hammer. "I reckon what you said

just earned yourself a look at the canyon," he told Roberto. "But you do any lying and the feller we're taking you to will make you sorry we didn't shoot you right here."

Skiff directed Virgil to hold his pistol on Roberto while Skiff himself splashed down into the creek. He stooped and dabbed one arm in the current. Soon he brought up Roberto's revolver like a slender, silver fish and shook the water out of it. "Ain't that a pretty thing," was all he said about it.

"He's kind of pretty hisself," Virgil said.

Once Skiff came back on his horse, Virgil took and maintained the lead, following a smooth-bottomed trace as narrow as a cow path. Roberto rode second, leading his pack horse, with Skiff behind him and holding his rifle at the ready.

On the whole, Roberto did not mind being escorted, even with a gun held on him. That Virgil and Skiff had been suspicious of him soon came to seem entirely understandable. In fact, Roberto decided it was good they had acted as they had. He was a wanted man himself, seeking refuge among others of his kind. If the outlaws of Palo Duro—or Rebels, or whatever they were—took precautions with outsiders, those same precautions would protect him as well as them.

Roberto began to feel pleased with himself. Being shot at had not shaken him up so badly. And soon he would reach his destination, for surely Skiff and Virgil, despite their raggedness and unmilitary appearance, were part of Jackson's force. Just as surely, they were taking the shortest route to the man who would shelter him.

As for the canyon itself, Palo Duro was a world. Roberto's former picture of a gash in the Panhandle prairie turned out to need revision. It was a gash, perhaps, a wound cut by water—but only if one had had the perspective of angels from which to examine it. What it was from Roberto's point of view, a rider along Prairie Dog Town Fork, was a vast place, with the sheltering canyon rims of red rock thrown wide, although climbing higher with every mile they traveled.

Besides being broad and open, the canyon offered prettier country than the prairie above it. In many places the bottom was greened over with what were tantamount to meadows. In these flat places, the creek meandered lazily, its banks shaded by elms and wild plums.

As they rode they saw wild turkey flutter into sycamores. A deer bounded along the creekbank. Once they saw a grouping of buffalo, placidly chewing and regarding them. At each sighting of game, Roberto's spirits improved. Palo Duro was beginning to seem a kind of Eden.

It was after sundown, with red light hanging like tapestry behind the screen of trees, and the sheltering walls of Palo Duro Canyon now no more than dim hulks, when they turned into what seemed a side canyon. They crossed a trickle of stream, then, within another half-mile, Roberto heard voices.

Seconds later, he and the men escorting him rode into a clearing. Around the fringes of this open space, low-roofed, log buildings were set at skewed angles to each other. On a porch fronting the largest building stood a young woman, pretty in a rough way, wearing a light-colored dress. What most took his eye, however, was a group of men standing in the dirt yard, with here and there among them a lighted lantern with insects crazying around it.

Every face in that group looked into the half-circle's hub, where a hatless and iron-bearded man stood rooted, his tall boots spread apart to suggest authority. Just as Roberto wondered if that man could be Jackson, he saw another figure within the half-circle. This one was stripped to the waist, sweating despite the cooling evening, and stood with his arms pinned by two other men.

Roberto looked amazed at the scene before him. He saw no Confederate uniforms, or even vestiges of uniforms. The faces rotated to take in Roberto, Skiff, and Virgil, then returned to defer to the bearded man, who for a moment stood wild-eyed and incredulous. Then he moved, stalking through the line of men, who parted for him like smoke. In seconds he stopped in front of Virgil's horse, his stance a confrontation. His voice was mild, and all the icier for that.

"What are you men bringing me?"

Virgil started badly. "We . . . he was coming up the creek and—"

"Says he's a law dodger," Skiff said warily. "Claims he was sent for."

"He claims that, does he?"

"I figured right off he was lying," Skiff added.

"They were fixing to shoot me," Roberto said. "I suppose I surprised them. I said what came into my head. Would . . . would you be Mr. Jackson?"

"This is a serious mistake," Jackson said, if it were he, "bringing this boy in here. You men will answer for it."

"I'm to say, sir, that my pa is Hollis Creigh, who rode with you in the war. He said you'd remember. And that you might be good enough to shelter me on account of—"

"Hollis Creigh," Jackson said speculatively. He was a new man in Roberto's experience, looking nothing like any rancher or granger he'd ever come across. One reason was his clothes, for he wore a blousy-sleeved shirt, boiled white and open at the collar. His dark trousers were bound by a gold sash that held a long revolver. His boots appeared as soft as kidskin and shone dully in the lantern light. The man resembled, in those clothes and that light, a long-haired preacher more than any other type Roberto had come across. What held Roberto's eyes was his face: the beak of nose, gaunt cheeks vertically scored, the forehead heavily browed, shading deep-set, fiery eyes. It was the face, Roberto thought—no, the visage—of a prophet.

"We figured best we bring him in, colonel," Virgil said. "Wasn't nobody with him, we made sure of that much. We figured if you didn't want him, we could shoot him here and bury him someplace."

"The two of you figured this together, did you?"

"Well, we did what we thought we oughta."

Jackson's response spooked Roberto to his bones. From the sash he whipped out the long-barreled revolver and extended it, homing on Roberto's face. The hammer racheted back. The muzzle wavered with some unidentifiable passion, tracking in small circles. Roberto looked from the gun muzzle to the man's glowering face and grasped that he was about to be murdered. It was dizzying.

"Dismount," Jackson said.

Shaking badly, Roberto swung down and nearly collapsed. He'd been on the horse for most of the day; his legs were unused to supporting his weight. Besides, standing before a cocked pistol made him feel spindly as a newborn colt, and his legs as weak as paper.

"I'll not tolerate a liar," Jackson said.

"We told him," Skiff said.

"Hush!" Jackson glared Skiff down, and then Virgil, in case he might have considered saying something. He returned his attention to Roberto, who felt the man's gaze like a cold wind.

"We're a tight-knit group here," Jackson said. "Somewhat threadbare compared to times past but disciplined nonetheless. Each one depending on the other. Do you see what I'm saying?"

Roberto managed a throat clearing. This was the military way of doing things, he told himself. He nodded.

"Any commander depends for his decisions upon information. If such information is faulty, do you see the havoc that raises?"

Roberto assured him he did.

Jackson took a step closer. "Lie to me even once and you become liable for strict discipline. Do you follow?"

"Yes, sir."

"I'm a stickler for it," Jackson said. He lowered his revolver's hammer. Roberto dared breathe. Jackson shifted the revolver to his left hand and hung his right theatrically in space. He said, "A lantern."

Roberto heard a scuffle of boots. The wire bail of a railroad lantern was set into Jackson's hand. Then yellow light was conveyed into Roberto's eyes.

"Hollis Creigh," Jackson said, and studied Roberto for long seconds, his face so close that Roberto smelled brandy.

"My father, sir. He said you'd remember a debt."

"A debt to be sure," Jackson said. "And now it's collection time, is that it?"

"Not . . . that's not at all how he looked at it," Roberto said. "My pa still counts you a great friend."

"Well, isn't that cozy?" Jackson leaned in even closer. "By Jehovah, I detect the resemblance," he said finally, with his voice magnified to make it an announcement. His eyes gleamed then, and his face smiled a smile that gave Roberto no reassurance.

Jackson turned to the men behind him. "Looks like old Hollis has been dipping his wick in dark places." The men laughed, the woman on the porch with them.

Roberto waited. "I'm named Roberto."

"I'm not surprised. And what is it you are running from?"

Roberto had to swallow. "I killed a man. It was self-defense."

"I hope your victim was a Yankee carpetbagger."

"No—"

"An uppity free nigger, then."

"The son of a neighboring rancher. He was—"

"A pity," Jackson said. "Well, Roberto Creigh, it seems you're a volunteer."

"Yes, sir. But if you can't shelter me, I'm sure I could get along on my own hook. I mean if you don't feel you could—"

"Are you a true friend of the southern nation, Roberto Creigh?"

Roberto breathed gratefully. "I sure am. My folks are native-born Texan. My pa—"

"All right," Jackson said, and he stepped back and nodded. "All right then."

"I guess we done right after all, colonel," Skiff said.

"You two get back out on duty," Jackson told them absently. "On second thought, get down for a moment. The more of you who see this, the better." Virgil and Skiff exchanged wary looks and swung down off their horses.

"You're just in time to see how it goes with men who forget where their loyalties lie," Jackson said. "Our young recruit will be interested." Jackson turned and stalked back through the line of men.

The interview left Roberto dizzied. On the one hand, Jackson hadn't shot him. On the other, Jackson recognized Roberto's father's name and yet wasn't curious about him the way any old friend would be. He supposed, though, that there would be time for visiting later.

"Mark well what you witness here, Roberto Creigh," Jackson called to him. The men had re-formed their half-circle, with Jackson again at its hub.

Roberto had forgotten the shirtless prisoner. This man now cringed and tried to jerk away. Jackson strode up and struck him savagely with the back of his hand. The man reeled but kept himself from falling.

"Let's settle it with pistols," Jackson said.

The prisoner hung his head. His mutter was inaudible.

"Someone give him a gun," Jackson said. The two men holding him captive warily backed away. Another proffered a revolver, but the shirtless man wouldn't look at it. He kept his eyes directed to the ground in front of him.

"Take it!" Jackson ordered. "Fight me like a man!"

The response was beseeching. "Don't make me, colonel."

"You'd rather snivel. All right. Then you'd best ask for your whipping. It's your choice—the pistol or the whip."

The man, hang-dog and pitiful, looked at the firelit faces. The evening was full dark by this time, and the faces lurid.

"By the Almighty, *ask, damn you!*"

The man's voice came smothered in sobs.

"Nobody heard you," Jackson said.

"Whip me," the man said.

Jackson said, "So be it," with evident satisfaction. He backed a step. At some signal invisible to Roberto, the two men who'd been holding the captive stepped in and draped him over a hitchrail, his back to Jackson. The rail was too high for kneeling, causing him to hang awkwardly with his knees off the ground, his arms extended and elbows over the rail. The sweat of fear gleamed off his back.

Jackson was handed a whip, a heavy teamster's black-snake. The men around him backed away, at the same time raising their lanterns.

Roberto stood stunned. The first lash sounded, pulling from Roberto an involuntary moan, while the victim cried out in a wrenching voice.

Jackson was lean and tall and apparently well conditioned. He stood with his legs apart and launched his weight forward, laying on the strokes. Roberto tried to close himself down—his vision, his hearing—to shut out the lashes, the voices yelling encouragement, the flogged man's ragged screams. But the sound of the whip cut through, so that he heard and felt all of it.

At the tenth or twelfth lash, the victim sagged off the hitchrail and had to be draped back on. From that point, Roberto could watch no more. He stepped to his horse and pretended some difficulty with the cinch strap, even though it was late, and he was one of the gang now and certainly not riding anywhere that night.

A hand on his shoulder made him start like a colt. The calico-dressed woman had come off the porch to him. She said, "This is bad for you, isn't it?" She would have touched him again had he not shied from her hand. Her words went straight by him, so that he stood blinking and bewildered. Then Jackson's whip lashed again, and a particularly wrenching cry from the man being punished lifted up like a desperate prayer.

"Would you lookit the boy flinch. I expect you've not seen the likes of old Shad before."

"No . . . I—" Roberto let it go, not sure of what he would have said anyway.

"He really lays it into them," the woman said. "Makes

work for us as has to tend them. That one he's whipping will be sick for a month." She looked over to the flogged man, who had fallen off the hitchrail again.

"Put him back," Jackson ordered.

"What—what's he being punished for?" Roberto asked.

"Old Shad imagines the feller sassed him. Insubordination, he calls it."

"God . . ." Roberto said.

"There's a corral yonder for your animals." She pointed off into the darkness. "And a shed for your trappings. You come back to the house and we'll find you some supper."

"I'm obliged, ma'am. I—"

"Don't be ma'aming me. I'm Faith. And don't go getting lost."

The whipped man had sagged to the ground again. Jackson retracted his whip and prepared to strike him where he lay. Roberto couldn't see how slashing up one of your own men into raw meat, so he was fit neither for work nor fighting for weeks to come, could have anything to do with reviving the Confederacy. He supposed he had much to learn about things military.

The woman looked at him expectantly. Roberto decided he was glad to go. He turned from the circle of lanterns and was momentarily sightless. But he drew his mount and his pack horse behind him and walked into the enshrouding dark, his legs hollow. The next whiplash, when it came, was muted enough by distance and night sounds that it did not cut him.

13 · NASH WHEELER

NASH TROTTED HIS HORSE UP THE CREIGH RANCH DOUBLE track, leading the spare. He'd debated over letting Hollis Creigh see the pack horse but in the end decided it might work to his advantage. The presence of the second animal, so obviously loaded for manhunting, would underline what Nash had to say.

A couple of dogs came out barking, followed by two greaser vaqueros, who set up a yelling in their lingo that soon brought Hector Garza from the shade by the barn where he'd been mending harness. Hector spat when he recognized Nash. Then he advanced into the sun and stood squinting fiercely.

"You would speak to Mr. Creigh," Hector said.

Nash nodded. Hector looked in no mood for pleasantries, which was fine with Nash. He had not come to pass the time about the weather or the cattle business.

Hector, moving stiff-backed to show his contempt, crossed the ranch yard. His spurs rang up the steps before he disappeared into the house. It gave Nash time to ease his weight in the saddle and roll a cigarette.

The cigarette was drawing when Hector reappeared with his employer, his brother-in-law, Hollis Creigh. It surprised Nash that he still thought of Hollis without the crutches; but of course, they'd been a part of him since the war's end. If Nash associated any objects with Hollis Creigh, it was cap and ball revolvers. Creigh, however, was not wearing a sidearm now, although Hector wore one. Nash felt an itch to ease his own revolver in its holster, but he fought it down. He merely had certain facts to relay, and then his proposal. All he needed in return was a yes or no answer—which Hollis Creigh, being the straightforward man he was, would certainly give him.

"By gosh—Nash Wheeler," Creigh said, taking a civil tone and not overdoing his surprise. It was as though they'd last talked a month back; instead, it'd been ten years.

Nash drew on the cigarette and studied his old enemy, finding him hale despite the way he had to sag into the crutches. Take Creigh for a cripple, Nash reflected, and you'd make a bad mistake.

"Thought I'd see how you're getting on," Nash said.

"You'll come inside," Creigh said. "Dominga will get us coffee."

"I reckon not."

"Whiskey, then."

"I reckon I won't take the time."

Creigh turned to Hector. *"Hermano,* Nash is an old friend."* Hector, reading the implication, shrugged and stomped down the porch steps, crossing the yard to where he'd been working. He looked sourly at Nash's pack horse as he went by.

"At least, I always figured we were," Creigh said. "We kind of went our different ways after the war, but I'm damned if I ever saw a reason for it."

Nash frowned. Hating a man who did not hate you back diluted your satisfaction. "I got something to say," Nash said.

Creigh nodded. "I figured."

"Libba come to see me. She don't want a trial for fear of your boy getting off, pleading self-defense. You get a pair of lawyers het up and going at each other, anything can happen."

"Self-defense was how it was," Creigh said. "You ought to know, having been there."

"It'd be hard to say just what it was," Nash said. "One person could talk it one way, another could talk it another."

"If you believe that, you've changed more than I thought," Creigh said, and his eyes bore at Nash with so cleanly flowing a power that Nash glanced away. He disguised the reflex as curiosity about the Creigh place. The ranch, on the face of it, seemed no richer than any other two-bit outfit shipping its beeves on a shares basis. But no poorer, either.

"I spoke my piece to the sheriff," Nash said. "It's in the law's hands now."

"Roberto told me Quirt and Lew Christmas saw it too."

"I ain't getting roped into discussing it," Nash said. "What I'm saying is, Libba don't want a trial. She might have herself all kinds of reasons. One being how that old business about Cole's real pa is liable to come out. Anyhow, you'd know more than me about that."

Creigh advanced a step to the porch railing. "That's ugly talk, Nash. I won't listen to it."

Nash shrugged. "Then let's just say Libba's got her reasons." He saw a curtain move at the open parlor window —Dominga Creigh eavesdropping. Dominga or the pretty daughter.

"Anyhow," Nash said, "I only come over to set out my position."

"Which is what?"

"Which is sort of betwixt and between. I expect you heard about the reward Libba posted?"

"She's looking to buy vigilante justice," Creigh said grimly. "By rights, the law ought to prevent her."

"She only put the word out," Nash said. "The law can't stop that. But Libba don't put much stock in bounty men in any case, as they're short on information. Which makes them go baying off on false trails. Way I heard it, most are hunting up in the Nations." Creigh did not react, but Nash snorted to show what he thought of bounty hunters. "I figure you wouldn't send your boy to the first place anybody'd look."

"It's time you stated your business," Creigh said. He shifted his eyes to Hector down at the barn, so that Nash had to turn in the saddle and look too. Hector and a couple vaqueros were watching.

"Business is just what I'm talking," Nash said. "Last night Libba offered me half the BR ranch if I was to bring in your Roberto. I mean in a condition in which he couldn't defend himself."

"You're a son of a wolf bitch, telling me that," Creigh said, with enough ice that Nash found it gratifying.

"Half the ranch," Nash said. "It's a temptation, for a fact." He grinned, letting gloat into his voice. "So like you see, I'm loaded for bear right now." He watched Creigh's eyes trouble up as they settled on the pack horse. "I could ride back to the BR, or on up the trail someplace. It all depends."

"You can ride straight to hell," Creigh said, his anger plainly building.

"Sounds like you ain't hardly appreciating my position," Nash said. "Now, a body might figure half the BR would sound good to a man in my boots. But you know what I had to own up to lately?" Creigh was steely and did not oblige him. "That ranching just don't shine like it used to," Nash said. "The truth is, it's too damned much work."

"And you've got the gall to ride up my road to see whether I'd make you a better offer," Creigh said. He nodded with the certainty of it.

Nash scratched his chin stubble. It was a comfort Creigh was not armed. "Well, I wondered whether you'd got more practical in your old age," Nash said. "After all, some things are worth more than money."

"You're sitting there bargaining for my boy's life."

"Like I said, I'm treating it like business."

"You've imagined me with that federal payroll so long that in your head it's become a fact."

"Oh, I figure it's cached here someplace," Nash said airily, and again looked around. Hector and his vaqueros stood by the barn. A chicken ventured under a corral rung. Hollis Creigh hung angrily on his crutches.

Then the curtains blowing out the open window caught Nash's eye. They were faded curtains; certainly the money was not being spent on foofaraw inside the ranch house.

Then there was a noise and then movement at the open doorway. Dominga Creigh appeared, her face twisted with feelings running every which way. She had a two-handed grip on an old army revolver. Creigh yelled something and lunged toward the doorway. He swung out one crutch to knock the gun barrel up just as the shot crashed.

Nash's horse shied sideways; it took him a moment to get it under control. He dropped one hand to his revolver, but Creigh had already wrested the gun from his wife and was cussing her out.

Then Nash heard urgent footsteps behind him and drew his gun in earnest. It was Hector, coming on a run on account of his sister—to protect her or comfort her, Nash didn't know which.

Hector loped up the yard in Mexican boots, levered himself on the handrail, and vaulted all four porch steps. Dominga was bawling and jabbering in her lingo, her noises all running together and her hair tangled across her face. Creigh tried to hold her but he'd lost a crutch, and when she twisted away from him, he had to grab the wall for support.

Hector pivoted on a boot heel and called out something to Nash in Spanish that had the sound of bloody threat to it, then Hector went by Creigh, taking his sister into the house.

"Damn you people—I come here to talk!" Nash said.

"You talked enough," Creigh told him. He was angry, and his color was up.

"The hell I have. I'm just getting to it," Nash said. He breathed a second. "Old Bloody Ben Poole's eighty thousand in Yankee coin—that's my interest. But even with you holding out on me all these years, I'd be willing to leave you enough to get by on. Let's say for the good job you done protecting it."

"You're crazy."

"Give me three-fourths of it," Nash said, "and I'll leave your boy alone. Hell, I'll leave this whole country."

"Everything I own wouldn't tally three thousand," Creigh said. "And I'm damned if I'd give you one-tenth of that."

Nash had to smile. He heard Dominga Creigh sobbing inside the house and then Hector's voice rising angrily. "Not even to save your boy's life?" Nash suggested.

"You bastard. I ought to let Hector shoot you."

"Or your wife. Seems everybody's doing your fighting but you, Hollis."

"You take this back to Libba," Creigh said. "Robbie did little to be ashamed of. We're putting our faith in Texas law. I'd advise her to do the same."

"You're talking like you're planning on bringing him back," Nash said.

"I'm through talking." Creigh stooped awkwardly, his weight against the house, and fished up the fallen crutch.

"Well, my lands, I am surprised." Nash grinned to see Creigh struggling. "You want to keep Bloody Ben's money almighty bad, but damned if I can see you got a use for it." He flicked the cigarette end onto the porch. It arced closer to Creigh than he'd really intended.

"You come up here again," Creigh said, "I swear I'll shoot you myself."

Nash turned his horse so that if he needed to he could split his attention between Creigh and the vaqueros. "You're bound you'll have this thing your own way," Nash said. "Just don't make out I didn't give fair warning."

14 · CASS

IN PLACES WHERE THEY COULD COVER THEIR TRACKS, AS IN creekbeds or on rocky ground, they held northwest on what they imagined was a straight line to Palo Duro, a pack horse furnished by the Creigh ranch drawn on a rawhide reata behind each man. Other times, Riley, being more cautious, made them hem and tack every which way in order to leave a puzzle more than a trail, all in the event they were being followed.

"I doubt we're being trailed anymore, even if we were earlier. We've come too darned far," Riley said finally, after riding in worried silence for over an hour. He said it with such plainly concocted hope that Cass squeaked around on his saddle and looked at him.

"You sound like somebody trying to convince himself."

"Do I?"

Cass nodded with some vigor. "You spend any more time looking behind us, your neck's going to be twisted permanent."

"It's just that I look back there and I get to feeling itchy."

"Then think about something pleasant. Like sixteen hundred dollars."

"I have thought about it," Riley said, looking critical. "You'll have to admit it doesn't have the same degree of shine on it as five thousand."

Cass puffed out a breath. In his way of thinking, they should ride hell for leather for Palo Duro Canyon and pay no mind to the trail they were leaving. Anybody following would be left in the dust.

"Maybe not," Cass said, "but the thing is, it's not like we're in the same camp with bounty hunters. We've got Creigh's directions to the big canyon. We've even got his letter of introduction to show to his boy. What we've got is a sure thing. Just think about it—what could go wrong?"

Riley mulled it too long before answering. Cass got impatient and had to answer himself. "You're always calling my plans pie in the sky," Cass said, "but this is one that isn't. That money's going to make up a danged nice nest egg for whatever we fix on doing next."

"Buffalo hunting, if we're smart."

"Damned sure not. If you'd talked to as many stinking buffalo men as I did, you'd change that tune. You've got to stand upwind of those boys just to say howdy. I don't care for any kind of work that makes my clothes draw flies."

Cass looked down at his horse's laboring withers and waited for Riley's inevitable saucy answer, probably something about Cass not caring for any kind of work, period. The withers labored some more. Cass got impatient again and looked behind him, seeing Riley still studying their backtrail. "You listening or what?"

"I think maybe you're right," Riley said, a statement apparently directed at all of East Texas.

"It's refreshing to hear you admit it," Cass said, then realized he wasn't sure what Riley was talking about.

"We really are being followed," Riley said, "and I'm just trying to convince myself we ain't."

"Oh, for pete's sake."

The day had nooned with a heat not genuine, for the cool of September lurked in the shade along the creek bottoms. Cass raised himself in the stirrups to ease his hinder. He took off his hat and wiped his brow on a forearm. "Tell you what. We'll tie the horses in that wash yonder. Then we'll hike back to this high spot under these elm trees—"

"They're oaks."

"—and have a bite to eat. Then I'll have a nap while you fret to your heart's content about riders coming up behind us."

"You're saying you'll get all rested up while I have to stand guard," Riley said owlishly.

Cass decided not to answer. He was only offering a lunch stop to humor Riley's suspicious nature. Some gratitude. Just look how Riley turned it around on him.

Cass guided his saddle horse into the sandy wash and tied it and the pack horse well apart, where they couldn't get into foolishness. He got the food bag and let Riley bring up a canteen. He noticed that Riley got his rifle too.

In two minutes they were sitting in patchy shade under rustling live oaks, looking at ten-mile horizons in all directions and eating Hollis Creigh's jerked beef and the bread baked by his missus.

"Looks like half of Texas is laid out for us," Cass said appreciatively.

Riley said, "You Texans and your Texas. The way I see it, Texas don't contain any more of anything than any other place else. All it has is more space to put it in."

Cass laughed, then had a pull from the canteen. "That's not far off the mark," he said. "You know how, with something too big, you have to back up to get a good look at it? Well, in Texas, you don't have to back up." He pulled his boots off with some effort, doubled the tops over so various critters couldn't crawl into them, and placed them where his head was going to go. He had a gnawing suspicion his statement about Texas hadn't turned out right. "On account of you already *are* backed up," Cass said, clarifying.

"Um," Riley said.

Cass lay back and settled his hat over his eyes, then groaned at the resulting comfort, putting ostentation into it. He said, "Not a bad life."

"Go ahead, get all settled in," Riley said. "Roll out your bedroll for the night, why don't you?"

Cass tipped his hat up and looked at Riley with one eye. He could tell by the warm feeling in the back of his head that he would fall asleep right away. Riley was chewing guardedly, while looking from some vague point to the southeast, to Cass, then back to the southeast again. "I'm sure you'll wake me should Comanches show up," Cass said.

He let his hat resettle. The inside of the crown smelled pleasantly of hair tonic, which reminded him of barbers and hotels and beds with crisp sheets, which reminded him of the sixteen hundred dollars, which reminded him of their quarry, Roberto Creigh.

In a moment he was rehearsing how they'd find him, a young man—a boy, really—who'd never been far from his family's ranch, probably good and homesick by that point and tired of being an outlaw. The boy was probably well spooked by the company he was keeping, too, if Cass knew the kind of men who hid up in bunches.

Then Cass's thinking shifted, to where it seemed he was already in the canyon, which was dark and lurking and narrow as a church window, its towering walls actually meeting overhead, making it no longer a canyon but a cave, resonating with danger. And then it was really murky and Cass was riding in thick canebrake country with a hundred outlaws after him, while somebody was kicking his sockfeet. Then Cass rose up into yellow light, with the smell of sun-cured oak leaves and the heat of midday bunched all around him.

"Wha . . . ?" Cass said.

"Shsshh!"

And then he was awake and ogling Riley with his sleep face screwed up into what must have been a peeved expression, and Riley was crouching behind an oak trunk, poking his rifle barrel around it and looking more worried than anytime that week.

"For cripe's sakes, what?"

"Rider," Riley said. The rifle muzzle was a pointer. Cass looked out and at first found the sparsely grassed prairie unchanged. Then he made out movement a good mile out—a single rider coming on slowly, but coming on.

"One man a mile away and you're shushing me?"

"You got a way of waking up hollering. A body can't be too careful."

Cass pulled his boots on, his mind still half bedded. Riley was saying, "I figure it's that Nash Wheeler that Creigh warned us about." Cass was about to ask why Riley assumed the first rider they saw had to be Nash Wheeler, but he saw he was only being argumentative. If not Nash Wheeler, touted by Hollis Creigh as the best white tracker in Texas, then who else would it be?

"This not being the Nations, I don't expect I could just shoot him for following," Riley said.

"Shoot him? For damned sure not." Cass finally got his feet stomped into his boots and his hat on and his gunbelt straightened.

"It's one cure for the situation," Riley said. "Sooner or later we're going to have some face-down with the man."

Cass struggled to think. "We'll catch him," he decided. "I mean rope him."

"Huh?"

"Rope him and then leave him afoot. Lead his horse on ahead a few miles with his guns and his boots stowed on it. A few miles walking barefoot ought to persuade him to leave our trail alone."

Riley tugged at one ear, which indicated bewilderment. "How do you see us getting the drop on him?"

"He'll follow our tracks into that dry wash, right? We'll hunker in there and stretch a rope across it. When he comes through, we'll tighten our line and snag him clean off his horse. Then when he falls, we'll charge out and throw down on him with pistols. It's simple."

Predictably, Riley was skeptical. "I don't know. Stretching a rope sounds like something out of one of them nickel romances."

"Nickel how muches?"

"Storybook stuff," Riley said. "You go after armed men with ropes and they'll likely shoot you dead."

"He'll be too surprised to," Cass said. "Anyhow, I don't hear you offering a better idea, other than shooting him, which is not under consideration."

Cass swiveled and looked back over the prairie. The rider had made a quarter-mile while they'd argued. That was the worst of him partnering up with Riley Stokes; while they hashed things out, opportunities bypassed them.

Cass picked up the food sack. Riley got the canteen. They jogged back to the dry wash, keeping their heads low.

"I don't know why I'm doing this," Riley said. "Stretching a damn rope."

Tethering the horses farther down the creekbed was the work of a couple of minutes. Cass found a narrowing of the wash with thick brush on both sides. As he thrashed into the brush with his end of the rope, he scared up a covey of quail. The surprise nearly burst his heart from his chest. The wings pounded, the quail buzzed in all directions, and Cass's first thought was of Nash Wheeler galloping down on them before they were half ready.

"Scared the bejesus out of me," Riley called to him, and Cass answered, "Me too."

While his heartbeat came down off a full gallop, Cass decided the reata strung haphazardly across the wash's narrowing looked innocent enough. With no indication yet of the rider approaching, he scurried out and threw sand over the rope at what he considered key spots. Then he sanded out his footprints while backing to his hiding spot. After that, the snare's appearance was perfect.

"I'll give the signal," Cass called, "and we'll haul on it for all we're worth."

From the brush across the wash, Riley's voice said, "I got a poor feeling about this."

Cass hunkered back on the wash bank, his throat dry and the rope becoming soggy in his sweating hands. Riley always being the worrier made it Cass's job to be the pooh-pooher, even though there were times Cass worried as well. The fact was, this was one of them. Straight down to his boots Cass was feeling, like Riley had said, that their ambush was sort of storybook stuff. If he let himself, he could get to feeling foolish with nothing but a rope in his hands and a dangerous man—to be exact, a former Confederate guerilla fighter—riding down on them. Everything he'd heard about Nash Wheeler made him sound like a bad man to tangle with.

Cass checked his gun and then eased it back in its holster so he could pull it quickly. He wished at that moment they had followed some fool plan of Riley's instead of this fool plan of his own. That way, if the plan failed, all the blame would be Riley's.

In a minute, Cass heard hooves in sand. Then the rider, for all his supposed guerilla wiles, came straight up the dry wash following the trail they'd laid for him. Cass's view was not the clearest, being complicated by brush, but he made out the horse's dark mane and buckskin coloration.

At that point, one straggler among the quail community exploded out of the wash. Cass suffered a gut-twinge of things going off-kilter. The approaching horse spooked at the quail's noise and reared high. Its rider uttered a cry, thin and startled, and hung on as the horse nearly surged out from under him.

"Pull!" Cass yelled, hauling on the rope in desperation, feeling Riley's tug in return. In the clear view he had ahead

of him he saw the rope rise up taut and quivering. An instant later, the horse came down out of its rearing, jumped straight to a gallop, and caught the rope across its nose. Cass was yanked so violently by a half-ton of charging horseflesh that it nearly pulled him out of his socks.

Cass sailed into the wash as if jerked by God, his hands splaying and grabbing at nothing. Riley spilled simultaneously from the opposite bank. The buckskin horse reared again, panicked by the rope. Cass hit gravelly wash bottom and rolled. He came up looking skyward, seeing the rider somehow high above him, a vision backlighted by high sun, the rider spilling from the saddle and floating down, the rider's hat separating from long, cascading hair. Cass's only thought was to roll out of the way, but it was a thought slow in arriving. A human body slammed into him, knocking the wind out of him, leaving him writhing in that helpless, flattened, alarming state he'd not felt since childhood.

The buckskin went over backward with flaring eyes and nostrils and the scream a horse makes in panic. Then it rolled and got its hooves under it and plunged away down the wash, stirrups flapping like wings and the saddle skewed to a two o'clock position.

Cass felt flat as a suit of clothes; he couldn't get breath into him. Angelina Creigh couldn't get enough breath out. *"Of all the—!"* she huffed. *"Damn you both! I ought to—"*

While trying to extricate herself, she stuck a boot in Cass's face. When she saw Riley's revolver where it had spilled in his fall, she instantly crawled for it. Cass was no help; he still fought for breath. Riley had to dive after her and wrestle the gun away.

"You've got no right—" Angelina screamed.

Riley muttered, "Danged . . . *vixen!*"

And all the while Cass was thrashing his arms and legs and could not get one whiff of air back into his body. Pressure was building in his face, to where he felt his head might pop. The world reeled. He grabbed out to hold onto something, but his hands came up with loose dirt.

Then Riley was standing over him, pulling him up by his

gunbelt. Cass felt the first breath of air come into him. He gulped for it.

"Ow! Hey!" Riley said. He crossed his arms to ward off the rocks that Angelina, in her fury, was throwing at him. Cass pulled a deep breath into himself, filling like forge bellows. He reached for his holster, finding it twisted under him. He got the comforting, grainy-wood feel of his pistol stocks in his hand, thumbed back the hammer, and raised the gun skyward. The shot, when it blasted, called a big halt to everything.

Riley said, "By gol, she is a *hellcat!*"

Angelina said something truly unladylike, then reached down for a crumpled hat and stuffed it angrily on her head.

"Just ... everybody ... stop ... everything," was all Cass could manage to say about it.

15 · ANGELINA

THE BOUNTY MEN, BICKERING LIKE AN OLD MARRIED COUPLE, took an hour to find and catch her buckskin gelding. Once they had roped the horse, the stock of Angelina's repeating rifle was found to have been broken when the horse rolled on it. Compounding the loss, the bounty men would not let her have the rifle back in any case.

And all the while they dithered at finding and catching the horse, they tried to explain the business proposition her father had offered them, a far-fetched story of being paid sixteen hundred dollars just to bring Roberto to the law.

"I doubt my father has sixteen hundred dollars," Angelina said.

"He'll have plenty when we collect that reward," the taller one said with satisfaction. Angelina humphed. Once men such as these had collected Libba Barlow's five thousand dollars, it was hardly likely they'd turn over the lion's share to her father. Probably they'd keep it and ride off, leaving her brother in the *calaboso,* looking at a noose, and with little hope of defending himself.

As for her father's supposed offer, why would he pay good money to have Roberto back when only a few days earlier he had sent Roberto away?

"Because your father's afraid some feller name of Nash Wheeler is hunting him," the taller of them said. "You know who Wheeler is, don't you?"

Yes, she knew who Wheeler was, and knew also that Wheeler bore her father some grudge, a matter dating back to the war, for both her mother and Tio Hector had at times made references to it.

"It was on account of Wheeler we took pains to hide our tracks," the shorter, darker of them said. "Now your tracks are going to lead him straight to us."

Angelina gave him her most scornful look. "I followed your tracks easily enough," she said.

The darker, shorter one looked sheepishly at the taller, lighter-haired one, who said, "I told you we should have rode hell for leather. Instead, we wasted time cross-trailing, and then let a danged girl catch up with us."

Once the bounty men resumed arguing, Angelina saw a chance to slip around to where they had stowed her rifle, but the darker-haired one caught her by the wrist and pulled her away.

"You may as well kill me now," Angelina told them. "Otherwise, I'll come up on you in the night and shoot you both."

The taller one said, "Oh, put a hobble on it," in a tired way, and then looked at the other one like he would go to arguing again. Only he didn't; instead he said that with the sun already lowering, they might as well give up traveling any farther that day. What they might as well do, he said, with an air of facing facts, was make camp for the night.

The darker one took a rifle and went away mumbling, while the other began picking up small sticks and dried buffalo dung for their evening fire. Angelina noticed he wouldn't touch the buffalo chips with his long, slender fingers but used sticks to pick them up instead.

With only the taller one guarding her, Angelina had an idea of working around to her rifle again. She was moving in that direction when a shot sounded. Without meaning to, she cried out. The tall, fair-haired one looked up grinning from the campfire he was preparing and said, "Spooked you, didn't it." Minutes later, a second shot sounded, but she was damned if she would jump at that one.

The darker one came back carrying two prairie hens with their heads neatly shot off, just as her Uncle Hector or Roberto would have done it. The bounty men had seemed helpless to her in some ways, but they were apparently capable with firearms. Angelina took note of it.

By the time the fire had burned down to a hot bed of coals for cooking, and the hens were fixed on green-willow spits, the sun was sinking below the rim of the plains. Angelina decided that to spite them she would eat nothing. In a couple of days they'd have a starving captive on their hands, which would show the world what brutes they were. But soon the sweet smell of the roasting hens reached her, giving her such a feeling of weakness that she had to sit down on the ground.

Presently the dark-haired one stepped over to offer a plate with pieces of roasted meat on it. A slice of her own mother's bread was on the plate as well. Before she knew it, she was eating hungrily, for two days had been a long time to go without warm food. In truth, she'd eaten very little of anything.

The darker one watched her, his expression amused. "I guess I should have hunted up another bird. What'd you do, light out without grub?"

At first she wouldn't look at him, but the longer the question hung unanswered, the more it seemed to make her actions appear rash and incompetent. "I had no time," she said. "You rode out in the night and I had to follow. I barely got my horse saddled."

"Anyhow, she's here now," the taller one said. "And danged if she doesn't put us in a fix."

The darker one nodded, his eyes narrowing. For a while they both brooded.

"Look here," the darker one said, and took up his coffee and stood up, as though to make what he had to say seem more important. "If we let you go, will you promise to head straight back to your folks's ranch?"

"I only promise to protect my brother from the likes of you," Angelina vowed. Their responses pleased her: the taller one puffed out his cheeks in exasperation, while the shorter one said an ugly word.

"We can't very well tie her up someplace or leave her afoot, either one," the taller one said. "She'd starve, if wolves didn't get her first."

The shorter one agreed. "Her being skinny already, she wouldn't last more than a couple days."

"I am not at all skinny," Angelina said firmly.

"I expect we got off on the wrong foot with her from the git-go," the taller one said. "Hunting her brother on their family land, then roping her off her horse."

"We roped the horse, if you'll remember."

"I'm saying where she's concerned we ought to just start over," the taller one said.

"Suits me."

"Look, he's called Riley," the taller one said. "And I'm Cass. We're not the bad sorts you seem to think."

"I know your kind," Angelina said.

The other one, Riley, looked up exasperated from stirring sugar into his coffee. "Can't you get it straight we're working for your father?"

"I'll never believe it."

The one called Cass said with conviction, "I got a notion to show her the letter."

"By gol, let's do it. I've had a bellyful of being called bad names." The one named Riley rummaged through saddlebags, finally coming up with a sheet of foolscap that reflected yellow in the firelight. Angelina glared at it to show her contempt.

"You'll have to come closer to the fire to read it," Cass said. "It's from your father to your brother. It introduces us and tells your brother he should trust us."

She wanted to defy them, but the letter drew her; it was something of her family. She set her plate down and stepped warily closer. The darker one, Riley, held out the letter. He had the expression a falsely accused person wears while being vindicated. "You just read it," he said. "You'll see how muleheaded you been acting."

Her fingers closed on it. She recognized her father's headlong hand, the letters leaning forward like a colt going too fast for new legs. She angled it to the fire to read it.

"Dear Robbie," was at the top, which made her throat catch. She made out the names the bounty men were using—Cass McCasland and Riley Stokes—though they probably used other names too. In the next paragraph she saw the amount of Libba Barlow's reward—$5,000—a figure that clamored alarmingly when set in ink on paper.

On this evidence, the bounty men had not lied, but the possibility—even probability—remained that they intended to cheat her father, or, far worse, bring Roberto back dead over a saddle. Angelina stared beyond the letter into the campfire, seeing how it would go, how the bounty men would make her turn back for home, while they would go on and find her brother. She would be left to straggle back to the Halfmoon and appear a fool, all the more for having left without her parents' blessing.

She looked at the bounty men, seeing triumph on their faces. The one called Cass had built his supper fire against a short piece of log. On the log's butt end, near where he sat, he had placed their speckle-enameled coffeepot. Angelina found it no trick at all to kick out a foot, upsetting their coffee.

"Hey—!" Cass yelled. He lunged for the coffeepot, but it dumped before he caught it. Angelina knelt swiftly and fed her father's letter to the fire.

Riley yelled, *"Cass—stop her!"* and charged in to save the paper. She tried to push a shoulder into him, but he was heavier and stronger. She lost her balance and crashed backward into dry oak leaves. Riley managed to come up with the paper, but flames like a spearpoint were already blazing from it. He whuffed his breath on it, only fanning it more, and then yelped as the flames licked his fingers. What was left of the letter dropped blazing to the ground. Riley stomped it out and picked up what was left—no more than a blackened scrap.

"You . . . Damn you!" Riley said. She scrambled to her feet and faced them, feeling now that it was she who was triumphant.

"Gol dang it, now what?" Cass said. "There goes our introduction to young Roberto Creigh."

"You'll never need it," Angelina said shrewdly. "Not as long as you take me with you."

16 · SHAD JACKSON

THE MAN CALLED SHAD JACKSON WAS OF TOWERING STATURE, AND as hawk-faced, lean-limbed, and as fierce-eyed as the popular notion of Moses. He trimmed his beard in a Vandyke, a style associated with cavaliers. His hair was gray as ashes and worn swept back and cascading to his collar in imitation of the statesman John C. Calhoun.

He was subject to depressions, widely considered a malady of females. He detested this weakness in himself, and, as best as he could, he resisted. His preventative was pinches of saltpeter stirred into cider vinegar and taken twice daily, which left him free of all need for fornication. His treatment, however, once depression began tugging him to its gloomy depths, was drink, taken in binges.

As regularly as the moon's phases, the world soured on

him. Underlings displeased him; events nationally took precipitant turns for the worse. At these times, Jackson would retreat to his room off the tavern, then retreat farther to the sanctum of his bed, taking whiskey with him, along with his journals and Kansas City newspapers dating back to the middle of the war. There, he would reduce himself to invalidism, emptying two bottles a day and often imagining —without thinking it through in words but rather picturing the act as though he were a player on a lighted stage—of taking his own life, a ball from his cavalry pistol sent screaming through an ear, cauterizing his festered brain.

Eventually, each bout subsided. His devils departed, leaving him exhausted, calling out in a wailing voice for the woman Faith to bring wet cloths for his brow, dampering out the excruciating light, and to administer handfuls of Dr. Hammond's Philadelphia Nerve and Brain Pills, of which he had wooden cases laid by in the tavern.

Then he'd lie day to night to day again in the afterthroes of drink, which, though hellish, were preferable to depression. And when tintype visions left him—serpents, men's faces, riders from the past—he would sleep a corpse's sleep, eighteen hours or longer, then arise excited and trembling, feeling sweet air caress his skin, hearing birdsong in the woods beyond the tavern. He would throw open his door upon startled followers, Lazaruslike, showing himself reborn, declaring to Toby he was hungry as a wolf.

On a morning following a cycle of depression, its antidote, then reprieve, Shad Jackson sat at breakfast in his tavern's common room, replenishing himself with coffee and eggs, and was attended by an untidy and large-bellied aide de camp named Toby Grier. Just as Toby was refilling Jackson's cup, the front door opened on harsh sunlight. Jackson looked up squinting as a young man, a stranger, stepped uncertainly into the room.

Jackson said, "Toby—who in the *deuce?*"

"Uh, colonel," the young man said, "I heard you were ailing. I'm glad to see—"

"Who in the devil's name are you?" Jackson demanded. His fist hit the table, rattling the silverware. "What business have you in my canyon?"

The young man's eyes rounded. "I'm . . . sir, I'm Roberto Creigh. We met the other night. My father . . . You don't remember?"

Jackson was greatly put upon. The boy was a nuisance at best, and at worst a threat, for if one outsider could invade his refuge, certainly others could as well. He shot an accusation at Toby, who backed from the table.

"He's been around for days, colonel," Toby said. "Beats all you don't recollect."

"I'll not have people taking advantage of my affliction," Jackson declared. "I won't stand for it."

"But we spoke," the young man said.

"I believe, young sir, had we spoken, I would recall it."

The boy stood amazed, which Jackson took as further reproof. He returned his attention to his food, spearing a chunk of fried potato with his fork and mouthing it; but because of the interruption, his appetite was gone. He looked again at the boy, noting the nickeled revolver in a cross-draw holster. This annoyance was spoiling his morning.

"Toby, I don't welcome having an armed stranger here unannounced, someone who like as not could assassinate me as I dine."

"I'm sure he means no harm," Toby said. Jackson took in another forkful, but the food had turned tasteless.

"Sir, my father, Hollis Creigh, had hoped you would shelter me. In return, I'm honored to serve."

Jackson's astonishment heightened. He wiped his beard and dropped the napkin with theatrical finality atop his food. He pushed his chair back and said, "Hollis Creigh." The name rattled his memory. Then his brain ticked and he had it, both the image of the man and the man's connection to himself. He smiled.

"Hollis Creigh's son?"

"Yes, sir."

"You must know I'm called Shadrach. Can you imagine the reason?" The boy stood mute and uncomfortable. "Because I have stood in the fire and yet was not singed," Jackson said, and then found the boy's bewilderment gratifying. "Shadrach, Meschach, and Abednego," Jackson said. His good mood was reviving. "Don't you know your Bible?"

"Parts of it."

"Study it, the Old Testament especially. Everything a person needs is in that book."

"I'll try, sir."

"Your father once did me a great service," Jackson said. He angled his head to find Toby. "He gave me death. This boy's father killed me, Toby."

"Nobody could do that, colonel."

"Nevertheless, Hollis Creigh did it." Jackson enjoyed a laugh over it. His head was clear, his thinking agile. "Like the Christ, I arose on the third day," Jackson said. In the back of the tavern Toby tried to laugh, too.

"Do you mind that I compare myself to Christ?" Jackson said.

The boy said, "Not if there's similarities."

"You ought to have said yes, you do mind," Jackson said. "Christ and country and virtuous womanhood—that's where a man's allegiances lie. And you don't allow anybody to sully any one of them."

"By country, I take it you mean the Confederacy."

Jackson scowled. He'd been about to say as much himself, and did not care to have his words snatched from him. But the boy stood so gamely that Jackson let it go. "The Confederacy, of course. At any rate, how is your father?"

"Well enough, I guess. I left him ten days ago."

"Leg still bother him?"

"I expect he's used to it."

"I expect he is," Jackson said. "A brave man, your father. Cautious and brave at once—a rare mixture. You can always get hotheads, but they don't last."

Jackson studied the boy another few seconds, till his assessment resolved into certainty. The boy was full of potential, perhaps, but nonetheless a boy; and he was no danger to Jackson in the slightest. Jackson glanced with regret at the napkin he'd dropped on his food. He was still hungry. What he would have was Toby's pie and buttermilk.

"What about your own fortitude?" Jackson asked him. "Are you willing to carry on the good fight?"

"For the South, yes sir."

"You can ride and shoot?"

"Colonel, I sure can. My pa had me practicing both when I was no bigger than—"

"And you swear you're Hollis Creigh's son."

"I sure do, sir."

"Come here closer." Looking apprehensive, the young man stepped to within four feet of the table and froze into a posture he must have imagined was military attention.

Jackson smiled indulgently. He said, "Closer yet. I don't bite." Then he studied the smooth face as a sculptor appraises unworked stone. He sought Hollis Creigh in that face, but he could not manage it. What he saw were the dark hair and eyes, the heritage of the sun.

"Unless I'm mistaken, you're a child of Ham," Jackson said.

"My mother's a Garza, sir. They're a big family where I come from."

"Roman Catholic, I'd imagine."

"Yes, sir."

"Ham was progenitor to the darker races. That too is in Scripture. You Papists wouldn't know, as your priests do all your Bible reading for you."

"Our family reads the Bible, sir."

"It doesn't matter. Fetch me some pie and buttermilk and then leave me. Toby will dish it up."

The boy bustled to get it. Jackson craned his neck toward the back of the room. "We'll have to find some use for him, Toby."

"He seems eager enough," Toby said.

"You say, young sir, that you're a true friend of the Southern Nation?"

"There's none truer," Roberto said. "You can depend on that."

"Oh, I doubt we'll depend upon it just yet," Jackson said. "What I aim to do first is test it."

17 · ROBERTO

ROBERTO USED HIS DAYS FOR EXPLORING THE SIDE CANYON. HE found it was no more than a half-mile across and perhaps two miles deep. On all sides, the rock wall formed steep palisades, so that any force attacking from above would have to leave their mounts on the rim and resort to lowering men on ropes.

Besides a sense of shelter, the side canyon afforded fresh water. Below chalky evidence of gypsum near the canyon rims, seeps darkened the walls, testimony to underground flowage. Near the head of the canyon a spring was birthed, first to pool up under shading plum trees, then spilling over and winding through cottonwood groves behind the outlaw buildings, finally making its way toward the main canyon and Prairie Dog Town Fork.

But when exploring palled, Roberto was drawn inevitably back to the tavern, a sturdy log structure with a ranch-house porch, an open-ceilinged main room, and lean-to rooms at the rear, one a long kitchen, the other Shad Jackson's private sanctum. The tavern served as sleeping accommodations for those men not choosy about bedding down on the plank floor. Its main function, however, was as the locus for meals, for drinking and gambling in the evening—for most of what went on in Jackson's outlaw domain.

Roberto was surprised to find, while sitting unobtrusively

in a corner and sipping his morning coffee, that men sheltering in Palo Duro had to pay for their keep. In truth, Colonel Jackson served not only as commander to his men but innkeeper as well. It must have provided him considerable income, for, by Roberto's reckoning, Jackson charged exorbitantly for everything.

Along with the rest of the outlaws, Roberto paid for his plate of fried buffalo meat and pinto beans in the evening, and for the raw, kerosene-smelling whiskey that he sampled along with the men, not wanting to draw attention to himself as a teetotaler. As a result, his money dwindled alarmingly.

How the other outlaws replenished their funds was made clear when a group of riders ventured out, to return two days later, galloping into the tavern yard whooping like Comanches and shooting off pistols in all directions. Roberto was currying his pair of horses in the corral when the ruckus broke out. At the first shot, he grabbed his rifle and dashed toward the tavern, thinking they were under attack by Rangers or a posse.

But his alarm faded when Shad Jackson himself emerged on the tavern porch, pointing a pistol skyward and triggering off rounds of his own. After emptying their pistols, the riders swung down and trooped into the tavern. Immediately, a fiddle sawed into life, and heavy boots thumped time on the tavern floor.

Curious, Roberto mounted the porch steps and stopped in the doorway. The outlaws had tapped a whiskey keg. Amber liquor was being ladled into cups, bowls, even cooking pots, while men were moving in time to the fiddle. "Pretty Roberto!" somebody shouted. A man grabbed Roberto's arm, and he was hauled unwilling into a swirling mass of dancers. He saw the woman Faith being slung violently from prancing outlaw to outlaw, while Shad Jackson sat on the bar, overseeing and sipping his liquor.

Toby Grier, his bulging front aproned, was dancing a woman's part, as were a couple of others. A burly outlaw got Roberto's hand and whipcracked him across the room so that he fetched up against a table, nearly spilling it. Immediately, unseen hands propelled him back into the dancers.

"Your skirt!" somebody shouted. This was Judah Spain, a brush-bearded outlaw usually the loudest in any bunch; Roberto had made a point to keep away from him. Spain extended a red square of calico. "Damn it, boy—your skirt!" he said again.

The fiddle yawed to a stop. Roberto stood warily, while the dancers around him wound down like some elaborate child's toy. Eyes weighed on him. He saw that Toby Grier wore a similar piece of red cloth around his waist. So did the other dancers who'd been taking a woman's part.

"Pretty Roberto's going to get skirted," Skiff predicted.

"I don't care to do it," Roberto said. He backed away from Judah Spain, only to bump up against a man behind him, who shoved him roughly into the center of the room.

"By gol, iffen you won't skirt up, I'll do it for you," Spain said thickly. Roberto turned, his mind on retreat, but a boot snaked out and tripped him. He rammed the floor, driving splinters into his hand. He got up warily, and then Spain was on him.

But it was not the grizzly vise Roberto had expected. Instead, inexplicably, Spain embraced him. The rough beard enveloped Roberto's cheek; the raw-grain smell of cheap whiskey washed him. Then Roberto felt himself kissed by this bearded outlaw. Judah Spain roared, and the others roared behind him.

Roberto was stunned; a hammer blow would not have hit him harder. He cocked his elbow and launched a punch, but his fist was caught by Spain's vast mitt, captured and crushed, so that Roberto cringed onto his tiptoes from the pain of it. Then he was tossed roughly away against a wall of men.

Roberto felt hot frustration. He charged his tormentor and was elbowed down. He got up tottering, his head ringing with men's laughter. Spain must have hit him then, for he was slammed again to the floor. He lay gasping while the room revolved.

Spain loomed. "You ain't so pretty with your face busted." Approval was voiced by two dozen others. Roberto felt himself picked up by his collar and the seat of his pants. He was hefted through the doorway and thrown down the steps.

His consciousness thickened. He was underwater, drowning. Abruptly, the sound of birds reached him. He struggled to sit, and he remained that way, sitting dazed in the dirt yard, in red afternoon light, seeing laughing outlaws milling onto the tavern porch, Judah Spain planted at their front, his legs spread in high boots. On Spain's right was Colonel Jackson, amused and watchful.

A silvery object streaked his way, and Roberto was hit by his own tossed revolver, which must have spilled out while he was being thrown around.

Spain said, "Next time you're going to dance like a lady. You got any objections?" The words came strangely; Roberto had to sort them.

The pistol lay temptingly, but Roberto shook his head. "Speak up," Spain said.

"No," Roberto said, through split lips that worked like meat. He drew his sleeve across them and found the fabric well bloodied.

"Partners for the next dance," Spain announced abruptly. He turned on a boot heel and shouldered into the tavern, the crowd funneling in after him. The only man to linger was Shad Jackson, who hovered in the doorway, regarding Roberto.

"There are times I allow them their fun," Jackson said. Roberto tried to manage a glare. "I trust you're all right?" Roberto nodded.

Jackson's look held another few seconds, then he turned and was absorbed by the tavern. Immediately, jagged fiddle music rebuilt; rough voices climbed. Soon, the building resounded with dancing men, their weight flexing the tavern floor like a great, thumping drum.

Roberto spat blood, expecting to see teeth in it. He got up

with effort, holstered his pistol, and staggered down the yard, his feet finding the footpath that led between the corral and the cabins. A fringe of cottonwoods showed him an opening. He ducked through, into a sheltering. The stream welcomed him. He dipped his bandanna and washed, finding his left cheek was as thick as beefsteak. The pulped flesh screamed when he touched it.

He moved again, going upstream, crossing whenever the banks meandered and not caring if he wetted his boots. He emerged into sunlight, learning then that he'd lost his hat in the fight—if a fight it had been, and not just a beating. The sun soon made his head pound. He retreated to the shady stream bank and sat on a rock, where he remained without thinking until the roaring in his head subsided. Then he watched the water, tumbling, stilling where it pooled. Water spiders skated for him. He spat blood and watched it revolve and then float away, changing shape where the water hurried it.

18 · FAITH

SHE FOUND HIM SITTING, CROUCHED INTO HIMSELF, IN THE GROWing evening along the rivulet. The sound of the water would have covered her approach, but spooking him even mildly seemed cruel after what he'd been through. Instead, she gently called his name. His head came around like he'd been struck afresh. He scowled to see her.

She said, "I figured you'd gone thisaway. Can I come up, or would you druther be alone?"

He made no answer. She said, "Roberto?"

He said, "I don't give a damn what you do," in a pronunciation thickened by damaged lips. She picked her way, once letting a foot skid off a slick rock and having to throw in two jabbed steps to recover herself.

"Oopsy," Faith said. When she got close enough for conversation, she did not cross his line of vision but instead came up behind him and found a rock of her own. She lowered her weight, then slipped off her shoes and eased her feet into the water. It was a blessing, for her feet were punished; men danced like oxen. She watched the current a moment, its stately movement suggesting that she take her time.

"You missed supper," she said, "not that it amounted to much." He looked at her and quickly away. "I believe you could go back anytime now," Faith suggested. "Half of them are dead drunk and sleeping." She jerked her head to indicate who "them" included, but he didn't see the gesture.

"Anyhow, I brung you a sandwich. Toby makes the best bread, lots better than me. Better than my ma used to, even. She died pretty early on, my ma. Her face in my mind is getting to where it's kind of foggy, but I remember her bread real well." She waited, remembering she was taking cues from the current.

"I'm not really hungry," Roberto said.

"You just think you ain't. Best way to get mending is to slip right back in the swing," Faith said. "I seen a lot of those celebrations. Mostly, they just make extra work for me and Toby. I mean messes to clean up. Men are hogs."

"What was it all about, anyway?" Roberto blurted, and he turned, showing the broken lips, a shining bruise, an eye puttied shut with purpled flesh. The other eye, a dark one, apparently uninjured, held on her, wanting to know.

She shrugged. "They wiped out some buffalo men's party. You didn't see them big rifles Judah was showing around?"

Roberto shook his head. "Wiped out? You mean killed?"

"They don't like nobody getting away to tell tales to the army," Faith said. "Judah and Amos Mapes don't, and the colonel don't neither."

"That's plain *murder*," Roberto said. "Were the hunters northerners, or what?"

"I doubt anybody thought to ask."

"How does that square with Jackson's fighting for the

Confederacy?" Exasperation was in his voice. "Those men could've been Texans or anybody."

"It squares with outlawing," she said. She put her shoes on while he considered it.

"You want to see something?" Faith looked west, gauging the sun. "We just about got time before dark."

"See what?"

"I ain't saying—I'm showing." She took his hand and led him, at first threading her way between the trees, where darkness had already displaced the day, then veering obliquely, a shortcut, where the ground rose away from the creek. The walls of Palo Duro showed pink and orange in the light of dusk, and the streaks of gypsum glowed like snow. The place she knew was where the side canyon headed up.

"What is it?" Roberto asked. She heard the interest liven his voice. Interest was good.

"Before we get there, I'll tell you something." Faith paused to assess him. "You'd be 'round about eighteen or so," she said, and Roberto didn't deny it. "Some are pretty much growed at that age. No offense, but you still ain't."

"I'm grown," Roberto contended.

She shook her head. "You got a man's shape, but you hain't yet growed into it." She still studied him. "It's on account of you just ain't had to. I figure the kind you are, you got a home someplace with a ma in it. Pa, too, if you're lucky."

"I'd better forget them. I won't see them again."

"How come you're here in the first place?"

"I killed somebody," Roberto said. "It was a fight, not murder."

"Funny how fights come mostly to young fellers." When he didn't respond, she said, "You'd best go back and face it."

"I can't—not for a while anyhow."

"Whatever's back there is better than what's here," Faith said, "and that's for damned sure." She turned then and ducked under wild plums, leading him. It was nearly dark under the trees. She turned again and kissed him. He held himself from her at first, then his arms encircled her shoulders.

"I'm being careful of your hurts," she said, and kissed him again. "You shouldn't be here with these kind of men."

"I'm not such a child as you think," Roberto said.

"You've been with a woman," she observed, "a girl can tell that much." He nodded with swagger in it, the grin lopsided, immediately a boy again. "You hain't really loved yet, though," Faith said. "You only had a taste."

"Seemed like the full treatment to me." His grin widened. "Cost me a week's wages."

To help his mending, she laughed with him. At least Roberto tried to laugh; his pulped face got more lopsided, and new blood appeared on his lower lip. "Pretty Roberto," Faith said. "I'm twelve years older, and it's about two lifetimes."

She backed from him, then recaptured his hand and led him. They emerged from the trees, seeing in front of them a variegated field, white predominating—the white, in fact, looking luminous in the sky's afterglow.

"What . . . what is it?"

"It's bones," she said. "Ain't they white and clean as anything?" He went, his steps uncertain. She saw he was dazed, and so had she been the first time she'd seen them. Acres of bones, strewn like kindling among boulders. It looked like the aftermath of a battle of giants.

He stooped for a skull, perfect except for the jagged bullet hole. Its whiteness was like marble. "They're horse skeletons," he said, amazed. "There must be . . . *hundreds.*"

"I took a notion one time to count the skulls," she told him. "I got to four hundert and some—the furthest I'd ever counted anything. I had to give up on account of it took too long. Old Shad might've been missing me. Anyhow, four hundert weren't the half of them. I figure there's maybe a thousand."

"But why? How did . . . ?"

"They're Quanah Parker's pony herd. You heard of him —big Comanche chief with the white mama? The story I got is Mackenzie's bluecoats caught the Comanches here in the canyon. The troopers come down that dinky trail yonder. You can just barely see it." She pointed to the canyon's headwall.

"I don't see anything," Roberto said.

"In better light you would. Anyhow, most of the bucks got away on foot, but the women and children got captured. To put a damper on the border raiding, MacKenzie drove the ponies into this blind canyon. His soldiers shot every one of them."

"God," Roberto said.

"What I'm showing you," Faith said, "is that them who like fighting come up with all kinds of big reasons for it. But mostly, it's innocents who get hurt. Like these ponies. Or them poor buffalo hunters today. Or like you."

He looked at her seriously. She said, "You hear the colonel talking fancy notions—'the southern nation' and whatnot. Mostly, men who pick up guns ain't much more than horse killers. Even when they put a good face on it like the colonel likes to." She stooped to pick up a leg bone, which was as clean and smooth as porcelain. She tossed it, and it clinked musically upon the others.

"So much death in one place," Faith said, "but now it's peaceful. I come here and just stand sometimes. There's a feeling here that beats a church."

Roberto tried to take her by her shoulders again, the bones forgotten. She saw he was becoming proprietary. "Not here," she said. "Anybody could see us."

With that implied promise, he was content to follow like a colt. She led him back under plum trees, where the creek whispered. It was practically full dark. She rose up on her tiptoes and they kissed, holding it a long time.

"That's all," she said. "Forever." His eyes wondered. "I'm Shad Jackson's woman, and that's the end of it."

"But I thought . . ."

"Don't think," she said. "Don't look at me or wait for me. Don't come at me when there's no others around. Old Shad suspects you of tomcatting near me, he'll hang our guts from these willow trees."

19 · ROBERTO

HE FOLLOWED, BUT AFTER WHAT SHE'D TOLD HIM, HE COULD think of nothing more to say. They moved from the trees into the open, walking toward the sky's afterglow. He ached for her, but she moved ahead of him with purpose. It was full dark when they approached the buildings. When they could see the tavern's yellowed windows, she told him she'd go in ahead so no one would suspect they'd been together.

He watched her as she went, her shoulders squared to hide resignation. He reflected that she'd brought him food; she'd told him some things; she'd showed him old bones. He guessed that would be the extent of it.

Roberto bowed to the creek for a drink. He wet his bandanna and again bathed his face, which was more painful than ever with the feeling coming back into it. Then he went toward the corral to check on his horses.

As he crossed the open yard, moving warily and mindful of his beating, he was astonished to see a blue-coated U.S. trooper gallop in, coming from the main canyon. The trooper let his reins trail in his hurry and bounded up the tavern steps. The porch planks boomed; the door squared yellow. Loiterers on benches tossed their smokes and disappeared inside, tugged along in the trooper's wake.

Within seconds, a dozen men reemerged onto the porch, talking with animation, some yelling toward the cabins. Immediately, others jogged up from the lower yard to converge on the excitement.

"What is it?" Roberto asked of a man who passed near him.

"One of the colonel's army spies. Probably means we're going to see some action."

A minute later, the blue trooper and Colonel Jackson himself came onto the tavern porch. Jackson put a hand on the man's shoulder, making an odd picture. "You men in Mapes's detachment look to your firearms," Jackson ordered. "In the morning, you will ride out on reconnaissance." He craned his neck a moment, trying to penetrate the gloom. "Is that young Roberto I see in the yard?"

Roberto only nodded, probably invisibly. Men turned to look at him.

"This will be your first mission, Roberto Creigh. A testing. See that you're ready."

"I will be, sir."

"As for the rest of you—once Mapes and his men get back, I intend to mount a foray requiring every rider in the outfit." At the announcement, a scattered cheer rose up, to the colonel's obvious satisfaction.

Jackson's gaze elevated and traveled, surveying. "We'll be striking a blow for the southern nation," Jackson said, gloat lifting his voice. "If I told you men precisely what's afoot, I doubt any of you'd believe it."

20 · CASS

AFTER THE ZIGZAGGING THEY'D DONE TO SATISFY RILEY'S SENSE of caution, Cass expected to find it a relief to ride straight for Palo Duro Canyon. Not that they had a road or a trace or landmarks to follow. What they had was Riley's brass compass, a watchlike affair with a chain and spring-loaded lid. But to Cass's annoyance, Riley consulted this guidepost seldom and reluctantly, as if relying on the instrument proved his scouting skills were faulty. As a result, their route seesawed nearly as badly as when they'd been trying to hide their back trail. By the second morning after teaming up with Angelina, Cass filched the compass out of Riley's saddlebags and took over as pathfinder.

"I make west-northwest about that far mesa," Cass said.

"The jaggedy one or the flat one?"

"All mesas are flat. If you knew two words of Spanish, you'd know mesa meant table." Cass turned and found Angelina, hoping his knowledge of Spanish might earn him approval. But she didn't seem to be listening.

Riley, too, swiveled in his saddle to look at Angelina. "I figured the way everybody said mesa here and mesa there, the word meant anything that stuck up above the horizon," Riley said. "Which, in Texas, don't amount to a whole lot."

"Texas," Cass said firmly, "has got plenty of everything a person would want to look at. There's regular mountains to the west. To the south we've got saltwater coast—"

"Oh, cripes," Riley said, which he usually did when Cass got going on Texas. "Anyhow, you mean the mesa with the buzzards circling over it."

Cass's head came around in surprise. He canted his hat to study the horizon. "I guess those are buzzards at that. I wasn't sure what they were."

"It means more buffalo men's leavings, I'd imagine," Angelina said.

Cass sniffed. What breeze there was came from the same direction he was looking. He could not yet detect the rotten-meat smell of buffalo carcasses, but he figured in another couple of miles it'd be so thick as to be sickening.

Riley's thinking must have run along the same lines. He said, "In that case, let's stop and eat here. I don't want another meal spoilt."

"We'll eat as we ride," Angelina said. "We have wasted enough time."

Once they'd topped a low rise, they saw the buzzards had not been towering over the mesa at all but over a spot in front of it where decent grass flourished and faint wagon tracks crisscrossed the valley. When the riders descended, the spiraling buzzards took notice and sailed off to the north. A few high-shouldered birds that had been feeding on the ground flapped off in the same direction.

As they guided their horses in, Cass found they were looking at the stripped, disjointed, and half-devoured carcasses of buffalo men themselves. The men had been in camp, Cass guessed, for an acre of fresh buffalo hides were pegged out to dry. Farther on lay the collapsed skeletons of burned-out wagons. The bare ribs of a sun-blackened horse arced out through the hide. It was the men's bodies, however—or what was left of them—that gave the sight its power.

"What is it?" Angelina said, although Cass figured she knew well enough; she was stunned, was all. Cass himself had been through four years of the worst war in America; even so, he was pretty much stunned too.

Angelina started her horse forward, but Cass angled his own mount to intercept her. He caught her horse's bridle, earning her fierce look, the one she used on him often.

"I will see for myself," Angelina declared. Cass was going to say she'd regret it, but instead he shrugged and let go of her bridle. She moved up only a few horse lengths before stopping. He saw her gag momentarily.

"Comanches, I'd imagine," Angelina said. She was trying to sound unaffected by the sight but not getting much voice behind her words.

Cass noted that little smell remained, since various scavengers had eaten most of the meat. The lack of smell was about the only blessing in the situation, so far as Cass could see. He counted what he figured had been four men, although wolves had so disjointed the bodies that it was hard to be sure.

Riley dismounted for a closer look. "They're not scalped," he said. "Anyhow, Indians would have taken those buffalo hides."

"You're saying white men did it?" Cass said.

Riley nodded and surveyed the horizons. "We must be closer to Palo Duro than we figured."

"My God," Angelina said. "You think whoever did this . . . ? You're saying they're the same men who are sheltering Roberto?"

"Without having somebody who can track like an Indian, there's no way of telling," Cass said.

"We ought to bury them," Riley said. "These men might've been decent sorts."

"It'd take hours," Cass pointed out. "I don't see a shovel or pick or anything lying around."

"They might've had an axe," Riley said.

Cass saw that Angelina wouldn't look again at the buffalo men. She had faced her mount west. "Those men are dead," Angelina said. "It's Roberto we need to worry about." She heel-thumped her horse's barrel and started off at a trot.

21 · ANGELINA

IT SEEMED TO HER THAT THOUGH THE MEN ARGUED ABOUT EVERY little thing that came up, they seldom argued about, or even discussed, matters of real consequence. When they finally got around to what she regarded as an important decision, they would chime in together in perfect agreement—as though the action to take next or the direction in which to head were perfectly obvious.

What worried her since finding the dead buffalo hunters was the nature of the men who sheltered Roberto. It seemed plain, in her mind, at least, that the buffalo party had been attacked by the outlaws from Palo Duro; who else was there in that part of the plains? This was an alarming conclusion, yet Cass and Riley showed no interest in speculating about it.

"The country's climbing," Cass noted cheerfully, as though they were out pleasure riding.

"How will we get into this Palo Duro Canyon if it's an

outlaw stronghold?" Angelina asked them. "Have either of you given any thought to that?"

"I expect we'll have to hope for the best," Cass said. Riley, normally the most argumentative, merely nodded. She found it maddening.

"What if they don't believe you when you tell them you're outlaws?" In Angelina's mind, this was another large worry.

"What else would we be?" Riley said. "I doubt anybody'd be traveling in this country lest they were buffalo hunters or on the run."

Angelina thought that hardly covered all contingencies. What if the outlaw band feared Cass and Riley were lawmen? Or, more likely, suspected they were what in fact they were—bounty hunters come to snatch one of their number from under their noses?

"If you're to be outlaws, then what about me?" Angelina asked. "If you're thinking to leave me outside the canyon while you go in together, you're badly mistaken."

"Oh, you'll likely get into less trouble sticking with us," Cass said. His assumption that this, too, was beyond debate infuriated her. She looked to Riley for an opposing opinion, but once again he did not object.

"So I'm to pose as someone you've abducted?"

Ahead of her, Cass's back revealed nothing. After a space filled only by clopping hooves, he said, "Too dangerous for you. These men are apt to be woman-starved."

"Then . . . what?" she asked. She had an inkling but was afraid to say it.

"We'd best pretend you're the lady friend of one of us," Cass said. "Else, some outlaw is going to try and latch onto you."

"Just like that. You've decided I'm to be the . . . the paramour of one of you."

"For appearances' sake," Cass said.

She looked at Riley, who adjusted his hat once her glare fell on him. He said, "I expect it'd be best."

"Well, the *brass* of some people!" Angelina decided she

ought to have been consulted. She further decided she was going to be mad about it. "You're saying I'm to have people thinking I'm . . . that I'm *living in sin* with the likes of one of you?"

"I told you she'd get her dander up," Riley said.

Cass said, "If you'll remember, I didn't dispute it."

"So which of you upstanding gentlemen is supposed to have captured my heart?"

The men consulted with wary looks. "I guess me," Cass said.

"Oh, wonderful. And just how did you pick the lucky man? You tossed a coin and fate declared Cass had won me, was that it?"

"Not exactly," Riley said. He'd gotten his sheepish look again. "We flipped for it, but for once, Cass lost."

22 · MAJOR HARVEY BLACK, U.S.A.

MAJOR BLACK WAS TAKING HIS EASE ON THE THIRD-BASE LINE when Sherman's detail caught him. More precisely, the major was sitting on a folding camp chair, special-ordered from the firm of Hartley and Graham of New York City, amid the commotion of a Sunday game of baseball. His attention had strayed from the game itself—though the inning was the eighth, and his Fort Griffin Stalwarts were tied seventeen-all for the summer championship—to the hatless and very bald head of the Stalwarts' catcher.

The man whose scalp reflected sunlight was a corporal, recently demoted from first sergeant in the wake of a drunken brawl in The Flat, the town that had attached itself, parasitelike, to Fort Griffin. He'd not been broken in rank on the ball field, however, as he was the most capable player Major Black had come across in the army's entire Department of Texas, a catcher with an arm to second base like a Springfield rifle and, as a batsman, a cannoneer. In fact, the talents of the bald corporal had been Major Black's inspiration for forming the Fort Griffin Stalwarts in the first place, thus, indirectly, also the cause for the raising of their perennial opposition, the team of pimps, hide hunters, and barkeeps called The Flat Buffalo.

At this moment, the major was not studying the catcher's throwing arm; it was the head that held him. The corporal's skull was lumpy enough to resemble a bag of horse chestnuts. There were so many lumps, and of such size, that Major Black had to wonder whether they'd been earned in saloon fights or if heredity alone were responsible.

Saloon fights seemed likely, that being what had cost the man his sergeant's stripes. But if the lumps were nature's work, perhaps they contributed to their victim's faulty judgment. Perhaps the corporal were doomed by the existence, the size, and the unfortunate placement of those lumps to be troublesome his whole life, a curse to himself, an exasperation to his superiors.

Phrenology, Major Black considered, had a questionable scientific basis. He regarded it as a lame theory devised to explain behavior not explainable otherwise, probably invented to boost the career of some popular surgeon. Now the major wondered whether there might be something to such skull-lump theories after all. He vowed to enter a query in his journal about it that evening. It'd be something to ask a post surgeon about if he ever got back to civilization.

The major's mind still pondered head lumps, but his idle eye was drawn to movement beyond first base. Simultaneously, the Stalwarts' pitcher cocked a leg, uncoiled, and threw. A sturdy Buffalo batter leaned into the pitch. The bat *whocked!* and sent the leather ball arcing down the right-field line.

Two hundred voices detonated. Major Black frowned and stood up to see better, noting that the Stalwart fielder showed perfect athletic form right up to the point when the ball went through his legs and bounded out on the prairie.

One base runner barreled home, breaking the tie, while the Buffalo player who'd struck the fly ball windmilled around second. Major Black groaned aloud. A loose ball in Texas might roll to the Nations.

Then the major saw guidons. Coming in from the limitless plains, against which first base was practically the only landmark, was a column of twos, the riders in army blue. The right fielder stopped agog, forgetting the ball, which rolled unimpeded and was eyed with curiosity by the Kickapoos. When the second runner scored, Major Black was furious.

Major Harvey Black, U.S.A., during the war brevetted full colonel, considered on-post baseball perfectly harmless, in fact actually health-promoting. He'd raised and coached the Stalwarts himself, even outfitted them at his own expense in hob shoes and proper caps. Now here came some meandering battalion to invade his carefully surveyed outfield—interrupting his recreation, his effort at army-town relations, and the pastime that had been the utter salvation, he considered, of his every boring Sunday.

"Orderly!" Major Black commanded, but his orderly was not within earshot, in that dinning crowd earshot being limited to three feet in any direction. Most of his command were screaming for the blood of the erring Stalwart fielder. Drowned out, his team now two runs down, Major Black stalked angrily onto the ball field, stopped, stood on his heels, and directed his glare at the invading column. In its vanguard he made out an officer in gauntlets, a civilian scout, and a pair of Indian guides, probably Kickapoos.

The major's appearance caused a general hush, although some Buffalo supporters recovered quickly enough to yell catcalls. But soon all heads craned to where the major was looking—at the guidons of Troop A, Headquarters Company of the Eighth Cavalry, fluttering onto the vague outer boundary of right field. The mounted troopers numbered no more than twenty, signifying a mission of small importance. Behind the soldiers came an army ambulance, and at the column's tail, heavily loaded pack mules.

The hush was followed by a vast jeering, the buffalo hunters and teamsters, even Major Black's troopers getting into the act, yelling for the column to get off the ball field. At the noise, the invading detail recognized its trespass, for it executed a neat oblique toward the foul line, demarcated at Major Black's order by a file of whitewashed rocks.

As Major Black himself strode to intercept the column, his orderly, finally recognizing official business, dashed from the sidelines to catch up with him. Major Black had seen the captain at the head of the troopers; his eye now picked out a lieutenant. He saw no officer his equal or superior, which made the interlopers a safe target for his anger. He decided he was justified in unloosing a whole blast of it.

"They've got their nerve," Major Black said. "This intrusion puts us two runs down."

"Yes sir," his orderly said.

"It never should have happened."

"No sir."

Ahead, the captain stopped his column. A sergeant sang, *"Dis-mount."* Major Black's right fielder began chatting to a trooper. A fence around the field's perimeter would prevent such calamities in the future, the major reflected as he stalked. A proper ball field required a board fence. But where would he get boards on the Texas plains? Finding enough fuel for kitchen use cost his wood cutters a half-day's ride.

Another dozen strides brought him to the head of the column. He was in full uniform, of course; Major Black did not let slip his standards, Sunday or not, frontier duty or not. Even so, he wished he had worn his saber that day. Nothing enhanced military bearing quite so well as a saber.

"I'm Captain Nelson, sir—Eighth Cavalry," the intruding captain informed him, his careless salute only stoking the major's anger. "You're Major Black, I take it." His offhand manner stoked it all the more.

"You're a very presumptuous young man," Major Black

said. "I'll thank you to get this detail off my ball field. We're playing for the summer championships."

To Major Black's surprise, the captain smiled; it was downright insubordinate. "In good time, sir," Captain Nelson said. "For the moment my orders are to halt us here."

"Orders?" Major Black thundered. "By whose authority?"

For an answer, the young captain merely deflected, inviting Major Black's attention to the ambulance. A door swung open. Captain Nelson's words came strangely. "Sir, that of the commanding general of the army."

A bespectacled man in a round hat and well-sweated civilian suit climbed out of the ambulance to critically survey the ball field, the makeshift fort perched on its mesa, the ragtag town beyond. Evidently, the scene affronted his idea of landscape; he looked as if he'd just as soon climb right back in again.

"See here," Major Black said, but the captain raised a gauntleted hand, suggesting patience would be rewarded.

The second man out was bareheaded, scruffy, and redbearded, showing a badly grayed undershirt beneath an unbuttoned officer's tunic that lacked insignia of any sort. Most unsoldierly, Major Black concluded, and surmised him to be a case of disorderly conduct being transported under arrest.

A third figure emerged, a proper-looking sergeant-major in a kepi cap, who closed the door behind him.

"If you think to toy with me, captain," Major Black said, "I can assure you that—"

But the trio from the ambulance was now striding toward him, and the insolent Captain Nelson interrupting. "Major Black—I have the honor of presenting General William Tecumseh Sherman."

In the major's startled mind, great weights shifted. The features of the shabbily dressed officer fumbling with his tunic buttons went into flux. Even so, the major was suddenly reminded of etched illustrations in *Harper's Weekly*. He took in the failing hairline, the reddish beard and rough-cropped hair, the redhead's fan of creases at the eye corners. The face's expression was infinitely hearty.

"Major Black," Sherman said, extending a bare hand to grasp the major's gloved one. "We've not met, I believe, but I've done my homework on you. You stand upon a distinguished war record. At Antietam, particularly."

Major Black said, "Yes, I—"

"It's Harvey, isn't it?"

"Harvey," the major managed.

"You'd best call me Cump," Sherman said. "I don't stand on ceremony." His eyes roved the ball field. "I see you've inaugurated Sunday sports."

"Uh. A frivolous business, admittedly."

"Nonsense," Sherman said. "Quite progressive. In fact, of such stuff morale is built. I'm told in the eastern states, baseball's quite the rage. There's even talk of a professional league, if you can feature grown men being paid to play games."

"I daresay," Major Black conceded, though what he dared say he had utterly no idea.

Sherman still fumbled with his tunic buttons. "Confounded things. Part of what's wrong with the military, eh? Too many buttons."

"Yes sir."

"Now that you've seen me in my undershirt, hardly worth struggling to button up, is it?"

Major Black shook his head, agreeing, and lying to his core.

"Well. Meet my companions. This sturdy specimen is Sergeant-Major Bricker, my traveling secretary and a pure wonder. Dictate him a letter anywhere and his penmanship will be presentable, even in a rolling conveyance like this one."

"Really," Major Black said.

"Mine looks like balled-up wire under the best circumstances," Sherman said. "If I'd had him in the Carolinas, we could have shortened the war by weeks. My subordinates could have read what the hell my orders were."

Captain Nelson and the civilian laughed briefly.

"The gent with the good sense to laugh at my jokes is Mark Thayer, correspondent for the *St. Louis Dispatch*," Sherman said. "These days, a soldier has to take a reporter in tow just to go to the privy. That son of a bitch Custer's to blame for that little innovation."

"I'd no idea," Major Black said.

"Damnable breed, reporters. Bound they'll write about you whether or not they know beans. Best thing's to keep your own scribe handy. You get misquoted less that way."

As Major Black commented, "I'll remember that," Sherman punched Thayer affably in the shoulder. The correspondent frowned tolerantly, then made precise corrections in the perch of his glasses.

"I take it you've met Captain Nelson?" Sherman said.

"Indeed so," Major Black said. It seemed the heat had intensified, making his head swim.

"The buckskinned frontiersman yonder is Looper, our chief of scouts," Sherman said. "Fascinating breed. Speaks Indian languages like a diplomat."

"Uh . . . quite incredible."

"Well," Sherman said. "It's clear we've interrupted your baseball match. We'll remedy that and you can carry on."

"It's of no importance at all, sir," Major Black assured him, and received one of Captain Nelson's frequent grins. "I'm afraid I had no word at all of the general's coming."

"All by design, of course," Sherman said. "Sorry to drop in unannounced."

"What—I mean, if I may inquire . . . ?"

"What the devil are we doing on the Texas plains, eh?" Sherman made a crinkly smile. "Officially, I'm inspecting army posts. In reality, I'm honoring an invitation to go wolf hunting with Indians."

"Wolf hunting!"

Sherman laughed. "From no less a personage than

Quanah Parker of the Kwahadi Comanches. I'm fulfilling a social obligation, you might say. It's absurd, of course—I'm probably the worst shot in the army. Haven't touched a weapon since I became a general."

"I believe you're having me on," Major Black said.

"Not at all. I've said publicly that I intend to be Quanah's worst foe, if that's how he wants it, or his best friend if he keeps to the reservation. It's one time the papers quoted me straight." Sherman winked at Mark Thayer. "I never actually said 'war is hell,' you know."

"Revision improves everybody," Thayer said.

"Anyhow, Quanah's kept his boys reined in so far. He deserves a pat on the back for it."

"We've had reports of depredations to the north," Major Black pointed out.

"As for that, Quanah blames white outlaws. He sends me letters posted from Fort Sill. I'm inclined to believe him."

"Of all things," Major Black said. "You're going up the Panhandle with no more than . . . with so small a force?"

"We've a score of top men," Sherman said.

"But an officer of your stature. You'd be a great prize to any hostiles."

"All the more reason not to clamor for attention," Sherman said. "These troopers are a picked group. I've no qualms at all."

Major Black said, "I can offer an escort of my full command."

"Counterproductive," Sherman said, in such a crisp and soldierly way that for years afterward Major Black would respond "counterproductive" to any subordinate's proposal he did not like. "If I arrive with too much force," Sherman said, "it might imply distrust of Quanah's intentions. Grant and I—I should say the president—we put our heads together on this. He agreed with me right down the line."

"Of all things," Major Black said again, sounding to himself like an utter idiot.

"At any rate," Sherman said, "I take it that's the extent of your Fort Griffin on the mesa over there."

The major looked beyond the ball field, where dozens of impatient spectators had straggled onto the diamond by this time. His glum collection of adobe buildings, his sorry command, crouched low on a prominence of ground, as if embarrassed to be so visible. Even the flag flapped without much enthusiasm. "I'm afraid so," the major said.

"Good," Sherman said. "Consider yourself inspected. You passed with top marks."

"I did?"

"We'll water our animals and push on immediately. We'll trouble you for grain if you can spare it," Sherman said. He turned on a heel. "Captain Nelson?"

"Yes sir."

"Let's get our arses off this man's outfield."

23 · ROBERTO

ROBERTO THOUGHT OF HIMSELF AS A SON OF TEXAS, AND ONLY secondarily as a son of the South. When he rode out of Shad Jackson's hideout with a handful of others, he was all for kicking the federal authorities out of Texas, but he didn't relish notions of robbing trains or express offices. That he might help do these things for the sake of accomplishing some military objective made him feel better, but doubts about it still clamored in him.

He imagined that employees of trains or express offices might feel duty bound to defend the property in their care, whether that property was carpetbag-owned or not. Inevitably, in any robbery, there would likely be shooting. Some fine Texas people might be injured or killed, right along with carpetbaggers.

Still, Roberto figured robbing and shooting was the outlaw life for you, and he might as well get used to it. Here he'd already shot one man and had run for his life, and probably had half the lawmen in the state looking for him. His father had sent him to hide with an outlaw band, probably never foreseeing that joining in on outlaw activities would be so unavoidable. But in Roberto's view, he had enough blood on his hands already. He resolved that in any shooting scrape, he would aim wide of anyone who seemed an innocent party.

The man leading the outlaws Roberto rode with was called Amos Mapes. Some called him lieutenant, while to others he was only Mapes or plain Amos. Roberto surmised that Mapes had been with Shad Jackson a long time—years, probably. They seemed to talk in riddles sometimes, a kind of separate language, which was how people talked when they went far back together. It was the same way his mother talked to her brother Hector when they got going about old times.

Mapes and Jackson must have hatched some plan, for Mapes rode with purpose. Oddly, he had not headed for the main canyon at all but was leading them ever deeper into the blind side canyon. Roberto did not remember the steep trail that Faith had told him about, the one ascending to the canyon rim that Ranald Mackenzie's troopers had used to attack Quanah's Comanches, until Mapes had led them past the beginnings of the field of horse skeletons. Then he looked up and saw it.

The riders approached to the base of the trail, then dismounted and led their horses, trudging, not wasting breath on words. At one elbow was an ever-increasing drop—enough to shatter a man if he got careless. At the other elbow was the raw, brick-colored rock of Palo Duro Canyon, in many places streaked white with gypsum.

It was a hard climb, the trail switchbacking in places because of the steepness, and the narrow ledge virtually disappearing where water had eroded it. Despite the difficulty, Roberto thought the trail made a clever way of getting out of Palo Duro. Were Texas Rangers or a sheriff's posse to show up unannounced, the location of that trail up the sheer rock could be a handy thing to know.

At the top they entered a different world—the kind of

wide-stretched plains through which Roberto had traveled before finding the canyon. The remainder of the day they rode east, riding hard and tending to business. Finally, with the shadow of each mounted man as tall as a church steeple, Mapes picked a place under oaks for their camp. After they'd made a poor supper on cornbread and cold buffalo meat, Roberto shook out his bedroll and lay down for the night, although the other outlaws seemed more interested in drinking whiskey and playing cards than in sleeping.

They were all up early, however, and soon riding again. By midday they descended to a lower country where caprocks and mesas stood all around. After being exposed on open plains, Roberto liked the sheltering feel of higher horizons. They gave him a sense that not much that was bad could happen there.

Something bad did happen, however. After they crossed a stream and began climbing again, the men became increasingly wary and silent. Finally, as they faced a high rim that would afford a perspective, Roberto felt sure, over the wide prairie beyond, Amos Mapes split them into pairs and sent them off in different directions.

Roberto drew as his partner a short-legged and spongy-bodied man called Badger. Mapes pointed out a draw in the rim flanking the river, and soon Roberto and Badger were making for that, urging their horses up a steep, rocky trail. Within a half-mile the going became as steep as the side trail leading out of Palo Duro had been, so that, for the final hundred yards, Roberto and Badger had to dismount and tow their unwilling horses. Then, when they came up to the head of the draw, they found it choked with brush and cactus, forcing them to pick their way. Badger had sweated his shirt dark and was puffing like a locomotive by the time they peeped over the rim. Even Roberto was laboring for breath.

As Roberto had imagined, their new vantage was wide, rolling prairie. A mile or so to the east he saw buffalo—a loose herd, grazing like cattle.

Under Badger's direction, they hobbled their horses below the lip of the brushy draw, where they'd be hidden from anyone on the prairie. Then they found a place to lie up in the shade of scrub oaks, where they could look out at the world over rifle barrels and be masters of a five-mile stretch of country. Badger looked like he was settling in for a long wait, so Roberto squinched around in the oak leaves, getting himself comfortable.

None of the outlaws on this trip were much for talking. Badger, though, found less to say than any of them. But there lay Roberto, a rifle in his hands and his hat pulled down to shade his eyes—and in his head, a hundred swirling questions.

"Just what is it we're looking for?" Roberto asked, once Badger had got enough breath back to answer.

"You'll know when you see it," Badger told him. Even that little bit started him puffing again. He fanned his face with his hat and looked unhappy. His eyes were sleepy, reflecting the marching clouds. "Most like, we're not going to see anything anyhow."

"Really?"

"Tomorrow, maybe," Badger said. "Still, you best look sharp while I close my eyes a spell. That sun's got my head humming."

"All right," Roberto said.

Badger closed his eyes for several minutes, but he huffed and snorted so much that Roberto could tell he was still awake.

"I was wondering what you liked best about the outlaw life," Roberto said. Badger lifted his hat and looked at him owlishly. "If you don't mind me asking."

"How the hell old are you?" Badger said.

"I turned eighteen last week," Roberto said. He was a little sad about not having celebrated his birthday. "I didn't think to tell anybody."

"Hard to feature," Badger said tiredly, then reset his hat over his face. "I'd a sworn you was about six."

Roberto smarted awhile. He resolved to say no more to Badger than he had to. If a grown man was so lazy as to sleep the day away, Roberto would do without his company.

Badger's snores soon mixed with the breeze that rattled the oak leaves. Roberto scanned the plains and wondered again what he was looking for. It seemed irresponsible that Badger would leave him on guard without explaining what he was on guard against. Roberto was just guarding, he guessed.

The leaves rustled in the breeze coming out of the caprock country. A pair of hawks *screed* and kited overhead. Badger's snoring mixed with all of it, till it became the kind of harmony of sounds that started thoughts to wandering. Left untended, Roberto's thoughts usually went straight back to his family's ranch near the North Trinity, invariably causing his heart to sadden.

To keep his mind sharp and his spirits up, he tried to count the distant buffalo. He counted thirty-seven, but they were so far off that the chore taxed his eyesight, and he couldn't be sure he hadn't counted some twice. Compounding his problems, the animals would disappear and then reappear again as they grazed among the swells of plains.

About a half-mile beyond the buffalo group Roberto thought he saw a line of other animals moving. They were too much in regular order to be buffalo. But whatever they were, they were soon obscured by intervening hills. He did not catch sight of them again, although he puzzled about the matter for some time.

After an hour or so, Roberto was building a comfortable dream in which he was an older version of himself, more used by that time to his life as an outlaw. He had grown a large mustache and had used his outlaw money to become successful in ranching. Then he'd returned to his family's old Halfmoon spread, which he found a modest outfit compared to his own. In the daydream, Roberto himself was so changed—harder-muscled and steely-eyed, and with that fierce black mustache—that no one but his family could recognize him.

Angelina was married and there with her children, who called Roberto 'Bill' to protect his outlaw identity. Then Roberto sat down and had a whiskey with his father, and talked about Shad Jackson.

It was all a pleasant notion, being somebody like Jesse James, hiding out right under the authorities' noses, a wanted man, yet able to walk the streets of Jacksboro and pass the time of day with the sheriff or anybody. And it was comforting till he realized that, while he would be older in this dream, his father and mother would be older too. In his imagination, they'd grown older and shrunken, kind of crumpled together, all from worrying about him. At that point the dream became upsetting, and Roberto left off thinking about it.

Minutes later, Badger uttered three abrupt snorts and then woke up. He looked at Roberto out of clouded eyes, his face as slack as a hunk of meat. It seemed two hours of sleep had only exhausted him.

"Seen anything?" Badger asked.

Roberto debated whether to tell Badger about the string of buffalo that had been lined up too regularly to have been buffalo. Then, when he turned to look where these mystery animals had been, all his nerves triggered off at once. He was looking at an Indian, a bare-kneed and bandy-legged young man in breechcloth and polka-dot shirt, standing no more than forty paces away.

Most Indians Roberto had seen wore wooden faces, but this one looked as surprised as any white man would have—his eyebrows elevated and his eyes got big as conchos. Roberto felt himself and the Indian locked together, held frozen by mutual disbelief.

Then they moved together, Roberto reaching in panic for his rifle and the Indian jerking a carbine to his shoulder. The Indian's carbine blasted. A force that was strong and angry threw up dirt next to Roberto's knee. Dust clouded his vision. Then, behind him, Badger's rifle detonated, the concussion slapping Roberto's ears and setting them pealing.

Roberto held his rifle in a thick dream. The Indian, suddenly slack-armed and sick-looking, lowered his carbine. Badger's rifle roared a second time, the shock of muzzle blast hitting Roberto like a hot wind with grit in it. The Indian turned lazily and dropped.

Badger said something that came as though underwater. Roberto whirled around, pointing his rifle in all directions. If there were more Indians, he was finally ready.

"Jesus," Badger said, "that's the last time I partner with kids. What was you fixing on—inviting him for coffee?"

Badger scuttled through the leaves to take shelter behind his tree. Roberto crawled behind a different one.

"The thing about redskins is there's never just one," Badger said grimly.

Despite dirt in his eyes, Roberto strained to see; he strained to hear despite the ringing in his ears. After a quarter-hour of watching, the shots seemed long faded, to the point that it began to seem impossible that what Roberto had witnessed had really happened. The Indian, though, still sprawled on the prairie, showing no movement except for a patch of his shirt that the breeze was rippling.

"You never kilt before?"

"Once."

"I wouldn't've guessed it," Badger said. He got up with his rifle cocked and crept onto the prairie as gingerly as if crossing a freshly frozen river. Not knowing what else to do, Roberto followed. Badger rolled the Indian over with his boot. Bloody splotches showed on his shoulder and chest.

"Kickapoo, I'd judge. What's your opinion?"

"I've no idea," Roberto said.

"You ain't much use a'tall, are you?" Badger stooped to pick up the Indian's carbine, then whistled when he examined it. "Damned near new army gun, regimental markings and everything. You got to ask yourself what a Kickapoo with an army Springfield is doing up here in Comanche country. You know something? Might be this feller is just the thing we're looking for."

Badger looked at the plains all around, seeming stuck in

indecision. "I expect we'll need to find that little buck's pony," he said finally.

They found the pony ground-tethered in a depression, probably an old buffalo wallow, munching grass and minding its business. Roberto eased up to it, grabbed its halter, and began leading it. When they returned to the dead Indian, Roberto helped Badger drape the body over the pony. They immediately started back down the draw, the same way they'd come up. Once past the cactus, they mounted and rode, leading the Indian pony.

The afternoon sun made it hot going, even downhill, but Badger pushed hard. He seemed relieved to have an excuse to return to where Amos Mapes waited.

When they were most of the way down the draw, and only a mile or so from the spot where they'd separated from Mapes, Badger dismounted and dumped the Indian's body into a patch of cactus. "His rifle's all the proof we need," was all Badger said about it. A few hundred yards farther, they ran into Mapes himself.

"I thought I heard shooting," Mapes said.

Badger showed him the army carbine, making sure Mapes saw the regimental markings, which Badger regarded as highly significant. "I figure Kickapoo," Badger said, "which is the bunch doing the army's scouting these days."

"By gol," Mapes said. But while he was studying the carbine, another pair of riders returned from the rim. They were excited, and one of them took Mapes off to one side for a conference. After he'd listened for a minute, Mapes dropped the army carbine and didn't look at it again. He raised his pistol and triggered three shots into the air. Roberto had thought they would camp there for the night, but Mapes tightened his horse's cinch and then studied the rimrock intently.

When the other outlaws straggled in from the different directions Mapes had sent them, Mapes walked a couple of the older ones up the dry wash a ways. Roberto could see them putting their heads together, though he couldn't make out any words.

"He's forgot about what we brung him," Badger muttered. Finally, Mapes gave these men extra water and the group's remaining tinned food and sent them up toward the rimrock again.

"When you strike them, keep a mile to their west and hang with them," was the last thing Mapes told the two men. Roberto watched them ride off, their faces unhappy.

"I wouldn't get too curiosified was I you," Badger told him.

"I was just wondering what we're up to on this trip."

"Tell you something," Badger said. "The sooner you let off wondering such things, the sooner you start being one of old Shad's soldiers."

24 · VIRGIL HOBBS

ONE OF THEIR HORSES STAMPED AND SWISHED ITS TAIL. A GRASShopper clacketed somewhere. Virgil turned to say something to his partner, Skiff, and found him fast asleep.

Virgil had been about to say that, as he saw it, sentry duty was in most ways no chore at all; in fact, it was a satisfaction. In his opinion, being out at the mouth of the canyon with their rifles handy and their horses already saddled gave him and Skiff options.

Say Texas Rangers were to raid Palo Duro, sneaking over the canyon rim somewhere at midnight, and all the outlaws had to *vamos* of a sudden. Not likely, but say it happened. Some of Jackson's men would be drunk or sleeping, some still playing cards in the tavern. Another might be in the privy with his suspenders around his boot tops. It tallied up in Virgil's mind to a picture of general unwariness. Surely most of the outlaws would be cut down quick if any shooting started.

The few who got away—and Virgil had been about to point out to Skiff that he and Skiff would likely be among them—would likely be thrown on their own hooks. In a run from lawmen, a horse under each man and a pair of rifles might be all they'd have to carry them over hundreds of miles of prairie. Virgil had intended to say that in case something like that happened, it was best to be ready.

The fly in that ointment, however, was Skiff, who was ready for anything so long as it was napping. The fact was, as partners went, Skiff was a weak peg for a man to hang his hat on. It was a realization Virgil had had before, but he realized it again now, watching Skiff sleep with his mouth open and drool stringing out. You could argue any person was as negligent as a dead dog about what happened while he was sleeping. Even so, Virgil felt Skiff carried such negligence further than most.

The trouble with Skiff was life tired him right out, and with no good cause that Virgil could see. It wasn't that Skiff overtaxed himself, for he drew the line at wood chopping or currying horses or anything strenuous. Sentry duty was about the most Skiff would bestir himself to do, and he only did that much because Virgil handled the lion's share of it. Skiff pretty much stuck to napping—mornings, afternoons, in fact anytime at all. In case of lawmen attacking, Virgil considered Skiff would likely get shot dead before he even woke up.

A thought that worrisome caused Virgil to crook his rifle in one arm and tug his hat brim down, and then study the trail critically in both directions. Abruptly, he jerked around. Thinking he'd heard voices, he dropped to his belly and wriggled behind the same tree Skiff was sleeping under, and then poked out a rifle barrel and listened intently.

Virgil had not heard or seen anybody since the spy dressed as a bluecoat had ridden in a day earlier. Alarming as that was, the bluecoat had shown Jackson's secret flag and had loudly announced the password. Then when the man had swung down off his horse, Virgil was amazed to see he was little Georgie Post, one of the cheerfullest of outlaws, whom Virgil had known five years or longer.

The only other rider Virgil had seen had been the youngster, a surprise of a whole different sort. Virgil remembered it'd been Skiff who'd captured the boy, which made Virgil feel a little better about having Skiff for a partner.

With his one eye squinched shut and the other looking down his rifle barrel, Virgil watched and listened. Things seemed in their places; the cottonwoods rustled and grasshoppers clacketed the same as usual. In a minute, Virgil was tempted to think he hadn't heard anything in the first place.

Then he noticed the horses, his and Skiff's, standing hobbled out away from the trees. Both animals had their heads raised alertly, their ears up like cornshucks, and were looking toward the creek, showing they'd heard the voices too.

At that point, Virgil debated about waking Skiff, for one man scouting wasn't as good as having two. Skiff's nerves, though, were unpredictable. He was apt to wake up in jerks, and do it loud.

Then Virgil heard the voices, unmistakably, and louder this time, coming from downstream. It sounded like people calling across the water, and all sort of loud and uncautious, causing Virgil to figure it must be riders from Jackson's outfit after all. On the face of it, this seemed a sound line of thinking: Probably men had been sent out on a foray that Virgil didn't know about.

He decided that before waking Skiff, he'd sneak up in the hackberry bushes and have himself a look. If they turned out interlopers, Virgil would wake Skiff in a big hurry.

Feeling nervous, Virgil cocked his rifle and skulked past where Skiff was sleeping. He went into the plum trees and then hunkered to listen. The voices were louder, but they did not sound like they were coming toward him; they sounded like they were still in the creek.

Virgil stalked forward to a place he knew and looked out over the water. What he saw nearly popped his eyes out. A slim girl in men's clothes, with her hat gone and long, dark hair spilling around her shoulders, was sitting a scared horse spang in the current's middle. In a confusion around her, hampered by having to hold the reins of pack horses, was this pair of . . . so help him, of *town gents,* in black coats and vests and striped britches now wet above the tops of their stovepipe boots!

The girl was heel-thumping her mount's sides and yelping and looking altogether furious, while her horse stayed planted stock-still in the stream, its eyes big as dinner plates, refusing to be ridden across or be led by its bridle or be pushed from behind or anything.

Virgil's reaction was to laugh, which he could do safely enough with the racket the travelers were making. Town gents always struck him as comical anyway. The men weren't any of Jackson's, Virgil could see that much; but neither were they lawmen, or they'd hardly be dressed like riverboat gamblers and have some sprout of a girl with them.

Virgil's thinking was just getting down to exactly *what* they were when the darker-haired gent got his horse positioned behind the girl's. He leaned out and leveled a revolver near the flanks of the girl's mount. Before Virgil could blink, the man shot, the girl yelped in surprise; powder flame spurted from between the revolver's barrel and cylinder and scorched the girl's horse on its rump.

Virgil conceded that shooting was a good way to get the horse moving; the trouble was, it overdid it. The scorch treatment sent the horse surging frantically for the bank, but the current coming at it, or the sun coming off the water, must have confused it. What the horse did was turn upstream, still making for the far bank but angling badly. The angle kept it in the water all the longer, which made it all the more frantic. Heedless of the girl's efforts to control it, the horse made a beeline for a wide, still pool where the water eddied, a pool Virgil knew was bottomed with quicksand.

Virgil grinned and ducked down behind his hackberries. The brush was sparser near the roots, allowing him a clear view. Just twenty yards in front of him, the girl's horse, still riled at having its rump singed, hit the quicksand. As its hooves sank, the horse got ever more frantic to pull them out, so that it did a kind of high-stepping dance of panic, the muck sucking its legs lower the faster it thrashed.

Still, safety seemed within reach, except that when the horse got within ten feet of the bank it reared up and dumped its surprised rider. Then with a mighty effort, the horse surged for the bank, clambered onto solid ground, and disappeared into the brush.

The panicked, muck-stepping horse had been an entrancing spectacle, leaving Virgil dumbfounded. The town gents, still on horseback in the middle of the stream, looked dumbfounded too. The girl in the quicksand got her legs under her, but there must have been no bottom at all, the muck having been well thrashed by her horse going through it. She tried to stand but immediately sank to her armpits, then screeched loud enough to break windows.

So much had happened in front of Virgil that the next thing caught him flat. His partner, Skiff, blink-eyed from having his nap interrupted, appeared on the far bank with his pistol drawn. Skiff was wet to his stomach from wading the creek. The expression on his face said that, whatever he'd expected to find raising all the commotion, it was not two gents in frock coats and a screaming girl in quicksand.

Skiff stuck out his pistol, aiming at the gent closest to him, the darker-haired one, just as the gent spurred his horse toward the girl. Skiff's gun banged. The gent's coat jumped like fingers had snatched at it. Both town gents twisted around in response to the shot, but the one who'd been shot at was the faster. He whipped out a long-barreled revolver and fired. Skiff's face went consternated. He sagged to his knees and then tried to raise his pistol, but it was as though it had become heavy as boulders. When the gent fired a second time, Skiff collapsed on the creek bank. His hat dropped into the current and went gaily downstream like a little boat. Then his fingers unclutched, and his pistol dropped into the water with hardly a splash.

There was still more to take in. The girl was thrashing and screaming. With all her movement, she'd sunk so that the muck was clear up to her chin. Then, suddenly, both town gents were spurring straight for the bank and straight for Virgil, as though they could spy clear through the hackberries and see him crouching.

With the town gents bearing down on him, Virgil broke and ran. Brush whipped his face, confusing him. He burst free of the pickers and stickers and staggered into the open, finding he'd taken a wrong turn in the brush, and was now nearly under the hooves of the taller man's horse, which came snorting and clambering up the bank with its nostrils as black as caves.

"Hold it!" the gent yelled. Virgil was sure he'd be shot dead like Skiff. He spun on one heel and tried to get his rifle pointed, but a gun blasted almost in his face. Hard ground thumped his hinder. Then he was sitting with his legs stretched out and a deep pain boring at the very center of him. He tried to yell, but he couldn't get the breath for it.

"You danged fool *idiot!*" the town gent hollered. "I said *hold it!* Can't you understand English?" The gent was so worked up, Virgil felt even sorrier about things. It was as though he'd gone and spoiled everything.

The other town gent, the darker-haired one, urged his horse up the bank beside the first one. To Virgil, the world seemed tippy. He watched in wonder as creekwater slid in sheets off a horse's hide, the water sliding slower than he'd seen water slide before. One of the gents hollered, "Quick—get a rope!"

Virgil felt weak and sick. He rolled to his stomach, but the pain was worse. His head reeled from all that had happened. Five minutes earlier he'd been thinking how glad he was to be doing sentry duty. Now he was shot in the chest, and all in the space it took town men to cross a creek.

He rolled to one side, and the hurt backed off a little, so that he seemed to watch the gents' activity from a far-off place. "Throw her a loop!" the tall one hollered. The shorter one threw a loop of rope, then hollered for the girl to grab it. The girl screamed about quicksand, like maybe the men hadn't noticed it. Then the taller one bellowed for the other one to pull the rope back and try another toss. Virgil winced at all the commotion. He felt like resting, but the hollering disturbed him.

The taller gent grabbed the rope away and pulled till the loop end came back. It took him a second to coil the rope, during which time the girl's voice cut off in midscream. Virgil couldn't see over the bank, but he figured the quicksand had gulped her. However things came out, he hoped the commotion would end soon.

The taller gent swung a big loop over his head like a Texas cowpoke; then he threw it. "Grab it!" he hollered. "Angelina, grab it!"

"Damn!" the shorter one said, "you're no better than me!"

"Hell, then," the other one said. He threw his gun on the bank and launched himself off the creek bank. There was a great, crashing *sploosh,* causing Virgil to moan. He had a powerful need to rest, and was peeved at the ruckus they were making.

The shorter gent caught a horse right in front of Virgil. He dallied a few turns of his rope around the saddle horn, then he grabbed the horse's bridle and tugged the animal roughly.

When the horse pulled, everything got out of Virgil's way. He saw the rope tightening; he heard a loud, sucking sound. Then the taller gent and the girl were dragged up onto the creek bank—at least, Virgil figured they were the gent and the girl; what they looked like were huge clumps of glistening mud. When they uncoupled, they turned into exhausted-looking mud people lying on muddy grass, the man coughing and the girl wailing and both of them covered head to foot with the red-brown mud.

"Angelina, you're all right!" the mud man was insisting. The girl, though, kept carrying on, wailing and such. Then the mud man tried to hold her, but she screamed and rolled away from him.

"Don't you touch me!" she yelled. She got to her feet, a tall mud girl, but one of her boots had been half sucked off by quicksand, and she promptly fell down again.

"You—" the mud man said. "I just saved your *ungrateful hide!*" He and she got up at the same time, but she backed away from him and turned, and then grabbed on to the shorter town gent, who was standing amazed. He had no choice but to hold her right back, even though it got mud all over him.

The ruckus had been entertaining, but Virgil's interest had faded. He closed his eyes. He had a tingly, comfortable feeling that he wanted to snuggle closer to. He remembered himself as a boy, being tucked in at night.

"Doggone it, Angelina," a gent's voice said. "I was the only one who wasn't muddy."

The world rolled over and Virgil looked up into the mud man's blue eyes. He had sky and high clouds framed behind him, and he looked very tall. The mud man might have fussed some with Virgil's shirt front. His voice said, "God, Riley—this feller's a mess."

A farther-away voice said, "We can't take time with them. No telling who heard those shots."

"Right."

Virgil was just plain not interested. He certainly wasn't going to make conversation with mud people. He'd just started having a new kind of comfortable feeling and had been interrupted. All he wanted was to get back to that feeling.

"I doubt we can do much for you, mister," the close-up voice told Virgil. "You hear me? *Mister?*"

25 · HOLLIS CREIGH

IN HOLLIS CREIGH'S EXPERIENCE AS A TEXAS RANCHER, HAVING company was a rarity. You didn't drive a buggy down a neighbor's ranch road without dogs yapping and somebody in the house seeing you. But except for a ranch hand dawdling near the old harness shed, he saw nobody as he drove into the BR's ranch yard. As for dogs, Libba's old setter, Bootsie, had probably died years ago. It was funny, Hollis thought, that she'd never got another one.

He clambered down and got his crutches off the buggy floor. The porch steps had a hand railing, enabling him to hop up the steps.

As he tucked the pads into his armpits and approached the door, he hoped Libba herself would answer his knock, for he always handled himself awkwardly around Sally, Libba's colored housemaid. Though he'd known Sally upward of twenty years, since well before Emancipation, Hollis had barely said a dozen words to her, and had gotten as few back. It was disapproval of him, he supposed, both of him then and later. He wondered what she'd think of him now.

At his knock it was Sally's face at the door, looking faintly indignant, showing no flicker of recognition. She held her hands away from her dress as though she had cake batter on them.

He asked for Mrs. Barlow, saying her married name as formally as a drummer selling cookstoves, and then stood with his hat in his hand while Sally let the muslined screen door slap and disappeared inside. In a moment Libba's voice said, "Well, don't leave him standing," and Sally hustled to say, "No, ma'am."

He was let into the foyer, which was more cramped than he'd remembered it and far darker than the outdoors. He made out a wall bristling with Coleman Barlow's deer antlers. Looking at them, Hollis could remember the hunts, usually Coleman, Hollis himself, and Nash Wheeler, with a BR hired man or two to help haul back the meat. Hollis selected an impressive eight-pointer and hung his hat. "I guess Bootsie died," he said.

"Him and most everybody," Sally told him.

"I'm in here," Libba called.

Libba's voice had come from the parlor. He crossed an oval, braided rug that he did not remember, being careful to

plant the crutches so that the rug wouldn't scoot out from
under him. He turned and she was there, silhouetted against
the west window.

"Hollis," Libba said.

"I've not entered this house in many a year," Hollis said.
It was a needless comment, but the house's effect on him
was powerful.

She was sitting on the piano stool, more a perch than a
seat, which gave the impression she was about to rise and
come to him, although she did not. She wore the clothes of
mourning—black, or what he took to be black in that
light—but if she had been crying she did not show it. What
she looked was composed, stopped in time.

He was conscious of Sally hovering in the dining room
behind him.

"I've got something that needs saying."

Libba's attention elevated. "We'll be a few minutes," she
said, her voice amplified for Sally.

"Yes, missus."

Say it now, Hollis told himself. He cleared his throat. If
she'd offered a drink, he would have taken it. "I wanted to
express how bad we all feel for your sake. My family.
Everybody."

"It'd be tempting to mock those sentiments."

"I suppose you'd have a right. At any rate, they're true
enough."

"I should have expected you'd come," Libba said. "You
always did have brass where I was concerned."

He wanted to say that he didn't remember her minding,
but he figured it would not have done any good. He said,
"Waiting a few days seemed the decent thing."

She made a sound, a skeptical expelling of breath. "Days
are about all I have left." Her eyes rested on him. "I suppose
that sounds self-pitying." Hollis tried to find a useful
response, then gave up and shrugged.

"You've come to ask me to call off my reward," Libba
said. "Drop the charges. Forgive and forget."

151

Again, Hollis hemmed in his throat. "Just dropping the reward would be a lot. It's . . . Well, the likely result would hardly be justice."

She said, "Justice," summoning scorn.

"One boy is dead," Hollis said. "Who's to profit by the death of another one?"

She startled him. "*I* would profit! My mind can't make sense of this any other way!"

He thought then that she might cry. She pivoted on her piano stool and faced the window. He had a notion to advance, to take her by the shoulders—a strong notion, but he checked it.

"As for not pressing charges, I think a trial's in Robbie's best interests," Hollis said gently. He was trying to reach her as he used to know her. "I believe it would clear his name. You must know, Libba, that it wasn't murder."

She revolved to face him. "My Cole is dead. I don't want a trial. What I want is something faster and cleaner."

"So Nash tells me."

The eyes showed surprise. "Nash went to you? What good could have come of that?"

"It seems he was real interested in Robbie's whereabouts," Hollis said. "The reward you're offering is considerable as it is, but it sounds like you're offering Nash substantially more."

It upset her enough to bring her to her feet. "I'll not be scolded by you. A man whose son killed my boy."

"*Your boy.* Yours only? Do I have to say it aloud? To you of all people?"

"Don't," Libba said. Her expression was pained; she shook her head. "After all these years it's meaningless now anyway. I made a point to forget it."

"I never did."

Her look was accusing. "Just what are you saying— forgive everything for your sake, on account of you and me?"

He blew out a breath. He realized he'd kept alive a notion

that people who used to care about one another would see a thing similarly. "Libba . . . Can I sit down?"

"No. Do the crutches pain you? My sympathy's spent." Her eyes lifted beyond him. He thought she might call for Sally, but it appeared that she changed her mind. In her eyes, something settled.

"I have in mind going back to Alabama," Libba said. "My mother's still living, and I've got a sister. There's no law saying you have to live your whole life in one place."

"I suppose not."

"This ranch is getting to be nothing but a graveyard," Libba said.

He considered the truth of that. There seemed little else he could say. "So you offered Nash an interest in the BR."

"He's earned it if anybody has."

"Has earned it, or is earning it as we speak?"

"I don't nursemaid Nash Wheeler," Libba said. "He goes where he has a mind to."

"He still works for you."

"Work? There's precious little work of any kind going on around here. What's the point?"

"Nash has already left, hasn't he?"

"I don't know where he is," Libba said. "If he went to see you, you'd know more about it than I would." Her eyes, looking uncomfortable, traveled beyond him. When she spoke again, she said, "Sally . . ."

"Wait," Hollis said. But Libba's housekeeper answered with a "Yes, missus" so promptly that Hollis figured she'd been listening. It hardly mattered; Sally was privy to all their secrets.

"See Mr. Creigh to the door," Libba said.

"Yes, ma'am."

Sally came up wearing an expectant look and stopped fifteen feet from him. At least she wasn't going to herd him.

He said, "Another death won't help anything, Libba," and went through the wide archway with its familiar oak moldings and turned toward the door. He realized then why the foyer seemed narrower: he'd been two-legged those earlier times; now he was three-legged, with his crutches splayed out like buttresses.

Sally beat him to the foyer's narrowing and held the door for him. The crutch thuds changed when he went onto the porch. Outside, the light was dazzling after the shrouded parlor.

"My hat," he said, remembering. He turned and saw that not only Sally was behind him; Libba had come up to the door too. Above the dark dress, and framed against the dark background of the house's interior, her face hung disembodied behind the muslin screen.

"Here it is," Sally's voice said. She must have passed it to Libba because when the door opened it was Libba's sleeve that extended, Libba's hand that held the hat.

He was about to reach for it, but her forearm and wrist cocked, and she sailed the hat past him. It floated over the porch steps, descending gently to the dust of the yard. His horse regarded its landing with surprise.

Hollis looked one more time. Libba's expression was set in triumph. When he turned to negotiate the porch steps, his thought was that they were like a brother and sister playing out some childhood spat; only a family could fight with such pettiness.

"It'll do me good to see you stoop for that," Libba said. He could read no emotion from the words whatever.

"In that case," Hollis said, "you just watch me."

26 · CASS

HE AND RILEY PULLED THE BODIES INTO BRUSH TO HIDE THEM. Then, with Angelina, they took cover in the hackberry brush, looking out over the creek on one side and the open meadow on the other. They kept their rifle barrels bristling, but if anyone had heard the shooting at the creek, they did not show themselves. After fifteen minutes of breezes swaying the plums and alders, the creek running and redwing blackbirds calling, the shots seemed long faded. Cass began to feel safer.

Once they edged out of the brush, Riley rounded up loose horses, while Angelina bewailed the loss of her hat. It was Cass who rode downstream and fished it out of the water, and then presented it to her with a flourish. She set her jaw and stomped away from him.

Next, just as Riley came up with the horses, Angelina announced she was going to bathe in the creek. "I've got to wash the mud from these clothes," she told them, adding that nobody had better try to spy on her.

"Just keep an eye out for more quicksand," Cass suggested. Without answering, she moved a ways down the creek, her back suggesting new defiance. Cass was interested in how they were going to get into Shad Jackson's camp under the new circumstances. After all, they had killed two men who were apparently part of the outlaw fold.

"How do you figure we ought to play it?" Cass wondered. "Make out we never saw these men, or what?" He figured he had just enough time to wash himself and his own clothes before Angelina came back. He sat down on the bank and pulled off his boots.

"I think we ought to drape them over their horses and ride in with them," Riley said. "Claim they jumped us and we had to kill them. The truth, in other words."

"Bold as brass?" Cass, stripped, waded into the creek, which was nearly as warm as bathwater. He held his clothes under the current and watched mud stream away from them.

Riley said, "We're supposed to be bad outlaws, aren't we? This here Jackson might get so peeved we killed his men that he'll forget to question our story."

It sounded to Cass like odd logic. "Might get so peeved he'll hang us," he said. He realized there were a lot of elements. They chewed the matter over awhile longer; Cass wouldn't have called it an argument. They were both too undecided to take firm positions.

Just when Cass realized he hadn't come up with any better plan than Riley's original one, a movement on the creek bank caught his eye. He looked up to see Angelina in wet clothes and with her hair dripping, and there he stood bare-hindered in the shallow edge of the creek.

"Dang it!" Cass said, and squatted.

"I'm not looking so don't flatter yourself," Angelina said. "I grew up with a brother." She angled her head to one side while she combed water from her hair. It looked like she was angry with the hair for not drying faster. Cass, cussing all the while, eased himself upstream to where trees shielded him.

"I've been thinking," Angelina announced.

The statement hung till Riley said, "Oh?"

"If I'm to pose as the paramour of one of you, then I will have some say in the matter. Otherwise, I won't do it."

"Fine with me," Cass said. "There's only the two of us, though."

"I'll go with Riley," Angelina said. "I mean I'll pretend to be his sweetheart, but not yours."

"Lucky old Riley," Cass said. He figured he'd gotten all the mud out of his white shirt that was going to come out. It ended up the color of horse teeth.

"I dive in the muck to save you, and you end up being grateful to Riley," Cass said. "Where's the fairness in that? He gets embraced, and me, I'm not supposed to touch you."

"I'm grateful," Angelina said. "But if I'm to pretend I'm somebody's sweetheart, it'll just have to be Riley."

"Fine," Cass said again. He figured since she'd said she wasn't looking, he would just wade out and dry himself. The truth was, he felt kind of like kicking a dog, if he'd had a dog. So, fine—let Riley humor her for a while. Fine, fine, it was all fine with him. He, Cass, would just keep his mouth shut and do his damned job and get their sixteen hundred dollars.

But as he climbed up the bank he had to go and ask, "So what's wrong with me all of a sudden?"

"It's that you're too presumptuous where women are concerned," Angelina said, keeping her back to him.

27 · DOMINGA CREIGH

DOMINGA SAT ON THE PORCH HER HUSBAND AND BROTHER HAD added to the house in 1868 and tended her knitting. More exactly, since the needles moved with eyes of their own, she watched the long and flaring shadow of a support post inch across the flooring, watched it slowly overtake a particular knothole on a particular board. She reflected that the moving shadows resembled in one way the moving events of a life: one could watch, but one was helpless to stop them.

For her vigil, she had chosen the porch over the house's interior because she could see down the double-track ranch road. She'd found she had to see, even though the road was empty. Dominga Creigh saw signs in everything, and that her husband had not returned before sundown seemed a particularly unfavorable one.

Despite his years, despite—or maybe because of—the leg, Hollis still cultivated a boyish streak. When the mood struck him, he was wont to lope the buggy team, shooing her protests, chucking the leader into ever more speed while she despaired over the dust and danger. It was a roundabout way of admitting to herself that, had he good news to bring her, he would have loped the team half the miles from the BR, and been home before the evening shadows.

A movement collected her. Dominga's brother Hector moved beside the corral carrying a farrier's hammer. Angelina's collie dog trotted at his heels. Hector started when he saw her still sitting on the porch. He looked to the setting sun, and then back to her, and the look he gave was a bad one.

"You have put too much hope into this matter," Hector said. He spoke softly, but the words carried up the yard. For some reason, she found the Spanish comforting.

She could have responded that it was a mother's place to hope, even when others had none—in fact, especially in those times. But she heard in her ears how such a thing would sound: like something a priest would say. She was tired for the time being of the things priests said.

Instead of replying she looked beyond Hector. There was movement on the double track. Or perhaps it was only this hope Hector had mentioned that coaxed her heart into seeing what her eyes did not.

But Angelina's collie barked. Dominga stood up, her needles clattering to the porch floor. Hector looked too, until Dominga was without doubt that it was her husband coming unhurried up the road, and without doubt, too, that Elizabeth Barlow had not pitied them.

They stood as fixed as tombstones till the buggy rattled into the yard, with the two dogs yelping and crossing and recrossing almost under the hooves of the horse. Had her husband given a sign, she would have flown across the yard to him; but his face was bad, giving her no reason.

As she stayed rooted on her porch, so Hollis showed no inclination to get down from the buggy, even when Angelina's dog jumped up on it and nuzzled him. What he did do, finally, was look at her in a way that was worse than anything he could have said.

"The reward stands," Hollis told Hector, who perhaps did not read as much in a face and in actions as Dominga was able to. "Libba's all mixed up on some things, but she was clear enough on that."

So as to have something to do, Hector reached out for the horse's bridle.

"There's worse, too," Hollis said. "Nash Wheeler's already started. Libba wouldn't say so, but I'm sure of it."

Dominga let her words flow down the yard. "I was certain of it also."

If her husband were surprised, he gave no indication. He sourly regarded the setting sun. It seemed he addressed the sun rather than Hector.

"You would do me great honor to accompany me, *hermano.*" Hollis spoke in Spanish, which he seldom used, even with Hector. The fact that it was not his language made the request more formal. Immediately, Dominga grew cold with the coming loneliness. Everyone was leaving.

Hector spat—"*Pah!*" He said roughly in English, "You could not keep me here."

Her husband's smile, though brief, was the best she'd seen since the shooting. "Good," Hollis said. "In the morning early, then."

28 · ANGELINA

CASS PROCLAIMED IT OBVIOUS THAT THE WELL-WORN TRAIL THEY had discovered would lead to Jackson's sanctuary. Once again, Riley did not dispute him.

They saw no one else as they rode into Palo Duro, but the two dead outlaws slung over their own horses made the riding a serious business. Angelina decided she had misjudged Cass and Riley twice already, having first thought they were bloodthirsty bounty men and later that they were smooth-tongued charletons who had hoodwinked her father. That they were also fighters had come as a surprise.

She realized that while Cass and Riley had had experience in dealing with the roughest sort of men, she herself had had none. As each mile went by she found herself more agitated, with a growing need to discuss her fears of what might lie ahead. The men, though, merely got squint-eyed and unhappy looking, and answered her queries with a grunt here or two words there, so that she gave up trying to talk with them.

For an hour they rode generally west. Having to lead both their pack horses and the grimly laden outlaw horses made for slow progress. Finally, the trial veered into a narrower side canyon. Riley and Cass looked ahead and made critical faces. They dismounted in unison and began unsaddling their horses.

"We're camping?" Angelina said. By the sun, it was no later than four o'clock.

"Switching mounts," Cass said. "If we have to shoot our way out, I want a fresh horse under me." Riley pulled the loads off what had been their pack horses. Cass eased up to one and slipped his saddle over it.

"Best you'd do the same," Riley said. "Pick either outlaw horse you like. If you're afraid to touch a dead man, I'll dump him off for you."

"I'm staying on my Lobo," Angelina said. "He's taken me this far."

"Suit yourself," Riley said.

Cass pulled his revolver, snapped open the gate, and looked at each round intently. Then he spun the cylinder before shucking the gun back in its holster. Riley checked his own pistol, then tore strips of white cloth off a dead outlaw's shirt and tied one to his rifle barrel. Cass tied a strip to his rifle too.

"You might remember I can shoot a Winchester," Angelina said. "Besides, I'm supposed to be an outlaw girl—a tough customer."

Cass and Riley looked at her, then at each another. "I doubt she'd murder us at this late date," Cass said.

Riley went to a pack horse and drew out her broken rifle. He barely glanced at it before throwing it into a clump of soapweed.

"That was my Uncle Hector's," Angelina said stoutly.

"Then your uncle can come fetch it," Riley said. He went to a dead outlaw's horse and drew out a rifle almost identical to her own, the brass-framed Winchester Tio Hector called a Yellow Boy.

"Ever shoot from off Lobo's back?" Riley asked her. He handed up the rifle.

"He'd never buck me."

"A horse not used to gunfire's apt to buck you to the moon," Riley said. She looked for his teasing expression, but his face stayed in a set. He swung up and watched Cass mount.

"One thing's for danged sure," Riley said. "If we get out of this mess, that's all she wrote for outlaws and bounty hunting and getting shot at. If we're staying partners, we're going to hunt buffalo." He nodded for emphasis and tugged down his hat.

Cass settled himself, then adjusted his holster's angle till he got it just so. "All right," he said grimly, alarming Angelina that he didn't care to argue.

They rode no more than half a mile before Angelina smelled woodsmoke. Riley worked his rifle's lever to chamber a cartridge. The ratcheting of steel was an ominous sound.

"Don't fire unless we do," Cass instructed her. "And remember, no one's to know Roberto's your brother. Don't let him run up and hug you or anything."

"No," she said.

"If you have to, call out in Spanish to warn him," Cass said. "It beats having them know what we're up to."

"Of course," Angelina promised. "I will."

29 · CASS

WITHIN ANOTHER QUARTER-MILE THEY HEARD VOICES. THE PATH veered around a stand of cottonwoods. Their horses waded a tributary of the main creek, muddying only to their fetlocks. Then the trees fell back and they entered a clearing.

It was as though they carried a spell. A man splitting

firewood looked up in amazement. Another stopped in midstride on his way across the yard. Somebody else took one alarmed look and jogged for a log house. Boots thundered up the porch steps. A voice yelled, "Colonel!"

"Hello the camp," Cass called out. He waved his rifle to show the white cloth.

"We're friends," Riley hollered. "We're coming in."

"By God, they got Virgil's horse!" somebody yelled near them, and another voice responded, "Hell, they got Virge hisself. Skiff too!"

In seconds they were surrounded by a score of rough-looking men, all voicing anger over the dead outlaws, all regarding Cass and Riley and Angelina with stony eyes. Cass tried to keep from looking around too much; he had to make himself hard, to appear to know what he was doing. Riley was doing the same. Angelina, though, was looking everywhere. Cass could see by her face that she'd not yet spotted her brother.

Then the men crowding them were looking at the central building. A tall, lean man in high boots had come out on the porch, standing with a woman at his elbow. The woman looked friendly enough; she said, "Company for supper." But the man was glowering.

An outlaw stepped up and raised the head of one of the dead outlaws, gripping him by his greasy hair. "Virgil Hobbs," he announced to the man on the porch. "Shot dead. They got Skiff too."

"You're Jackson?" Cass asked.

The man on the porch's first response was to nod to Angelina. "Ma'am," he said, and his bow was courtly. But his eyes traveled to Cass and Riley, and his face changed. "For the moment, my name is my concern. This is a terrible cargo you've brought in here. I believe I shall hang both of you."

"These men are dead through their own doing," Cass said. "They didn't challenge us or announce themselves. They just cut loose on us."

"They had orders to."

"Then they should have shot straighter," Riley said. "It appears you were poorly guarded."

"Don't come here telling me my business," Jackson said. His eyes were as flint-hard as any Cass had seen.

"All I'm saying is was I you, I'd consider these fellers let me down," Riley said. "As fighters, they didn't amount to much."

Cass was afraid Riley might take that line too far. "We're on the run from Fort Worth," he put in. "We had a misunderstanding with a deputy sheriff."

"Pistoleers, are you?" Jackson said skeptically. "I suppose you killed the deputy too."

"He claimed to recognize us from a wanted dodger," Riley said. He shrugged theatrically. "It was awful rash of him."

"That makes you common outlaws," Jackson said. "Abducting a lady as well. I won't abide disrespecting womanhood."

"Never mind about Angelina," Cass said. "She's Riley's sweetheart. He's Riley Stokes," he added. "I'm Cass McCasland, at one time of the Confederate cavalry. As for being outlaws, we figured it's no crime robbing banks in Texas. It's all Yankee money."

"You're saying that to get on my good side," Jackson said. "You think to bluff your way. You've got sand in your craws, I'll say that much."

"Obliged," Cass said. He glanced around with what he felt was a mild expression. Angelina still looked shocked and lost. She'd obviously expected to see her brother immediately.

"The truth is, we're all rode down," Cass said. "We could use some food and a rest. We've heard a man on the run gets a fair shake here."

Jackson said, "Word of our presence here is all over the settlements, is it?"

"Not at all," Cass said. "We made inquiries."

"A man gets a fair shake only if he's a true friend of the southern nation," Jackson said.

Cass answered quickly. "You're looking at two of them."

"And pays his own way."

"Like we said," Riley said, "Yankee money."

"And most of all, if he proves he's one of us," Jackson said. "As to that, we'll soon be mounting a force of riders. You look to your weapons and animals. In a couple of days you can show us your mettle."

"Fine with us," Cass said.

"We'll find out whether you're the bold badmen you claim to be," Jackson said. "Until then, you're on a trial basis. As for the lady, she is most welcome."

"I believe your men would just as soon lynch us," Cass said.

"You'll not be harmed. Those sheltering in Palo Duro obey my commands," Jackson said sharply. "As for the men you killed, bury them behind the corral yonder. Supper's at six. Board's a dollar a day. If you don't like it, move on."

"Sounds fine," Riley said.

"Since you have a lady with you, we'll see about a cabin. I repeat that you're on trial. Whatever you do, you'll be watched."

"That's understood," Cass said.

"It had damned well better be. You'll pardon my language, ma'am." Jackson bowed again to Angelina, then designated a couple of men as replacements for the slain guards. With that, Shad Jackson turned and went through the door behind him, as though he had no more interest in anything beyond supper.

"Ma'am," Cass said to the woman on the porch. He turned his mount, and they walked their horses past a gauntlet of narrow-eyed men. Riley expelled a long breath when they reached the corral. Cass got down and untied the gate. When he turned, he saw Angelina's expression, crushed and brittle.

"No sign of him?"

"There's—there's one Halfmoon horse in the corral. Just

one. And Robbie had two." Muscles around her mouth were jumping.

"That's actually good," Riley said. "I mean, about the horse."

"How can you say that?" Angelina said. Cass heard in her voice raveled emotion.

"If both animals were here and him not, it could mean they hung or shot him," Riley said. "This way it means he's off hunting rabbits or something."

Angelina let out an explosive, scornful breath. "I must ask about him."

"Ask?" Cass said. "You damned well won't *ask anybody.*" He had to keep his voice low because of a handful of sullen men watching. "What we've got going here is a big play-act. We've got to be exactly what we told Jackson, else he'll string us to a cottonwood." He pulled off his saddle and hefted it to a corral rung.

"We came for Roberto," Angelina said.

"Of course. But you'll have to be patient."

While they were stripping the rigging off their mounts, two men came into the corral and handed them spades. Cass and Riley had to carry the dead men to an open plot beyond the spindly rail fence. One outlaw remained to watch them. He hunkered with his back against a corral post, his eyes slitted against low sun, and chewed a weed thoughtfully. Riley planted his spade, putting his weight into it.

"You bury them deep so's coyotes don't get them," the outlaw directed. "Me and Skiff, we was first cousins."

30 · RILEY

IT WAS LONG AFTER SUPPERTIME WHEN THEY LEFT CASS IN THE tavern and left him also to his own devices for the night. Riley figured there was little any of them could do about Cass's sleeping arrangements, since they'd let it be known that Angelina and he, Riley, were cozy. Or rather, he and Cass had let it be known. Angelina, according to Riley's view of it, had been doing her best to act like a tramp.

They found the cabin Jackson had assigned them. It was rickety, but at least it had walls and a roof. Riley closed the door behind them, shutting off what little light came from a high field of stars. He heard Angelina grope to the table. When the candle flame mounted, she turned. Her eyes widened at seeing his anger.

"What?" she said.

"You know danged well what! We're supposed to be pretending to be lovey-dovey, then you go practically advertising yourself to these damned outlaw killers!" His pacing made the floorboards creak. He turned and said, *"Jesus,"* putting a lot into it.

"I'm the one who took the risk!" Angelina said. "I had to learn whatever I could. Roberto's either—"

"Dang it, we all took the risk! There's Cass and me in that tavern trying to play like we're big outlaws, while you're circulating like a six-bit flirt. 'Don't you have any little Spanish boys for me to love?'" Riley mimicked a girl's voice, his face twisted to pantomime coyness. "For cripes' sakes, Jackson said they're watching us!"

At that point it got to her. She sat down on the only chair and studied the floor.

"You know what you just went and did?" Now that he'd unpacked his mad, Riley was going to give it a good airing.

"Only a couple of them heard what I said," she said, looking up. He saw she'd managed to get her chin reset. "Besides, nobody told me anything."

"All the worse!" Riley said. "What you did, you just let those wolves in the tavern know you're up for grabs. Now I'll have to fight half those sons of bitches before we get out of here. Are you blind? You don't see how they look at you?"

"I see," she said stiffly.

"You're just mud-headed enough to be flattered," Riley said. "I ought to let the whole bunch have you. They probably been woman-starved for weeks or months."

"I don't care what they think," Angelina said. "I care about Roberto."

"Dang it, not caring is exactly what's going to get us *killed!*"

"Don't you yell at me. He's my brother. Your feelings aren't in this at all!"

Riley paced. Angelina's words echoed till he supposed she was right. Angelina thought only about her brother. Cass's mind was set on his sixteen hundred precious dollars. Riley's own feelings in these situations mostly tended toward saving his neck.

He puffed out a breath so vehemently that the candle guttered. There was a space in which he began to hear crickets.

"Roberto's dead," Angelina said in a stricken voice. "I feel it." She stood up and went hollowly to the bed, which was no more than a bunk padded with straw, with a buffalo robe thrown over it. She sat down, then collapsed to lie on her side. It was as though a breeze had toppled her.

Riley guiltily regarded her back. Then her shoulders heaved and he heard her sobbing. "Oh, for pete's sake," Riley said. He went to his trappings, got the pistol he'd saved for her, and went back to the bed. The shack was so small it only took him eight steps.

"You'd better have this," Riley said. She kept her back to him. He offered the pistol but she wouldn't turn to look at it. "It's a pocket pistol. I took it off the outlaw I shot. You ought to carry it in your boot or something, in case somebody comes at you."

She snuffled, maybe words.

Dumbly, he said, "Huh?"

"I said, and use it on myself?"

"What?" Riley said. "Angelina, for pete's sake . . ." He sat on a corner of the bed. She turned. He saw how she'd flooded her eyes and then had daubed them with a sleeve. She took the pistol as negligently as if it were a stick and turned to the wall again.

In a strangled voice, she said, "Comfort me."

"What?" Riley leaned over her, thinking he was not sure he'd heard, and then was dead sure that he had. For it was as though they'd crossed some barrier that they'd both been contemplating for a week or longer. He put an arm behind her head, and her hair in his fingers was a sudden treasure.

Then he was with her on the tiny bed so there was no moving away for either of them. He sought her mouth with his. He kissed her, he smelled her tears.

"You don't really want this."

"Yes," she said, but her real answer was her movement, so that they met on middle ground on the bed, and in time made each other bare and vulnerable, and finally meshed, and after that coupling lay entangled for a long time without him feeling there was anything that needed saying. At some point the candle had burned out. Outside, there were crickets, and starlight filtering through the cracks in the cabin.

A knock rattled the door. Riley groped for his gun, then realized it was out of reach on the chair. A space opened. Cass's voice, sounding stretched and hurt and laboring to be joky about it, said, "Everybody decent?"

Riley looked at Angelina, whose eyes were conspiratorial. He cleared his throat. "Sort of occupied." He kept his voice low because outlaws might have been lurking nearby.

"Occupied?" Cass said. The jokiness in his voice had drained right out.

"Afraid so."

"All right," Cass said. They heard hesitant footsteps moving away. Riley was left feeling sorry for him. In Riley's ear, Angelina giggled.

"Poor old Cass," Riley said.

She said, "Do you think there's room for him in bed with us?"

Riley chuckled, thinking of it. The fact was, at that moment, lying naked and tangled up with Angelina Creigh Garza, Riley felt sorry for any man who wasn't Riley.

"You've had many women," Angelina said, matter-of-fact.

It stumped him. "I guess I'm no plaster saint," Riley allowed, then regretted the cavalier sound of it. "The ladies mostly go for Cass over me," he said, amending. Which was true enough, at least sometimes. "Women see Cass as sort of a gaudier specimen."

"Cass is arrogant," Angelina said. "All men are, but he's so especially."

"I'd say he's more like pig-headed," Riley said. "And once he gets a whiff of easy money he's like a bloodhound."

"Arrogant. All men are."

"Even me?" Riley said.

"All of you," Angelina assured him.

"Now why would you say that?" It seemed to Riley he got his comeuppances often enough. He had his faults too, and was mostly well aware of them.

"I didn't mean to scold," she said. "You're a nice enough man."

"But mighty tall in my own eyes."

"In your way, yes."

"You're going to have to explain that one," Riley said. It seemed ungrateful for her to call him names after what they'd just done together. He didn't know what was arrogant about what they'd done, for he'd certainly appreciated her. As far as he could tell, she'd appreciated him right back.

"It's something one can't explain," Angelina said. She was sticking to her guns.

"Take a whack at it," Riley said. "I'll sort it out."

"You're arrogant about love, because you think this . . . doing this, is something clever, and that men thought it up."

"Well now, I hardly think—"

"Yes," she said. "To your thinking, this is love—all this moving."

"The moving part is mighty comforting, I'll say that. You said earlier to comfort you, and darned if—"

"It was ill advised," Angelina said. She sat up and found a comb somewhere and began combing out her hair. Electricity crackled. He saw her as a long and lovely shadow.

"Speaking purely from my end of it, the moving part is

about the nicest," Riley said. He hated to hear a woman run down the moving part, especially if she'd just been with him. "I didn't notice you holding your breath any."

"All right, it's nice," Angelina said, "but even animals can do that part."

The comparison to animals, he thought, was downright uncalled for. It was as if he were being accused of being a rutting boar or something.

"What I mean is a man thinks this is his great gift to his woman, this kind of loving," Angelina told him.

Riley blinked. He supposed that was about how he saw it.

"That's the easy part," Angelina said. "You just follow nature."

"It does tend to take its course," Riley said with satisfaction.

The comment only made her combing more vigorous. Just when Riley was afraid she might yank some hair out, she stood up and moved to the table. The loss of her already pained him. He said, "We could take another try at it without so much moving this time."

"Then that would be twice the mistake." Her voice had sounded a little cold, he thought. Then he heard her busying with the basin, washing away all traces of him.

At that point he sat up. "Then I expect what you're really talking about is the marriage part," Riley said. It was as serious a word as he'd uttered lately, and it seemed to make her move all the more forcefully. The basin rang in anger a couple of times. He could just make out Angelina drawing up her undergarments, covering her flanks.

"I certainly am not," Angelina said. "Once again you manage to see loving without all the richness it might have. No wonder men make laws about it, about marriage and loving and when you should and should not. It's men who are the judges, and it's men priests who decide the rules. It's not just you, it's all of you."

"I . . . we do?"

"What I'm talking about is true closeness," Angelina said. "Not even many marriages have that."

"True closeness?"

She struck a match and rummaged for another candle. When the light finally came up her expression was a thing to see: a radiation of some poor kind of triumph.

"Just listen to yourself," she said. "Listen and you'll hear you don't know anything."

She opened the door with force, staggering the candle flame. She went out and closed it, staggering the flame again.

Feeling a bit of a fool, or feeling something but having no idea what, Riley took the opportunity to pull his britches and shirt on. He put the pistol he'd tried to give her on the rickety table. She came back in a minute; probably she'd only gone out to squat in the bushes.

"I'd feel better if you'd take this pistol," Riley told her.

"It was all ill advised," she said again. "A weak moment."

It grieved him to hear it. "I don't know how you can say that," Riley said.

She shook her head. Her own assessment was all that mattered to her. She said, "We're only pretending to be lovers. Don't think I'm going to share the bed with you."

"Son of a bitch," Riley said.

"Why say such an ugly thing as that?"

"It's only I'm a little whirly-headed," Riley said. "Maybe I stood up too quick."

31 · CASS

Cass woke up in the weeds with his face to the shed. A chicken was pecking nearby, but he didn't think the chicken had woke him. If he had thought so, he would have wrung its scrawny neck.

He got up and took a stance to make water on Skiff's grave. Just as he let go he remembered Skiff had an outlaw cousin. Too late now, Cass reflected, but he glanced all around until he finished.

Then he tried to straighten himself around inside his clothes. After being slept in, clothes never fit in the morning the way they did when you went to bed. It was because they got damp, Cass supposed, and stretched in the wrong places.

When Riley and Angelina had shut him out of the shack, he'd gone hunting for a bedding ground. One spot looked about as unwelcome as another, but since he was going to bed so late, outlaw style, he wanted a place where he'd be shaded in the morning. A person couldn't sleep late with the sun baking him.

Waking up damp was the inevitable bad side of sleeping in the deep shade, Cass figured. It was like life in general: there were advantages and disadvantages to everything, and often it was just too tedious to weigh everything out. Sometimes you had a mind to hunt up the perfect bedding ground, and other times you had a mind just to go straight off to sleep, especially when your saddle partner did something to show he valued your friendship as worth about two cents.

Cass saw a snake near the horse trough. It wasn't a rattler, and therefore not worth wasting a bullet on. He washed his face in the end of the trough that had no scum on it, keeping one eye on the snake in case it changed into a rattler. He combed his hair with his fingers, put his hat on, and felt a little better.

The shack door was still closed against him. Fine, Cass thought; he would just go up to breakfast by his lonesome. Cass McCasland had been on his own hook since he'd gone off to war at age sixteen. He could wipe his own nose and tend his own hinder. One other thing he could do was entertain himself, at breakfast or anywhere, and for long stretches, if he had to. The fact was, he could have a high old time with no help from anybody.

But while Cass was still owlishly regarding the shack door, the hinges creaked and Riley stepped out, looking, to judge by his sour face, like he felt even poorer than Cass did. Not wanting to see Riley at that moment, whether hangdog or not, Cass was sorry he hadn't moved along quicker toward breakfast. He hadn't been looking for Riley's company and didn't want Riley getting any notions that he had. Cass could breakfast quite tolerably, thank you, without the company of Riley Stokes.

Here they were, though, he and Riley face to face, and both obviously pretty groggy.

"Morning," Riley said.

Cass nodded. Even under the circumstances, he could give away that much.

"You going up to breakfast?"

"I was," Cass said. "I wasn't going to wake you, though. On account of you might've been occupied."

"Huh?"

"Occupied," Cass said.

Riley looked sheepish. "Naw."

"I might just go on ahead," Cass said. "You'll be waiting for her, I expect."

Riley made a limp gesture. "She's already up and out." He glanced at the shack and then made the gesture again, even limper than the first time.

"I found a good place to bed down beside the shed," Cass said. "I had a good sleep."

Riley stretched in a way that Cass saw was ungenuine. "Dang, those board floors are hard on a man's back." Riley's yawn wasn't bona fide either.

"You spent a poor night?" Cass said.

"Pretty much."

"Too bad."

That seemed to rouse him. "I doubt I need you feeling sorry for me," Riley said. "I've spent worse."

"I'll bet."

Riley scowled. He looked toward the tavern. "Are you going up to breakfast or not?"

"I said I was," Cass said. He pulled his hat down to cut the low sun and they walked toward their breakfasts, keeping a couple of yards of ground between them. Despite Cass's longer legs, they walked at exactly the same pace. They'd gotten used to each other, Cass supposed.

He supposed, too, that he and Riley were, after all, only business partners. What Riley and Angelina did together was their personal matter and none of his own; there was no point in feeling hangdog about it.

But then he remembered Angelina was actually a business matter herself, that she was key to their getting Roberto Creigh to go back with them, thus key to their getting paid their sixteen hundred dollars. Bounty hunting was their job of work, and sixteen hundred was their salary. Riley had been a fool to go and jeopardize it.

"She says I'm arrogant," Riley confided. "You too."

Cass saw Riley was trying to get Cass and himself back into the same boat, and get Angelina into a boat by herself. But while Cass was figuring that, Riley said, "You wouldn't be sort of jealous?" He kept his voice down because of two of Jackson's men who were sitting on the porch.

"Me?"

"Peeved, maybe?"

Cass shook his head.

"You might figure you had a right to be," Riley suggested.

"I damned well am not jealous nor peeved," Cass said.

"Prickly too," Riley observed.

Just as Cass stomped up the tavern steps, the door opened and they met Angelina, looking as though she'd bathed and breakfasted and been up for hours.

"I'm glad somebody slept good," Riley said.

Cass, though, read something in her face. He said, "What?"

She took in the outlaws on the porch, both admiring her openly. "We'd better go check on that lame horse of ours," she said, like it was a public announcement.

"What lame horse?" Riley said. She led them about two rods into the open clearing, over ground pocked with hoofprints. Riley said again, "Horse?"

"The lame one," she said, her face brimming with significance.

Finally Cass said, "Good idea."

With Angelina beside them, they started toward the corral, walking a little faster than they would have without her.

"You shouldn't go in the tavern with those men," Riley said. "I told you last night—"

"I was hungry. You were sleeping like the dead. So was Cass, down by the shed."

"Then you'd better not have been flirting around again."

"I was clever."

"Oh, cripes," Riley said.

"I talked to Jackson's woman this time. Her name is Faith. I asked, 'Isn't there someone here I can speak Spanish with?' I said I was dying for a lack of speaking Spanish."

"Now that was a darned fool thing," Cass said.

"It was just the thing to ask," Angelina said. She was letting out more and more excitement. "Faith said a dark-eyed boy had gone out with a bunch of others. 'Pretty Roberto,' she called him. It's got to be him."

"Then he's safe?" Riley said.

Angelina nodded, triumphant. "He's expected back with the others, tomorrow at the latest. It was clever of me, don't you think?"

"It's pretty fair news," Riley acknowledged.

"Clever," she insisted.

Cass was thinking of sixteen hundred dollars and bed sheets and clean clothes, and of taking his meals in some hotel dining room in Fort Worth. It was a reminder he was hungry. "I'm for eating breakfast," Cass said to them.

32 · ROBERTO

To Roberto's amazement, Amos Mapes drove his riders through most of the night, past rock formations that lurked like passing ships. At the first easing of darkness in the false dawn, Mapes took his coiled rope and chased off the dead Indian's pony. Then they rode hard again, despite the tiredness of both men and horses.

It was early morning when Roberto began getting a sense of familiarity. Amos Mapes stopped them so that he could tie a red cloth to a piece of tree branch, making a signal flag. Then he triggered three pistol shots into the air. Soon after, they were riding up what Roberto thought was surely the Prairie Dog Town Fork of the Red River. In another few minutes they came upon Shad Jackson's sentries at the shallow mouth of the big canyon. Then Roberto was stunned to see a familiar figure standing with them. Nash Wheeler, foreman of the BR ranch, stood tightening his cinch strap. His holster was empty, his rifle scabbard too.

"By gosh—young Bob the Kid," Nash Wheeler said when he saw him, while Roberto's head reeled at seeing so familiar a face that far from home.

Nash grinned like they'd been best chums for years. "Lucky deal I run onto you. Tell these jumpy fellers with their guns out I ain't no Texas Ranger."

33 · HECTOR GARZA

"NASH HAS TO TRACK, WHEREAS WE KNOW RIGHT WHERE WE'RE going," Creigh said. "That's our one advantage." He took a last swig of water, then jammed the stopper on his canteen.

Hector did not need to be told this thing of their one advantage. But he understood that Creigh was thinking aloud, testing the logic of his words against the reality of the day's warmth and the breeze coming off the distant Llano.

Creigh got up before Hector could move to help him. He hobbled to his horse and struggled with the *cincha,* having to lean into the crutches to free his hands for working. Being forced to work so awkwardly put Creigh in a bottled rage. Hector, seeing the force Creigh expended in his movements, kept his distance. He recognized when Creigh would allow himself to be helped, and when he would not.

Instead of watching the seething man, which would have tried Hector's own patience, Hector wrapped the cold beef in its oiled paper and wrapped his sister's bread in a cloth and stowed them in his saddle pockets. Then he dallied three wraps of his canteen strap around the saddle horn to keep the canteen from flopping.

By that time, Creigh had tightened his *cincha.* He shucked his crutches into a leather scabbard Hector had made for that purpose, then he faced the saddle and pretended some adjustment in the stirrup till Hector came around to help him.

Hector laced his fingers to receive the booted foot. Creigh gripped the mane with one hand and the horn with the other. Just before hauling himself up enough to proffer the foot, he gave Hector a fierce look, his eye-corners crinkled and the eyes themselves glinting.

"Hermano," Hector said, "allowing oneself to be helped ought not cost such pain."

"It damned well does me, though." Creigh picked a spot of ground and spat, and it looked to Hector as though he'd got something out of him besides spit, for his eyes eased. Or maybe it was that Hector's use of *hermano*—brother—had not gone unnoticed. This was a thing Creigh often called Hector; they were brothers-in-law, after all. But so tender a term was sometimes said too cheaply for Hector's taste, although Creigh, being a white Texican, could not be expected to know it. What Hector called Creigh was mostly *señor,* or when he was feeling very easy, *cabeza,* the head one or chief, or behind his back, *cabezota,* the stubborn-head—when, for example, they had argued over some detail of running the ranch together.

"There is a saying," Hector said. "The true gift weighs nothing." Creigh took a breath and hauled himself up, what he called his Scots-Irish face reddening with the effort. Hector received the weight and strained to lift. They grunted in unison, then Creigh was up and got his stump swung over and settled himself in the saddle.

Creigh breathed a moment before he said, "Without strings attached, you mean?"

"Yes, that too." Hector straightened against a hint of a difficulty in his back and then got his horse and mounted.

"I'm obliged anyhow," Creigh said. He did not look so fierce now, Hector decided. Hector set them a trot, then turned in his saddle.

"Pah!—I do it not for you, señor," Hector said, grinning. "It is for the sake of Angelina and Roberto."

34 · TWO HORNS

SCOUTING FOR THE ARMY HAD GOT TWO HORNS AND HIS BROTHER the use of very fine carbines. It got them much food to eat, and blue army jackets to wear in cold weather. There were many fine things to be gained when working for the soldiers, but Two Horns had felt sure that, in the end, only bad things would come of it.

Two Horns found the place where his brother's pony had waited. With all the droppings around, he would not have needed to be Kickapoo to find that. Then as soon as he'd dismounted he saw the hard-heeled tracks of white men. There had been two of them, one much heavier than the other. The tracks proclaimed the white men had led Two Horns' brother's pony up a little rise.

Two Horns had felt very bad since Hawk had not returned to the army column. Now, following the white men's boot prints and the hooves of his brother's pony, the bad feeling worsened. Near the top of the rise, with the bad feeling drumming in him, Two Horns cut off to the left and circled. The prints were a day old at least, yet it would not do to walk into the bad welcome that had greeted his brother Hawk.

In Two Horns' thinking, Hawk was already dead, so he did not mourn when he found the blood splotch. Before mourning he had a duty, which was to find his brother's body in order that it could be properly buried and the soul thus freed for its flight to the afterlife.

Keeping his mourning in check, Two Horns picked up an empty army cartridge case that lay beside the blood splotch. He noted where the white men had loaded the body onto Hawk's pony and the direction the tracks led. Then he again skirted to intercept the track farther ahead, in case the white men were still in that country.

As he moved, Two Horns' heart was heavy, for the blood

splotch was old and dried. That his brother had been killed was sad news, but it was acceptable to him. Death was not so tragic; all men must die, and few die at a time of their own choosing. What concerned him more was that the body had been taken up by white men,—and for what reason? Even if the white men had discarded it, Hawk's body would have gone unguarded and unburied one whole day, meaning it surely would have been torn by coyotes by that time or picked by vultures or crows.

As he was thinking these bad things and grieving over how poorly the soul of one whose body is mutilated fares in the afterlife, Two Horns found the place from which the white men had fired, for a pair of brass cartridge cases lay bright as tiny suns in the oak leaves. From that point, the trail led down a steep arroyo into the broken, rocky country below.

Before fetching his pony for the ride down the arroyo, Two Horns spent some time studying the descending trail and the country beyond. He saw a big, empty valley with jagged rock rimming it and much thick brush lining a creek.

Other than the shod hoofprints leading down to the valley, he saw no white men or signs of them, and no coyotes or vultures. What he did see was an excitement among crows. This activity was at a spot near the foot of the descending trail. Some crows hopped about that spot, making short flights from one bush to another. Others floated above it, their fingered wings fixed for riding a breeze that flowed down there. All these crows, whether floating above or flitting about in bushes, spoke in their language of a good thing to eat that lay in that brush.

With a sad heart, Two Horns went to get his pony. He felt bad for the soul of his brother, and also, he was angry with himself. His feeling of only bad things coming from scouting for white soldiers had been a strong one, and yet he, Two Horns, had not heeded it.

35 · ROBERTO

ONCE ROBERTO EXPLAINED THAT NASH WHEELER WAS NEITHER A Texas Ranger nor any other kind of lawman, Shad Jackson's outlaws showed little more interest in him. Roberto heard Amos Mapes mutter that the whole damned country must know about the outlaw hideout, judging by the rate strangers kept arriving.

Other than that comment, Mapes seemed in such a hurry to get back to Jackson's headquarters that he stopped his riders only long enough to water their horses. Then Nash's pistol and Winchester rifle were returned to him, and all but the two sentries rode on toward Jackson's tavern, taking Nash with them.

But if the outlaws were not much curious about Nash's appearance at Palo Duro, Roberto Creigh certainly was. It seemed wrong on the face of it. Here was a man he'd known most of his life as the Barlow family's foreman, as an old war comrade of his father's, but more recently as a man who had shunned his father for ten years—certainly a declaration of animosity. And more recently still, as the man who'd sat his horse and done nothing while Roberto and Cole Barlow, Nash's boss's son, had exchanged fire and Cole had fallen. The unanswered questions bottled high in Roberto's throat gave him a queasy feeling.

Soon, though, they were riding into the canyon. With the outlaws exhausted from their long ride, some dozing in the saddle, Roberto pretended his horse was favoring a hoof. He dismounted alongside the path, picked up a hoof, and looked at it critically, all the while letting Nash catch up with him.

"Just tender, I reckon," Roberto said, in case anyone was paying him mind, but he slid his eyes to Nash, who reined in and sat his saddle with his palms crossed on the horn and his face holding amusement.

"Well, Bob, I own it was careless of me getting took prisoner," Nash said. Roberto shrugged; outlaws getting the drop on him was not what he wanted to talk about.

"You're wondering what I'm doing here, two-hundert-some miles from the BR, and fall roundup coming on," Nash said.

"You followed me," Roberto said.

"In a roundabout way," Nash conceded. "The long and short of it is I'm saving your hide."

"Cole died, didn't he?"

"Pretty much dead when he hit the ground. I guess you never knew it."

"So you mean you'd testify for me?"

"Might not have to," Nash allowed. "The game's changing. But first off, let me ask you something. You seen those fellers rode in with your sister?"

Roberto, in the act of remounting, was sledgehammered. His sister? Angelina, here? If he'd been swim-headed at seeing Nash Wheeler pop up as sudden as a cactus bloom, he was ten times more swim-headed now.

"If you been out of the canyon, could be you wouldn't know," Nash said easily. "She's here right enough, in tow of a pair of bounty hunters. Only they ain't leveled with her. Angelina probably figures they're here to take you back to mama."

"I think you'd better explain yourself," Roberto said sternly.

"It's good news, mostly. Libba—Mrs. Barlow—had a change of heart and took her reward off you. Of course, being you run off, you wouldn't have knowed about the reward either."

"I expected she'd offer one."

"Yeah—five thousand in hard money. And the shine of that much drew bounty men from all over, including the two gents who are here with your sister."

"I can't believe Angelina's here," Roberto said. "She wouldn't have—"

"Believe it," Nash said. "I followed their tracks two hundert miles or better. Anyhow, the thing was, Libba got to remembering what a hothead her Cole was. So she finally got around to asking me if it was a fair fight you had with him. 'Course, I had to own it was."

"You did."

"Don't look so muddle-faced. Cole pulled his gun and you shot right together, didn't you? I for damned sure saw that much. So Libba says would I have to say as much in court? I says I reckon I would. So she says in that case there's no point in a trial that'd just make Cole look worse."

"Really?"

"I see her point. Here's Cole already looking like he's damned stupid, and it turns out he's slow, too."

"I expect he'd been drinking."

"We all had," Nash said, "Cole more than anybody. But I know what I saw. And with a hand on a Bible I won't say different, not even to tickle Libba. Hell, she don't *own* me."

Roberto considered it. "I'd be obliged."

"No need to thank me just for saying God's truth. And the thing now is, this pair of bounty men must've talked your old man into letting on where you was, with the notion of saving you from all the other bounty men. Or so they must've said."

"Nobody puts anything past Pa. He's—"

"Your pa always did let his heart rule his head, and that's God's truth too," Nash said. "So now, you ride in wherever these boys are taking us, and them two bounty men are apt to shoot you dead."

"But you say the reward's called off."

"Hell, *they* don't know that, on account of they left before I did. Anyhow, they're hardly going to take my word for it. They see me, they're going to try and tell you I'm after the reward myself. You watch."

"I see," Roberto said, but it was some complicated, having to consider who knew what and who didn't.

"Then what do you think I should do?" Roberto said.

Nash glanced up the line of riders, then leaned from his saddle to close the distance between them. "Skedaddle out of here, you and me. The quicker the better."

"If Angelina's here, we'd have to take her with us," Roberto pointed out. Nash frowned at that. "I couldn't leave her," Roberto said. "A girl alone."

"She's with the two bounty gents."

"All the worse," Roberto said.

Nash looked irritated, but he puffed a breath and resettled himself. "I expect you're right," he said finally, "but it makes things tougher. You know a way out of this canyon where we don't have to pass them guards?"

Roberto thought of the switchbacked trail they'd taken out of the side canyon two days earlier. It had seemed a comforting secret. "Maybe," Roberto said.

"Tonight then," Nash said. "Or soon as we can slip away."

"My horse is beat," Roberto said. He could have added that, after a long night of riding, he was used up himself.

"Mine too. It can't be helped." Nash looked cautiously up the line of riders. "You keep yourself ready," Nash said. "Meanwhile, I believe we been seen jawing enough together." He tugged his hat and urged his horse farther up the line.

It left Roberto in a stew. Here he'd just started getting comfortable with being a tough outlaw and a soldier for the South. It hadn't been bad so far except for being shot at, and seeing an Indian shot down right in front of him.

Now here was the chance, apparently, to go back to his family without facing charges. From what Nash had said, Libba Barlow seemed resigned to Cole's death. It seemed impossible after what Roberto had been through, the idea that his old, normal world had continued on from where he'd left it, and even more impossible that he could ease right back into it.

But he found that the sneaking out part bothered him, and a second later the reason loomed up. He spurred his fatigued horse to catch up with Nash.

"If there's another way, I'd rather not sneak out," Roberto said. "I couldn't rightly leave without telling Colonel Jackson."

Nash appeared instantly angry but then throttled back on it. He looked ahead and then behind him—needlessly, Roberto thought, for half of the outlaws were asleep in their saddles. "Oh, hell no," Nash said, "you couldn't tell anybody."

"But I'm obligated," Roberto said. "I as good as joined up. He'd think I deserted. And here this Jackson and my pa were bordermen in Missouri during the war. I sure owe him some kind of explanation."

Nash's face went startled. "They were? And he's boss over all these owlhoots?"

"More like a commander," Roberto said. "They're not regular outlaws, they're fighting for the Southern cause."

"That's horse turds," Nash said with scorn.

"It's so for a fact," Roberto said, then remembered something important. "By gosh, you were there too—in Missouri in the war. You must know him. Colonel Shad Jackson?"

Nash shook his head. "Not by any such name as that. I'm real interested, though, in seeing just who this feller might turn out to be."

36 · CAPTAIN NELSON

CAPTAIN ESTES NELSON FELT TUGGED IN A DIRECTION HE DID NOT want to go. He'd been having an intriguing dream featuring a mysterious woman, and he wanted desperately to get back to it.

Then, cruelly, he was awake, looking at the mahogany features of an Indian not two feet from his own face. Nelson gave a start, a strangled, powerless exclamation that did not register in any way on the face of the Indian.

"One is coming," White Owl Feathers said.

Nelson remembered Kickapoo scouts, General Sherman, the trip to Quanah Parker. "Wha—who?" he managed.

"Someone," White Owl Feathers said. "You follow."

The Indian had been there—at least Captain Nelson thought he had; then he vanished. Captain Nelson blinked twice before fumbling for boots.

When he groped his way to the perimeter, Looper was there looking grim-faced, hefting a big Sharps rifle. Half the picketed horses had their ears up and were studying the darkness to the west. White Owl Feathers and the remaining Kickapoo crouched motionless, looking off to the plains, their carbines held ready.

"Who?" Captain Nelson asked, but White Owl Feathers shushed him. So Captain Nelson crouched too; it seemed appropriate. He drew his revolver. The dark was impenetrable.

"I don't see or hear a thing," Nelson whispered.

"Old Owly Feathers says somebody's coming," Looper said around a mouthful of tobacco. "He says a bad thing's happened."

What bad thing, Captain Nelson wanted to ask. He was suddenly out of patience with scouts and Indians; he wanted to shake information out of them. Only then did he remember the missing scout, the Kickapoo named Hawk, and that Hawk's brother, called Two Horns, had gone off in search of him.

Captain Nelson looked into the darkness, but the murk offered him nothing. Looper and his Indians held motionless. Within two minutes Nelson heard a hoof scrape. Then the immense shape of a horseman loomed up so close that Captain Nelson startled badly. He cocked his revolver.

"Not shoot!" White Owl Feathers said. Looper swore. Captain Nelson stood up, his legs hollow from surprise. White Owl Feathers spoke in Kickapoo, then Two Horns, from his height on horseback, responded briefly.

Looper said, "He says white men are watching you."

For some reason Captain Nelson stepped toward the

pony. Then the oddness of the phrasing struck him. "Watching *me?* Or watching the whole detail?"

No one responded. Captain Nelson said, "Hadn't we better tell Sherman?"

"I reckon morning's soon enough," Looper said.

At that point, Captain Nelson divined that the shapeless burden slung over Two Horns' pony was a human corpse. He said, "Oh, God."

Two Horns slid from the pony and spoke again in Kickapoo. Captain Nelson looked to Looper. "He says look what happened to his poor brother," Looper said, and spat.

Some force pulled the captain toward the body on the pony. "I'll help you," Captain Nelson said. White Owl Feathers peered intently into Nelson's face, then moved out of his way.

Although Two Horns understood no English, the captain's intention must have been plain enough, for Two Horns supported his brother's body by the knees and Captain Nelson took the shoulders. Together they eased it off over the pony's rump.

Captain Nelson could feel he had most of the weight, and once he had it, he didn't know what to do with it. He guessed the main thing was to show respect for the dead. Once they'd lowered their burden to the ground, Two Horns began to turn the body over. Captain Nelson squatted and helped with that too.

When the face came around it was all chewed meat—skinless, lipless to the bare teeth, staring out of shouting, bloody eye sockets. Captain Nelson gagged and stooped over. The remnants of his supper made a false start, then surged. He vomited.

While he was sputtering for breath he heard Two Horns say something in Kickapoo, the tone matter-of-fact. Then White Owl Feathers said something. Captain Nelson, conscious of looking ridiculous, tried to straighten up, but another wave caught him, mostly an empty spasm by that time.

As he labored and spat, ghostly-skinned bare feet stepped

into his view. He looked up to see General Sherman, his face impassive.

"You're too young, captain, to have seen the war."

"Yes sir," Captain Nelson said.

"Anytime men go to fighting," Sherman said heavily, "the crows and buzzards make a damned good living."

37 · TOBY GRIER

HE WAS UP TO HIS BELLY IN NOON DINNERTIME. SOME MEN WERE just now stomping into the tavern, while others grabbed a last biscuit, then gave up their places at the tables. "I don't know whether we're running a pigsty, a soldiers' mess, or a hostelry," Toby remarked to the dark-haired girl, who laughed and smiled so nicely that it made him feel he'd said something clever.

The girl, a young woman, really, was a willing worker who made the chores normally apportioned between him and Faith go quicker. Why she helped out at all was more than Toby could see. Just so she'd have another female to talk to, Toby supposed. Well, it was fine by him.

Toby had been at the colonel's side since the middle of the war. In those early days, he'd had fewer doubts as to what they were about. It was simpler—they were Missouri bordermen. But when he looked back, he decided that had not been so straightforward a business either, for being Missouri bordermen or bushwhackers or whatever you called them amounted to being about half soldier and half cutthroat and thief. He guessed things around the colonel were always complicated.

After Appomattox, when they learned the amnesty didn't apply to bushwhackers, the colonel and his men had so-journed in Arkansas—Missouri being safe enough for little outfits like the James brothers and the Youngers but not for big bunches like the colonel's. Eventually, with carpetbag Regulators riding everywhere, half of them armed niggers, they'd had to ease over into Indian territory, from where they hit northern-owned banks and railroads and crossed back again without much trouble.

But then came the Pinkertons, book-learned men in city shoes who paid for information in hard Yankee money and soon converged on the colonel's hideouts. So now it was Texas, and Palo Duro, and damned little activity, which meant, for Toby Grier, too many men underfoot in the tavern all the time, and a lot of surly lip to put up with.

The colonel had attracted hard cases in the war, too, of course. Men like Arch Clement and Cole Younger were as hard as men came. But lately the colonel had let his standards slip alarmingly, to Toby's way of thinking—taking in, on the one hand, men who were no better than animals, and on the other, that smooth-faced son of Hollis Creigh, a kid scarce dry behind the ears. Now here was this pair of frock-coated town gents and the dark-eyed beauty with them. The fact was, Toby couldn't predict the colonel's thinking at all anymore.

There was worse, too, all combining to give Toby a sense of things going wrong. The colonel now got his affliction every fortnight at least, causing drinking spells that went on for days. It got to where Toby wondered what he'd do if the colonel were struck down one day from too much liquor. He'd surely never stay in this place. If Toby were doomed to be cook, saloon swamper, and nose wiper to hard cases, he might as well go do it amid the comforts of a town somewhere.

Toby heard the hound and then a commotion of riders in the yard. Faith said something to the dark-eyed girl—Angelina, her name was—who pivoted in something like alarm toward the tavern's front door. A scraping of chairs arose off the plank floor as men went to the windows. Toby didn't bestir himself; he supposed it was just Amos Mapes's bunch coming back from foraging on the prairies.

Then Toby was interested to see something afoot between the town gents and Angelina, for the taller one gawked out the window and then gave Angelina a look of big significance. She leaned out and looked too, then said something quiet but excited. The taller gent spoke sharply to the shorter one, who jumped up from the table. Then Angelina practically flew toward the back of the room.

"What—he can't see you in an apron?" Faith said, and snorted through her nose like she did when skeptical. Angelina stayed intent on whatever bedeviled her— Indians, maybe—and pushed right on by. When she went through the kitchen doorway, Toby said, "Can't get out that way." He chuckled when the girl's face reappeared, looking stricken. "Washtub's set spang up against the door," Toby said.

Toby had no more time to wonder about it. Spurs and boot heels sounded on the porch. The door opened on Amos Mapes, looking drag-tailed and sweated, his hair creased where his hat had been. Behind him came two or three others, then the Creigh youngster with his eyes round, looking like he was into outlawry way over his head. And then there was a tall, sun-browned man who carried familiarity with him as powerfully as a strong wind.

"Where's the colonel?" Mapes said.

"Ailing," Toby said. He jerked his head to indicate the colonel's bedroom, but his eyes never left the new man. "You going in there, it's none of my doing."

"We found a snooper down the canyon," Mapes said. "Colonel don't want nobody here without his say-so."

"Likely he'll be mad if you tell him and mad if you don't," Toby said. He scratched his neck and plumbed his memory, still bothered by the new man. Before Mapes could answer, Toby cupped a palm to one ear.

"What?" Mapes said.

"Colonel's calling," Toby said warily. "He must've got woke up by all the yapping."

When Toby turned back, it was like witnessing a facedown—the town gents and Roberto and Angelina and this new man all bristling back and forth with looks that crackled like lightning, right there in the room.

"I'd better go on in," Mapes said. He was oblivious to everything but his own problems. "Wheeler, you too."

Mapes moved on heavy boot heels toward the closed inner door, and as the new man followed him, a vista over new territory opened in Toby Grier's mind. He said, "By God—*Nash Wheeler.*"

"Howdy, Toby. How's the outlaw life?"

"A lot like being a danged cook," Toby said.

"Looks like you been sampling your own wares," Wheeler said, and nudged Toby's stomach with the back of his hand.

Mapes opened the door to the colonel's room a few inches and spoke softly to the man inside. Toby heard the rasp of the colonel's voice. Mapes said, "Another recruit," and then something Toby didn't catch.

Nash Wheeler passed by him, still lean and hard-looking as ever—if anything, harder—and with his swagger still intact after all the years.

"Mapes tell you who's in bed in there?" Toby said.

"Somebody name of Jackson," Wheeler said.

Toby laughed. He looked from Wheeler to Angelina and Roberto—in fact, he looked at all the newcomers—and he got the delicious feeling that comes from holding secrets.

"Come on in and meet the colonel," Mapes told Wheeler.

Roberto said, "I better go along and vouch for him."

"You stay," Mapes said.

Toby, who went to the colonel's sickbed no oftener than he had to, found reason to go in now. The look on Nash Wheeler's face promised to be the kind of treat a person rarely got.

He filed in with them—Mapes, then Wheeler, then Toby, who gently shut the door. The room was cavelike. The bed was a battleground: sheet and blanket twisted, one pillow on the floor. The colonel lay as composed as a corpse, his face ash gray, a cloth folded over his eyes. At the intrusion, one spindly arm hooked out and removed the cloth. Jackson's eyelashes flickered, working at sight.

Amos Mapes began an explanation, but the colonel raised a hand. On the colonel's face was an odd smile. "Nash Wheeler," the colonel said. "It's been a long time."

Wheeler's brow knuckled, as though his brain were being asked to digest a thing too big for it. His voice, when it came, whispered, "You!"

Toby chuckled, starting deep in his belly.

"You're dead," Nash said.

"Sometimes damned near," the colonel acknowledged. "But as you see, I always manage to rise again."

38 · CASS

THE TAVERN GLOWED YELLOW AT THE WINDOWS AND EMITTED THE usual evening ruckus. Cass made sure no one was looking as he crossed the yard. Then he slipped into the shack and closed the door behind him. Riley and Angelina sat flanking a single candle, their faces expectant.

"Well?" Riley said.

"I reckon anytime now," Cass said.

Cass fished out one of his twisty cigars and lit it with the candle. There was a knock. Angelina's voice issued a softly spoken challenge in Spanish. She was answered in Spanish in return. Cass drew a long revolver before opening the door, letting Roberto Creigh burst in to embrace his sister.

"You've been hurt," she said, putting a hand to his cheek.

"A fight," Roberto said. "This was so crazy of you, coming here after me."

"I just had to, for your safety."

"I don't know who to believe," Roberto said.

"First listen," Cass said, and he told Roberto how bounty men were hunting him, and that his father now wanted him to take his chances with the law. He explained about Elizabeth Barlow's reward, how the money would go—or most of it—to pay for the best Fort Worth lawyer his father could hire.

"Nash told me you'd say something like that," Roberto said, "and that you couldn't prove any of it."

"The sprout's a regular lawyer himself," Riley said.

"Believe us, not Nash," Angelina said, beseeching.

"Your pa gave us a letter of introduction," Cass said. "That would've proved it—excepting that she burned it."

"Roberto—I've traveled so far with these men. How could I be wrong about them?"

"If you're sleeping with one of them, you'd be blind to everything."

Her hand streaked out and spanked him a good one, heedless of his bruised cheek. The sound came stinging off the walls.

"Oh, mother," Riley said.

"Now do you believe me?"

"I believe I'd better stand farther away," Roberto said.

"Nash Wheeler is your enemy!" Angelina said. "He's doing this for Libba's reward money!"

"I just don't know what to think about anything," Roberto said. "According to Nash—"

"Lies! Just look at his face!"

"Look," Cass said, "if you can't trust us, then don't trust Wheeler either. That's reasonable, isn't it?"

"It's pretty much my only choice," Roberto said.

"Meanwhile, your biggest enemy might be neither Wheeler nor us either one," Cass said. It stilled everybody. "I'm talking about Colonel Jackson," Cass said. "Something big is in the wind."

"The outlaws are getting ready for some kind of action," Roberto said, "a foray, Jackson calls it. I heard he's got guards posted back in the trees with orders to shoot deserters."

"Meaning me and Cass will have to go along with whatever Jackson's planning or else get our necks stretched," Riley said. Then he added sarcastically, "But not Angelina—her being a prime specimen of southern womanhood." She made a face at him. "One thing Jackson dotes on is southern womanhood," Riley told Roberto.

"I'm afraid Riley's right on the money," Cass said. "If Jackson launches some kind of raid, we'll probably have to be in on it."

Riley said, "Wonderful," summoning his best sarcasm.

"Anyhow, that's enough gabbing for tonight," Cass said. "Jackson's men are suspicious enough as it is."

"Just look at the way that Judah Spain looks at us," Riley said. "Mapes too."

"Right," Cass said. "We'd best not get caught powwowing."

Riley said, "I'll douse the light while you both slip out."

"One moment." Holding the candle, Angelina stepped closer to her brother. "Look into my eyes and know I speak the truth about these men. You must trust them."

"That's such kid stuff," Roberto said.

"Look into them!"

He looked, his expression sobering. Then she turned and blew out the flame, slamming them into darkness. "I believe you believe it," Roberto's voice said. "But that doesn't mean I have to."

"*Idiot!*" Angelina's voice said; it was the Spanish pronunciation. Cass figured, though, as he and Roberto slipped out and quietly closed the door, that it would have meant and sounded the same in any language.

39 · NASH WHEELER

WHEN THE SULFUR END OF A WOODEN LUCIFER BURST TO LIFE, Nash applied the flame to his cigarette. The sleeping man's features squinched, protesting the sudden light, then he tried to roll to his side in the narrow bunk. Nash reached out, a kind of idle experiment, and held the blazing match inches from the man's face. The eyes fluttered, then went from sleep to terror in the space of a second.

"Christ Jesus!" Toby convulsed, his legs thrashing under the bedding. Then he delved under the pillow for whatever weapon a timid man like Toby Grier would keep—a derringer, most likely.

Nash cocked his army-size revolver. "Leave it," he said.

"You scared . . . by God, years out of me!" Toby breathed. He let his head collapse back to the rolled sheepskin he used for a pillow.

Nash transferred the match's flame to a candle at Toby's bedside. He said, "I'd keep your voice down, lest somebody took a notion we was plotting together."

"Plotting?"

"People get all kinds of notions," Nash said.

"What in the devil are you fixing on, Wheeler?"

"I'm here to tell you," Nash said. He exhaled smoke over the man in the bunk. "You must've enjoyed your little surprise today, bringing me in to see the colonel."

"You . . . you're not sore about it?"

"Sore? More like tickled to death," Nash said. "Seeing my old saddlemates after all this time, one of which I thought had been in his grave ten years. You don't know how I mourned that man."

"I'll bet," Toby said.

"Here I thought he'd went straight to heaven and taken

that eighty thousand with him," Nash said. "No angel in heaven needs eighty thousand Yankee dollars. If I ain't mistaken, a lot of it was in gold."

"You been drinking?" Toby said.

Nash pushed the gun forward, inserting the front sight into Toby Grier's chins, costing him a sharp intake of breath. "Don't playact," Nash said. "As I recall, you was at Greenville with everybody else."

"The federal payroll," Toby acknowledged. He had to grunt it.

"Progress at last." Nash eased the gun slightly out of his victim's throat. "Can you believe all these years I thought Hollis Creigh had it?"

"Creigh? I don't believe he even—"

"My mistake," Nash said. "So now here's Toby, grown in girth and grown in wisdom, sticking by his old commander down the years. I ask myself what could inspire that kind of loyalty." He prodded with the gun barrel. "The colonel ain't exactly Marse Robert E. Lee, is he?"

Toby's shrug of ignorance was barely perceptible.

"My notion is it's greed," Nash said. "The chance for a big payday."

Toby choked. Nash let off pressure with the gun barrel while his man finished coughing. Toby sat up glaring, his eyes watery.

"I'm asking flat out," Nash said. "Where's the money?"

Toby shook his head. "That's the kind of thing I don't even think about. You know him. He'd kill anyone who crossed him."

"You thought you'd wait and see if he don't die," Nash said. "Then you'd have yourself a good, long look around."

Toby tried to glare again, but outrage was leaking away from him. "Judging by your face," Nash said, "I'm damned near the mark."

"Somebody was to tell the colonel what you're here for," Toby said, "he'd string you up before you could blink."

"Somebody was to tell him that," Nash said, "I'd let on

how old Toby's been poisoning his food. Causing his broody spells, is what you've been up to."

"That's a dirty lie!"

"It hardly matters if it is or ain't," Nash pointed out. "A man who drinks as much as the colonel, he'd believe in camels and tigers."

The look of fear and vulnerability that came over Toby's face was a thing to savor. Nash stubbed his cigarette on the keg at the bedside. Then he licked his fingertips and pinched out the candle, shutting Toby Grier into absolute darkness.

"Sleep tight," Nash said. He stood up and felt his way to the door. "We'll chat again in a day or so. You'd best think up some notions about where to find that money."

40 · CASS

CASS FASTENED HIS SADDLEBAGS, THEN HE STEPPED HIGH FOR HIS stirrup and threw a leg over, joining Riley, Roberto, and the rest of them already in their saddles. It felt good to be on horseback after days of lounging around the tavern. Less good was riding out of Palo Duro in company with Colonel Jackson and two dozen misguided Confederate irregulars. A foray, Jackson had called it, enjoying his mystery. For all Cass knew, they were off to capture Texas.

When Jackson himself came onto the porch he was a picture that filled Cass's cavalryman's eye. He wore an entire Confederate officer's uniform—saber, twenty-button gray coat, knee boots and gauntlets, even a rakish plumed hat with the brim tacked up. He carried a flagstaff with the flag sheathed in satin.

Cass had hardly taken it all in when he heard hoofbeats, then three riders pounded into the tavern clearing, Amos Mapes in the lead. When they reined in, Mapes said, "Colonel, his tracks lead straight out of the canyon."

"Wheeler always was contrary minded," Jackson said. He descended the porch steps and accepted the reins of a magnificent white gelding. "If he's no longer got stomach for a fight, we are well rid of him. All others accounted for?"

"Every man," Mapes said.

Cass hooked Riley with a questioning look and kept his voice down. "Wheeler rode out?"

"Must have. Doesn't figure, does it?"

"I doubt Nash would have left without me," Roberto said worriedly.

"He'd maybe got his fill of being a Reb in the war," Riley said, and then cringed when Cass scowled at him for saying Reb. But if any of the outlaws noticed, Cass couldn't discern it.

The colonel mounted. Angelina and the woman Faith remained on the porch. Angelina had to keep up the fiction that she was waving to Riley; actually, Cass could see her farewell was mostly for Roberto.

The women were joined by Toby Grier, who came out wiping his hands on an apron. "Good hunting, colonel."

"Thank you, Toby."

"Colonel, you come back in one piece now," Faith said.

Jackson swept off his plumed headgear. "Ladies," he said, then handed the flag to a mounted outlaw with something like reverence. "Soldier, unfurl the colors."

The man pulled off the satin cover, exposing a Confederate flag that was sun-faded and ragged with bullet holes. As the light air caught it and the fabric flapped tentatively, it gave Cass a haunting feeling of the war being on again.

"Let us vow not to disgrace this hallowed banner," Jackson said.

Somebody responded, "Amen to that."

Jackson turned his mount and, for a moment, danced it. Then from his throat was reborn the savage, falsetto shriek of the Rebel yell, echoing of banshees and wolves and Comanche war cries. A half-second behind him the men took it up, till it swelled to fill the tavern yard, till Cass's back was shivered and his heart stirred, and he was moved enough by native loyalties to rise up in his stirrups and throw his voice in with them.

Over the din, Mapes called, "For-ward!" Colonel Jackson spurred to a trot, taking the lead. They fell into a column of twos, Riley with Cass and Roberto flanking the outlaw called Badger. They wheeled and, like a snake uncoiling, flowed out of the tavern yard, following the banner.

Riley looked at Cass with open disgust, then looked ahead at the trotting column, then again at Cass. "If you aren't something," Riley said. He shook his head.

"You better mind the company and button your lip," Cass told him.

"Don't think I didn't see you," Riley said, "yelling your head off with the rest of them like a bunch of danged coyotes." Cass scowled again at him, but Riley said, "This is turning into some kind of holy secessionist mission for you, isn't it?"

"It damned well is not," Cass said. "It's all playact, and you'd better start getting good at it."

Riley rode awhile without answering. Finally, he nodded grimly. "Maybe so—but you'd better appreciate it's a strain on a former Union man. Guess it could've been worse, though."

"How d'you mean?

"I was ascairt for awhile there we'd all have to sing Dixie."

41 · ANGELINA

THE KITCHEN WAS A LEAN-TO, ATTACHED TO THE MAIN STRUCTURE of the tavern like a tick to a dog. It was lighted by a mismatched pair of oil lamps, each with a glass base and a fragile glass chimney. These double points of light combined to cast shadows that loomed across the floor, struck the walls at bent angles, and waltzed and crisscrossed as the workers moved past them. They were putting away the supper dishes.

A crash behind her made Angelina jump. A three-gallon coffeepot banged across the plank floor. "Goodness!" Angelina said.

"Toby," Faith said, "you have been clumsy-handed and bejittered the livelong day. Wasn't four minutes ago you broke a bowl."

Toby grunted something as he stooped to retrieve the pot. His face came up strained, his eyes injured. Angelina wondered if he'd been drinking.

"Beg your pardon?" Faith said.

"I said I didn't wake up my right self this a.m.," Toby said. "I didn't enjoy much of a sleep."

"Likely the ruckus of Angelina and her sweetheart sporting kept you awake."

Toby set the coffeepot on the planks that served as a counter and gave Faith a collapsed, gray look.

"That's all in your imagination," Angelina said. "There was nothing worth hearing."

"Ha," Faith said cheerfully. "Anyhow, myself, I don't catch a good breath except when the gang goes off foraging like this. And then old Shad, I don't know whether I'd ruther have him up and flying off the handle or drunk abed and moaning. He's a trial either way."

Faith looked at Toby expectantly. It seemed to Angelina she was inviting him to side with her, to say something against the colonel, but Toby just looked depressed.

"You're down a hole for a fact," Faith decided. "Was we in a town, I'd fetch you a tonic. One of my girlfriends was partial to Doctor Glover's Patent Rejuvenator. Anytime she run out of it, she'd get the shakes." Faith laughed as she went into the tavern's main room, carrying freshly washed tumblers.

Toby turned a ruined face to Angelina. "You seen anything of that new man today?"

"Which?" Angelina said, but then supposed she knew.

"Name of Wheeler."

"Didn't he ride out with the others?"

Instead of answering, Toby went through the low doorway into the tavern, his round shape even rounder in his barkeep's apron. Faith's voice echoed in the big room. "Don't know what you keep expecting to see out that window, Toby. The boys won't be back for days, most like."

Angelina put away the last of the plates. Even scullery work was preferable to doing nothing. When the men came back, she and Roberto, along with Cass and Riley, would find a way to sneak out of the canyon and away from Jackson's outlaws. Until then, she wanted to keep her fingers busy.

Faith came back into the kitchen, leaned her backside against the drainboard, and looked at the cobwebbed rafters. "What a worrywart," she said. Then Toby came in carrying a bottle and a glass in the same hand. The other hand cradled a sawed-off shotgun.

"Toby, you are tetched tonight," Faith said. Toby sat on a salt-pork barrel with the shotgun across his knees and poured himself a shot.

"Tending the colonel is one thing for a woman. I expect it's even a bitterer portion for a man," Faith said, speaking to Angelina as though Toby weren't there. Angelina turned her back and poured the bucket of greasy wash water on the drainboard. She heard it run onto the ground outside, sounding remarkably like rain. There was a subject in the back of her mind that bothered her. She hunted it and found it was Nash Wheeler: where he'd gone, and why.

"Not that me and Toby tend the colonel's same needs," Faith said. She laughed a snorting laugh but was immediately thoughtful again.

"Your man Riley, now. Was I you, I'd hang onto him," Faith said. "Easy-moving like that. Never beats you. Appears like a man with good prospects."

"Prospects?"

"Outlawing can't last forever," Faith said. "Riley looks like you drop him off a roof, he'd land on his feet."

Angelina said, "I suppose that's true."

"It sure ain't none of my business," Faith said, "but he looks at you more'n you look at him. Appears the one you're after is Pretty Roberto."

To show unconcern, Angelina shrugged.

"I suppose young and comely as you are, you take men for granted," Faith said. She watched Toby pour another drink, the bottle's neck rattling against the tumbler. "Life's bitter portion comes a little later."

Angelina hung the dish towels near the cookstove to dry. She had no more reason to stay in the low-roofed kitchen, except for Faith's and Toby's company. The night was not cold, but she imagined having a fire in the tavern, just for the sake of coziness. "We could play cards," Angelina suggested. "Pass an evening just the three of us."

"I wouldn't mind it," Faith said. She regarded Toby as he drank off another shot. "Bump-on-a-log here ain't exactly being sociable."

Toby regarded her sullenly, then his head jerked toward the window. He said, "What in hell was that?"

Faith said she hadn't heard a blessed thing, but Toby shushed her. Somewhere down the yard, the hound barked.

"By God!" Toby whispered.

"Possum," Faith said.

"Shush!"

"Possum, coon, skunk—every one of 'em's night prowlers."

"Will you shut your damned yap so I can hear?" Toby picked up a lamp in one hand. He had the shotgun in the other, the buttstock elbowed tightly against his sidemeat. He went to the doorway and peeked into the empty main room. The dog barked again, sounding uncertain.

"Well he ain't barking at the tavern," Faith said. Toby went into the larger room beyond the doorway, leaving the women in reduced light. They heard him take tentative steps. Faith said, "Men and their drinking."

Angelina felt drawn toward the doorway of the main room. The bark came again, low and gruff—a muttered threat. Then the dog's voice climbed to a sharp yelp and broke off suddenly. There'd been violence in it. From behind Angelina's shoulder, Faith said, "What in the world?"

Angelina went into the main room with Faith right behind her. Toby was like a puppy on a string; he took two steps one way and then jerked around and went a new direction, then stopped again. He set his lamp on a table, then picked it up. But he kept hold of the shotgun; he hugged it like a baby.

Toby cocked both hammers and went to a front window. Faith said, "Don't you go shooting somebody, jumpy as you are." After the words died, there was no sound at all.

"Who's out there?" Toby yelled, his voice rising ragged and high-pitched at the end of it. He said, "We maybe better douse the lights."

"For pity's sake," Faith said, still skeptical.

Toby blew out the lamp and set it on a table. Then he stepped his aproned bulk onto a chair to reach for one of the hanging lanterns. There were two, the railroad kind, hanging on wire bails from the open rafters. Angelina heard a noise from the kitchen and spun to face the doorway. Two steps sounded distinctly and then Nash Wheeler filled the kitchen doorway, stooping because of his hat. His face was shining and giddy with triumph.

"Damned hound bit me," Nash said. Toby moved, his arms jerking. Nash extended a revolver to arm's length and fired.

Toby Grier was standing on a spoke-backed chair, his head a foot under the railroad lantern, so that he seemed blessed by yellow light. Wheeler's pistol ball tore through him, snatching the fabric of his vest behind him as it exited.

Toby's expression unhinged. The shotgun dropped, hitting on its muzzle and discharging one barrel, then recoiling away and causing a great concussion and billowing of smoke in the closed room. Toby, with both hands exploring his chest for the bullet hole, tilted sideways like a structure poorly carpentered. He was a big man—not tall, but meaty as a salt-pork keg; when he fell, the impact shook the tavern.

Smoke swirled like coiled rope. "Ladies," Nash said, and

touched his hat. He crossed fifteen feet of rough plank flooring. He switched his pistol to his left hand, then picked up Toby's shotgun. "Is this what you were aiming to do me with?"

Toby gasped for life. His killer directed the shotgun muzzle at Toby's belly and triggered off the second barrel. Again, the sound was a great blow to the ears, thundering off the floor and walls. Toby's legs spasmed, and then he was still. Nash shifted the shotgun in his hand so that he held it like a spear; then he launched it at one of the windows. The glass crashed out. The gun disappeared into the dark; Angelina heard it hit somewhere. In a moment, night sounds came in.

Nash stood under the lantern while powder smoke carouseled. He shifted his revolver to his right hand. He said, "You—clear out."

Faith, her face stunned, sidled along a wall.

"I mean it," Nash said. "You git."

Faith slid, keeping her back to the wall. When she was halfway down the room, she broke into running steps and was quickly through the door. The door slamming behind her caused Angelina's nerves to pulse. A cry escaped her.

"Spooked you," Nash said, and grinned. "So, little Miss Angel, daughter of my old *compadre*. Who'd've thought you'd wind up on a treasure hunt with Nash Wheeler?"

Angelina was numbed from the shooting and could not respond.

"First, though, you can hunt me up the best bottle in the house." Nash lowered himself to a chair and kept his pistol on her. "Once you've fetched that, you come here and take my britches down. Have a look where the damned dog bit me."

42 · CASS

THEY RODE EAST INTO EVENING, TILL THE SKY FLAMED BEHIND them and gradually burned out. Cass could hear the colonel's voice up ahead sometimes, but except for him, talk had fallen off to nothing.

It was after midnight when they splashed across one of the rare creeks with water in it. When they'd crossed, Amos Mapes called for a dismount. The men stripped the rigging from their horses and picketed them, then searched out bedding grounds. Cass and Riley found a spot under oak trees, leaving space for Roberto. They'd just unrolled their blankets when word was passed to form up. Riley swore and said something about it being as bad as a regular army. Cass shushed him. But Roberto, Cass could see, was big-eyed with excitement.

Cass, Riley, and Roberto assembled with the others under a pair of cottonwoods as a night breeze with a feeling of autumn in it rustled the leaves. Mapes held a lantern and called for quiet. Colonel Jackson paced in front of his outlaws, his saber drawn and flashing in the light.

"We'll bivouac till four o'clock," Jackson told them. "No fires or noises. Whether we vanquish the enemy or he vanquishes us depends on a surprise attack."

"Just who is the enemy?" one of the outlaws asked.

"I suppose it's time you knew," Jackson said. "Very well. Let me begin by saying that you men are making history. I've called this a foray. In reality it's the greatest strike for the southern cause since the end of the war." He surveyed them for a reaction. "I would be gratified to hear you cheer."

They opened their voices to it, Riley, Cass saw, right along with the rest of them, while Jackson paced, showing satisfaction. When the cheer died away, Jackson turned on a heel, his eyes boring into them. "One of you—Mr. Spain—tell me how you kill a snake."

"Me personal?"

"A poisonous viper," Jackson said.

Judah Spain was wary; one hand curried his beard. "Reckon blow its damn head off."

"Exactly. What we're about this morning is beheading the snake."

Among the men there was a shifting of weight. A tethered horse nearby whinnied and blew. Spain said, "Any snake in particular?"

Jackson took a formal stance. "Lincoln is dead, blessed be the Lord. Grant is in the White House and unfortunately out of reach. But one monster remains." At Cass's elbow, Roberto gave a wondering look.

"General William Tecumseh Sherman," Jackson said, "the Satan of Atlanta, despoiler of the South!"

Badger said, "Sherman's in Texas?"

"He sleeps not more than four miles from us," Jackson said, "guarded by a lesser force than we've got here."

From the outlaws, muttering sounded. Cass jerked his head around, wary of what could happen. Then a voice broke clear: "You mean to hold Sherman for ransom?"

"By Jehovah," Jackson said, "I mean to take an eye for an eye."

"With all respect, colonel, what's in it for us?"

Jackson went incredulous. "Why—glory, you fool! The satisfaction of vengeance." Still, some voices grumbled. "Quiet!" Jackson demanded. "Where's the spirit in you men? We are presented an opportunity of fabulous proportions."

"I reckon most of us'd druther have a payroll or a bank," an outlaw said. "Something we can split up."

"May God damn the lot of you!" Jackson thundered, and he raised his sword threateningly, till outlaws in the front rank pressed back. "You're small men, the lot of you, who can't see beyond your own pocketbooks. Sherman's death will be reported by every newspaper in Christendom, forc-

ing the world to recognize the South as an occupied nation. England will rush to aid us. France almost certainly. Beginning with the dawn, we unloose a wave that shall wash the tyrant from our midst!"

Riley leaned to Cass's ear. "Cripes, if we aren't in the soup."

"Therefore, I want to see backbone," Jackson said, "and by God, you'll show it! Anyone doing less than his duty will be summarily shot." He stood, defying them to protest. "If that's understood, then go to your beds. And by the Almighty, you'll wake up soldiers!"

He glared at them a moment longer and then stalked off, plumed hat, saber, and all. Amos Mapes was left alone in front of the men. He watched Jackson diminishing, till it seemed Mapes was more one of the outlaws than he really was an officer. "Dismissed," Mapes said, but the group was already unraveling.

Riley was swearing under his breath, but Cass wasn't worried about Riley. It was Roberto who looked hollow as a stovepipe, his eyes like a spooked horse's.

"What would Sherman be doing out here on the plains?" Roberto asked. "It doesn't make sense."

Cass shook his head. "Maybe Sherman's only here in the danged colonel's mind."

"If he's real, it sure puts us in a pickle," Riley chimed in. "Either we go along and commit treason, or we don't and get shot for it."

43 · ANGELINA

SHE HAD BROUGHT HIM A CLEAN GLASS FOR THE WHISKEY, BUT Nash had not used it, preferring to swig his liquor straight from the bottle. He'd already put down more than half of it.

Nash drank again, then got carefully to his feet. He said, "Whoa, Nelly," in mock concern at his drunkeness, then his gaze touched Toby Grier, lying murdered on the tavern floor. Nash bent, deliberately comical, to peer at the corpse's face. "Looks like Toby finds being dead mighty unexpected," Nash said, and laughed.

Angelina cringed behind the plank bar. She tried to think of what weapon the tavern might hold, but thinking was so difficult. Her mind stayed locked on Nash, as though if she focused on him strongly enough, it would hold him from her. As for guns, she could remember seeing only Toby's shotgun, the one Nash had lately thrown out a window. The pistol Riley had tried to give her was still down at the cabin.

"So, Angel—this must come as a disappointment, you winding up with an old saddle bum like me." Nash worked up a belch. "Here I bet you been saving yourself for"—the bottle weaved, seeking his words for him—"oh, some grandee's son or other."

She thought of knives, kept in a box in the lean-to kitchen. She could run in there; she'd beat him easily. But Nash, of course, had his revolver.

"Anyhow, pretty quick here, you and me are going to want our privacy." Nash set his bottle on a table, then wrestled against the whiskey fogging him to position the oaken bar in its supports, barring the front door.

"Heavyish thing," Nash said. "But we can't have you changing your mind in the midst of the proceedings. What I hear, young brides are known for it."

Angelina began sidling along the bar's length toward the kitchen doorway. She kept her eyes locked on him, her expression frozen.

"Marrying ain't given enough credit," Nash said. "Besides its other comforts, it is a slick way to come into money." He drew himself up, as though expecting to be refuted. "By God, it's how Coleman Barlow done it," Nash declared. "Time was he wasn't no more than a wild settler's sprout. Then he hitched up with Libba, and he was in clover." Nash's eyes drifted, surveying a past time. "Say, was you aware lots of men had their turn with her?"

Angelina shook her head. She wanted to keep a conversation going, keep up the pretense this was not happening. But in her terror of him, her voice would not catch.

"Before Coleman come along, there was me, there was your pa—hell, your pa had his claim staked, practically. Fact is, Cole Junior wasn't none of Coleman's at all. He was your half brother." Nash's laugh was scornful. "I'd wager hearing that is an education to your ears."

His talk was gibberish to her. She slid along the bar, gaining a half-step, a step. A glimmering in the doorway testified that a lamp burned in the kitchen. She would break for the doorway; she would dash the lamp to the floor, spreading a river of fire; then she'd get out the backdoor before he could catch her. But only if she were fast enough and Nash slowed enough, drunk enough.

"I guess your pa settled for second best on that account," Nash said, "marrying Hector Garza's little sister and getting no dowry to speak of. And here you're settling too. You don't get some landowner's boy after all. What you get is me. Things got a way of working out funny."

Nash turned to struggle with a table. She caught her breath, seeing opportunity but still gripped in indecision. He tried to move the table by pulling from one end, to further block the door. "'Course, I'm danged near a man of wealth myself," Nash said with his back to her. "If I figure right, the colonel's got money hereabouts."

She broke, running in a dream's slowness. But in six steps she was through the doorway and into the lean-to kitchen, whimpers escaping her in her panic. She heard his shout, then heard his boots—running steps pounding floorboards. She grabbed the lamp, its flame wicked, its glass base and chimney infinitely fragile. The outside door loomed, but it was barred—Nash had barred it! She turned her back to it, an animal at bay, and her cry was wrenching and hopeless.

Nash burst in, red-faced and laboring, glowering down a long revolver barrel, a fury on him. She stood with the lamp held in her two hands in front of her, expecting death's clap. She shuddered. He advanced on her, the gun wavering in his anger. Her plea came strangled.

"Speak clear," Nash ordered.

"I said shoot. Go on and shoot."

"You set that lamp down easy."

Her response was a jagged beginning of tears. Nash was nearly on her, on his face a dawning of victory. She squeezed her eyes to shut him out and felt the lamp being taken from her fingers. She covered her face and sobbed. Then his breath came hot on her ear. His weight pinned her body. His wet nuzzling began at her neck, and the whiskey reek of him was sharp and sour—a smell of vegetable rot, like corn silage, the nourishment of swine.

Angelina fought him, pummeling out blindly, but his grip prisoned her wrists. "By God," his voice growled in her ear, "you make me wrassle for it, it's going to go worse." She rammed a knee where she knew he was vulnerable. His response was galvanic: a sharp intake of breath, a convulsive stooping. She twisted from his grip and bolted for the inner doorway and the tavern's main room.

She cried out when she saw the front door—the table in front of it, the bar firmly placed—but fortune guided her. She turned, wrestled with the doorknob to the colonel's room, opened it, was through it. This door's locking bar, she remembered, hung on a swivel. She revolved it into place just before Nash rammed his weight. The door's oaken boards pulsed violently inward, but the bar held.

"Damn you!" Nash bellowed. He came at the door three times, the door shuddering, the man grunting like a rutting bull at each expenditure of force. A pause, then he crashed again, but with diminished strength. She heard him swear, heard his ragged, furious breathing. Then two gunshots exploded through the door, showering her with splinters. She cried out and sagged against the wall, sobbing freely.

Time tracked. Nash's voice said, "It's cozy in there, I'd wager," in a pretense of good humor. The sound brought her out of herself. She looked about her, finding Shad Jackson's sanctum a crypt, windowless, nearly airless. The barest strip of light showed under the door; Nash's bullet holes in the door glowed like misplaced eyes. Shapes assumed murky definition: a bed, a chair, an upended box that served Jackson as a bureau. Clothing hung from nails driven into the logs.

She crawled, then pulled herself up along the wooden box, supporting her weight against the wall. Her fingers scrabbled across the box's top, finding matches. She struggled against shaking fingers to strike one alight; she broke it, tried another. The third match burst to life, revealing objects looming starkly against their own trembling shadows. She found a bottle stoppered with a stub of candle; she touched her flame to its wick. Fire's spear point wavered, then steadied. She dared to exhale.

"You got to come out sometime," Nash's voice pointed out. "What I'll do, I'll have a nap against the door. I had kind of a big day anyhow."

She held her candle like a beacon, finding no closet, no useful detail or feature or break in the walls. The logs were adobe-chinked; the ceiling was low, without a stovepipe hole; the floor was bare pine boards, close-set.

She became systematic. She moved the chair. The bed resisted her, but by sitting with her back to the wall and her legs extended for pushing, she found she could move it. She pushed, coaxing the heavy-framed bed toward the door, wooden legs groaning a bass note on wooden floor. If she could not get out, neither would the man get in. A standoff was victory.

"You moving furniture?" Nash's voice said. "Just like a female. Move in and right away redo everything."

Then, discovery. Where the bed had been, a square, a yard on each side, had been sawed into the floorboards. One side was hinged: a trapdoor. She put fingertips to the crack, but the door was unyielding. She sought a tool, finding a tortoise-shell comb, its tines greasy from Shad Jackson's use. She wedged the comb into the crack and pried, gaining an inch of purchase. Then she got her fingers under it, lifted, laid the door open fully, releasing a dankness of earth.

She got her candle and examined, finding, instead of the underground passage she'd hoped for, merely a cavity—square, unlined, leading nowhere, a grave dug to receive a leather-bound trunk.

Before a thought could form she was leaning forward. The trunk's lid was unpadlocked and lifted easily. The trunk's odor was somberly metallic. The pay packets of waxed paper, marked U.S. PROPERTY and stuffed with federal greenbacks, meant little to her. The rows of canvas bags heavy with uncirculated gold coins were nothing she could use.

Her gaze was pulled to a miniature pistol, its barrel a snout, its grip curved to a parrot's head, with an old-fashioned offset hammer and percussion lock. Her breathing became rapt; her mind stilled to nothing. The object weighting her hand was tiny, more talisman than weapon. She brought the pistol to her candle, reading H. DERINGER, PHILADELPHIA in its iron, and in an engraved scroll, OSCEOLA. She discovered the copper gleam of a percussion cap on its nipple and understood it was loaded.

Angelina moved to the door, hearing Nash's snoring. Her boots were lace-ups, a style called the Velours Calf. She undid the uppermost eyelets of the left boot and inserted there the tiny pistol. Her trouser cuffs covered it easily.

Then she climbed into bed, Shad Jackson's bed, with its shouting memories of its former occupant. She puffed out the candle and lay back to think. For a moment, everything swirled; then her mind raced ahead of her, investigating, anticipating, discovering possibilities.

44 · CASS

CASS CAME AWARE OF MOVEMENT AROUND HIM, THEN SOMEBODY kicked his boots. Memory surged in. He lay in his bedroll among Shad Jackson's outlaws. He'd intended to sneak himself and Riley and Roberto out of the camp once they'd all bedded down, but the colonel had posted four sentries, shabby men with Winchester rifles, their eyes full of misgivings. Now here was the whole camp stirring, the lot of them poised, incredibly, to attack General William Tecumseh Sherman and a Federal escort, and it was all happening a decade too late.

Cass reflected that he'd once been Confederate to the core. Ten years earlier he would have paid for the privilege of a shot at Sherman, no matter what gun you gave him, no matter the range. Cass reasoned that whatever Sherman had been guilty of during the war, he was still guilty of now, so why not go along with Shad Jackson and do his fair share of the shooting? Cass had attacked Federals before; just because a sheepskin document proclaimed the war was over, what difference did that make?

He rolled to his side to see Riley get up onto an elbow. Ten years earlier, Cass would not have bedrolled next to a bluebelly Kentucky infantry private. To compound that novelty, this particular bluebelly had already saved Cass's hide a time or two, in various scrapes on the western frontier. Riley's eyes looked like wounds that had healed badly; he was never enthused about early rising. "Son of a bitch," Riley said, looking around in disgust. "It's still the middle of the night!"

Cass decided then that the war being over made the whole difference. He'd been Confederate and had done his damnedest, but he'd gotten outnumbered, outequipped, and in the end outlasted. Now he was Confederate no more, just Texan and American. And Sherman was not the sacker of Atlanta but the commanding general of the army. Not the Yankee army, particularly, but the plain old, gol-danged army—made up of northerners and southerners, Irishmen and whatnot, the louse-infested and underpaid army whose soldiers blew off their wages like cowboys, then straggled out on the windy plains to protect Texas from Comanches.

No sir, Cass figured, the war being over made every difference that counted. He grunted to get up. And it made a criminal of Mr. Colonel Shad Jackson.

Roberto was already bustling, rolling up his bedroll. Cass said, "You didn't sleep at all, did you?"

"I tried to."

Cass was about to say he would not have slept either at Roberto's age, with a fight due in the morning. But the dose of older and wiser in it changed his mind for him. Instead, he produced his watch. "Three hours wouldn't have helped you much anyhow," Cass said.

Roberto showed a tight face. "Cass, what do you think we ought do? I mean once shooting starts."

Cass surveyed the camp as it came alive. Hulking forms picked up guns and saddles. "Watch our chances and skedaddle if we can," Cass said. Roberto did not look reassured. "And shoot wide, if it comes to that. Don't kill anybody you'll be sorry for."

"If it was just a regular battle," Roberto said, "I wouldn't be half so scared."

"I know you wouldn't." Cass saw Amos Mapes circulating among the outlaws, scolding dawdlers. He picked up his bedroll. "Anyhow, we'd best not powwow overmuch. Stick tight to me and Riley and we'll come through all right."

In a quarter of an hour they were moving by twos, the horses stepping reluctantly in the full dark. They advanced against a thinning of night on the eastern horizon. Cass and Riley munched sandwiches of cold pork that Angelina had filched from the tavern's larder for them. Roberto, though, said he had no appetite.

Cass sensed their circling, a great arc on a radius of a mile or more, requiring a half-hour to execute. They were putting the coming dawn to their backs, and to their enemies' faces.

As they trotted, Amos Mapes came up on their right. "What we fixing to do about that army detail's Injun scouts?" Badger's voice said in the dark. "We come charging in, likely they'll give warning."

"Don't fret about them boys," Mapes said. "The colonel's got it all figured."

Cass saw Roberto's eyes widen in the half-dark. Riley's look was not much more confident.

Then Colonel Jackson was coming up, his white horse tossing its head. "We're going to snatch Sherman right off the plains," Jackson said with satisfaction. "Those bigwigs in Washington City will mess their britches when they hear about it."

45 · LOOPER

LOOPER KNELT AND ADDRESSED HIS SCOUTS IN A FLOW OF KICKA-poo that was seasoned with Spanish and English, keeping his voice low so as not to wake any troopers. The three Indians blinked their eyes open, rolled out, and picked up their carbines. It amazed Looper every time how the Indians rolled out and were ready—no bugle calls or suspender buttons or hog-bristle toothbrushes, no groping for mess kits. Looper figured if you wanted the world's truest fighter, you forgot about any kind of soldier. What you wanted was an Indian.

"Sentry see fire much south," Looper told them, pointing. "Big fire. Sentry wake lieutenant, lieutenant wake poor old chief of scouts." White Owl Feathers blinked in incomprehension. "That's me," Looper said, thumping his own breastbone. "The upshot is, we better have a look-see."

For Looper it was an oration. He spat to clear the words away. Then he mounted. The Indians slung up on their ponies, and Looper led them out of camp. It had taken half a minute.

A point of orange fire showed to the south, looking like a hot coal. Looper judged it four miles. They held their horses to a walk till the camp slipped behind them, till they could no longer smell the previous night's campfire ashes and the accumulating piles of horse biscuits.

When they rode into a low spot, the point of fire vanished. The low spot furrowed into a coulee. With his Indians in tow, Looper crossed the wash, climbed a rise, and reined in, looking out over a murky expanse of plains that was more felt than seen.

A mile to the north, the army bivouac was a light-colored swath of tents. To the south, the bonfire, if that's what it was, looked no closer than it had before. Looper cut a chaw off that day's plug of tobacco. He decided the fire was either farther off than he'd figured, or was fading out, or both. In any case, they'd have to ride harder to reach it than he'd planned on.

He set them to a ground-eating lope. Most likely the fire marked the camp of some poor buffalo runners hit by renegades—probably white-led renegades at that, meaning Comancheros, a rum bunch. Looper had tried to serve warning about Comancheros in that region; in fact, the body of Hawk being brought in by Two Horns should have clinched his arguments. But Captain Nelson wouldn't listen, explaining that Sherman didn't want to hear about renegades on this trip. Sherman had his mind set on meeting with Quanah Parker. *Huh,* Looper thought. He could pretty much picture that: two high mucky-mucks face-to-face, one Comanche and the other white, each pretending things were dandy. Any talk of renegades was likely an embarrassment to both of them.

Looper held his horse to a lope and imagined the scalped remains of buffalo runners, a grisly sight on which to begin a new day. Thinking of it, he got a bad taste and spat a line of tobacco juice. He'd warned about white-led renegades, Looper had, and had been ignored. Being able to tell Captain Nelson he'd told him so was poor satisfaction.

46 · RILEY

AMOS MAPES POINTED TO WHAT HE SAID WAS THE ARMY CAMP TWO miles distant. All Riley could define was a horizontal smudge lighter in color than the surrounding prairie. Mapes passed word they were splitting the force. All riders on the left of each pair were to swing off and follow him. Those on the right would be led by Colonel Jackson himself.

Cass got a spooked, wary look. Riley had only enough time to glance around him to see how the split would go. Then he watched helplessly as first Cass and then Roberto peeled off to follow Mapes, their horses trotting.

"Close up there," Badger said behind him. With grim-faced outlaws riding behind and ahead of him, Riley was forced to keep to the column following Jackson, a man harboring the insane notion he was leading Confederate cavalry.

Jackson may have been crazy on the grand scale, but in smaller ways, Riley saw, he knew what he was doing. The file, with orders to keep carbines from rattling, trotted to the crest of a rise and reined in. The growing light allowed Riley an impression of the dozen or so riders under Amos Mapes, now forming up a half-mile to his right.

"Unfurl the colors," Jackson ordered. The Stars and Bars was allowed its freedom in the light air.

"I want Sherman alive," Jackson said. "Killing him is a privilege I reserve for myself." His horse fought the reins. Jackson collected his mount with irritation, then whirled it, looking off to where Mapes and his men had drawn up.

"I've lived half a century for this moment," Jackson said. Then his voice vaulted with emotion. "Give 'em the rebel yell, boys! *Charge!*"

Jackson spurred and leaped ahead. Needing no urging, Riley's horse galloped off with the rest of them, the whole whooping pack heedless of prairie dog holes.

At first the riders bunched tightly, but as the horses pounded on, they began stringing out, each animal finding its own speed. Riley tugged down his hat. Beside him, Badger had drawn a revolver. Riley looked off in murky distance toward Mapes and his men, Cass and Roberto anonymous among them, seeing that they too had kicked their mounts to a gallop. Both charging lines of horsemen would strike the army camp together.

Riley's first notion was that once the firing started, he would shoot his own horse, pretending a soldier's bullet had found it. But while that might keep him clear of the fighting, he saw in other respects it was a poor plan. Even providing he weren't busted up in the spill, he'd be afoot on the plains, in no position to find Cass quickly, or to protect Roberto. The fact was, Riley could see no other option than to spur on with the rest of them, to act his part as one of Jackson's bushwhackers—and, as Cass had said, not to shoot anybody he'd be sorry for.

They galloped on, a drumming of hoofbeats, the horses' breathing beginning to labor. In the rising light, Riley made out details of the army camp: shelter halves affixed into two-man tents, a U.S. flag and a regimental guidon wafting. Then he discerned uniformed figures running, others pausing to kneel, aiming carbines.

The charging riders were at two hundred yards when the first cotton bolls of smoke blossomed from the camp. Bullets sang by. Colonel Jackson turned in the saddle, yelling something, but his words were overrun in the rumble of hooves.

Another carbine ball whined past Riley's ear. He'd been infantry in the war; he'd repulsed cavalry charges but had never been part of one. The pounding of horses, the exhilaration of speed, sent his blood to coursing. He felt the momentum of the charge taking him. He drew his revolver. Fierce cries came from outlaw throats; Riley could barely stifle a wild yell of his own.

At a hundred paces, the two wings of the attack knitted ends. They swept in, a racing wave. Ahead, carbines sputtered. On Riley's left, an outlaw rider tumbled from his saddle. At fifty yards, the soldiers became individual, moving crabbed, their faces masks of effort. The first return shots sounded from the attacking horsemen, then it rose to a salvo as the wave broke over the camp.

47 · ROBERTO

MANY OF THE OUTLAWS GALLOPED STRAIGHT THROUGH THE tents. A bay horse was caught in guy lines and fell as though heel-roped, rolling on its rider. Blue soldiers looked up into revolver muzzles and crumpled and died. The firing clapped the eardrums. The smoke built to a fog bank, without breeze enough to drift it.

Roberto, with no side to fight for, reined back at the last instant. It seemed as though every rule or law had been suspended, whether laid down by man or God. Before him, men struggled to slaughter each other, exchanging fire at a few yards' distance, standing in gunsmoke like fiends in hell.

A soldier looked up his carbine barrel, sending a bullet scorching past Roberto's ear. He whirled his mount, looking for Cass but instead finding Riley, who jumped his horse over a kneeling soldier without a hoof touching.

Roberto's enemy, Judah Spain, loomed on horseback, bearing down on a soldier caught reloading. To Roberto's amazement, Riley extended his revolver, tracked momentarily, then fired. Consternation broke on Spain's face, then he spilled from the saddle.

"Stay close to me!" Riley yelled. Roberto pulled his

revolver and spurred toward Riley, as Riley swung his pistol to bear on the same soldier he'd saved moments earlier. Roberto's head wheeled in confusion; it seemed Riley was gunning men indiscriminately.

"Surrender!" Riley commanded. The soldier let his carbine drop, his panic obvious. "Hands behind your head! Roberto, you guard him!"

Roberto heard the command like a sound heard under water. He must have sat like wood. *"Damn it—jump down and guard him!"* Riley yelled. "Hold a prisoner in front of you and you both might get through!"

Roberto swung down; he was moving dazed, unable to tell if his feet touched ground. Riley slid out of his saddle, pulling his Winchester from its scabbard in the same motion. Outlaw riders broke through roiling smoke, then were swallowed again. Roberto gamely pointed his revolver at the prisoner, then saw the man was Roberto's own age, and shaking with terror. Roberto was shamefaced. He let the hand holding the revolver drop to his side.

"You all right?" Riley demanded. Roberto nodded. Riley looked at him, his concern obvious.

"I'll be fine," Roberto said. Riley turned and raised his rifle. He steadied on a distant outlaw and fired, knocking the man from his mount.

"Somebody sees you do that, we'll be skinned!" Cass yelled. He emerged, tall on horseback, from a hell of powder smoke.

Seeing both Riley and Cass calm in the center of battle made Roberto feel steadier. He saw it was as though they were doing a job. He took his prisoner by the arm, guiding him. "Don't worry," Roberto told him, though the young man looked spooked to his boots. "We're on your side."

Roberto came aware that the firing was dropping off, leaving a howling of rebel yells.

"Stick tight to that prisoner," Cass said, "else he'll likely be slaughtered." Riley, with his mouth set tight and his Winchester held in front of him, helped Roberto march the prisoner toward the center of camp. The smoke was thinning; in many places, the dawning sun slashed through it. Seconds later, a breeze stirred and the smoke drifted off, so that Roberto beheld the entire camp: tents flattened, loose horses still caught up in fright, men in various combinations of uniforms and underwear being herded at gunpoint.

A new surge of outlaw voices accompanied the hauling down of the Stars and Stripes. In its place, the Stars and Bars ascended the camp flagpole. Roberto perceived a general pulling toward that vortex, a movement of men on horseback and afoot toward the Confederate flag. The prisoner Roberto and Riley were herding drew Amos Mapes's attention. "We got us a bluebelly," Riley told him.

"Good work," Mapes said. "Take him up to the colonel."

48 · LOOPER

LOOPER LED HIS KICKAPOOS FOUR MILES BY HIS RECKONING. THEN he reined in, studied the southwest, and admitted he no longer saw the bonfire. He figured the flames had burned themselves out.

"Fire lies that way," White Owl Feathers said, pointing with an army carbine. He commanded scant English, but what he had he liked to trot out when he could.

"No sir, it was thataway yonder." Looper pointed with his own rifle. The discrepancy was eight or ten compass points, a considerable margin of dispute between plainsmen.

Looper scratched his chin whiskers. He hated to disagree with an Indian about anything under nature's dominion, whether it was animal tracks or directions or what was likely in the way of tomorrow's weather. The fact was, he hated to disagree with a redskin over anything more consequential than a presidential election, Indians being well known as oblivious to politics. But Looper was no tenderfoot; he'd spent half his life on the plains. He figured he knew where that bonfire had been, whether Indians backed him up or bucked him. The bonfire had been thataway yonder.

"That way," White Owl Feathers repeated, jabbing his rifle vigorously. Glumly, Looper disagreed. Two Horns said something in Kickapoo and pointed in the same direction White Owl Feathers had. Then young Blade piped up, speaking his own piece. The Indians powwowed in Kickapoo a moment, so vehemently and rapidly that Looper followed only half of it. Then, and with his satisfaction evident, White Owl Feathers pointed again. His estimate of the correct direction had not altered by the thickness of an arrowhead.

Three to one, Looper noted, and leaned out and spurted tobacco. He looked to the horizon, first in the direction he thought they should take, then in the one supported by the Indians. While he was looking in this second direction, movement showed. In a moment, the moving objects resolved into a pair of riders. Looper watched in some amazement, making out one man in a high-peaked Mex sombrero and the other in a flat-brimmed cattleman's hat. The riders were leading pack horses, coming on at a brisk walk and making steady progress.

A disadvantage of riding with Indians was you were all too likely to get shot at. Most whites, and Mexicans even more so, didn't care to see an Indian except over a set of buckhorn sights. Looper considered it hardly improved matters that his own Indians were Kickapoos, freshly pacified by no less a personage than Ranald Mackenzie. Once they unlimbered their rifles, few frontiersmen made distinctions.

Looper peeled off his bandanna and tied it to his Sharps barrel. It was a blue bandanna, but he figured his intent to parley would show clear enough. He trotted out in front of his Indians, then stood in his stirrups and waved the bandanna. The two riders stopped their progress. Looper saw them unshuck rifles from their saddle scabbards.

"Hold your fire!" Looper yelled, and tick-tocked the rifle

barrel over his head with vigor. Then he turned and called to Two Horns, who was apt to be unpredictable. "It ain't likely these two kilt your brother," Looper said, then repeated it in Kickapoo for good measure.

The riders stopped on the far edge of hailing distance. "Friend or foe?" one yelled.

"Army," Looper hollered. "J. Looper, chief of scouts. Attached to Eighth Cavalry." He saw the riders consulting. "We're coming up!" Looper yelled. He encouraged his mount and his Kickapoos fell in behind him.

"Morning," Looper said when the distance had closed. He got cool nods in return, but at least the men weren't shooting.

"Cattlemen?" Looper asked; to his eyes, they had a cowman look. The Mexican glanced at the other one, a fellow with a jutting stub where one leg should have been. The war, Looper figured automatically.

"Just traveling," the one-legged man said. "We've seen your tracks. About twenty riders with army horseshoes, a few mules, and a wagon."

"That's us," Looper said. "Seen anything of a fire down your way this morning?"

Again, the riders consulted with looks. The white Texican said, "Damnedest thing. Somebody poured coal oil on a creosote bush. We rode up expecting burnt-out wagons and found nothing more than a blackened piece of ground."

In his surprise, Looper let a trickle of tobacco juice get down the wrong way. He coughed till his eyes watered. Then, with his expression probably gawking wide enough for everybody to laugh at, he looked at the Kickapoos, who, being Indians in white men's presence, showed no reaction. Then he looked at the Mexican and the one-legged Texan. "Damnation!" Looper squawked, with his voice still choky from juice down the wrong pipe. "I believe I just been euchered by renegades."

He turned to look in the direction from which they'd come. And as he looked, there came a distant rattle of small arms fire. Beside him, the Indians stiffened.

"What is this shooting?" the Mex said.

"Why—I can't hardly credit it," Looper said. "Somebody's attacking my army boys."

The one-legged man said, "Sounds like a hell of a fight."

Looper eyed the newcomers' Winchesters, then the stump of the Texan's leg. He thrust his own rifle into his saddle boot to secure it for fast riding. He figured a quarter-hour, alternating a lope with a gallop, would bring them back to the army camp. "I kind of hate to ask," Looper said, "but you fellers wouldn't be game for a fight?"

The one-legged man said, "Hector?" The Mexican shrugged. "Appears we're going in your direction anyway," the one-legged man said.

"I'd be obliged," Looper said. He leaned out and spat his whole wad; he didn't want to go swallowing it while they were hard riding.

"You say renegades?" the one-legged man asked.

"One kind or another," Looper agreed. He reined his horse around. The firing was louder, a steady crackle to the northeast. "I couldn't say whether they're red or white or some of both."

"We have many times fought each," the Mexican said, like it was all the same to him.

"You just lead on," the other said. "If I drop behind on account of this leg, you save me a couple targets."

"That I will do," Looper promised. He dug spurs to his mount and they started off running, seeming to race their tall morning shadows across the grass.

49 · ROBERTO

THE FIRING DROPPED AWAY, LEAVING AN EERIE QUIET. ROBERTO heard the moans of injured men. When an outlaw fired a final shot, dispatching a wounded horse, Roberto's nerves all jumped at once. He heard somebody tell Amos Mapes that six of their own men had been hit. Roberto saw one who lay on the ground holding his belly, thrashing his legs and crying out hideously. He counted the bodies of eight soldiers down and no longer moving. Several others lay wounded. An officer sat on the ground and nursed a leg wound. But if the commanding general of the U.S. Army were among the shattered detail, Roberto did not see him. He figured the outlaws must have shut him up in the ambulance.

Cass whispered that if they saw a clear chance, he, Riley, and Roberto would hightail it out of there. No horse could outrace a rifle bullet, however; and the army camp sat flat on the plains. Cass said he figured that, at least for that day, they were fair caught. Come nightfall, he and Riley would do what they had to to get them away.

Riley herded his prisoner into a grouping of other captured soldiers. Then he and Cass stood nearby with their rifles crooked, standing so carelessly that it appeared they were only passing the time. Roberto understood, though, that they preferred to do as much of the guarding as possible, not trusting the outlaws, some of whom looked ready to shoot the captured soldiers on the spot.

Others among the outlaws were more interested in booty. Some were ripping through the soldiers' tents, stealing whatever they could find. Colonel Jackson strode about in tall boots, shouting orders in a voice lifted with elation. He was particularly pleased to have captured a news correspondent. At Jackson's demand, the reporter was pressed into writing a description of the fight, a job at which he sweated with a shaking hand, adjusting his spectacles constantly and never looking up.

"Damned shame there's no photographer to record this moment," Jackson said.

"Yes, sir," the correspondent said.

Jackson adjusted the set of his hat. "I believe it's time, Mapes. Let's bring him out."

"Uh-oh," Riley said. He stepped closer to Roberto but kept his face averted. "I don't like the looks of this."

Cass nodded agreement. He was studying the sergeant-major, who appeared able enough to make a useful ally, providing Cass could convince him they were not part of the outlaws.

Amos Mapes drew a revolver and stepped to the ambulance door. He said only, "Get out here."

The door swung open uncertainly, and then a figure Roberto understood to be William Tecumseh Sherman stepped onto the prairie sod. Roberto had expected a sputtering tin general; instead, Sherman was cool and grim-eyed, fitting Roberto's notion of a horse trader. Under prodding from Mapes's pistol barrel, Sherman moved toward Colonel Jackson—but moved warily and on his own terms.

Jackson stood in brushed Confederate officer's uniform, black knee boots and plumed hat. Sherman was barefooted, wearing blue army trousers and an ordinary undershirt. He walked to within six feet of Colonel Jackson and surveyed him with contempt. "Who in bloody hell might you be, sir?"

"Beg your pardon, general, but you're a prisoner of the Confederate States of America. I'd advise you to show your captors proper deference."

"I'll not defer to murdering trash," Sherman said. He scanned the outlaws, his gaze touching Roberto, then passing on. "The lot of you will hang for this. The soldiers you killed were protecting Texas."

Jackson expelled a skeptical breath. "Speaking of hanging, I'd thought to hang you. But there seems to be a scarcity of trees hereabouts. Instead, you'll die by fire. A fitting end for the Satan of Atlanta."

"I'll be judged by God for my actions," Sherman said, "not by the likes of you."

"True enough," Jackson said. "And today, I'm the Lord's avenging angel. Mapes, have that ambulance doused with coal oil."

"Right away, colonel."

"Now then, as for the identity of your captor, my men know me as Jackson, a name I assumed at the war's end, in honor of the great Stonewall. With this victory, such deception is no longer required." Roberto heard surprise rippling among the outlaws. The colonel looked about him, for the second time in a few hours savoring a surprise.

"It takes a coward to ride under false colors," Sherman said. Instantly, Jackson lashed out, a gauntleted hand raking Sherman's face, felling him to one knee.

"Mister, I know you for a madman and a traitor," Sherman said. "You desecrate a uniform that was worn with honor by thousands. Beyond that, I'm no longer curious."

"You shall know the name of your executioner because it gives me pleasure that you shall know it," Jackson said. "Let history record that William Tecumseh Sherman, the most monstrous fiend ever to flourish on this continent, was sent screaming to perdition at the hand of Colonel Benjamin Poole, First Missouri Mounted Irregulars."

Roberto felt mule-kicked. Riley gave him a look with the same incomprehension a fence post might give you. Sherman's brow furrowed to understand. The colonel stood smiling.

"I'm known as Bloody Ben Poole by some," the colonel said mildly. "It's an appellation I'm not ashamed of."

Sherman shook his head. "Poole was killed in sixty-five."

"On the contrary, he stands before you."

"By God," Riley said.

Colonel Poole, called Bloody Ben, looked around at gaping outlaws. "Mapes, I doubt even you suspected. Nor, I believe, does my Faith. It was my and Toby's little secret. Ah, and here's young Roberto Creigh, as astonished as the rest. It's fitting you're here, for your father, my old captain, discovered the man we left dead to serve as my corpse."

Roberto felt eyes shift to him. He managed to say, "My pa . . . ?"

"Missouri was becoming risky," Poole said. "In the East, whole Southern regiments were surrendering. But the damned Federals would not allow it of guerilla units. They branded us criminals! They hanged brave soldiers from trees!" Poole brandished his saber in Sherman's face. "I was not even recognized as part of the Confederacy—by an enemy I had fought for *four long years!"*

"Nor should you have been," Sherman said. "Your prey was mostly innocents."

Poole nodded in satisfaction, a man hearing his grievances confirmed. "So this boy's father brought me a man—a farmer with Union loyalties. The resemblance was strong. After mutilation of his features, it was perfect. We ruined a splendid Confederate officer's uniform while shooting him up as we did, but it served our cause well."

Behind Roberto, the sergeant-major said, "You creeping bastard!"

"Sergeant, you've got a disrespectful mouth," Poole said. "Once our honored guest has danced for us, I'll shoot you myself."

"This is insanity," Sherman said. "The war's been done with ten years."

"Done with?" Poole said, incredulity making his voice tremble. *"Done with?* By the Almighty, that war never ended *at all!"*

"You're mad," Sherman said.

But Poole turned from him. "Enough talk. Mapes—shut him in the ambulance!"

"At least spare these other men," Sherman said. It caused Poole to pivot and study him, reappraising. "Most of these troopers were too young for the war," Sherman said.

"I'll admit I'd hoped to find you a cringing coward," Poole said. "But it's no matter—I've executed brave men before. Someone prepare a torch."

It was then, with sickening pressure building in Roberto's chest and his head hollowing with the unreality of it, that he noticed the riders. They were hundreds of yards out, a line of them, pitifully thin against the sweep of the plains but coming on at a fast lope and making straight for the army camp.

Roberto hooked Cass, indicating, with his eyes alone, his interest in the south plains. Cass snuck a look, his face going questioning, then he nudged Riley. Within seconds, some of the soldier-prisoners were looking off to the south as well.

"If Sherman tries to break out, shoot his legs," Poole ordered. Roberto glanced back to the ambulance. An outlaw stood on its roof, pouring clear liquid over the whole vehicle.

"Amos," Colonel Poole said, "the torch."

"Colonel!" An outlaw gestured excitedly. "Riders, colonel!"

Bloody Ben Poole shaded his eyes. Roberto saw that the riders, six of them, were still a long rifle shot out, but their pace had not flagged.

"Fetch my glass!" Poole commanded. An outlaw jogged obediently to Poole's horse. Cass slid an eye to the pile of captured army weapons, among them a number of ammunition belts.

Poole was handed a telescope. He extended the instrument and peered at the horizon. "Merely a distraction," he said, then passed the telescope to Mapes.

"Looks like Indians," Mapes said, with his face twisted in concentration. "Some of them, anyhow."

"No doubt the scouts we decoyed," Poole said. "Very well—we shall deal with it. Keep three men on Sherman."

Cass elbowed Riley, then he said, "We're holding the prisoners for you, colonel," loud and eager, like he was the brightest-eyed outlaw in the bunch.

"Good," Poole said. "If they show resistance, shoot to kill. The rest of you, form skirmish line!"

At the command, general movement broke out. Outlaws jogged to form a rank. Cass pulled his revolver and passed it to the startled sergeant-major. "Trust me, damn it," Cass said. "We're no part of these men."

Taking the cue, Riley handed his own revolver to a likely looking soldier. Roberto gave his to the captain with the leg wound, then pulled his Winchester repeater from his saddle scabbard. He hefted the rifle's weight and was grateful for the clear feeling that flowed through him: this time he knew what he was fighting for.

"Once I shoot, you get Sherman out of that ambulance," Cass said quietly.

The sergeant-major stretched a grim smile. "A pleasure, mister."

Riley said, "When the ball opens, you enlisteds break for that pile of carbines."

"I don't generally back-shoot," Cass said. "But if ever there was a time for it . . ." He was squint-eyed, gauging events. Poole's outlaws were kneeling, already aiming at the incoming riders. Colonel Bloody Ben Poole was poised, sword aloft.

Cass threw his rifle to his shoulder and shot an outlaw. The man arched his back in agony, then toppled. When the riflemen in the skirmish line turned in confusion, Riley and Cass levered shots into them. Roberto slung up his rifle and fired, knocking down an outlaw. With a yell, the knot of soldier-prisoners burst forward to reclaim their carbines. One soldier was cut down just as he reached a weapon, but the others armed themselves, tripped open breeches, and thrust cartridges home. The first sharp cracks of Springfields sounded.

Roberto felt a bullet tug his sleeve. Riley, kneeling beside him, was a demon on a repeating rifle, dropping outlaw after outlaw with a half-dozen shots. Poole's men, caught in crossfire, had momentum against them. From their front, the six riders were charging, firing rifles one-handed. From their rear, Winchesters mowed, augmented by the heavier Springfields.

"Fight, you shiftless cowards!" Poole's voice cut through the bedlam. Cass saw his saber whip down to slash one of his own men. But despite Poole's efforts to rally them, the outlaw skirmishers broke and ran, though the plains offered scant protection. Then Roberto beheld a vision: his uncle Hector loped in to run down an outlaw, then finish him with a revolver shot.

Riley levered a fresh cartridge and toppled a running outlaw. Some few of Poole's men managed to mount their horses, but at least half were spilled from their saddles before they could get away.

Roberto coughed from powder smoke. He saw Bloody Ben Poole drop his saber, grab up the reins to a magnificent white horse, and mount. Poole pulled an army revolver, then jerked the animal around and fired three times at the ambulance. Reports pounded in reply out of the swirling smoke, but with no effect that Roberto could see.

Someone had set the coal oil to blazing; from around the army ambulance, black clouds unrolled. The sergeant-major wrenched the door open, and the commanding general of the army scuttled out, red-faced from the fire's heat, looking highly relieved to breathe free air.

But when Roberto looked back at the heart of the fight, Bloody Ben Poole was spurring his horse. He crossed the camp in five strides, making for the open plains. Riley threw his Winchester's lever, sank to one knee, and steadied, but the hammer fell on an empty chamber. A couple of soldiers sent carbine bullets after him. Poole, however, galloped unscathed.

"Count on him to save his skin," Cass said. As Roberto watched, two other outlaw riders altered course, joining their fleeing leader.

"Looks like Mapes, too," Riley said. "Dang it. Heading back where we just came from."

50 · CASS

ROBERTO CREIGH'S REUNION WITH HIS FATHER AND UNCLE WAS something Cass felt obliged to look away from. He figured the scrape they'd just come through had been close enough that, had he a pa still on this earth, he would have hugged him too.

"Your boy turned out a hell of a scrapper," Riley told

Hollis Creigh. "Fighting must run in the family." Creigh struggled to say something, maybe that he'd never doubted it, but right then, emotion prevented him.

Garza, though, immediately wanted to know about Angelina. His eyes slitted when he was told she had remained in the outlaw camp. Riley gave Cass a look, the one that meant his mind was made up. He said, "I'll fetch our pistols back."

Cass figured because Riley and Angelina had been sweethearts, at least in some degree and for a little while, that Riley was feeling responsible. The truth was, Riley Stokes had a soft spot for innocent parties generally.

For once Cass didn't argue. He sucked a breath and called loudly for the best judge of horseflesh in camp to pick him out a pair of fast mounts for the run to Palo Duro. Sherman protested, arguing that capturing Poole and rescuing innocents was the army's job, but in the excitement no one paid him much attention. Cass pointed out that Sherman's detail had dead to bury, wounded to tend, and prisoners to guard. He said it looked like the soldiers had their hands full.

"Pa says when it comes to judging horses," Roberto said, "he'll pit Uncle Hector against any man in Texas." At that, Garza got a grave and honored look and strolled about the camp, appraising animals like he was there for an auction. He was back in a minute, leading a bay gelding and a black mare. Cass saw both were Halfmoon horses, and he nodded his appreciation.

The sergeant-major, whose name was Bricker, bustled up with a pair of troopers carrying saddlebags and canteens. "You'll be needing rations," Bricker said. "Oats for your animals, too."

"Robbie's exhausted," Creigh said, "but I'm going with you, and I don't want to hear argument."

Cass avoided glancing at the stump of leg. He looked Creigh in the eyes. "You'd slow us."

"Damn it, man—she's my daughter."

"All the more reason to think of her welfare," Riley said.

"You saw the horse Ben Poole rode out of here. Probably thoroughbred. Cass and I are going to need all the speed we can muster."

Creigh's face sagged, and he looked away. In a minute, he said, "In any case, we're forgetting there's a wild card in all this. Nash Wheeler."

Riley threw in that they'd seen Wheeler in Palo Duro but that he'd weaseled out of joining the raid on Sherman. "Looked like he hadn't the sand for it," Riley said.

"Nash Wheeler's got sand enough for anything," Creigh said. "Besides which, Libba Barlow offered him half the BR Ranch if he'd bring Robbie back across a saddle."

Cass shrugged. "You heard Riley. Wheeler rode out."

"It doesn't square," Creigh said. "Nash would have stuck tight to Robbie."

Cass fiddled with a saddlebag, aware the sun was climbing. "All the more reason you and Garza ought to stay here with Roberto," Cass said. "Protect him in case Wheeler's got some move in mind." He let his eyes rove the plains. "He's maybe out there watching his chances right now."

"I suppose it's possible," Creigh said. Cass saw him reach some conclusion, then, reluctantly, step back, giving Cass room to mount.

Riley swung up. "You ready?"

"I guess I have to be."

"Good luck," Creigh said, and Garza said, "Go with God."

Cass set spurs to the long-legged bay Hector Garza had chosen for him and led Riley at a lope. After a few hundred yards, he looked back, seeing the smoke of breakfast fires. Somebody had replaced the American flag on its pole, and the morning breeze exercised it.

A half-hour of steady loping put the army camp out of sight, but it did little to alter the western horizon. Riley pulled his mare to a walk, letting her blow, then took the reins in his teeth to free his hands for digging into a towsack. He said something, but the reins ruined his pronunciation.

"Come again?"

"Jerked beef," Riley said. He made a face.

"Beggars and choosers," Cass said. "Et cetera."

"I could just as well have eaten the danged reins," Riley said. With his teeth, he tore off a chunk of beef, making a show of its toughness.

"Tough or not," Cass said, "I wouldn't turn down a bite of it." Riley handed over a piece, saying it looked like dried-out harness leather.

"You'll admit we're getting off the trail here," Cass said.

"Off the trail, my foot. Jackson's tracks lead—"

"I mean of our sixteen hundred dollars. All we bargained for was fetching Roberto back to his pa. That job's done."

"What—you'd leave Angelina to those wolves?"

"I'm only saying from here on out it's your venture," Cass said. "You been blaming me the whole trip. At this point, we're doing your good Samaritan work."

Riley chewed thoughtfully. "This is actually tenderer than reins or harness leather. It's more in the category of boot tops."

"Riley, you are dodging the issue."

"You're saying I'm saving her hide only on account of I got tangled up with her," Riley said. "One time."

"It's one more time than I did," Cass said.

"Hells bells—was I off someplace else, you'd go after her yourself, you know you would. You are not quite the money-grubbing, nickel-plated son of a bitch you like to make out. Close, but not quite."

"Very much obliged," Cass said. "But I'm saying you owe me for going. Once we're out of this, I'm treating myself to a hotel room and new shirts and fancy meals, and it's coming off the top of the sixteen hundred, not off my split."

"That's agreeable."

"And all the days of poker playing I feel like without you pestering me nor getting antsy."

"All right," Riley said.

Cass blinked; he could hardly believe it. Even so, it was

his style to try to sweeten any deal. "And by gol, something else too."

"Don't push it," Riley said.

"Something big," Cass said.

"The day's wasting," Riley said. He swigged from his canteen to wash down the jerked beef. He wiped his mouth with the back of his hand, and then kicked up his horse to a lope again, going on ahead. Fact was, Cass saw, it was more of a gallop.

Then Cass thought of it: what he wanted from Riley. Just the thing. It was perfect.

"Hey!" Cass hollered, but at the rate Riley was riding, Cass might never get to name it.

51 · NASH WHEELER

"YOU SHOWED GOOD SENSE GIVING UP LIKE YOU DONE," NASH said, but she went on walking, a body with its mind dead, down the tavern steps, the bags weighting her arms and rounding her shoulders. He hadn't expected an answer anyway. She tied a bag with twine. He hefted it on the horse. They made another trip.

"Another hour and I would've burnt the place down and you in it," Nash said. "All this pretty gold would've melted. It'd still be gold, though. That's one thing about it—you can't ruin it. All you can do is lose it, or else somebody else takes it."

They went for the tenth or twelfth trip into the bedroom, seeing Bloody Ben's mess of a bed. "Every time we come in, you're ascairt I'm going to rape you." He took her by the shoulders and rotated her toward him. "Ain't you?"

It was getting infuriating, the glassy eyes, the not answering. He slapped her. For a moment, the eyes flared up and fixed him. Then they were flat eyes again.

When he released her, she got her two bags and hefted them with difficulty, the weight making the veins prominent in her wrists. "You can ease your mind," Nash told her. "With this kind of money to nursemaid, old Nash can stand to be a buck nun awhile longer."

He laughed, hurting himself on account of his whiskey head. He made her back away to the room's corner while he caught two bags around the necks with one hand. The other hand had the job of holding the revolver.

"Just like the other times," Nash said. "Easy does it." They went through the tavern's common room, past old dead Toby. In two more trips they had all the coins and currency. Some of Ben Poole's journals and other junk Nash left in the bottom of the trunk. Then inspiration struck him.

"Turn your back."

She regarded his gun, then him. "You'll need me to lead one of the horses."

Nash said, "Hell, I know that." There was a pleasure in having a living thing so completely in his thrall—and a damned beautiful thing at that. "I ain't shot you yet, have I? Just turn your damned back."

She complied. He fumbled at his pants buttons. It took him a moment, what with her standing there, but then his stream arced in front of him. She startled at the sound when it first hit, spattering into the bottom of Colonel Bloody Ben's trunk, wetting the journals and other papers. Nash laughed as he did it.

"What's old Ben going to think of that, huh? Come on, let's get this last stuff draped over the horses."

They started, each leading a horse. The only other horse remaining in the corral was her own animal, a gelding she called Lobo. She said he was lame, that she'd barely made it to Palo Duro on him at all. Nash figured she was lying, under some idiot notion she was saving the horse, but he could hardly take the chance that the horse might lame up on him. As she described it, the trail leading up the walled sides of Palo Duro figured to be treacherous enough without either of them having to lead two horses.

"If he's that lame, you won't mind if I shoot him," Nash said.

"You shoot him," Angelina said, "and I'll sit down right here."

"You would." Nash laughed, again hurting his head. "Hell, I wouldn't put it past you."

As they passed the corral, he tugged the gate open, figuring if her gelding wanted to browse, let it. They went out together, each leading a heavily loaded horse. He reckoned thirty-some thousand was packed on each animal, making them the prettiest damned four-leggeds he'd seen or ever would see. Compared to them, a half-blood *señorita* wearing men's clothing was downright homely.

52 · BLOODY BEN

A FULL CYCLE TURNED, DAY TO NIGHT TO NEW MORNING, BEFORE the rider pounded through the shallow, indeterminate beginnings of Palo Duro Canyon. As he rode, he admired his own pacing shadow: the smoothly laboring horse surmounted by the rushing rider, the plumed hat, the cavalryman's cape sweeping behind like wings. It was a picture he appreciated—a picture of the cavalier.

That the hunter was once again the hunted was no setback to him. He had been hunted all through the war; here, he had the vastness of the western plains in which to elude his enemies. At his mind's core, he was undefeated, his mission only postponed. That his enemy still lived was, unexpectedly, an exhilaration—for if Sherman lived, then Poole's hatred survived as well, and with it, the potency of who and what Ben Poole was.

He reined in. The horse's blood was up with the thrill of the run, but Poole snubbed its tossing head. Then it wanted water from Prairie Dog Town Fork, but Poole held it back. They had miles yet to run; water now might founder it.

With the gelding's barrel heaving under him, he studied his backtrail. The riders dogging him topped a rise and started down. They had slowed him; Poole had waited for them several times, letting them draw within a quarter-mile before he loped off again, his horse clearly superior. Though their identities were still closed to him, he suspected one was Mapes, who was canny enough to have saved himself. They had slowed him, but having a couple of fighters still answering his commands might well prove useful.

Poole used the pause to punch empty casings from his revolver. He refilled the cylinder, then eased the hammer down between loaded chambers—a dangerous practice, but these were dangerous hours. The men were coming up now. He smiled to recognize the forward rider, Amos Mapes sure enough, riding hatless. The trailing rider was a big lout of a youngster called Willie Lock.

Poole snapped shut the loading gate and holstered the revolver. The riders reined in, horses' forelegs banking up dust. Then riders and horses labored for breath while the same dust overtook them. Before he spoke, Ben Poole noted Mapes carried his revolver drawn.

"You men guard this entrance," Poole said. "I've got my papers to fetch from the tavern. I'll rejoin you on my way out."

Mapes broke into a tight grin. Strangely, he said, "How do we know you won't slip out the side trail and leave us to do the fighting?"

Poole blinked. *"What?"*

"Finding out you're Ben Poole," Mapes said, "I mistrust you even more'n I used to."

Poole looked at this new Amos Mapes, the grin set lopsided, verging on a sneer. Again Poole noted the unholstered revolver. It was a lot to take in, and he was still more surprised by it than furious. "By God, this is *insubordination!*"

Mapes shrugged. "There ain't hardly time to horsewhip me. You ain't got enough help in any case."

Poole shifted his glare to Willie Lock, who wilted, not having much iron in him. Poole fixed Mapes. "All right, Amos, what is it you want?"

"The outfit's shot to smithereens, and the army's probably trailing. Things have went to hell generally. So me and Willie are through playing soldier. I figure best we all skedaddle like three pards. Even steven."

"You figure."

Mapes nodded. "I figure, too, we're owed a share of whatever you're going back to the tavern for. It for damn sure ain't papers. Toby's cooking, neither."

"Of a sudden you're quite fond of figuring."

"I been right along," Mapes said. "Anyhow, we'd do better scratching each other's back than each other's eyes out."

Poole fixed Lock again. "You fond of figuring too?"

"I feel same as Amos," Lock said.

Poole smiled. So they'd put their heads together; for the moment, so be it. New men were recruited easily enough, and those no longer useful were disposed of just as readily. Ben Poole had recognized early in the war that in any great undertaking, men came cheap.

"We won't discuss it further," Poole said. He wheeled his mount, which came around unwillingly, having its mind still fixed on water. He set them a lope down the canyon path, past the first narrowing and the better grass where the stream meandered. He thought: the fools, for there was no chance he would let them live once they'd seen the payroll money. More reliable would be Toby and Faith, still waiting at the tavern, although neither a fat cook nor a woman would be essential to him either, not once they'd helped him haul the money out of Palo Duro.

By the time he led them off the main trail and pounded up the side canyon, the sun was nooning and shadows squatted. Breezes were banished by sheltering rock. The day hung expectant.

The buildings hove in sight. As they reined in, Poole

shouted for Toby. Strangely, no one came onto the tavern porch. Poole swung down in the yard, with Mapes and Lock right behind him.

Mapes said something about the tavern, but Poole, caught in the strangeness and silence of the place, didn't follow it. Poole draped his reins over the hitching post and took the steps double. The tavern's interior was a battlefield of tables upended, chairs on their backs like dead animals. Toby Grier lay with his stomach mounded above him and his mouth open. His eyes were fixed a hundred miles up, appearing absorbed in counting seraphim.

Mapes and Willie Lock pushed into the room. Mapes said, "Bloody Jesus!"

Poole windmilled in knee boots toward his private treasure, hearing Mapes running behind him. The bed had been shoved against a wall. He stuck a knife point under the trapdoor and swung it wide. The trunk was there. He grabbed the haft and lifted, and was struck by the astringent, pickled smell of urine. A few of his journals lay sogged in the bottom. There was not a gold coin or a scrap of Federal currency.

Poole arose, at first tentative. Then he kicked the bed in a fury. He was Bloody Ben Poole, the one man bold enough to strike when circumstances offered a target. He was the South's last warrior, and he was stymied by *imbeciles!* He hollered, "Faith!" then noted the irony of her name.

"By God, you kept the whole payroll," Mapes said, startled. Poole looked through him, his mind far ahead. "The damned Union payroll from Greenville!" Mapes said, getting his whole voice behind it. "I heard about it, but I figured Yankees got it."

"I spent nothing on myself!" Poole said. "I supported the southern nation and that was all! I could have sailed to Europe, do you understand that? I could have been the toast of London. Of royalty!"

"So who in hell's got it?" Mapes said. Then his eyes found conviction. "Damnation—it's that old rider friend of yours. What's his name? Wheeler."

"Nash Wheeler," Poole said. He lunged through the tavern in long steps and out the front door, with Mapes and Willie Lock scrambling to follow.

The side canyon's red-rock rims told him nothing. The clouds sailed mutely. A sea of hoof pocks was registered in the dirt of the tavern yard. He looked for a hint of direction. *Something.* On the ground before him, a point of light winked. Poole stooped; his fingers reclaimed a coin, a Federal three-dollar gold piece, compact as a shirt button, new and uncirculated. Another glimmered a few steps beyond. Farther out in the yard, a canvas bag bearing the letters U.S. lay spent, a handful of gold coins spreading from its mouth. Mapes and Willie Lock dashed to the discovery, elbowing each other in their haste to scrabble up the coins.

Bloody Ben Poole detoured around his men the way he might have bypassed rooting hogs. To his mind, the string of finds implied a route. He said, "By Jehovah, the side trail! I should have known it."

He swung into his saddle. "Lock, you lead us. Your eyes are youngest." He was gratified when Willie Lock obeyed. Nash Wheeler was a different matter than Faith or Toby. Poole did not intend to get shot from ambush.

Lock led them trotting down the path toward the cabins and the corral, past the leaning privy and a lone, grazing horse. Amos Mapes went second. Six or eight rods farther on, Ben Poole was heartened to see another coin gleam at him, but he did not mention it or stop for it. One bagful, more or less, did not concern him. What mattered was the bulk of it.

53 · ANGELINA

"GO ON UP," WHEELER TOLD HER, AND NUDGED HER WITH THE revolver barrel. She looked up the trail they were to ascend, following its faint line to the canyon rim. Roberto had told her of it; it was the route that troops under Ranald Mackenzie had descended when attacking Quanah Parker. Roberto had told her of it—its location and history—but his words had not prepared her for its precariousness. It was no more than a deer trail, a thin succession of footholds climbing strenuously to the top.

"Get moving," he said again, "and keep sensible. You cause a horse to go over and I will by God send you tumbling after it."

She started on foot, tugging the unwilling horse behind her. At the horse's resistance, she looked back, seeing its eyes peeled wide with fright. "Maybe we ought to blindfold the animals."

"That's a trick I never put stock in," Nash said. "You show a horse it ain't got a choice, it'll go just about anywhere."

They ascended, tugging their lead ropes. The horses, in Angelina's opinion, were too heavily laden; each of them must have carried several hundred pounds. Above all, she wondered what would happen when he no longer needed her. Would he release her or take her with him? Or would he simply kill her, as he'd done poor Toby?

54 · MAPES

WILLIE LOCK LED THEM ALONG THE NARROW SLASH OF CREEK that gentled between wild plums. They crossed and recrossed the water, iron shoes scraping rock, mud sucking the hooves. Mapes figured they'd gone a mile or more, far enough that they had only to break clear of the trees and they'd see the steep side trail ascending out of Palo Duro. He was about to suggest they go from there on foot, when, from behind him, Poole called for Lock to do just that.

"I have a presentiment," Poole told them, with his silly hat plume waving and his brow knuckled with seriousness. He tied his mount to a smooth-barked plum tree. While dismounting, Mapes caught Willie Lock's eye, communicating ridicule. In his notion, only women had presentiments.

"I don't have to tell you you'll need rifles," Poole said.

"Right enough," Mapes said. "You damn well don't have to tell us."

They threaded the trees, watching for movement. When they reached the fringes where the rubble of rock began, and beyond that the pony bones, Poole unshucked his telescope. Mapes figured they hardly needed it, for with his unaided eyes, Mapes could make out the oblique slash of side trail and the two plodding horses and the two human figures already upon it.

"It's Wheeler and that dark-eyed beauty," the colonel said, with his voice pinched, as though he were speaking through the telescope. "He's forcing her at gunpoint."

Mapes found he was cheered at the sight of the pretty señorita. Once he got the money, she'd come in handy for celebrating. "We ought to just let them do the sweating," Mapes suggested. "Then go on up and catch them up on the plains."

Poole's look fulminated. "By God, I'll give the orders!

What you're suggesting is tactically foolhardy. If they turned on us, we'd be defenseless on that trail."

Mapes shrugged, figuring old Bloody Ben might have a point and he might not. Either way, Mapes did not intend to put up with such bossing much longer. "So let's just shoot them now," Mapes suggested.

"Maybe so," Poole said, and nodded while still appraising the two climbing figures and their horses. Then Poole looked at Willie Lock—hopefully, Mapes thought. "Which of you is the better shot?"

"That'd be me," Mapes said. "Fact is, I'm the better man all around." Mapes was proud of his single-shot rifle; he'd had an Arkansas gunsmith equip it with a fancy ladder sight. He raised the ladder and set the sliding aperture for three hundred fifty yards. "This here Ballard shoots right on the money. Even so, I'll want to get a mite closer."

Mapes had a light heart as he stepped into the open. There was a scattering of red boulders about sixty yards ahead of him, about where the pony bones started. Any boulder among them would do for a rest.

"You fool—they'll see you!"

"Let 'em," Mapes said. He kept his back to Poole and Willie Lock and walked into the open, taking his time. He said, "There's not a damned thing they can do about it."

55 · PALO DURO

RILEY ERUPTED FROM THE TAVERN WITH HIS PISTOL IN HIS HAND, but he came to an uncertain stop on the porch. With worried eyes, he surveyed all he could see of the outlaw camp.

"Well?" Cass said.

"That fat man Toby is lying shot dead in there," Riley said. "Otherwise, there's nobody."

Cass slid off and massaged his hinder. His horse gave him a look that said it was owed feed and water. "I don't claim

I'm a top tracker," he said, "but it hardly takes an Indian to see Poole and his boys came in here. And the tracks say they didn't come out." He picked a weed and sucked on it while he studied the cabins and the privy, all of which were silent and unhelpful. He drew a breath and hollered, "Angelina!" The only response was blackbirds.

Riley had directed his squint to the canyon rims, which were pinkish and slashed with white, like slabs of raw bacon. "It would have been smart of Poole to have a secret way out," Riley said.

Then a distant shot reverberated—the report of a heavy rifle fired a long way off, then a dying succession of echoes.

"Head of the side canyon!" Riley said. "Let's go!"

Cass figured his horse would just have to bear up a while longer. He swung into the saddle, and they went up the tavern yard at a run. Where the bare yard greened up and their way narrowed to a weedy path between the cabins and the corral, Angelina's pet gelding stood calmly cropping grass.

Cass eyed the horse and then eyed Riley, who said, "By gol, I do hate to see that."

"She's maybe still here in camp," Cass said.

"More likely she's up ahead, mixed up in that shooting." Riley spurred his exhausted horse, passing Cass. They galloped toward the blind head of the canyon, then slowed to enter trees paralleling the creek. Riley immediately saw the freshly mucked hoof holes of a party of riders. "How much farther?" Cass asked.

Riley ducked low lest a branch grab his hat. "Still a ways." It was cool under the trees. Birdsong accompanied them. Within minutes, the shot seemed historical.

Dark shapes loomed. They came upon three lathered horses tied to trees, pulling at leaves out of boredom. "Here's as far as we're riding," Riley said. He swung down and pulled his Winchester.

Cass did likewise. "Something tells me we ought to scatter their horses."

"Then we better scatter our own with them," Riley said. "A man escaping would take one as soon as another."

They untied all the horses and tried to shoo them in the direction they'd come in. The horses bolted only a few yards from the men, then turned and regarded them.

"They're set on hanging around," Cass said of the horses. "It's the grass and water in here."

Riley shrugged. He threw the lever of his Winchester to chamber a cartridge, then topped off the magazine with another round.

Cass said, "I haven't told you yet what I'm asking for."

"Huh?"

"That other concession besides hotels and poker."

"But now you're fixed to, is that it?" Riley tugged his hat down and started, leading Cass on foot and crouching to clear the lowest branches.

"We can deputy, or deal faro, or clerk in a dry goods, far as I'm concerned," Cass said. "But we are for damned sure not going buffalo hunting. After all this, I'm primed for indoor living."

"The first shot's just to make our point," Mapes said. "They're going to see right off what a fix they're in." He set his hat on the boulder he crouched behind. He laid his rifle's forearm across the hat and sighted.

The longer Mapes sighted, the more it seemed to Ben Poole that shooting was the wrong choice. It was his gold up there, not Mapes's, and below that gold was a two-hundred-foot drop. Poole recognized it as a tricky situation, but for once he couldn't say that any idea of his own was likely to be better.

Mapes made some fine adjustment with his rifle sight. "All right, fools—catch this." Mapes spoke with the rifle cheeked and his voice directed into the stock. Poole peered through the telescope, half fearing to watch.

The report was not singular but a half-dozen chained together, all whanging off the enclosed end of the canyon. There was a second's suspense while the bullet traveled;

Poole was surprised to see the bullet as a streak of sunlight in his telescope. Then dust spouted off rock two feet over Nash Wheeler's head.

Wheeler ducked in reaction. The horse he'd been leading tried to rear up on hind legs, but the man yanked his lead rope, controlling the animal and tugging its hooves down. Wheeler yelled to the girl; Poole heard the bark of his voice. Then they moved, a hurried procession—first the girl leading her horse, then the man leading his. They jogged and struggled against the pull of the slope, dragging abbreviated shadows.

"Gol dang—they're running!" Willie Lock said. He cheeked his Winchester and thumbed back the hammer.

"Wait!" Poole ordered, but waiting didn't help them. There must have been a wider spot on that trail, invisible from Poole's angle. The girl and Wheeler achieved this wide spot and stopped, the girl standing fully exposed to rifle fire, holding the lead rope to her pack horse. Wheeler, however, used the wide spot to slip behind the second horse so that his body was shielded.

"Should've shot," Mapes said flatly. "There's what comes from listening to your damned cautions."

"We'll talk to him," Poole said. He looked at his men, Lock bewildered, Mapes sniggering and defiant.

"Go on and talk," Mapes said.

Poole put his voice behind it. "Nash!" The word crashed and echoed.

Wheeler's voice drifted back. "That you, Bloody Ben?"

"He's got your number," Mapes said.

"Come down!" Poole hollered. "There's enough for everybody!"

Wheeler's response was a shot, a flat report without much echo trailing it. A bullet whined pitifully off a rock many yards in front of them.

"Damn fool's spitting pistol balls at us," Willie Lock said.

"For sure talking ain't gaining us nothing," Mapes said. He snuggled back into his rifle, shutting one eye.

"You fool!" Poole shouted. "The money!"

Mapes's rifle roared. He turned a hot face and said, "You yelled right in my frigging ear!"

Poole shushed him, thinking he'd heard the slap of a bullet against flesh. He swung up the telescope to see the black horse that had shielded Wheeler rise up on hind legs, its load shifting rearward. This time, its master was in poor position to control it. There was a moment in which man appeared to wrestle horse and the horse pawed for footing.

Through Poole's glass, it appeared a rear hoof slipped off the trail. Then the animal was falling, its hooves still churning for purchase, but falling. It screamed its horse scream, then tumbled, becoming gravity's plaything. Where the rock face went vertical, the horse dropped clear, turning once in midair and making time go sluggish in the slowness of its fall, then hitting an outcropping.

At the first impact, money bags, already flailing by their cords, burst asunder, so that Poole and his men beheld a cascade of gold coins, obverse and reverse catching the sunlight. Then all descended together—flailing horse, money bags, a shower of coins and falling rock—till these elements struck with a combined crash against the red-rock scree and bleached pony bones at the head of the canyon. The resultant dust cloud rose up big as a barn, then drifted, slowly dissolving.

"Son of a bitch," Mapes said hollowly.

"Gol dang—that was gold!" Willie Lock exclaimed. Abruptly, he scrambled over his boulder parapet and down the other side, his rifle held one-handed for ballast. He reappeared running, heading into the field of bones, scrambling through the tumbledown of rocks, debris over centuries from the rim above.

Mapes said, "Damned if Willie's getting all that!" and dashed forward too. Willie Lock was yelling about gold, while Mapes yelled about Willie Lock.

"Fools!" Poole screamed at them. "Imbeciles!" But his men ran on into the field of bones.

* * *

Cass and Riley had advanced to the edge of the trees when the second shot sounded. Where the powder smoke blossomed some sixty yards in front of them, they saw the humped backs of Ben Poole and two of his outlaws. They saw the black horse dance off the ledge, saw it tumble, saw the gold rain, saw the crash. The quick chain of events left a figure Cass reckoned was Nash Wheeler standing unprotected on the sheer face of the canyon wall. The slimmer figure uphill of him Cass took to be Angelina.

"You see that gold?" Cass said. His voice was excited; he couldn't help it."

"Must've been Bloody Ben's," Riley said.

"I'd wager it's the eighty thousand Creigh told us about," Cass said. But just as he was figuring how to get his hands on some of it, a dispute broke out among the crouching outlaws. Then one bolted over his rock and began running toward the spilled gold. In seconds, another followed.

"Best chance we'll get," Cass said.

Riley shouldered his rifle. "Mine's the far one."

"Who's arguing?"

Riley, always a keener eye over a Winchester rifle, let go with the first shot. The farther outlaw was just topping a boulder. He fell like he'd been heel-roped.

Rattled by such accuracy, Cass let go an early shot—a miss. Amos Mapes whirled, his expression dumbfounded, his rifle muzzle sweeping a hundred degrees. Cass worked the lever, sought a convergence of sights and target, achieved it, fired. Mapes drew himself up straight and stiff, as if he had something important to say. Then he toppled, making a brittle crash in what looked like heaps of bleached-out bones.

A veil of smoke drifted. Cass said, "Where's Poole?"

"Scuttled behind those rocks. Looked like us shooting his men was the surprise of his life."

"He's got a rifle?"

"Just a sixgun," Riley said.

The plume of Poole's hat paraded behind a rock. Cass threw a shot, causing the plume to vanish.

"Missed," Riley muttered.

Cass got a hair irritated. "Sometimes hitting isn't the idea. I wanted to keep him pinned while you got closer."

"Me?" Riley said. "I don't relish crossing that open ground just to get myself shot."

Cass nodded. "In that case, I'd judge it's a stalemate in the Bloody Ben department." Then he shaded his eyes and looked to the side trail, seeing two figures and a pack horse resuming their ascent.

Angelina watched in horror as the black horse went over. Her first notion, when she could collect any wits at all, was that rifle fire would pick them off the rock face one at a time—Wheeler, the remaining horse, Angelina herself.

Then one of the outlaws broke from the boulders where they were sheltering, and before she could grasp the meaning of it, a second one followed, both men running and yelling. A third man yelled too—something unintelligible from behind his cover of rocks. Then, inexplicably, smoke popped out like popcorn from the fringe of trees. She saw the smoke first, and then the sounds reached her. There were three shots. The two outlaws twisted and dropped amid the field of bleached bones, and their rifles fell clattering.

Then Angelina's chance to act, if there'd been one, was taken from her. Nash Wheeler came up swearing, his face grimed and sweaty, edging past the remaining horse with his pistol aimed at her. She saw his fury over losing half the gold. Nash yanked the lead rope from her and pushed her ahead of him. He had the rope and the pistol in one hand, while the other hand gripped her shoulder.

"You know who's down there?" Nash said. His breath came ragged. She was afraid to look at him. "You got a notion, I'd wager. It's that damned pair of town gents!" Then she dared look, and he was awful; lines ridged his face.

"Move!" Wheeler ordered, and roughly turned her. She was desperate to push her mind out in front, to foresee what would happen. With only one outlaw left to shoot at them, and Riley and Cass at the edge of the trees, she and Nash would probably succeed in reaching the top. But then? She'd be shot, probably, or pushed over the edge. Or dragged along farther, prolonging her ordeal.

In the great bowl below them, quiet drifted. Bird noises reached them. They labored on the ledge, her breathing and his overlaid like that of needful lovers, the gravel scrunching underfoot, the horse's head sawing with its effort.

From below, another shot rang out. Nash, diverted to the sound, said, "They're shooting at old Bloody Ben. By Christ, I hope they get him." She saw it was all the chance she was likely to get. She affected a stumble, tearing from his grasp and crumpling to her knees, then crying out and collapsing full length. Nash almost stepped on her.

"Damn it, get up!" He jerked her by an arm.

She pretended helplessness, letting her weight sag. "I'm hurt! It's my ankle."

"By God, I'll pitch you down on them bones yonder!" He yanked her by one arm, so that half of her weight was suspended from it, but she let the other hand trail to her boot. Her fingers closed on the derringer's wooden handle. Her mind racketed with the risk of it.

She pivoted. In two heartbeats, Nash Wheeler's expression drained to disbelief. She drew back the little gun's hammer, poked the muzzle ahead of her, and triggered. The hammer snapped, useless. In her desperation, she shrieked.

He said, "Why, you damned little pup—" He drew back an arm to backhand her brutally. But Angelina thumbed the hammer a second time and in panic pressed the trigger. This time the gun banged and throbbed in her grasp, but without implying much power. It was as though all she'd fired were smoke.

The horse whinnied surprise. Wheeler took a backward step and stumbled. Immediately, gravity yanked him, and he fell hard on the trail sloping away behind him, his feet swinging uphill in momentum and his body half somersaulting into the horse's forelegs. His hat rolled and went down, sailing into space. Angelina watched in fascination, the blood pounding in her temples, hoping to see him spill over the edge.

But Nash collected his body's movement, and his roll subsided. He lay full length on his back with his legs uphill of him and looked up at her, his face reddening with the effort, his neck cords standing out like blades. She threw the little gun at him, but it rattled away and down. He cocked his revolver and aimed squarely at her face.

Riley witnessed them moving, Nash Wheeler slipping past the remaining horse and taking its lead rope, and shoving Angelina up the trail ahead of him with his gun to her ribs.

"Somebody's got to keep Bloody Ben pinned," Riley observed. "He works his way back to those men we killed and he'll pick up a rifle. At that point, he's a big danger to everybody."

"That's the easy job," Cass said. "Somebody else had better scurry up that trail and try to help Angelina."

"Whoever goes," Riley said, "his hinder's going to be an easy target."

"We'll flip for it," Cass suggested.

Riley considered. "Naw, you'd only win. Anyhow, we'd want our best marksman to sneak up that trail, in case he gets a clear shot at Wheeler or at Poole either one."

"You're volunteering?" It sounded like Cass could hardly believe it.

"And being as how it's Angelina who's in the soup . . ." Riley let the thought hang while he studied it. He decided it seemed only right. "I'm kind of involved already," he concluded.

Cass said, "I'll admit I'm impressed."

"Yeah, well—don't be." Riley fed fresh rounds into his rifle.

"You'd better go if you're going." Before Cass's words died, a minor pop of a noise sounded from the side-hill trail. Riley looked up to see a puff of smoke. Then Wheeler tumbled backward on his hinder, nearly turning a somer-sault. Cass said, "What in the hell . . . ?"

"I'll have to go anyhow," Riley said. "Burn up a few rounds to cover me."

There were times when Riley could not understand why he'd hooked up with Cass McCasland; then there were times when he could. Feeling he was depending on somebody who was rock solid was about all he had to feel good about.

"On three," Riley said. He counted aloud, then bolted. Cass stood up and levered shots into the rocks that sheltered Ben Poole. Riley sprinted for the side hill, for the point where the trail started in a rubble of rock.

Nash hadn't known what to think when Angelina turned on him. Then there'd been a pug-nosed pistol and the misfire, and, just when he'd been about to bat her off the ledge in his fury, there was the concussion of a shot right in his face. Now he had a pistol ball in him, for cripes' sakes. He figured he would just go ahead and murder her.

He looked at Angelina down the length of his revolver, feeling his blood raging and his eyes popping. By God, he'd just give her a ball square in the face.

She regarded him the way a snake probably got looked at. In return, his hatred of her was so strong that a head shot seemed too merciful. He lowered his sights, thinking there, between her breasts. Bang. Or a bullet in her woman's works there in the crotch, since it wasn't doing him any good anyway.

He settled on the knee, and closed one eye, the better to aim. "I'll cripple you up, then watch you go over," Nash said, and he intended to do it. He swore he would.

But she went on looking at him in that steady way, till he found he was cooling a little. Goddamn, his chest hurt! Meanwhile, the girl was a pair of hands and a pair of legs. He still had the weight of thirty-some thousand in gold to handle, and only one horse to help him. And now, a gol-danged popgun bullet in his chest. Damn!

Keeping the gun square on her, Nash strained to rise. He

got his legs slipped over the edge, careful of overbalancing, and then achieved a sitting position. There wasn't much blood, but a soreness like twenty hornet stings was camped just right of his breastbone.

Though he'd lost the lead rope in his fall, the horse stood placidly a few steps below him on the trail, probably marveling at the doings of humans. Nash made sure the gun was pointed right spang on Angelina before he tried getting up. He said, "I expect you been waiting all day to shoot me with that." He meant it for grim humor, but he was surprised how weak his voice sounded.

She made no answer. He said, "Help me up, damn you."

She shook her head, defying him. She was like some spunky filly before a good buster got to her.

He swore, throwing everything into it, but it didn't move her. He got one heel under him and pushed. It would have been easier to swivel his legs downhill from her and get up that way, but he didn't dare take the gun off her. He got a knee under him and then pushed with one hand. He came up, weaving on account of the trail's angle. He struggled for breath, and no wonder—his breathing had a whistle in it. "Nicked a lung," Nash said. "Damn you."

From the canyon floor, a barrage of shots sounded. Nash expected bullets pelting all around him, but the shooting, he saw, was directed elsewhere. He saw smoke push out from a rifleman, probably one of the town gents, standing at the edge of the trees. Maybe eighty yards closer to the head of the canyon, the plumed form of Bloody Ben Poole was moving on his haunches, keeping behind sheltering rocks and at the same time trying to circle, while bullets kicked up dust around him. Meanwhile, the other town gent bent low and sprinted for the base of the trail.

Nash knew better than to shoot. His rifle had gone down with the black horse; he had only his pistol. Assessing it all, he had to laugh, although the pain cost him, making him hold his ribs and creasing his face.

He retreated two steps and got the lead rope. "You come

here," he told Angelina. When she held that stubborn face, he could plainly see old Hollis in it.

"I'm through fooling," Nash said, and breathed a moment. "Come here or I'll put a ball plumb through your shoulder." He extended the gun, aiming. This time, she divined he'd do it. She sidled lower on the trail, till he caught her arm and brought it up sharply behind her back, her breathing catching in pain when he did it.

"All right," Nash said, and nodded while he worked for breath. "We're going to sashay to the top, you and me tight together." He had to breathe again before he said, "Long as I got you, nothing more's going to happen."

Cass came aware he was sending a lot of slugs smacking into the boulders without much result. Since nobody was shooting back, he thought he'd hold up.

He knelt and thumbed fresh rounds into the loading gate, partially replacing what he'd just fired. Then he peeked over his rock again. He couldn't see Ben Poole or even Poole's hat plume. All he saw was Amos Mapes on his pile of bones and the outlaw Riley had shot lying farther up the canyon. Where had all the horse bones come from, anyhow?

Then he craned his neck to find Riley, who had reached the foot of the side trail and had started climbing. Riley had gained maybe seventy-five paces up the trail, which put him twenty-five yards or so above the canyon floor. He wasn't climbing now, though; he was gesturing like a crazy man toward some point beyond Cass.

"What?" Cass hollered.

Riley yelled something back and jabbed and pointed like he was bound he'd shake his arm off. Cass pivoted, at first seeing nothing he hadn't seen earlier. Then a flicker of movement attracted him. Far to his right, where he wouldn't have expected to see anything, a hunched shape blurred between boulders, scuttling intently. Ben Poole was circling, making for the trees.

Cass threw a shot, making Poole hug a rock. But in a

second, Poole was up and scuttling again, still circling, so that Cass thought of the horses strung out along the creek, drinking to their hearts' content and munching fresh grass.

Afraid of being outflanked, Cass turned and dashed for the trees. This time it was Poole who threw a shot. For a miss, it wasn't half bad; Cass heard the music of it go past him. It got his blood going. He was angered to think that after what he and Riley had been through, Bloody Ben Poole might throw a lucky shot and kill somebody. He'd be even angrier, Cass reflected, if that somebody were him.

Though his blood was heating, Cass went warily, moving like a skirmisher. Before he crept any deeper into the trees, he looked behind him, getting a fix on Riley, who was climbing again up the steep side hill. Cass could see by the slow way Riley climbed just how steep it was.

Then he turned and plunged deeper into the trees. Compared to those from the open canyon floor, the sounds in the trees were intimate and contained. Birds chirped back and forth; creek water gurgled. Then Cass realized caution worked against him, for the slower he went, the greater was the chance Poole would catch a horse and escape. Cass would hardly dare follow, not with Angelina still in jeopardy high on the side trail.

He hurried. The trees were no bigger than a man's leg, affording skimpy cover. Cass threaded between them, running where he could, dashing across the upstart creek.

On his right, screened by trees, a form took sudden shape; the form was not running but had resolved into a stance, the head tucked and the arm extended, aiming. Cass dove as the shot came. A bullet whacked trees harmlessly, but then Cass's head hit something far too solid. His head exploded. Cass lay and racked from side to side, gripping his head, his mind clawing to hold on to consciousness.

Then a feeling shouted out even the roaring in his head, a feeling of the dangerous Bloody Ben. Cass heard Poole coming, warily but steadily, thinking he'd made a good shot, intending to finish the job. Cass found his rifle was broken where he'd fallen on it, the stock snapped at the wrist. He fished for his revolver, then raised it and fired skyward, the report so close to his stricken head that vermilion flashed across his vision. But the shot was a powerful signal that he still lived. The response was a thrashing, the noise soon diminishing. Cass raised his head to see Ben Poole loping away in tall boots, penetrating deeper into the trees.

"Gol dang," Cass breathed. He got to one knee and tried to steady himself. He'd rammed his head, apparently, when diving from Poole's bullet. Probably only J. B. Stetson's best plainsman's hat had kept him from knocking himself out completely.

Cass got up against a swimming head and soreness in his chest where he'd fallen on the rifle. He used cusswords appropriate to the occasion. Then he moved to his right, circling, trying to anticipate Poole's direction. The horses had been ridden hard and would stick close to water; he knew that much. Where he'd find the horses, he'd find Ben Poole.

Cass heard a whinny, saw a hole open in the woods. Three rods ahead, sunlight shafted into a meadow. A nondescript bay with its head up stood in lush grass. Cass perceived an unnaturalness in the extension of the horse's neck. Then he realized the horse was tugging against its reins, and the reins were held by the man who would ride it.

Cass seized a fist-sized rock and threw to his left, his idea of diversion. He was Cass McCasland, who mostly played sure bets, who liked boiled shirts and hotel meals. Heroics, for damned sure, were out of Cass's line. But he cocked his revolver and galloped into the clearing on long legs, catching Ben Poole, in his frocked officer's coat and knee-flap boots, his eyebrows clamped in concentration and one foot probing for a stirrup.

They fired together. The horse bolted. Sharp pain caught Cass's side, felling him. As he wheeled, he tried to keep track of Poole's direction. The ground came up and then grass embraced him; green smells tugged his nostrils. The meadow revolved, then steadied. Cass looked up into gunsmoke yellowed by sunlight, then he rolled over, still alive, still strong.

Near the ground, the smoke thinned. Cass saw Bloody Ben standing astounded, apparently untouched. In panic, Cass thrust his pistol ahead of him and worked the hammer. There was a stiffness in Poole's stance. He took a step, but at that point his legs rubbered on him. Ben Poole crumpled, going down like an empty suit of clothes.

Cass put a hand to his side, feeling sticky blood ooze through his fingers. He got up grunting. Poole lay outspread like a small child making snow angels. Leaf-dappled sunlight made a picture of him, a long-limbed man in polished boots, Confederate officer's uniform and flamboyant sash. The picture's sole flaw was a growing splotch, scarlet as spilled paint, between the high collar of his military blouse and the kinked hairs where his beard began.

Poole's hand still gripped the revolver. Cass stepped almost reverently on the exposed, milky wrist, not putting his full weight down. He knelt against the pain in his side, captured Poole's gun, and tossed it out of reach. He stood up again, noticing that fierce life still lingered in Poole's eyes. The lips struggled at communication.

"What?" Cass said.

The lips said, "Kill me."

Cass directed the barrel of his revolver to Ben Poole's brow. A man like Bloody Ben Poole, hell, he'd prefer death this way, rather than being hanged for his crimes during wartime, for plenty more committed since, and now for trying to assassinate the commanding general of the army. Cass saw it would be a blessing for a man like Poole to be hurled into eternity by the sudden mercy of a bullet, thus shortcutting the slow ticking of official justice, the deliberations of judge and jury. The mere fact that Poole wanted it caused Cass to deny him.

"No sir," Cass said aloud. He let the hammer down, mating it into the gun's frame in a series of clicks. Then he frowned. It was the gray uniform that bothered him. He figured the uniform was owed an explanation, although to hell with the man who wore it.

"I rode four years for the Confederacy," Cass said, "and I gave it one hell of a go. But it got to a place where we all hurt too much." He reholstered the revolver. "So when Lee quit, I quit. I reckoned it was time."

Cass stepped back. Fresh blood was still pulsing onto the grass, and Poole's eyes burned on. Whether the intelligence behind them had heard and understood, Cass had no idea. He guessed it didn't much matter anyhow.

Poole's sash suggested itself. Cass stooped for it, feeling a twinge of risk to hover that near the man. Then he tore off one of his own shirtsleeves—it seemed he was always tearing off shirtsleeves—and bandaged his bloodied side as best he could with the wadded sleeve, using the sash to bind it.

And when he looked back at Ben Poole, the fires had ebbed. The expression was unaltered—it was a face locked in protest—but the lips had frozen, and the eyes had filmed. Cass recalled there'd been an earlier occasion on which Ben Poole had feigned death. Even so, Cass figured the man who could do it this way, with this much conviction, hell, that man had not been born.

Riley heard Cass's racketing in the woods, the spurts of gunfire, and was not reassured. In his position on the canyon's side wall, he felt painfully exposed. Riley decided that whatever Cass's troubles, they were, for the moment, beyond Riley's help. He fixed his eyes on the trail and climbed, regretting past cigars and whiskeys, regretting his stovepipe drover's boots that restricted his calf muscles.

Despite the elevation Riley had gained, his view of what really mattered to him was maddeningly obscure. Wheeler was sandwiched between Angelina and the pack horse, making Riley's perspective little more than horse rump, the buttocks laboring in steady alternation and the tail switching like a landlady's broom.

Riley was laboring too; sweat flowed under his hat; he

took off his vest and left it in the trail. But the fact was, Wheeler was going so slowly, Riley saw he could easily catch up. He could draw to within, say, sixty yards, then throw on a burst of speed. Within half a minute he'd be up with them.

But to what end? When he'd been with Cass on the canyon floor, climbing the side hill in pursuit had seemed a good idea. Now it was hard to see what good he was doing. If he got too close, Wheeler would shoot Angelina or just elbow her over the ledge, the better to defend himself.

Where the trail kinked inward, accommodating an old water course in the canyon wall, Riley got a glimpse of Wheeler, gun in hand, gripping Angelina like a prize. They were struggling with the incline, Wheeler especially, his head pumping with each step.

Then Riley saw the droplets, lone outriders to begin with, then splotches. He stooped and daubed his fingers in it, convincing himself. He decided he'd let Wheeler know he knew; there might prove some advantage in it.

"Blood!" Riley hollered, when the trail kinked inward again and he could see Wheeler and Angelina clearly. Wheeler turned and pointed a pistol at him. The distance was absurdly long—a hundred paces. But the pistol blossomed smoke, and a slug sizzled off the canyon wall a foot from Riley's elbow. To get out of range, Riley had to bound back down the trail, losing hard-won elevation. He pulled up, skidding in gravel, and raised his rifle.

"Stay back!" Wheeler shouted. "By God, I'll kill her."

After that, Riley had to keep his distance. He wondered what the outcome would be once Wheeler and Angelina reached the canyon's rim. In Wheeler's place, Riley would have mounted the pack horse and ridden off. Riley, of course, wouldn't have hurt a woman. But Nash Wheeler? There was no telling.

Riley came around the last of the dry water courses, the trail narrowing to practically nothing where rains had eroded the footholds. He negotiated it, having to edge his boots. At that trickiest part, Wheeler threw another shot.

Riley flinched, but there was nowhere to hide. Then he saw Angelina giving Wheeler some trouble, and Wheeler having to tussle with her. Then Wheeler shoved her ahead of him and they were moving again. Back to the stalemate, but it would work in Wheeler's favor.

They went twenty laboring steps, thirty, Riley going warily in fear of Wheeler's gun. Then, ahead of him, first Angelina and Wheeler broke the horizon, followed by the pack horse—their shapes going dark against the lighter sky. The shapes quickly foreshortened, then vanished, going out on the prairie.

It was Riley's cue for speed. He dug into the slope and chugged, the rifle in his hand pumping like an engine rod. Between his rasping breath and the gravel underfoot, the noise he made was alarming. At any moment he expected Wheeler to reappear, to lift his gun and fire down the trail at him, where Riley made a slow, vulnerable target.

But Riley gained the rim. He broke out over the sweep of plains, meeting cooling breezes, and beheld Wheeler, Angelina, and the heavily loaded pack horse in the same tight grouping. Wheeler still held Angelina with one arm twisted behind her. His revolver still nudged her ribs.

Thirty yards to the right, however, Hector Garza was planted like a post, in his hands a Winchester rifle. Hollis Creigh sat on horseback some seventy paces out on the prairie, holding the reins of a pair of horses. Beside him, on a horse of her own, was the woman Faith, Ben Poole's woman. Roberto was on the left, kneeling, looking down a rifle barrel at Nash Wheeler.

"Angel, honey," Creigh said, "are you all right?" She tried to say she was, but her voice didn't catch. Creigh said, "Nash, I'm apt to get riled, seeing my daughter like this."

"Then for her sake," Wheeler said, "you'd best believe I will do what I need to."

Garza said, "He sounds sick, this one."

"I'd judge he's been shot," Riley said.

"By a woman," Wheeler said, and his nerves were so tight

that he found it funny. His laugh, though, quickly evolved to a cough. He worked it out and then spat—spitting red, Riley noticed.

Creigh said, "Those bags the payroll money?"

"Half of it," Wheeler said. "Enough to last me."

"Mr. Stokes," Creigh said. "I asked myself what Nash would think once he'd laid eyes on Bloody Ben. The answer was he'd forget Robbie. He'd set his sights on the Greenville payroll."

"And you never had any of it," Wheeler said. "I'll admit I was fooled."

Creigh said, "It was Robbie's notion you'd come out this way. Then we met Poole's woman."

"I'm tickled he thought of it," Nash said. "Angel and me can use the extra horses you got with you."

"With a ball in your lung," Riley said, "you won't make twenty miles."

Nash ignored him. "Fact is, Hector's going to lay down his guns and lead two horses in here closer." Wheeler's head rotated to find Hector. "Do it now."

A muscle flexed along Hector Garza's jawline. *"Hermano,"* Creigh warned him. Hector spat, then, moving warily, he stooped to lay his rifle on the prairie, then his revolver beside it. While Hector walked off to get the horses, Roberto's fingers clasped and reclasped the stock of his rifle.

Wheeler's breathing had a sucking sound. When he barked, "Hurry it up!" Riley saw how tautly Angelina was stretched, for the sudden words convulsed her. "Nothing slower than a Mexican," Wheeler observed. Riley tried to shove his mind ahead to think what would happen. Anticipate well enough and you could maybe change it.

Hector came back leading two horses, moving carefully. Ten paces from Wheeler and Angelina, he knelt and stuck his knife in the ground, then he wrapped both sets of reins around its handle.

"Back away," Wheeler said. Hector complied, but Riley saw his eyes shift, locating where he'd left his guns.

Wheeler began moving them—himself, Angelina, and the

pack horse bearing the money—in an awkward shuffling toward the tethered horses. When he reached the knife, Wheeler sank to a knee and gathered the reins. He got up with effort, his face ridging, dragging on Angelina for support.

Wheeler breathed. Then he said, "We're gonna ride on the same horse, Angel and me all lovey-dovey, and nobody's going to start anything."

Hollis Creigh said something so softly that Riley didn't catch it. Wheeler swiveled his head to ensure Creigh had not moved. He said, "Huh?"

"I said I need you, Nash." Despite the words, Creigh's voice had no plea in it. "I need you to testify what really happened when Robbie shot Cole Barlow."

"Yeah, I'll bet." Wheeler tugged a horse in close; he and Angelina were surrounded by horses. "Swing up easy," he directed her. "My gun's right on you."

Angelina regarded him, then looked to her father, who nodded. Her head disappeared momentarily as she put a foot in the stirrup. "Easy," Wheeler said. She swung her leg, and then was sitting tall, forking the saddle.

Wheeler said, "Clear the damn stirrup for me."

The pack horse, attracted by a tuft of grass, stepped out of Riley's line of sight. Freshly aerated lung blood showed on the money bags where Wheeler had supported his weight. Wheeler kept his gun muzzle touching Angelina's back. Riley could see how he aimed to swing up so they'd be sitting tight together.

"In fact, you testify for Robbie," Creigh said, "and I'll do what I can for you."

"That's right," Riley put in. "So far in this, you've only killed an outlaw. The law might find two ways to look at it."

Wheeler shifted his attention to the stirrup and prepared to mount. How weak he'd become was clear the moment he lifted a foot; he couldn't raise it high enough. "Damn," Wheeler said.

He tried three times, hauling up from the saddle horn with one hand, having to keep the gun on Angelina with the other. His first attempt was his best, but it failed by four inches. The succeeding two were feeble. He paused to breathe, chest laboring, presenting his back. Riley cocked his rifle's hammer. He could plainly hear the lung whistle.

Roberto rose from his kneeling position. Hector Garza closed four steps and crouched near his guns. Riley advanced as closely as he dared. Wheeler growled, "Stay back, damn it!" Ignoring the warning, Creigh clucked his horse and circled at a walk, getting a better angle.

"Somebody help me up," Wheeler said. "Or by God, I swear I'll shoot her."

Roberto said, "Somebody helps you, I'll shoot them myself."

Wheeler took care to keep the gun on Angelina, but he craned his neck to look at each of them. His eyes were dampered by pain.

"Give it up," Creigh said.

Something changed. Wheeler still gripped the gun, but its muzzle angled off at the sky. "Hollis, I ain't hurt your boy or your girl either one. I'll let her go. Your word's good enough."

"My word on what?"

"That if I let her go, you'll put me on a damn horse. All I want's a fair shake to reach Kansas."

"I couldn't do it. Like I say, I need you."

Wheeler's shoulders might have shuddered. He rested his forehead on his extended gun arm. "Hell, I ought to've knowed money don't come to old cowpokes."

There was a finality in it. The breeze carried the call of a meadowlark. Wheeler stood unmoving, his head bowed. Under different circumstances, Riley might have felt pity.

Creigh said, "It's bad money, Nash."

When Wheeler lowered his gun, Riley bounded in. Angelina thumped the horse with her heels and surged away. The animal had been Wheeler's support; denied it, he pivoted slowly, collapsing. Riley about half caught him, taking care to wrest away the gun. He lowered Wheeler to a sitting position on the Texas prairie, where the man blew out a long breath and then lay back like something fragile, his expression distant.

Riley kept his gun on Wheeler, but he heard Angelina's menfolk converging on her and then heard she was getting a big welcome. Her voice broke up into laughing and sobbing at the same time. Then Roberto's voice was whooping and going giddy. Creigh kept saying, "Angel, Angel," over and over, with a lot of feeling in it, while Hector had reverted to Spanish and was talking right over the top of all of them.

Riley kept his pistol on Wheeler's bloodied chest, but it hardly seemed needed. In half a minute, Roberto came up and gave Wheeler a drink from a canteen. "Sorry I ever doubted you," Roberto said to Riley.

"A thing like that doesn't even need saying," Riley said.

Then they were beside Riley, Angelina out in front of them, and Riley got his embrace. In her gratitude, she wet his shirt front, though it was well sweated anyway. "This one," Angelina said, speaking to her father and brother—speaking to the horses and the prairie too, for all Riley knew. "This one's the best," Angelina said. She embraced him again and kissed his cheek, wetting him some more. Riley got his chin nestled over her shoulder, and the smell of her hair giddied him the same way it always did.

When she let him go, Riley stood, momentarily awkward. Wheeler's voice came as wistful as wind. "Hollis." Dutifully, Creigh came swinging up on his crutches.

"Just tell me," Wheeler said. He had to set his teeth against the pain.

"You rest," Creigh said. "We'll get you in some shade here pretty quick. When I said I needed you, I meant it."

But Wheeler was insistent. "I want to know, being you never had the money—what kept you going? Hell, ranching in the BR's shadow on your tumbledown place. Your people depending on you for a roof and meat, and you crippled up." Wheeler's eyes sharpened when he looked up. "I just . . . to me, it don't figure."

Angelina had come up to stand beside her father; Roberto and Hector too. Creigh said, "Nash, I've never been crippled a day in my life."

Wheeler's eyes might have shown disappointment at the answer; then they shifted, as though his thinking had traveled to other subjects.

"Robbie, get a horse in here and get some shade on him," Creigh said. Hector stepped in and took over guarding, though Riley could see it wasn't necessary.

Angelina and her father were hugging again, and Roberto wrapped his arms around both of them. They were family and Riley wasn't, so he turned and walked on hollow legs to the rim of the big canyon. Far below, a figure led a horse into the open. When footsteps came up beside Riley, he turned in surprise, finding it was Poole's woman, Faith.

"That's either Cass down there, or it's Bloody Ben," Riley said. As Riley watched, the man hurried to ground-tether his horse, then began moving faster, scrambling over broken rock toward the bodies of Amos Mapes and the other outlaw. Riley waved his rifle, but the man was too intent to glance upward. It looked as though he would stop where Mapes lay, but he did not. He continued toward the very head of the canyon, clambering over boulders, scuttling across the pony bones.

"He don't move like the colonel," Faith observed. "It gives me a notion that the colonel's dead."

It was too far to make out detail; nevertheless, Riley breathed relief. "Oh, I reckon that's Cass all right. Look at him scramble for Yankee gold."

56 · ROBERTO

Tio Hector was on his feet again. He circled the trestle table and ducked the elm branches, refilling wine glasses wherever he could. At the end of the table he stooped to give his sister, Roberto's mother, a wet smacker on the cheek. She was beaming anyway: proud and happy and excited. She could hardly sit still for making sure Cass and Riley ate enough, did not want for anything. She must have made ten trips to the house already.

Roberto's father was speaking, his face serious, telling how it had been in the war's last days. "That man resembled Ben Poole, and I spotted it," his father said. "I maybe didn't kill him with my own hand, but on account of me seeing that resemblance, the man was killed, and I helped cause it. My punishment was the musket ball that shattered my leg. That and lying to my family about it, and then having to live with the lie."

"And you're saying the man might have favored the southern cause all along?" Cass said. "That's ironic."

"Whether he did or not is beside the point—which was that he was in no man's army, and therefore innocent no matter which way his sympathies went. To think that at one time I would have done that much for Bloody Ben . . ." Roberto's father shook his head. "So I don't judge any man harshly, not any more." His eyes stopped on Roberto. "Son, you want to judge somebody, you can judge me."

"It was war, Pa."

"There are lines even in war," his father said.

Riley said, "What Robbie did was straightforward in comparison."

His father nodded to agree. "Self-defense, and no court could have seen it otherwise."

"If it's fessing-up time, I got a confession myself," Cass

said. He got a mysterious look, then reached down by his feet, coming up with an old wool sock cram-full of something. He set it on the table with a heavy, metallic thud. Riley's expression flopped open, he was that surprised.

"Don't tell me," Roberto's father said.

"Seems I forgot to turn in one teensy portion to Sherman's army boys," Cass said. He opened the bag and displayed a gold coin.

"You dog," Riley said.

"Taking it back now would be danged awkward," Cass pointed out. "And seeing as how Mrs. Barlow never did pay her reward . . ." He looked from one face to another, gauging reactions. "Well, what I'm proposing is an even split," he said grandly. "Half for me and Riley, half for the Creighs."

"I don't want any part of that money," Roberto's father said, with enough starch that it stilled the whole table. Cass looked thunderstruck. Roberto's mother and Angelina froze like they were expecting a tree to fall. Riley cleared his throat. Then Tio Hector's eyes found Roberto. Oddly, he winked.

Roberto sensed an easing of his father's features. "I, uh, I can't argue that you two didn't earn it," his father said. "But the fact remains . . ." He frowned. "Well, hell—here I was just talking about not judging people."

Cass said meekly, "I see it as sort of a finder's fee."

Another pause stretched down the table, ending with Angelina and Roberto stifling laughter. Cass looked blankly at them. Riley studied his hands.

Abruptly, Roberto's father smacked the table. He said, "Dominga—what about that coffee?"

"Of course," his mother said, and then stood up.

In the lower yard a dog racketed. The second one added its voice. Angelina turned to study the ranch road. Roberto looked out to see a one-horse buggy progressing up the double track. Tio Hector got up and buckled on his gun belt. "Who could that be?" Roberto's father said.

"It's Mrs. Barlow's quarter-top buggy," Roberto said. "Looks like Quirt Hanson driving."

They stood up, all but Riley and Cass, who stayed out of it. "Must be Libba's got something to say," Roberto's father said. His mother got a stricken look, so his father said, "Now, Dominga, we're not letting this spoil our celebration."

There was a point where Quirt saw them at their table alongside the house, with all the dinner things set out, for he changed course, then eased the buggy to where the dirt edged into grass and reined up. The horse shook its harness and stood warily, keeping track of the dogs.

The family moved down the yard, Roberto's father and mother hand-in-hand, and Tio Hector with Angelina. Quirt Hanson had never borne them any ill will so far as Roberto knew; Roberto gave him a nod and got one in return. But there were graver looks between his parents and Mrs. Barlow. It charged the air, like a weather change coming.

"Libba," Roberto's father acknowledged. Roberto's mother spoke in Spanish, setting out an invitation. "Dominga says you're just in time to join us," his father said.

"I didn't come to impose," Mrs. Barlow said. "The fact is, I'm sorry for interrupting. But I was . . . Quirt was taking me to town anyway."

"It's fine," Roberto's father said.

"Anyhow, people talk," Mrs. Barlow said. "I thought I'd stop and tell you my news myself . . . so that you get the true story." She looked from one to the next, at all except Roberto.

"I'm staying on at the BR," Libba said. "I had mentioned earlier about going back to Alabama."

"I'm glad," his father said.

"I realized that besides graves to tend, I've got a home here. Coleman was no quitter, and I'm not letting him down." Her awareness seemed to widen to include Quirt. "Besides, the BR's breaking in a new foreman."

"You mean Quirt's foreman?" Roberto said. At that point she looked at him, her upper lip struggling, he thought, to hold its expression.

Quirt fiddled with his hat and said, "With a lot of help from the rest of the boys."

Roberto's father said, "Surely you have time for coffee."

"No, I . . . It'd be awkward. In any case, I've got to be going." Hollis nodded. "You can't change the past," Mrs. Barlow said.

"In a way you can," Roberto's father said. "You can come to see it differently."

At first she appeared to sift his words, but then Roberto could see her veer away, and she was merely impatient to be going. Quirt poised the reins. "There's still the matter of range rights to be worked out," Mrs. Barlow said.

"Plenty of time," Roberto's father said. "We'll get around to it."

She fixed her eyes straight ahead, but there must have been some signal, for Quirt snapped his reins and gee-upped, turning the buggy in a wide circle, the dogs accompanying. Then he wheeled them down the double track and away.

57 · THE GENTS

CASS, WOULDN'T YOU KNOW IT, WITH HIS WOUNDED SIDEMEAT swaddled picturesquely in Dominga Creigh-Garza's bandages, had eased himself into a shady chair next to Hollis Creigh. They sat smoking and gabbing about the war, winning battles that had been lost originally. What with the leg, Hollis would not have been much help clearing away the dinner things anyway. Roberto, whom Cass and Riley had taken to calling Robbie, same as his pa did, was hefting one end of the trestle table, sharing the load with his uncle Hector.

Angelina wore a white blouse that had a lot of Old Mexico in it, and a skirt that brushed the toes of soft shoes. She moved differently, like a bell swinging, as women do in long skirts, and at the same time straw-bossing, as Riley knew women inevitably straw-bossed occasions involving food. She was requiring that Robbie and Hector reset the table just so, chasing the moving shade under the elms before they had their coffee and sweets. After they'd set the table down, Angelina had them make two small adjustments before she was really satisfied.

Dominga Creigh was in the house, back at the cookstove, probably. It was Dominga's singing voice that floated out of the windows along the side of the house, and her coffee that sent its seductions down the yard, making Riley feel practically hungry all over again, although he'd just eaten enough to choke a spring bear.

In short, it was everybody in his place or her place, everybody with a niche. Except poor Riley, who was left standing useless with his elbows gawked out. He tried to scratch a passing set of dog ears, figuring the dog hadn't been born that didn't like its ears scratched. But this dog was Angelina's and had evidently taken upon itself the job of Angelina's protection. When Riley took two steps to intercept it, the dog gave him a look of steep suspicion—and probably jealousy, too, having seen him try to corner its mistress into a clinch on the porch that morning, when Riley had thought no one was looking.

Then, when Riley stuck his hand out, the danged mutt nipped at him. Riley yelped. Cass chuckled from his chair.

Angelina let loose with a cannonade of scolding Spanish, featuring many repetitions of the dog's name, which was Fredo—or, at this moment, Fredo *malo*. The dog crawled away with its belly dragging, forehead ribbed in contrition, eyes baleful. Riley was not sorry for it; he knew a playact when he saw one. He recognized the dog's ill will toward him remained undiminished, and vowed to have truck only with English-speaking mutts from then on.

"Fredo bit you? Riley, I'm sorry."

"Didn't quite catch me," Riley said. "Almost."

"You cried out."

"He spooked me."

"Come with me a minute."

"What for?"

"Just come along." She walked with intention, the skirt tolling, leading Riley across the yard toward the barn and corral. Riley ambled after her in the way he'd ambled through both sleepy, recuperative days that he and Cass had spent at the Creigh place. He had to spur himself twice before he caught up with her.

The corral was attached to a low-roofed barn. She put a foot on the bottom rail, cowpoke style. Riley draped his arms over the top rail and set his chin on his forearm, a picture of a dawdler, but inside he was humming. He was four times more conscious of her in such feminine clothes, the Mexican blouse, particularly. A couple of vaqueros were looking at them, making Riley proud to be seen with her. He'd forgiven her for the dog.

"Don't you ever miss having a home? I know I would."

"Lots of times," Riley lied.

Two horses and a mule inhabited the corral, and Riley was a stranger to all of them. For his benefit, the horses circled, showing off their lines. He admitted they were nice-looking horses, even if they seemed to know it. The mule was different, not going out of its way for him or anybody; mules knew they had few admirers. Like a lot of others, Riley had no use for mules, although in his case, it had nothing to do with looks. He just found them too opinionated.

He said, "Splendid animals," for something to say about the horses, and then could have gagged, for he sounded to himself like some big-pants auctioneer. The truth was, he hadn't been easy with her since that night in Palo Duro. Of course, he hadn't been easy then, either.

"There's something I ought to tell you," Angelina said, her manner so serious that his inner bells clanged, warning him not to answer too quickly. She said, "You were wrong about some things—"

"You've been telling me that right along."

"If that's so, I'm sorry. But let me finish." He waited, letting her finish. "But I was wrong about some things too," Angelina said. She looked down, seeming to blame her wrongness on her shoes. The statement hung, accumulating importance. Riley prickled, sensing implications looming all over the place. The horses were more interested in being admired than in overhearing conversation; they trailed back to the barn's shade to take up stances beside the mule, who gave them a look of I-told-you-so.

Riley said, "What things exactly?"

"I think you must know," Angelina said, and the fetching blouse shrugged up at the fetchingly bare shoulders. Riley had a pretty good inkling, but it seemed important to pretend he didn't. His expression probably gave off befuddlement. She put a palm to his cheek and drew him to her. Her kiss was sisterly. Riley had sisters aplenty, back in Kentucky. He figured, too, that Angelina had a brother and didn't much require a second one.

She said, "Do you understand what things now?"

"Darned near."

His hand, with a vision and a will of its own, went deftly to the slimmest part of her back, where it coaxed her into him. He was hoping she'd remember. She must have, for this kiss evolved to where there was nothing sisterly about it.

He held her that way till the vaqueros hooted, then the same hand that had had the big notions allowed her to lean back from him. They breathed for a second. They were both pretty surprised about it.

"Just tell me this much," Riley said. "Was I exactly right about anything?"

"Oh, yes—definitely."

She smiled to signify she'd told him all she meant to. Not that he felt short-changed; it'd been quite a lot, really.

She took his hand and they walked up toward the house, taking their time about it. Riley felt the consternation of the vaqueros play across his back, which was a feeling worth money. Angelina's mutt glowered at him from under the porch. The cast-iron yard pump suddenly needed Hector's close attention. Robbie looked embarrassed and tickled at the same time. Cass's expression had gone all scowly. Hollis Creigh looked like he'd had his skull sledgehammered and just hadn't fallen down yet.

Floating up the yard in tow with Angelina Creigh Garza, Riley felt practically like a bridegroom. Angelina's mother came out of the house carrying a bluestone coffeepot. When she saw them, her face looked as pleased as anything. But when she let the screen door clap, it was a noise that woke up everybody.

Roberto howled coyote style, expressing the same comment the vaqueros had. Angelina's mother went on beaming, and Hollis cleared his throat. Cass, always noted for quick recoveries, said, "Pardner, if we're going to hunt buffalo, I think it's high time we got started."